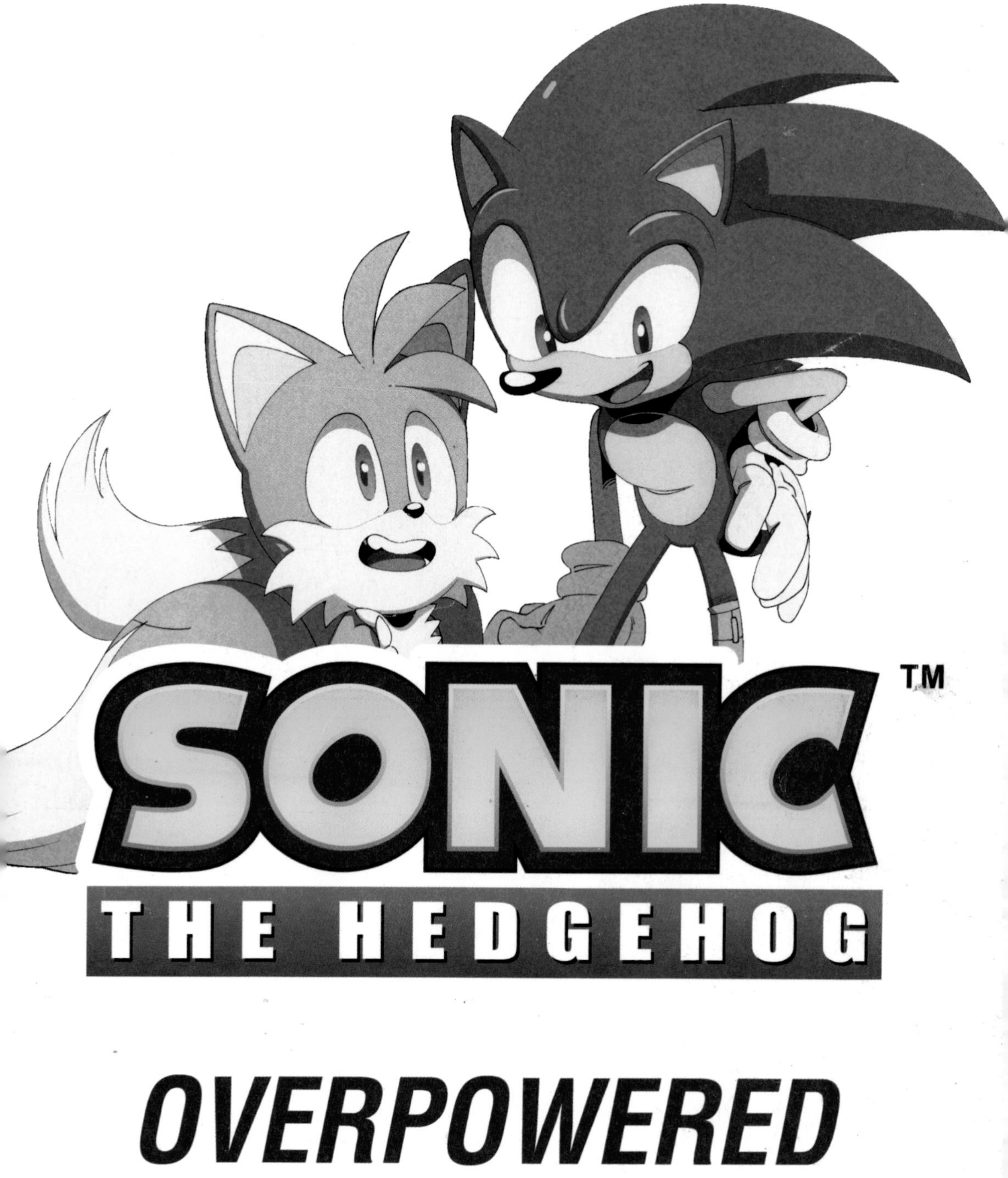

SONIC™ THE HEDGEHOG

OVERPOWERED

SEGA®

@IDWpublishing
IDWpublishing.com

Cover Art by
Aaron Hammerstrom

Cover Colors by
Matt Herms

Series Edits by
David Mariotte
and **Riley Farmer**

Collection Edits by
Alonzo Simon

Collection Goup Editor
Kris Simon

Collection Design by
Shawn Lee

ISBN: 978-1-68405-985-0   26 25 24 23   1 2 3 4

Originally published as SONIC THE HEDGEHOG issues #52–56.

Nachie Marsham, Publisher
Blake Kobashigawa, SVP Sales, Marketing & Strategy
Mark Doyle, VP Editorial & Creative Strategy
Tara McCrillis, VP Publishing Operations
Anna Morrow, VP Marketing & Publicity
Alex Hargett, VP Sales
Jamie S. Rich, Executive Editorial Director
Scott Dunbier, Director, Special Projects
Greg Gustin, Sr. Director, Content Strategy
Kevin Schwoer, Sr. Director of Talent Relations
Lauren LePera, Sr. Managing Editor
Keith Davidsen, Director, Marketing & PR
Topher Alford, Sr. Digital Marketing Manager
Patrick O'Connell, Sr. Manager, Direct Market Sales
Shauna Monteforte, Sr. Director of Manufacturing Operations
Greg Foreman, Director DTC Sales & Operations
Nathan Widick, Director of Design
Neil Uyetake, Sr. Art Director, Design & Production
Shawn Lee, Art Director, Design & Production
Jack Levesque, Art Director, Marketing

Ted Adams and Robbie Robbins, IDW Founders

Special thanks to Mai Kiyotaki, Michael Cisneros,
Sandra Jo, Sonic Team,
and everyone at Sega
for their invaluable
assistance.

For international
rights, contact
licensing@
idwpublishing.com.

STORY **EVAN STANLEY**

ART **EVAN STANLEY** (#52, 54 & 56)
ADAM BRYCE THOMAS (#53 & 55)
NATALIE HAINES (#54)

ADDITIONAL INKS **RIK MACK** (#52)
MARIA KEANE (#52)

COLORS **REGGIE GRAHAM**

LETTERS **SHAWN LEE**

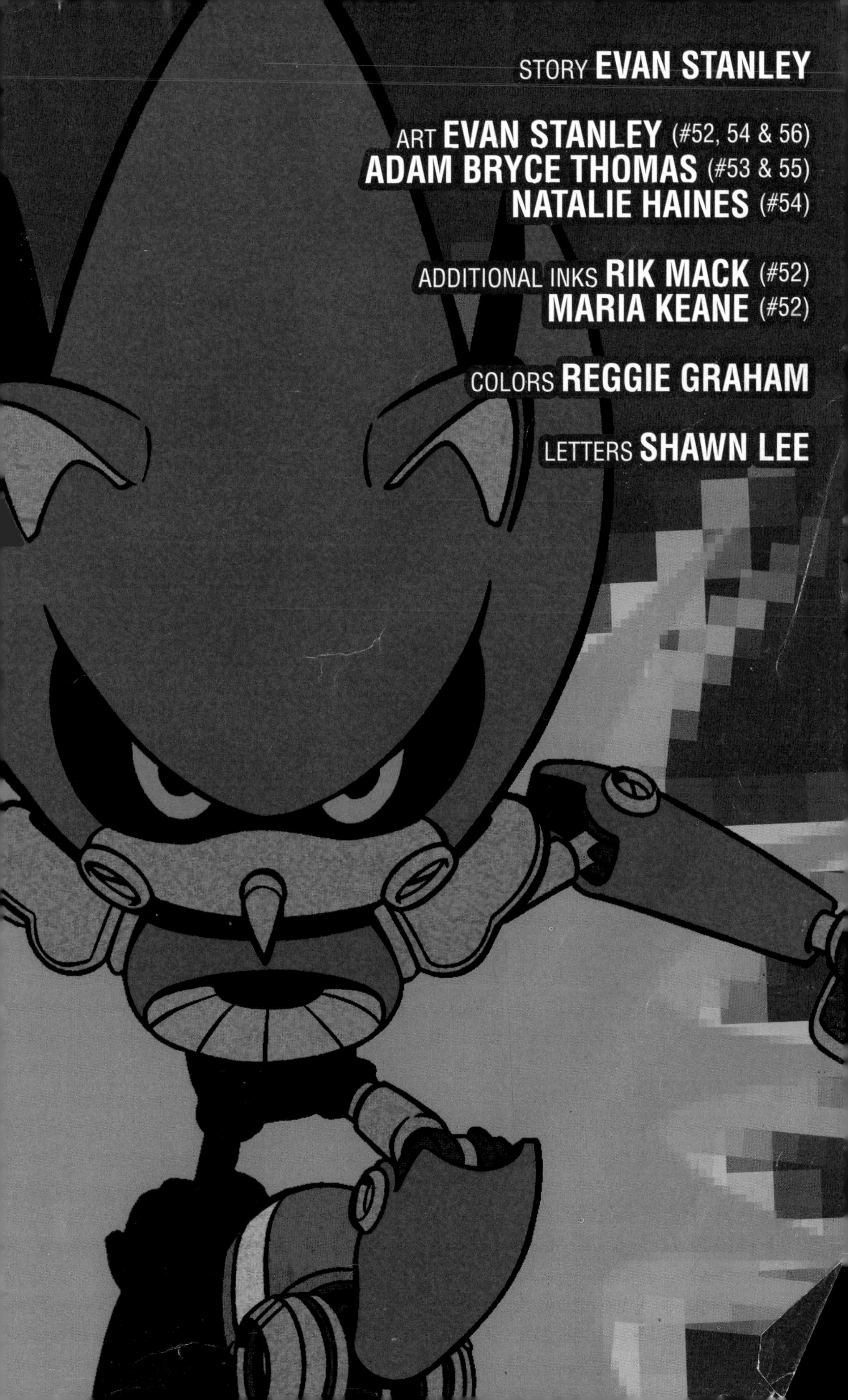

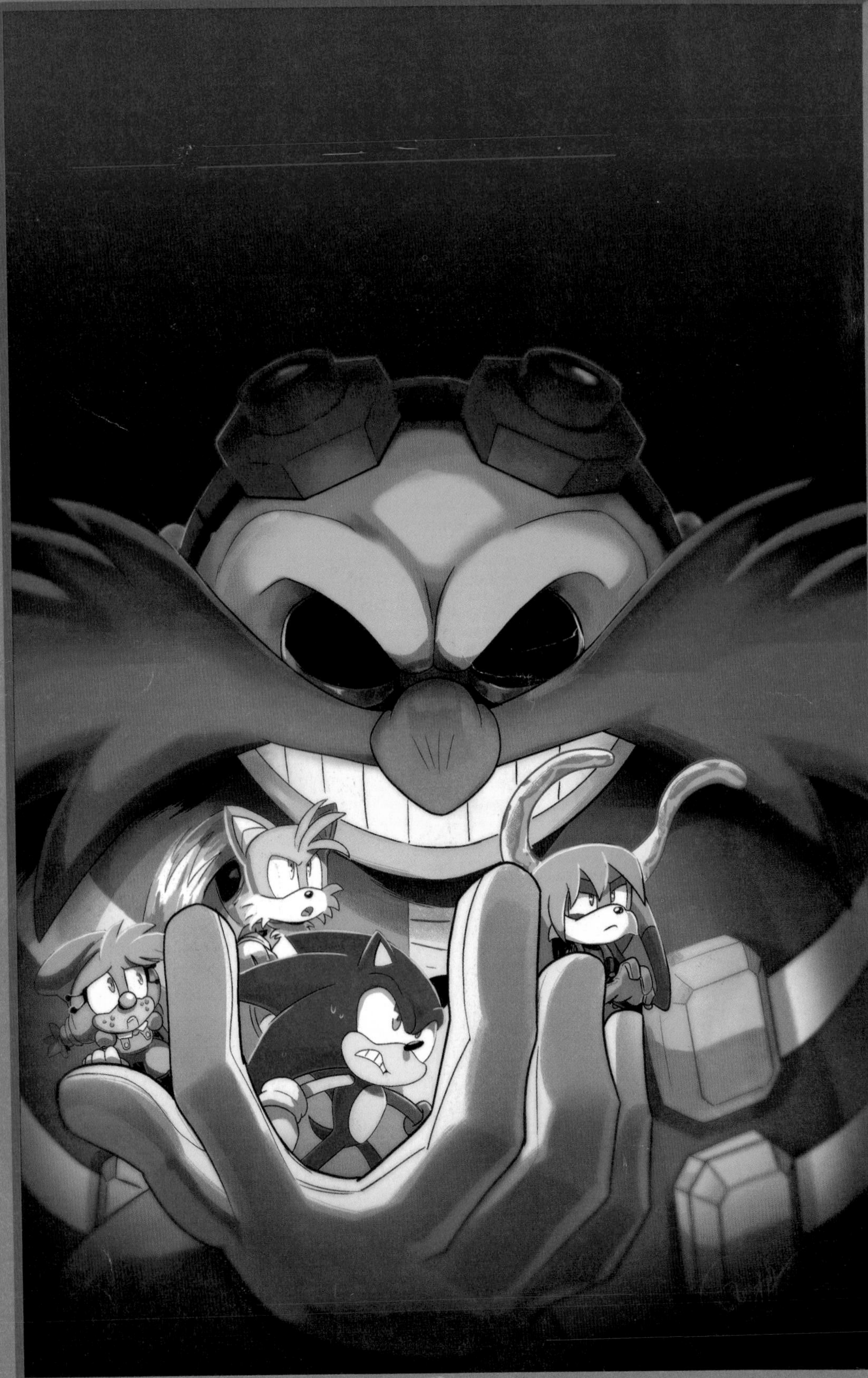

ART BY **GIGI DUTREIX**

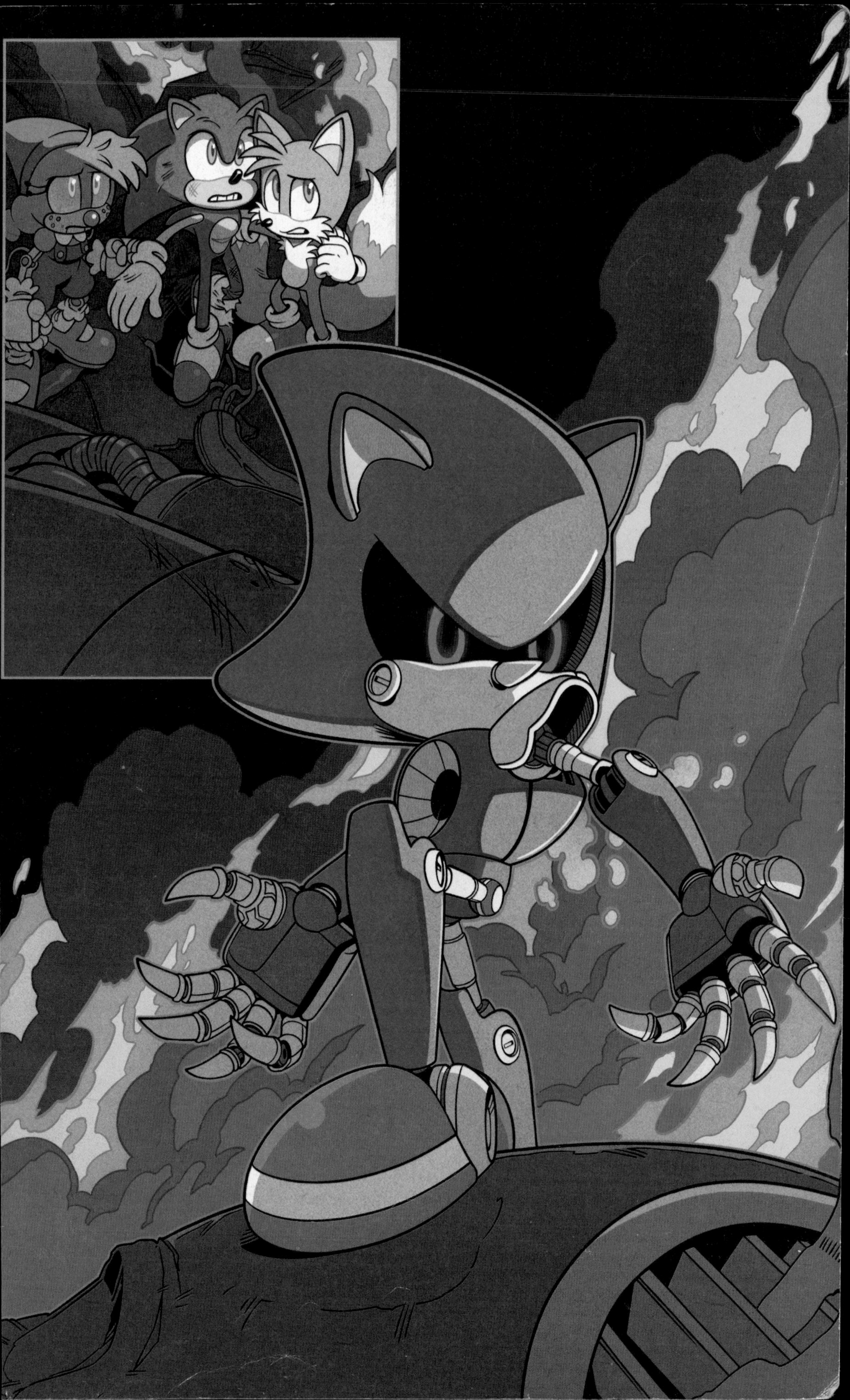

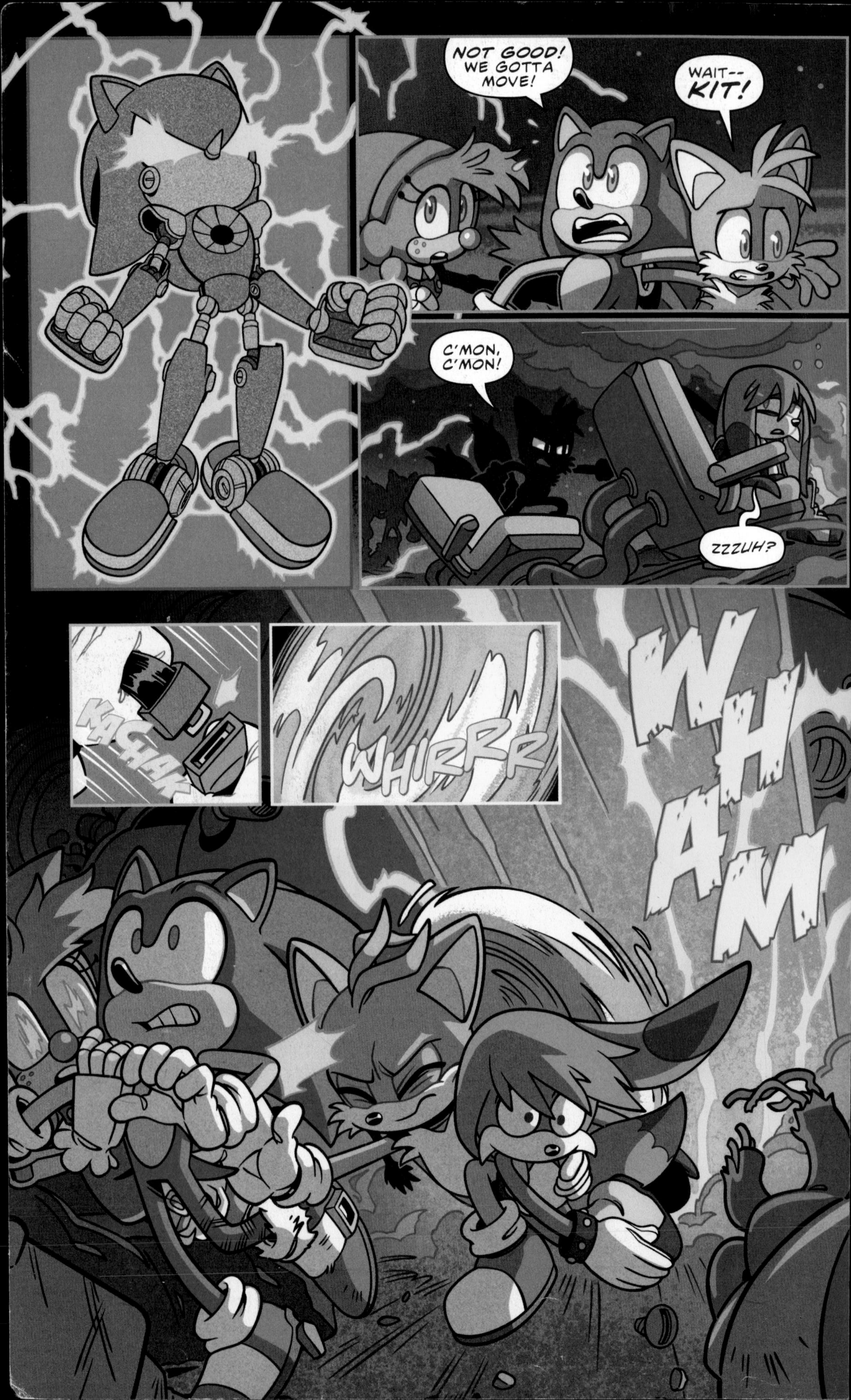
NOT GOOD! WE GOTTA MOVE!
WAIT-- KIT!
C'MON, C'MON!
ZZZUH?
KA-CHAK
WHIRRR
WHAM

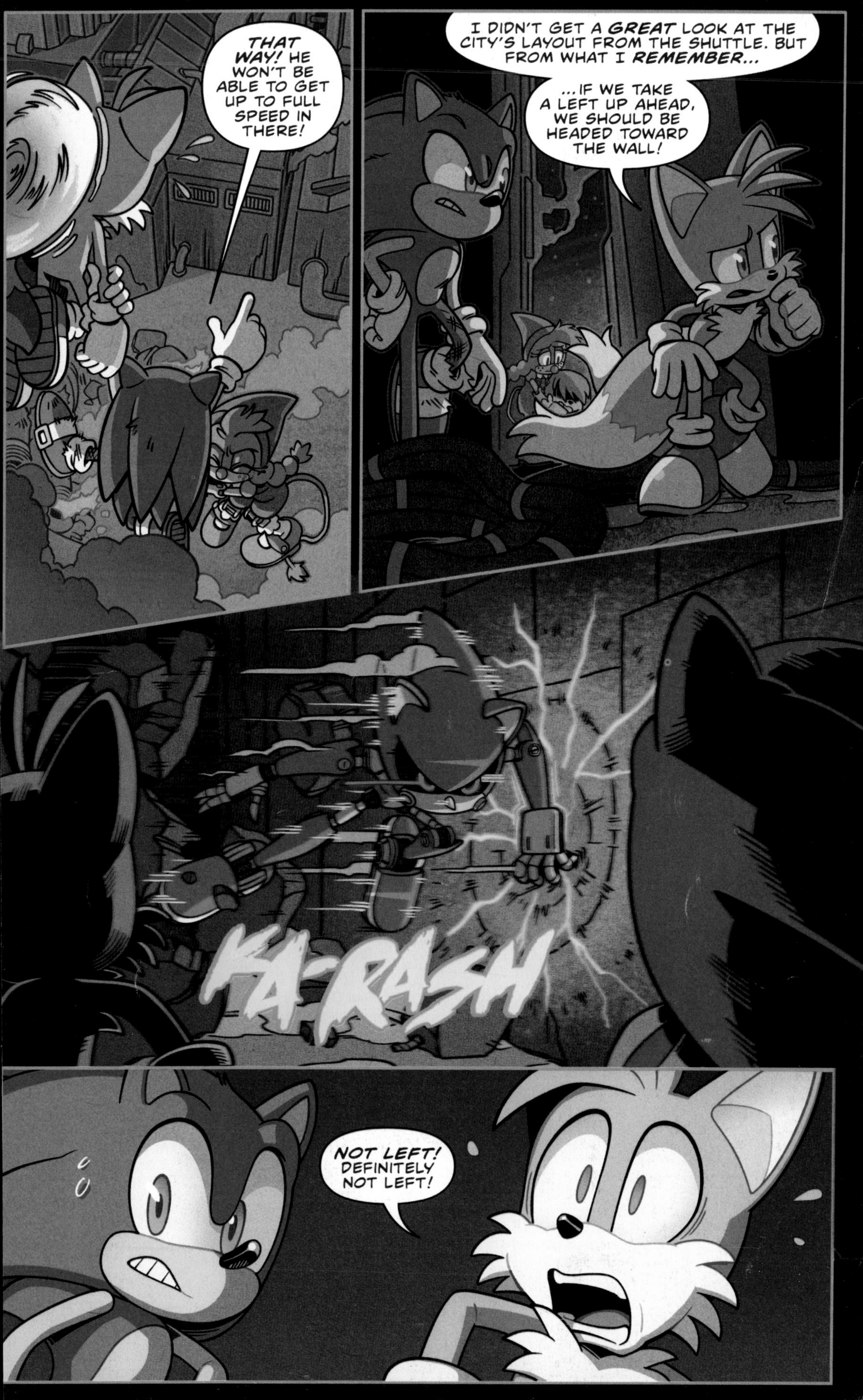
THAT WAY! HE WON'T BE ABLE TO GET UP TO FULL SPEED IN THERE!
I DIDN'T GET A GREAT LOOK AT THE CITY'S LAYOUT FROM THE SHUTTLE. BUT FROM WHAT I REMEMBER...
...IF WE TAKE A LEFT UP AHEAD, WE SHOULD BE HEADED TOWARD THE WALL!
KA-RASH
NOT LEFT! DEFINITELY NOT LEFT!

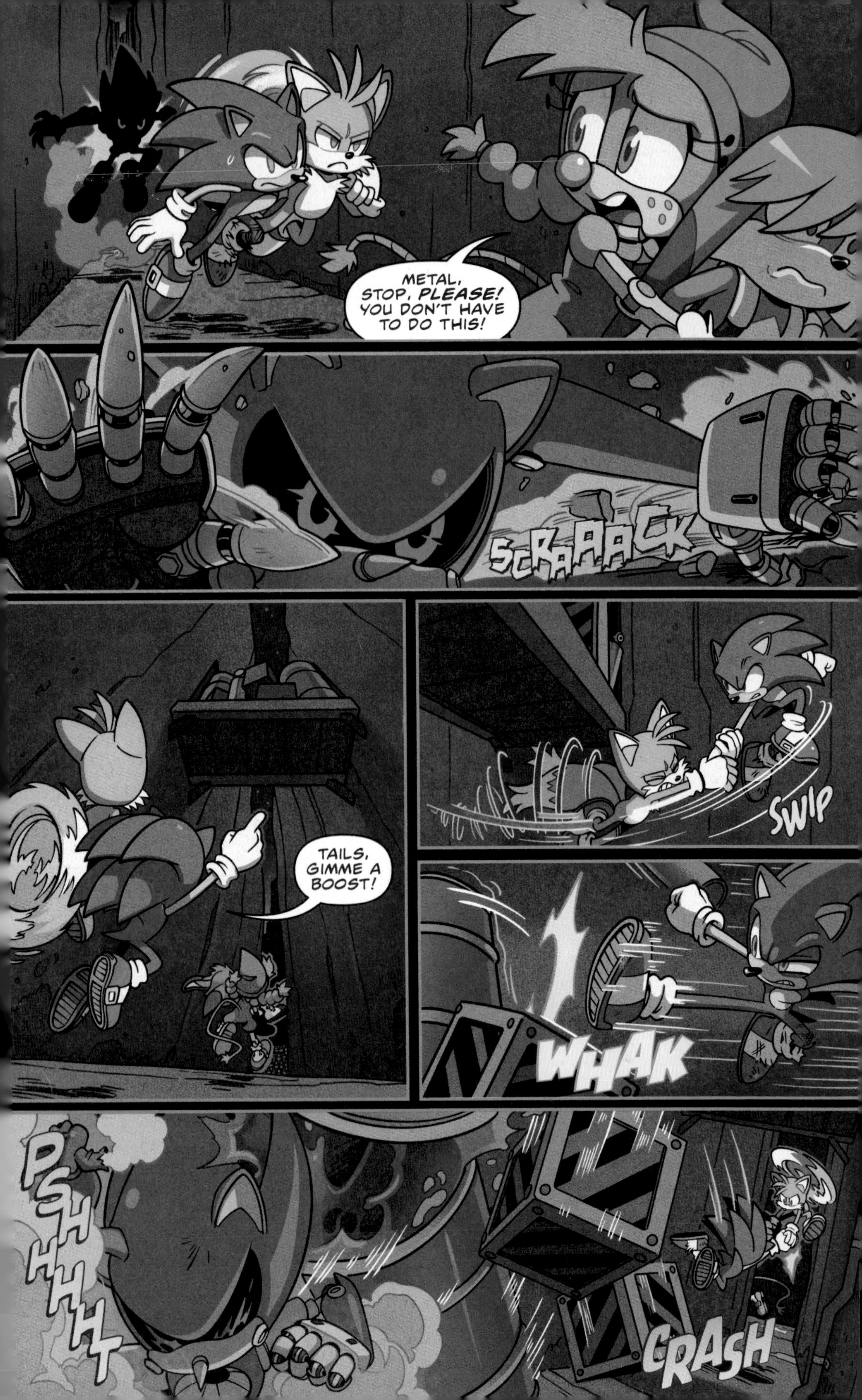
METAL, STOP, PLEASE! YOU DON'T HAVE TO DO THIS!
SCRAAACK
TAILS, GIMME A BOOST!
SWIP
WHAK
PSHHHHT
CRASH

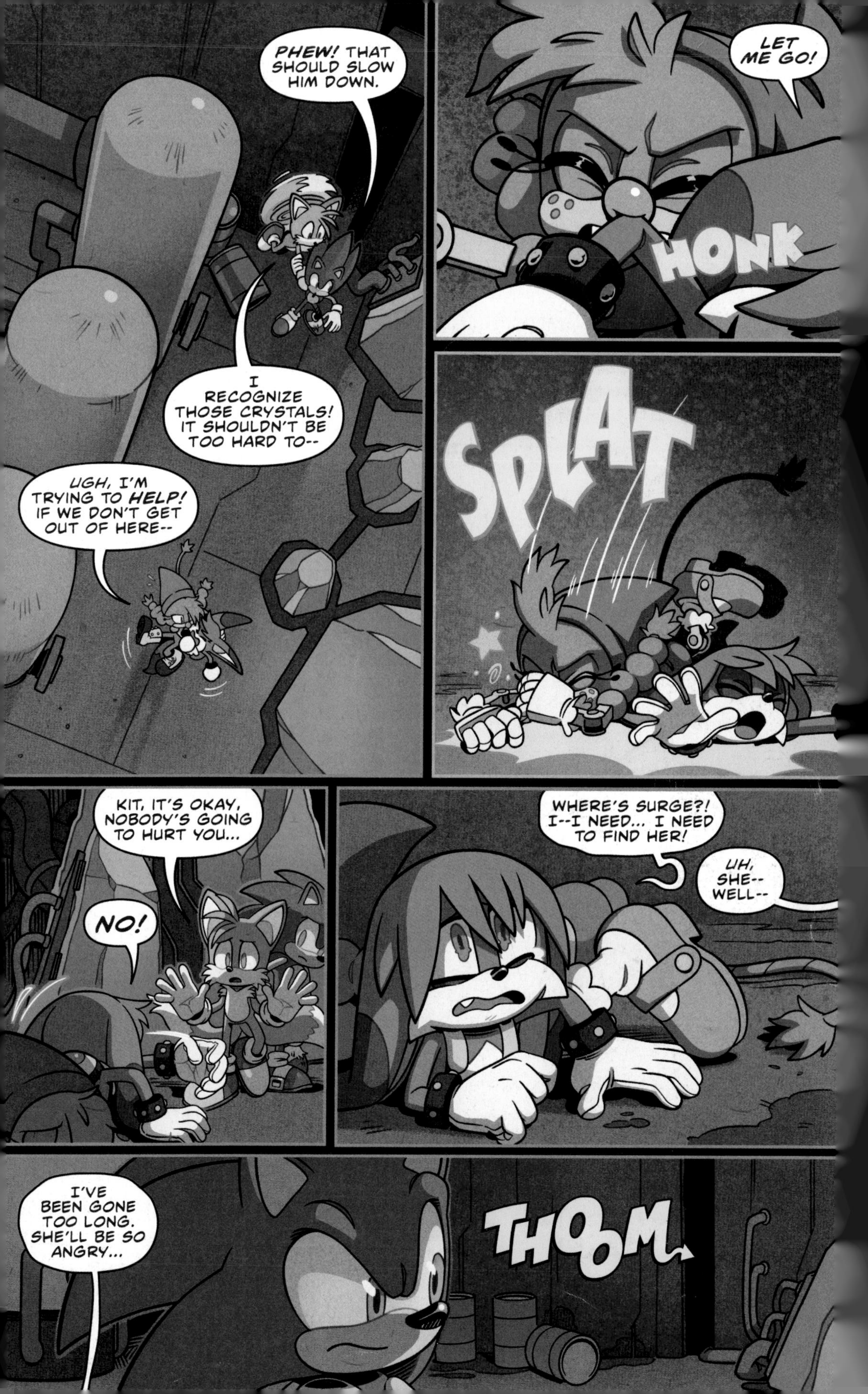
PHEW! THAT SHOULD SLOW HIM DOWN.
I RECOGNIZE THOSE CRYSTALS! IT SHOULDN'T BE TOO HARD TO--
UGH, I'M TRYING TO HELP! IF WE DON'T GET OUT OF HERE--
LET ME GO!
HONK
SPLAT
KIT, IT'S OKAY, NOBODY'S GOING TO HURT YOU...
NO!
WHERE'S SURGE?! I--I NEED... I NEED TO FIND HER!
UH, SHE-- WELL--
I'VE BEEN GONE TOO LONG. SHE'LL BE SO ANGRY...
THOOM

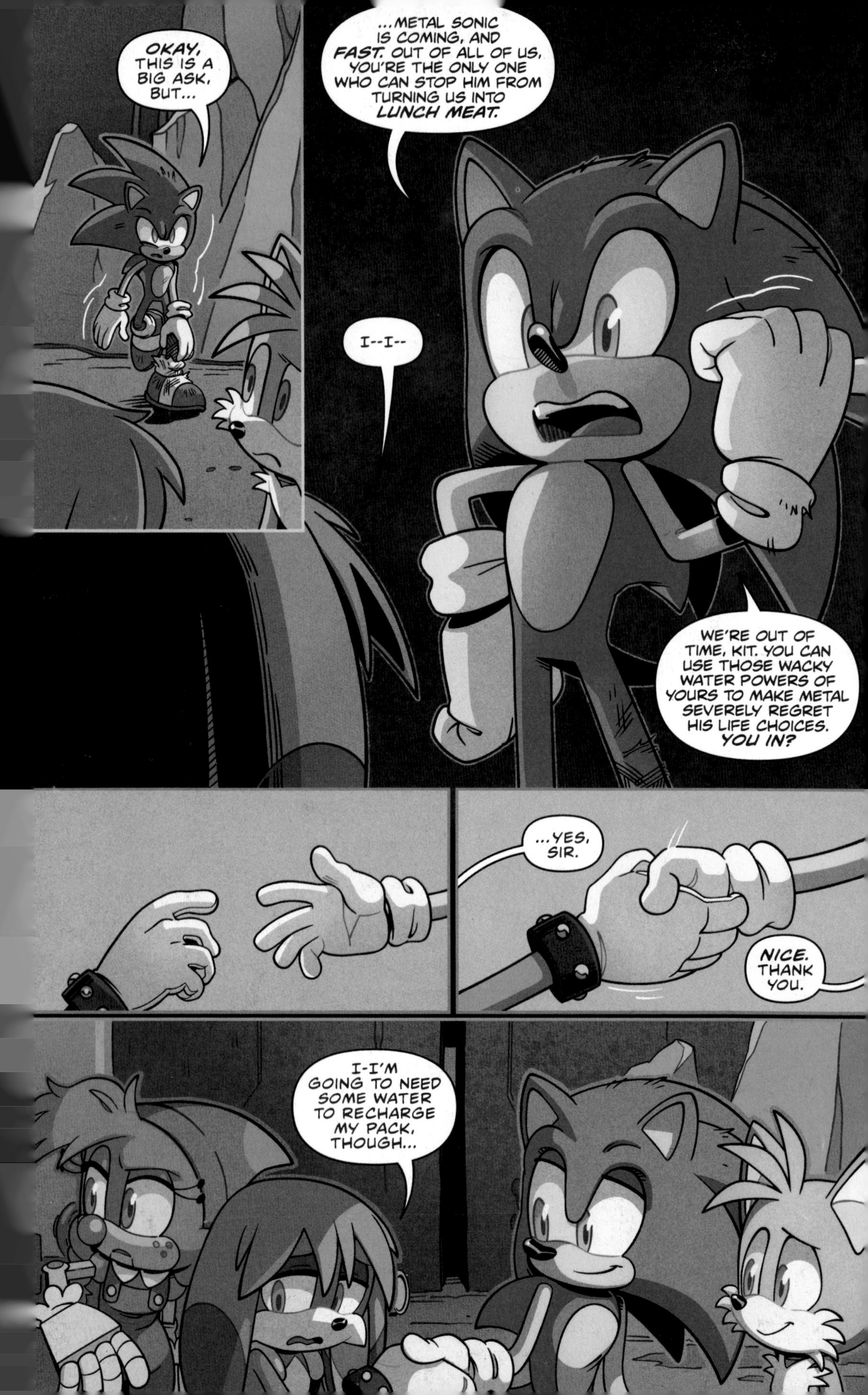

OKAY, THIS IS A BIG ASK, BUT...
...METAL SONIC IS COMING, AND FAST. OUT OF ALL OF US, YOU'RE THE ONLY ONE WHO CAN STOP HIM FROM TURNING US INTO LUNCH MEAT.
I--I--
WE'RE OUT OF TIME, KIT. YOU CAN USE THOSE WACKY WATER POWERS OF YOURS TO MAKE METAL SEVERELY REGRET HIS LIFE CHOICES. YOU IN?
...YES, SIR.
NICE. THANK YOU.
I-I'M GOING TO NEED SOME WATER TO RECHARGE MY PACK, THOUGH...

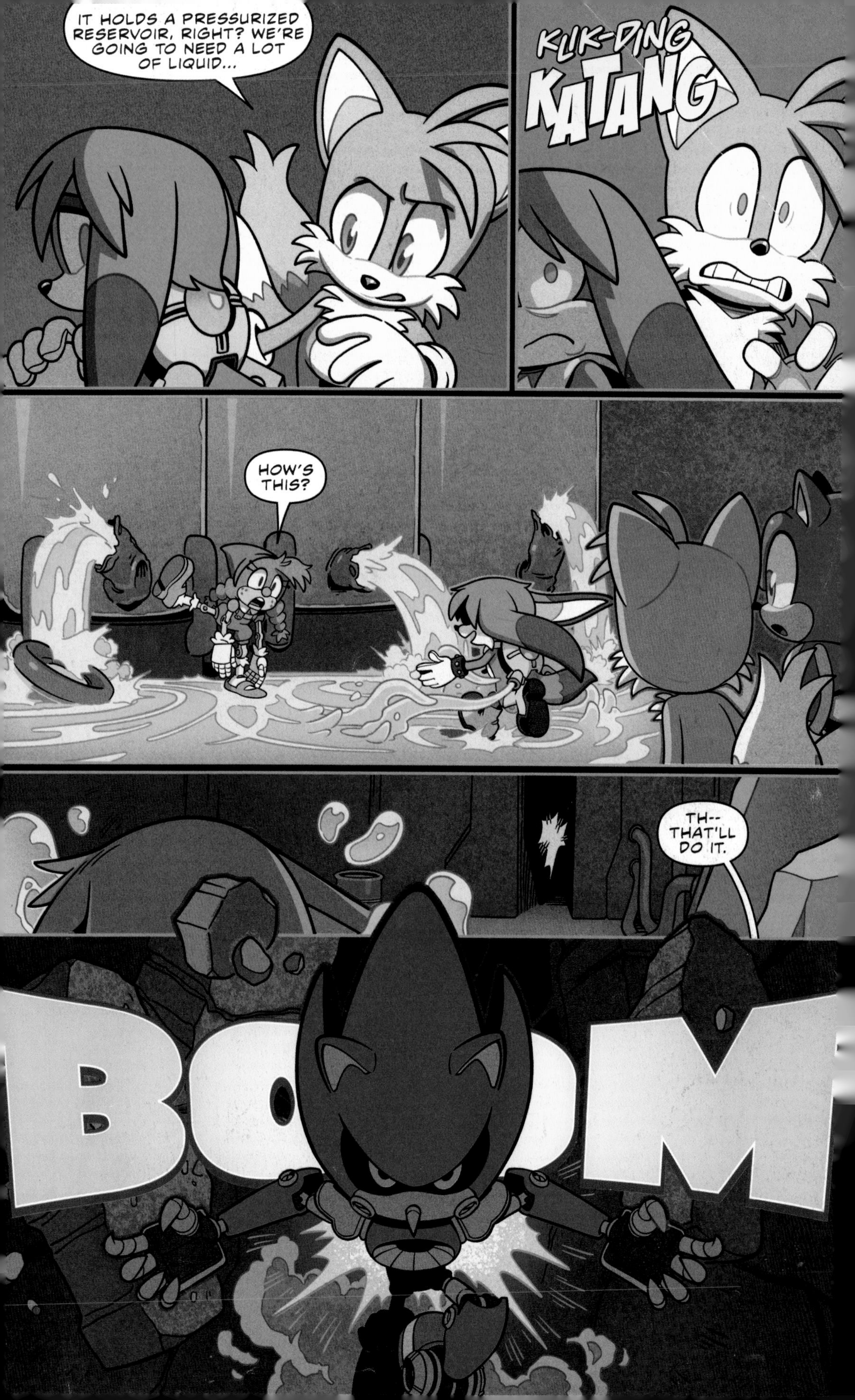

IT HOLDS A PRESSURIZED RESERVOIR, RIGHT? WE'RE GOING TO NEED A LOT OF LIQUID...
KLIK-DING
KATANG
HOW'S THIS?
TH-- THAT'LL DO IT.
BOOM

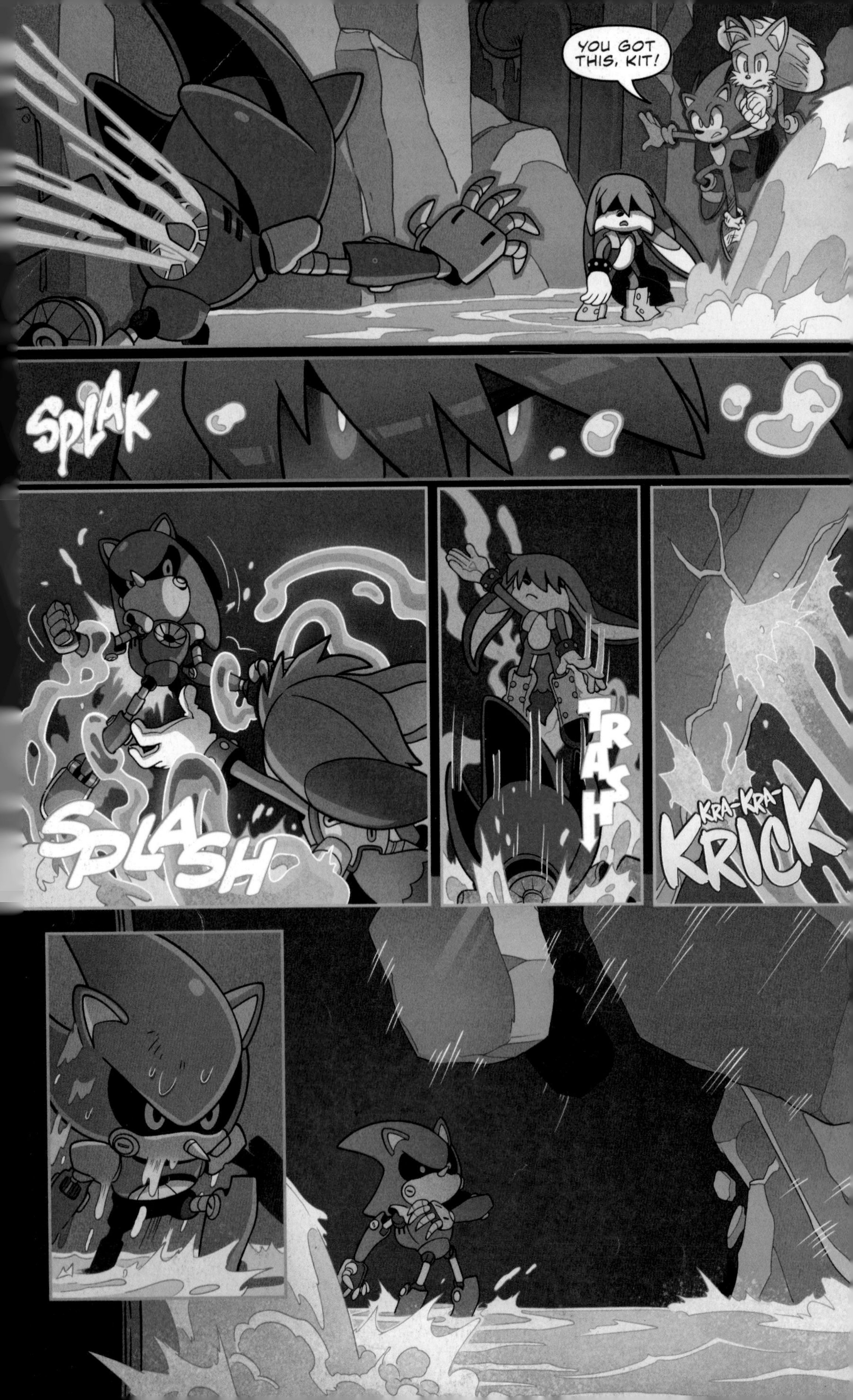
YOU GOT THIS, KIT!
SPLAK
SPLASH
TRASH
KRA-KRA-KRICK

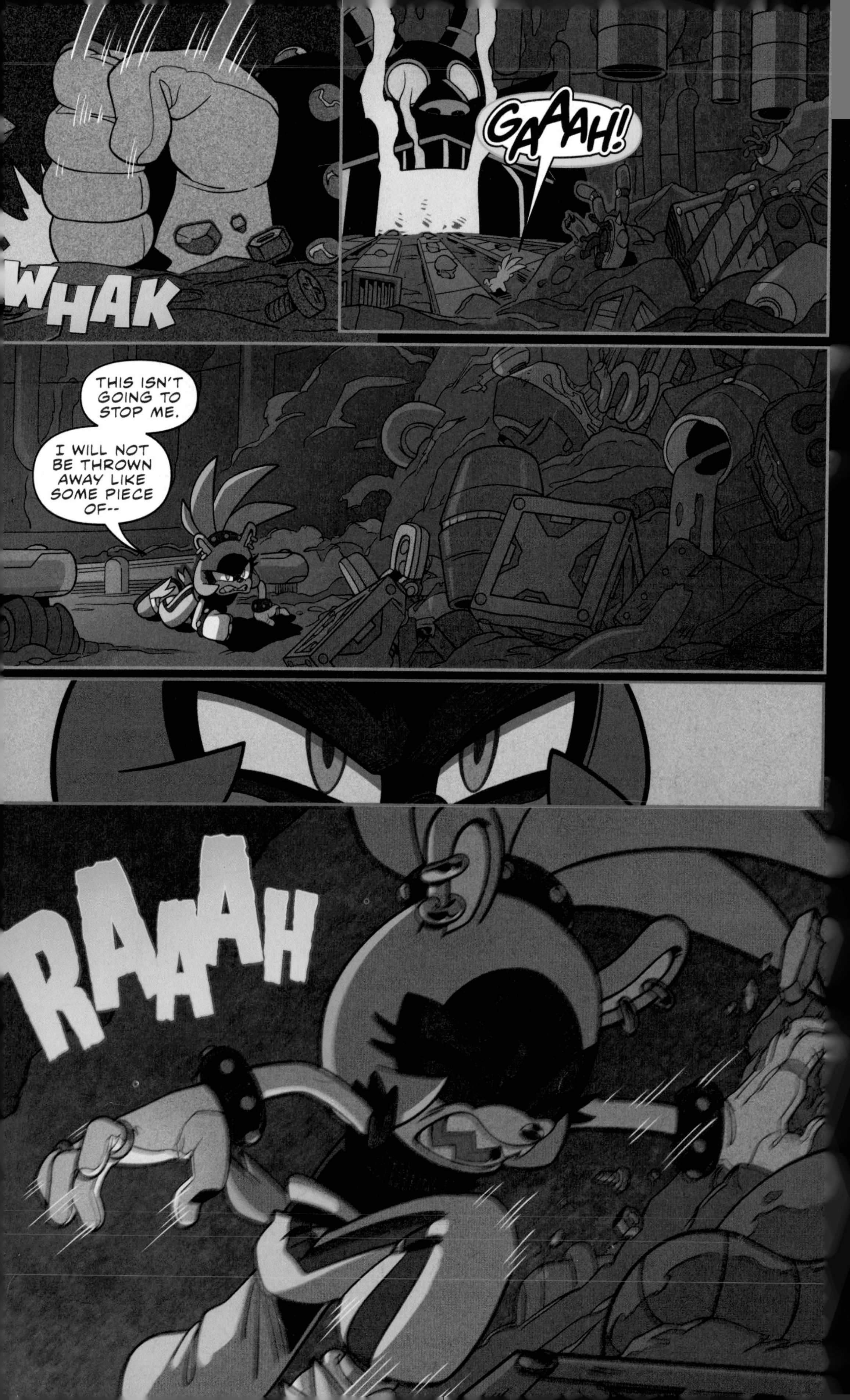
WHAK
GAAAH!
THIS ISN'T GOING TO STOP ME.
I WILL NOT BE THROWN AWAY LIKE SOME PIECE OF--
RAAAAH

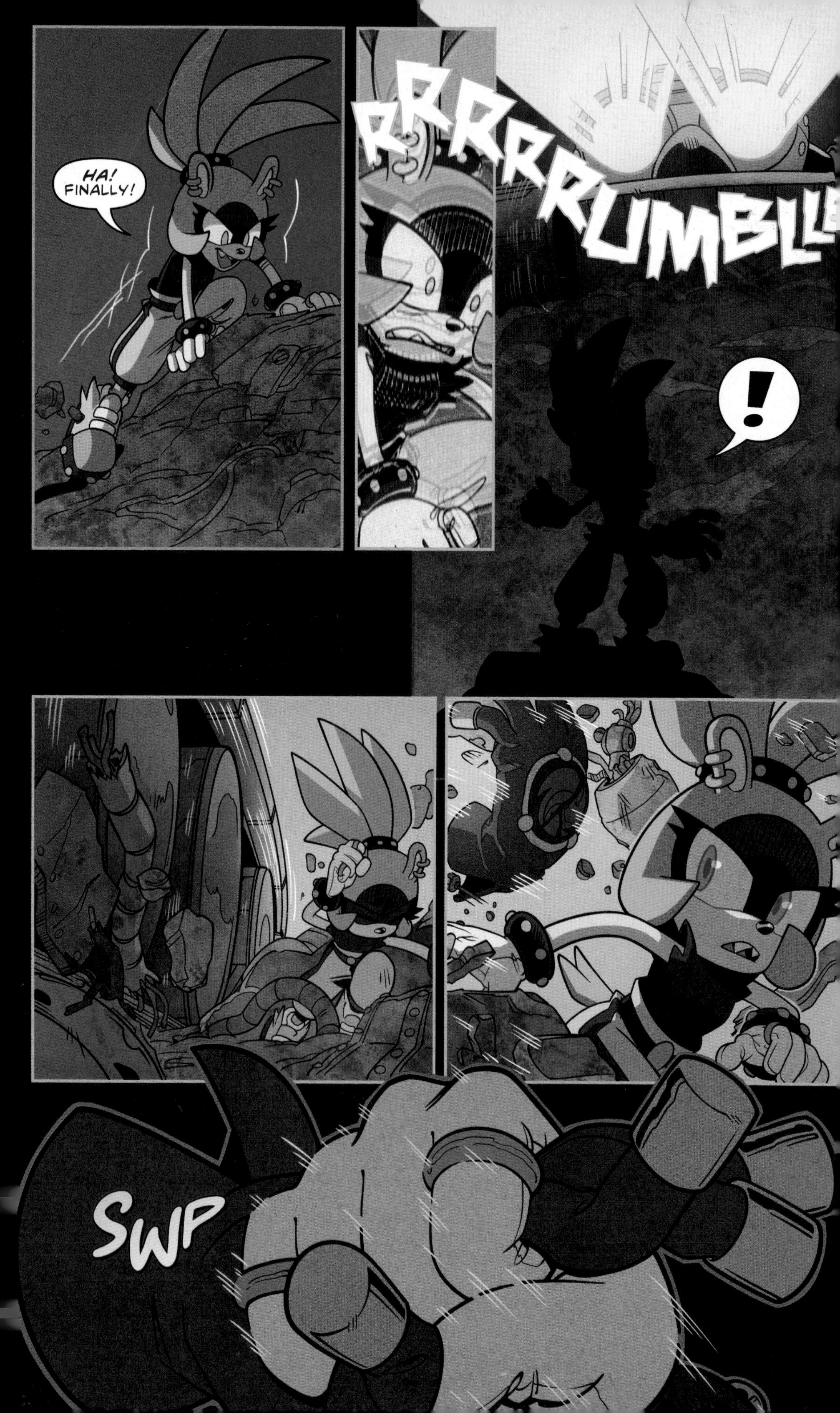

HA! FINALLY!
RRRRRRUMBLLE
!
SWP

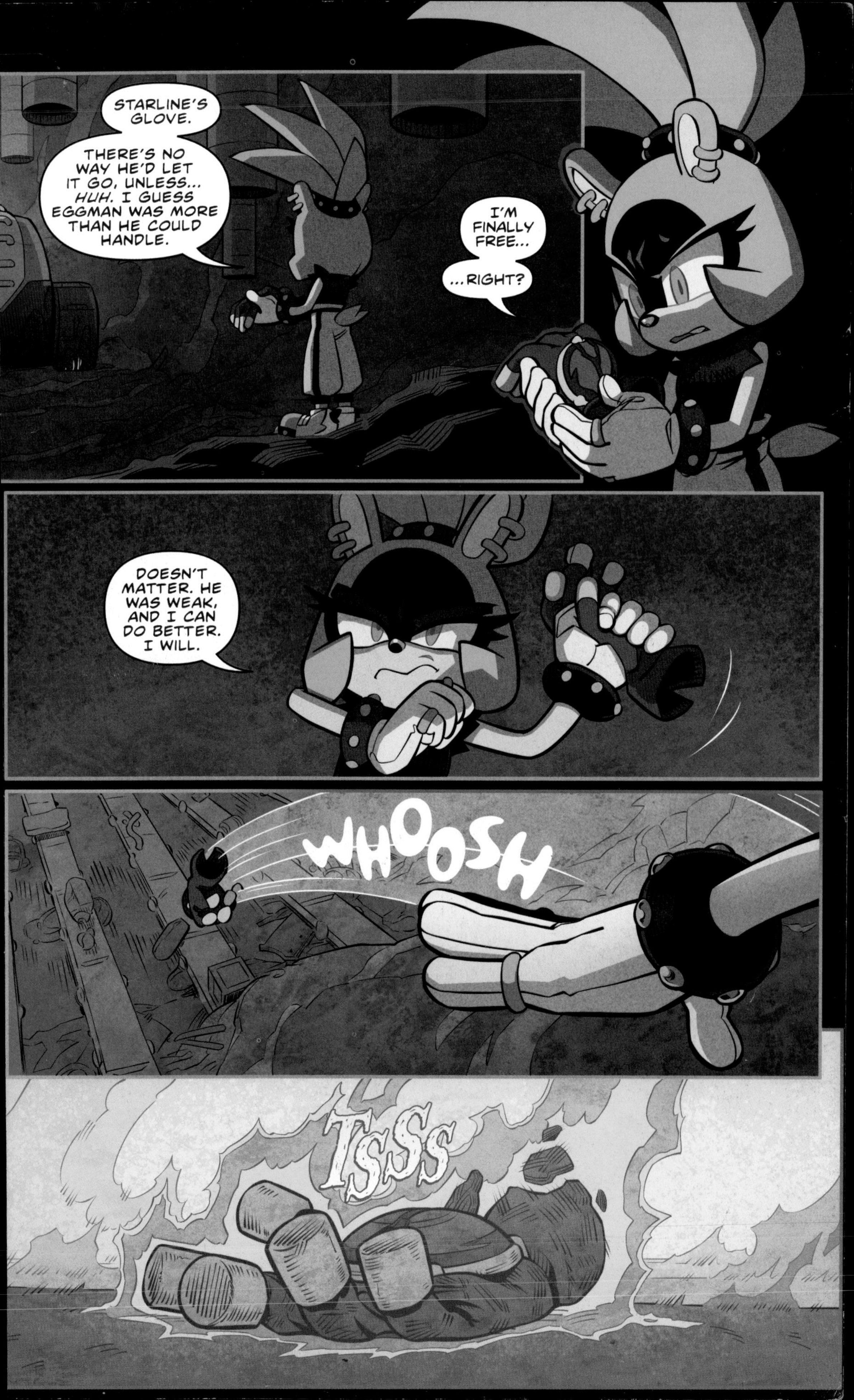
STARLINE'S GLOVE.
THERE'S NO WAY HE'D LET IT GO, UNLESS... *HUH*. I GUESS EGGMAN WAS MORE THAN HE COULD HANDLE.
I'M FINALLY FREE...
...RIGHT?
DOESN'T MATTER. HE WAS WEAK, AND I CAN DO BETTER. I WILL.
WHOOSH
TSSS

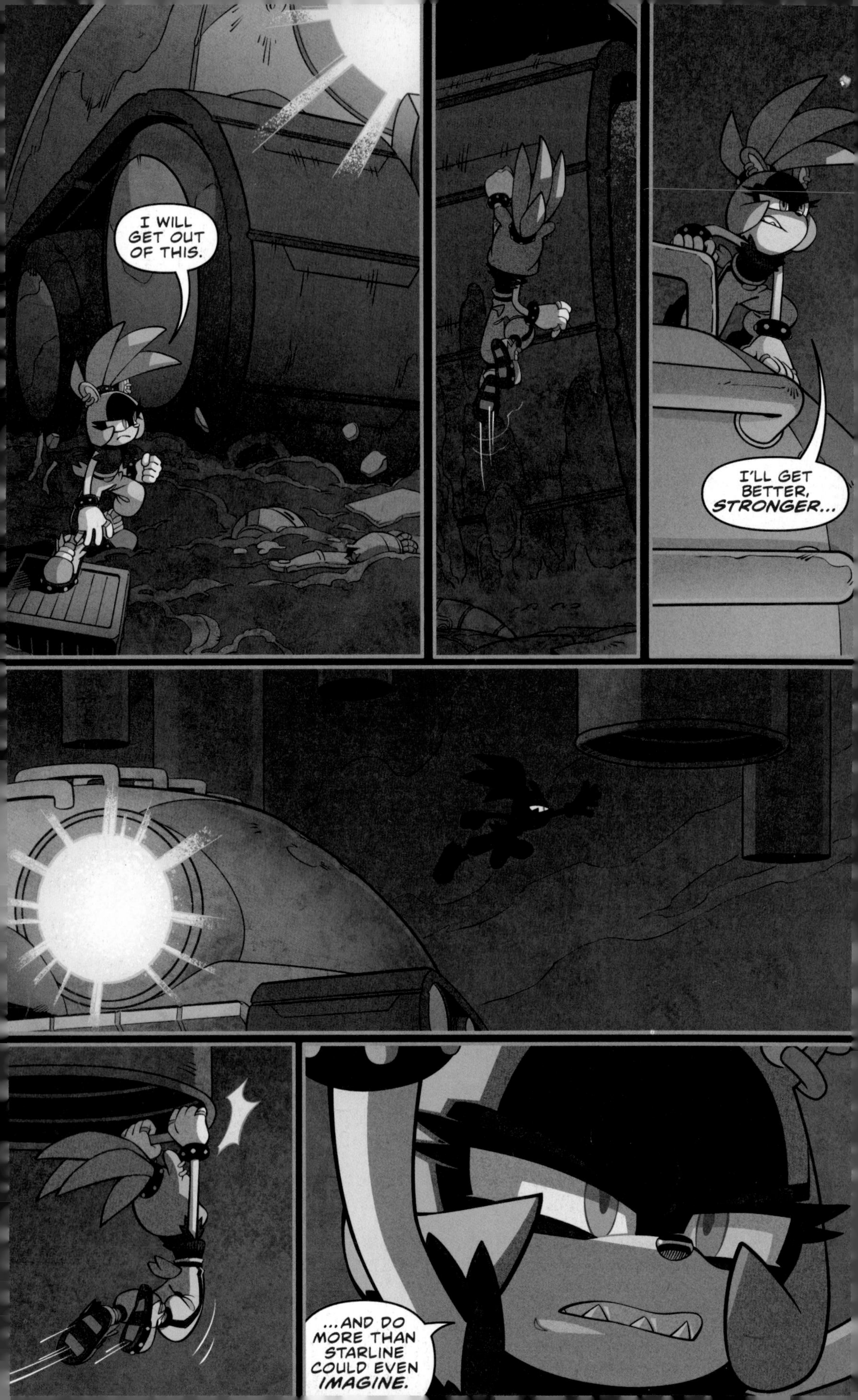
I WILL GET OUT OF THIS.
I'LL GET BETTER, *STRONGER*...
...AND DO MORE THAN STARLINE COULD EVEN *IMAGINE*.

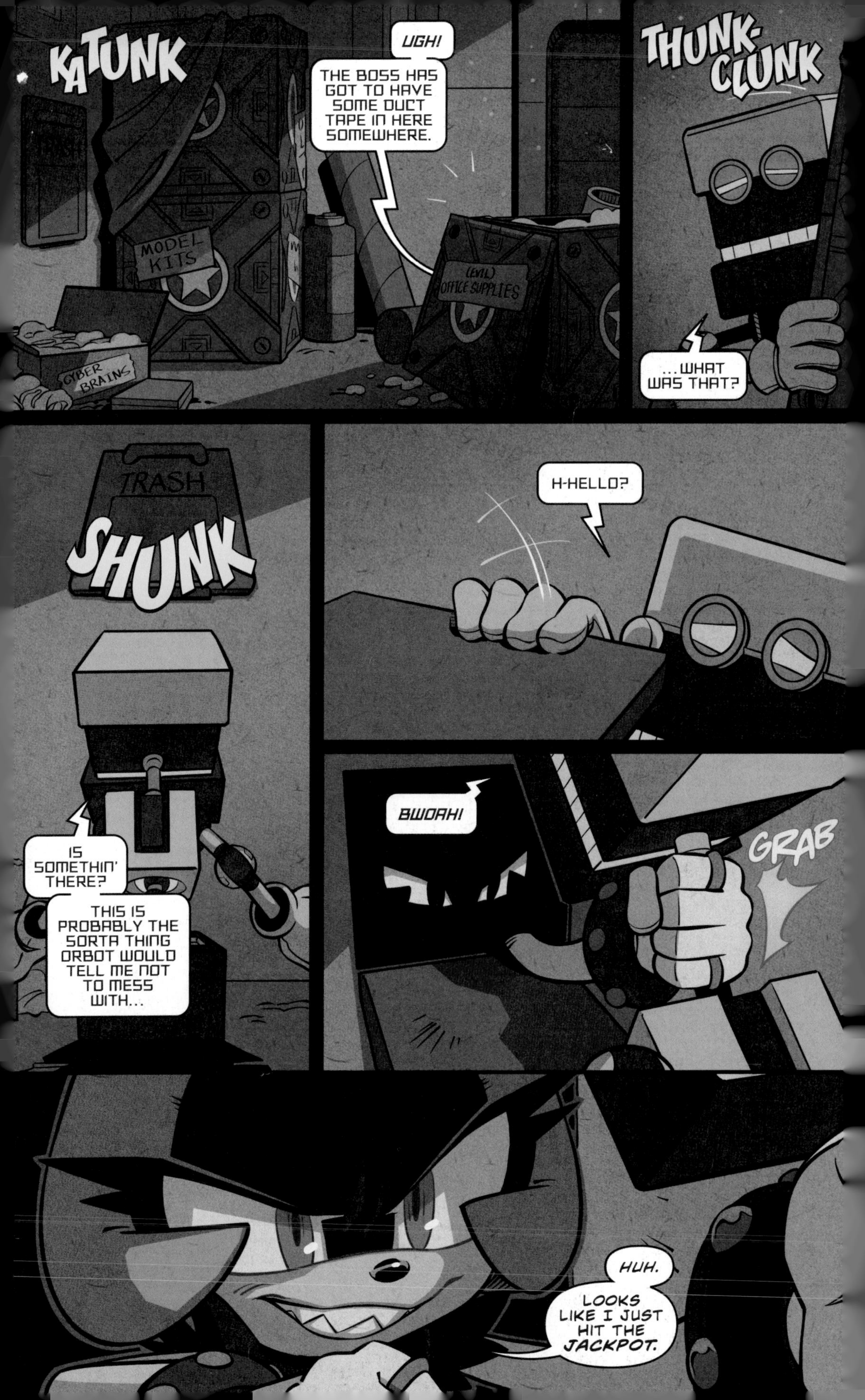
KATUNK
MODEL KITS
CYBER BRAINS
TRASH
UGH!
THE BOSS HAS GOT TO HAVE SOME DUCT TAPE IN HERE SOMEWHERE.
(EVIL) OFFICE SUPPLIES
THUNK-CLUNK
...WHAT WAS THAT?
TRASH
SHUNK
IS SOMETHIN' THERE?
THIS IS PROBABLY THE SORTA THING ORBOT WOULD TELL ME NOT TO MESS WITH...
H-HELLO?
BWORH!
GRAB
HUH.
LOOKS LIKE I JUST HIT THE JACKPOT.

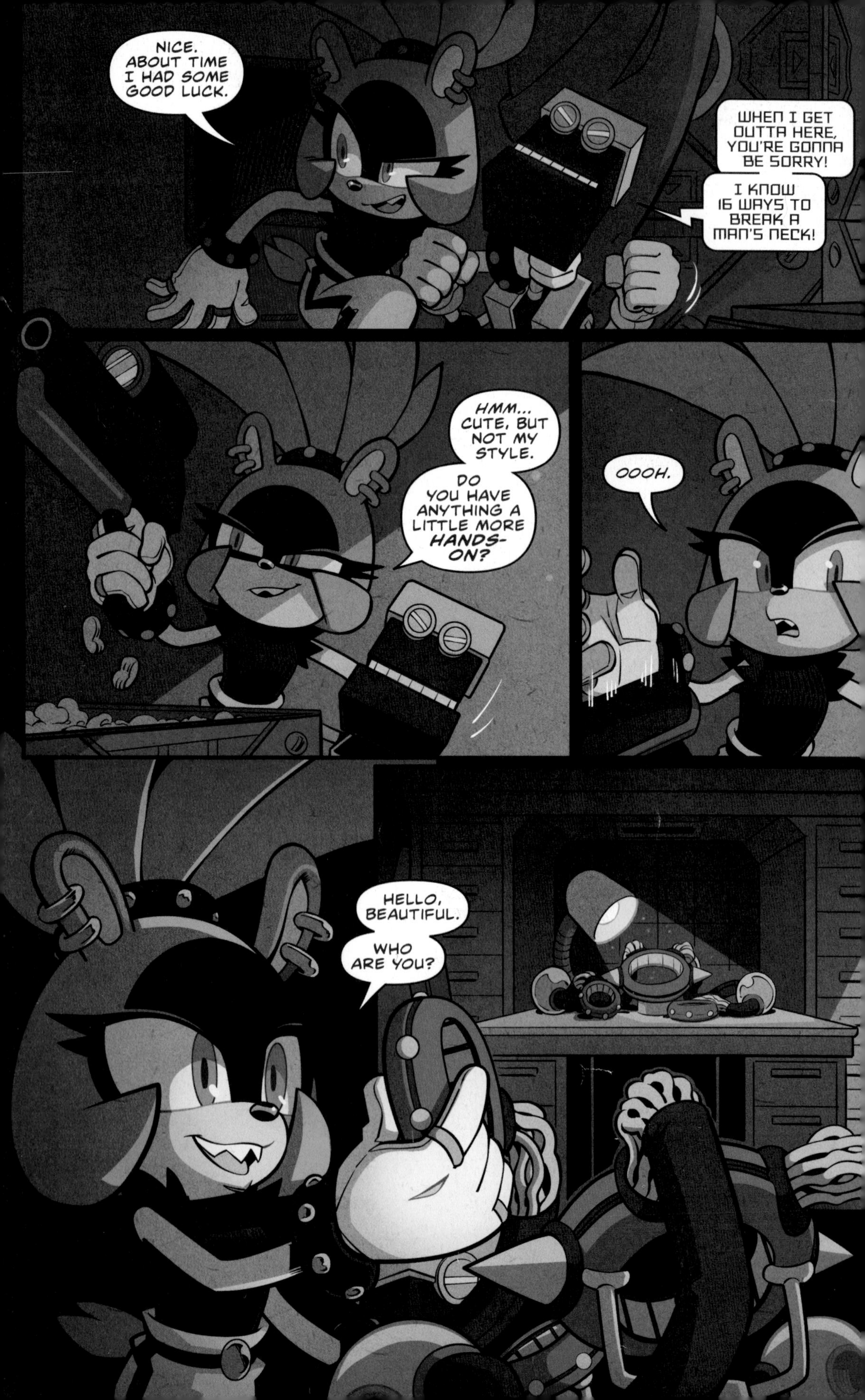
NICE. ABOUT TIME I HAD SOME GOOD LUCK.
WHEN I GET OUTTA HERE, YOU'RE GONNA BE SORRY!
I KNOW 16 WAYS TO BREAK A MAN'S NECK!
HMM... CUTE, BUT NOT MY STYLE.
DO YOU HAVE ANYTHING A LITTLE MORE HANDS-ON?
OOOH.
HELLO, BEAUTIFUL.
WHO ARE YOU?

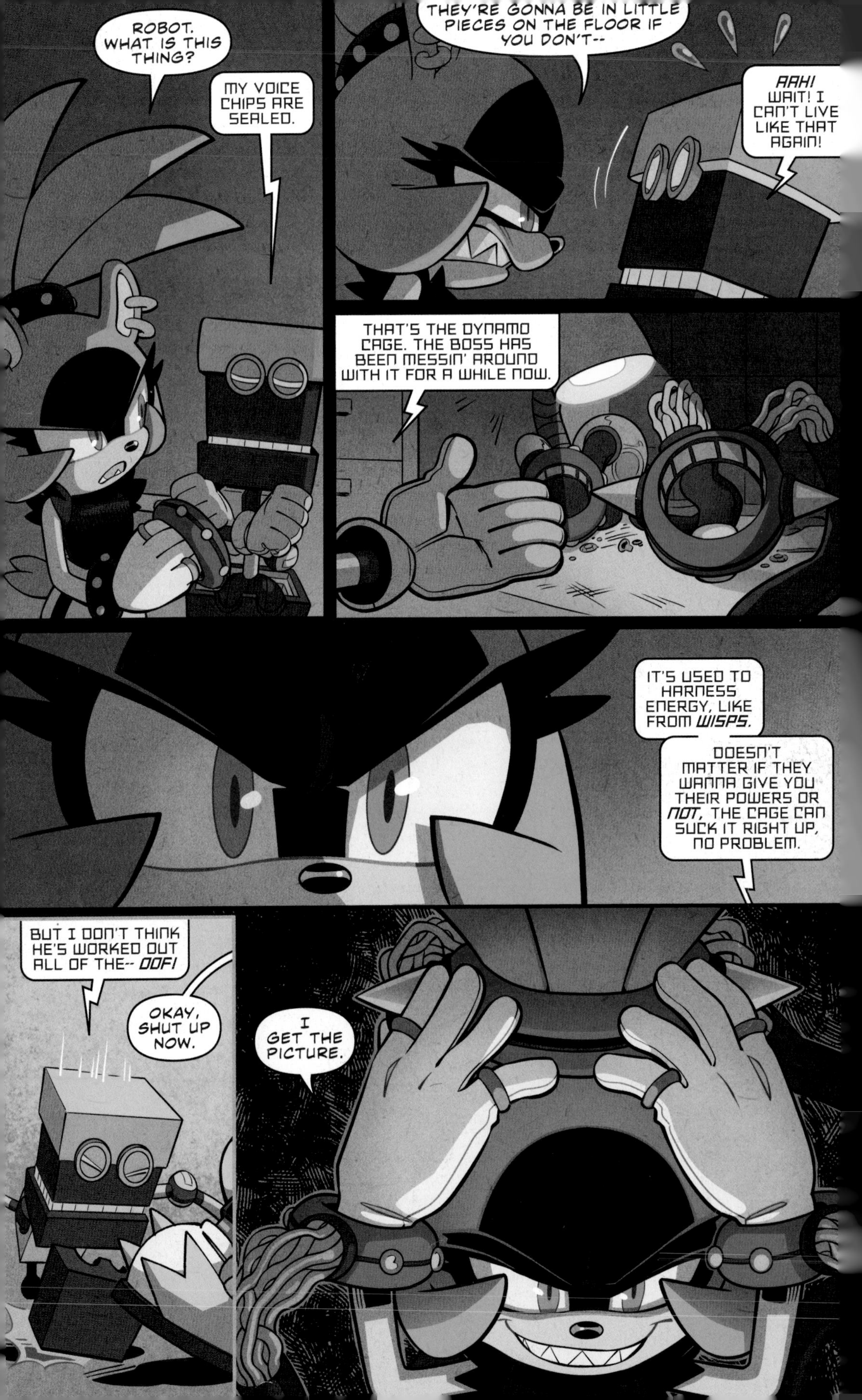
ROBOT. WHAT IS THIS THING?
MY VOICE CHIPS ARE SEALED.
THEY'RE GONNA BE IN LITTLE PIECES ON THE FLOOR IF YOU DON'T--
AAH! WAIT! I CAN'T LIVE LIKE THAT AGAIN!
THAT'S THE DYNAMO CAGE. THE BOSS HAS BEEN MESSIN' AROUND WITH IT FOR A WHILE NOW.
IT'S USED TO HARNESS ENERGY, LIKE FROM WISPS.
DOESN'T MATTER IF THEY WANNA GIVE YOU THEIR POWERS OR NOT, THE CAGE CAN SUCK IT RIGHT UP, NO PROBLEM.
BUT I DON'T THINK HE'S WORKED OUT ALL OF THE-- OOF!
OKAY, SHUT UP NOW.
I GET THE PICTURE.

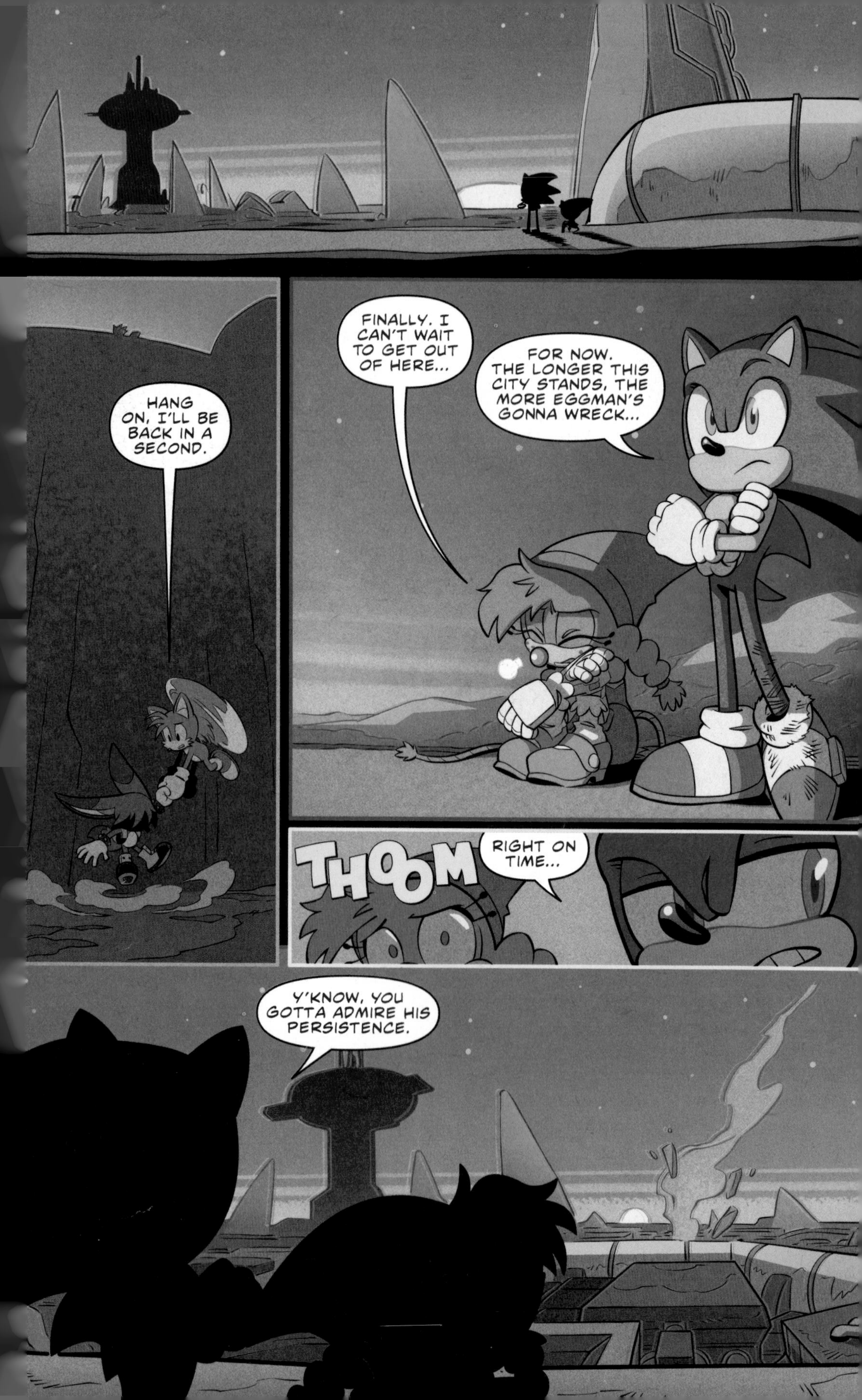
HANG ON, I'LL BE BACK IN A SECOND.
FINALLY. I CAN'T WAIT TO GET OUT OF HERE...
FOR NOW. THE LONGER THIS CITY STANDS, THE MORE EGGMAN'S GONNA WRECK...
THOOM
RIGHT ON TIME...
Y'KNOW, YOU GOTTA ADMIRE HIS PERSISTENCE.

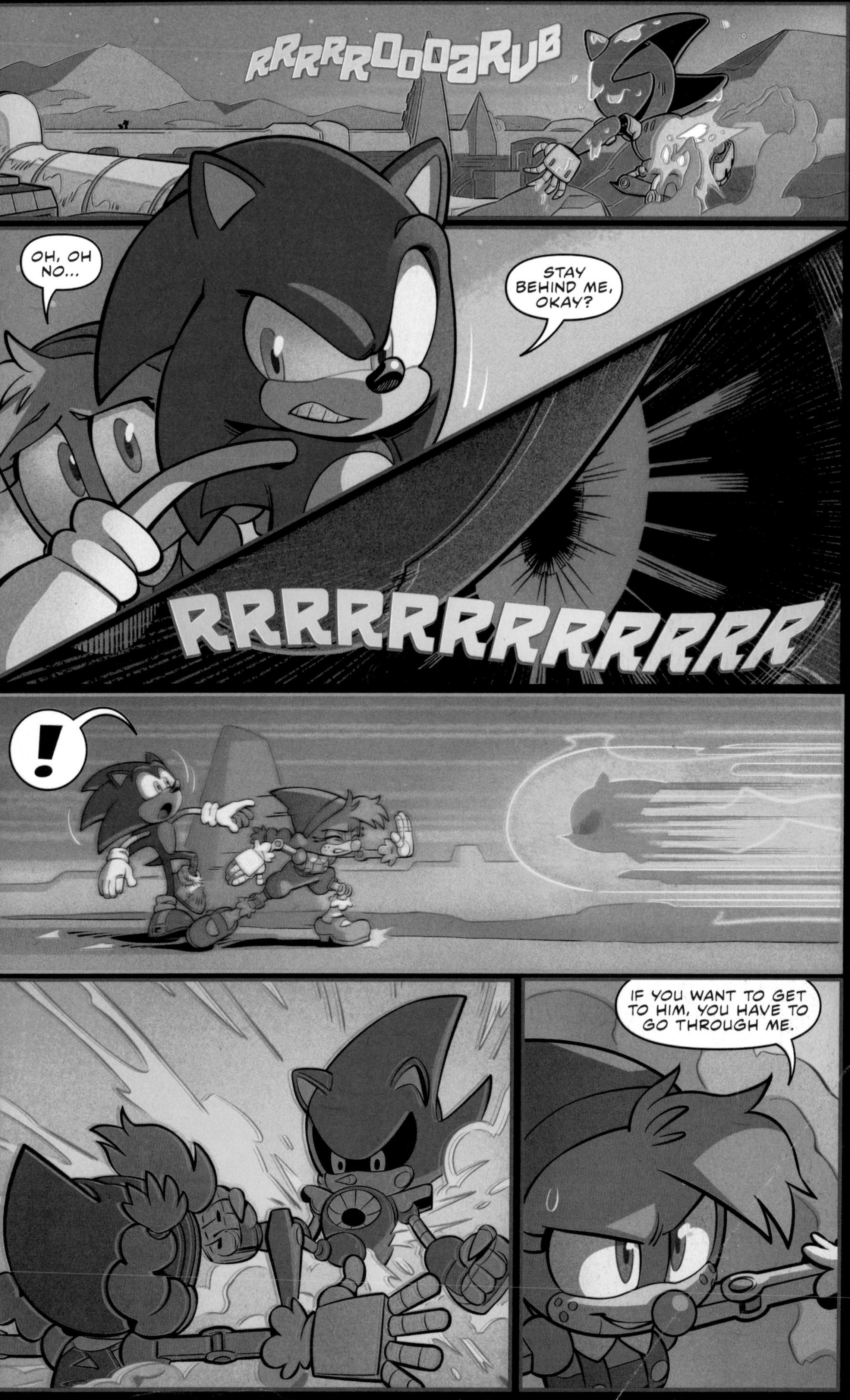
RRRRROOOARVB
OH, OH NO...
STAY BEHIND ME, OKAY?
RRRRRRRRRRRRR
!
IF YOU WANT TO GET TO HIM, YOU HAVE TO GO THROUGH ME.

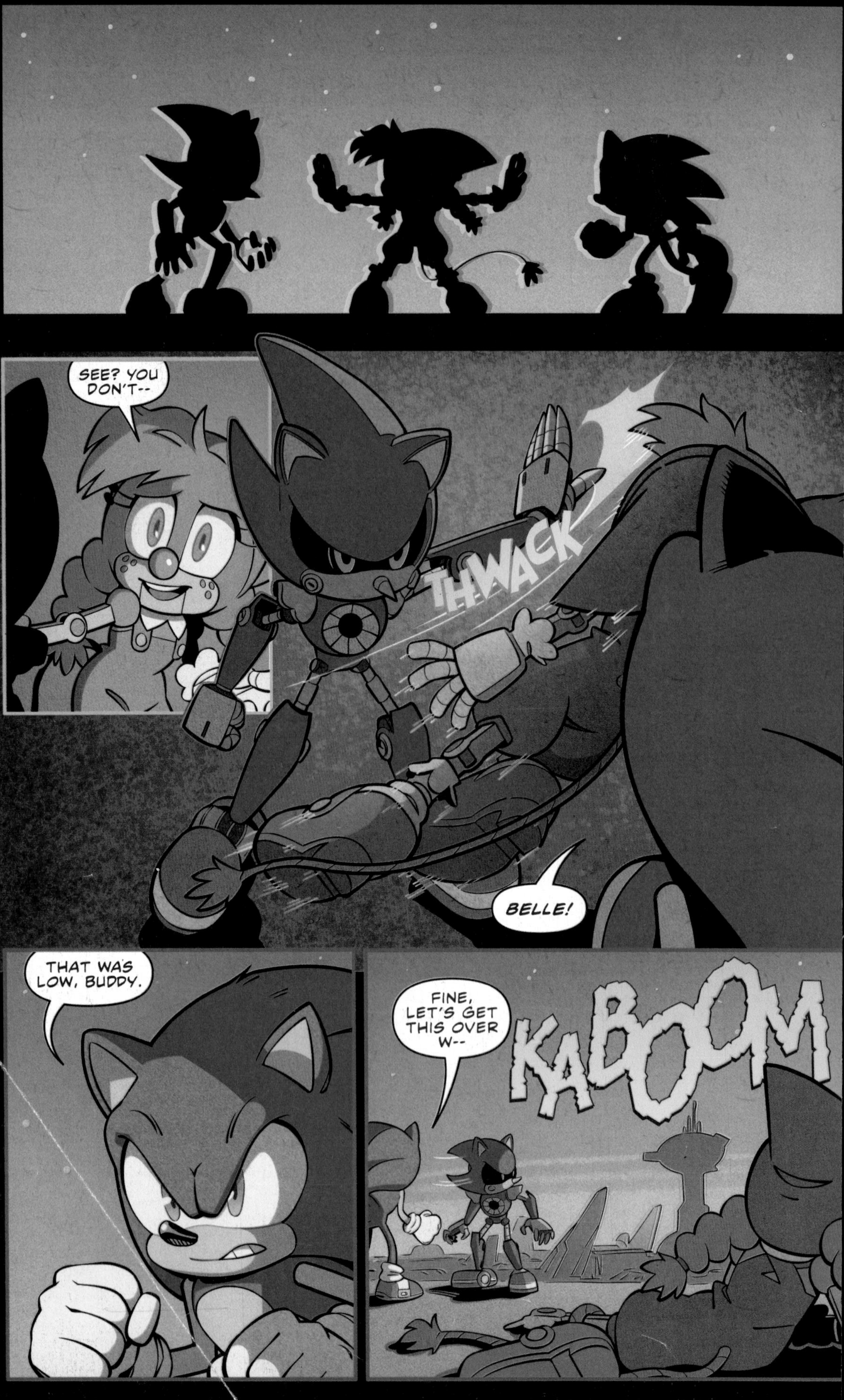
SEE? YOU DON'T--
THWACK
BELLE!
THAT WAS LOW, BUDDY.
FINE, LET'S GET THIS OVER W--
KABOOM

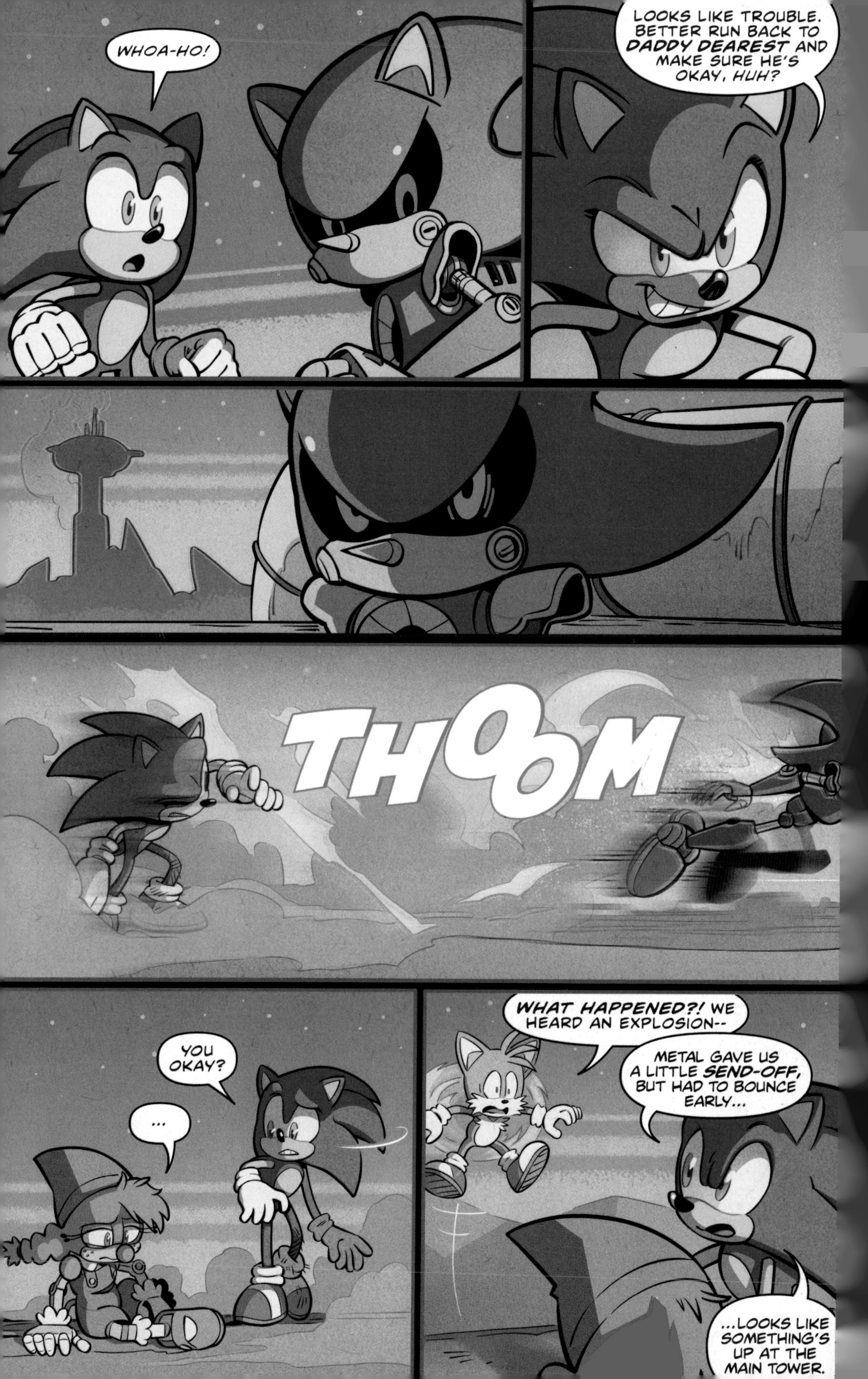
WHOA-HO!
LOOKS LIKE TROUBLE. BETTER RUN BACK TO DADDY DEAREST AND MAKE SURE HE'S OKAY, HUH?
THOOOM
YOU OKAY?
...
WHAT HAPPENED?! WE HEARD AN EXPLOSION--
METAL GAVE US A LITTLE SEND-OFF, BUT HAD TO BOUNCE EARLY...
...LOOKS LIKE SOMETHING'S UP AT THE MAIN TOWER.

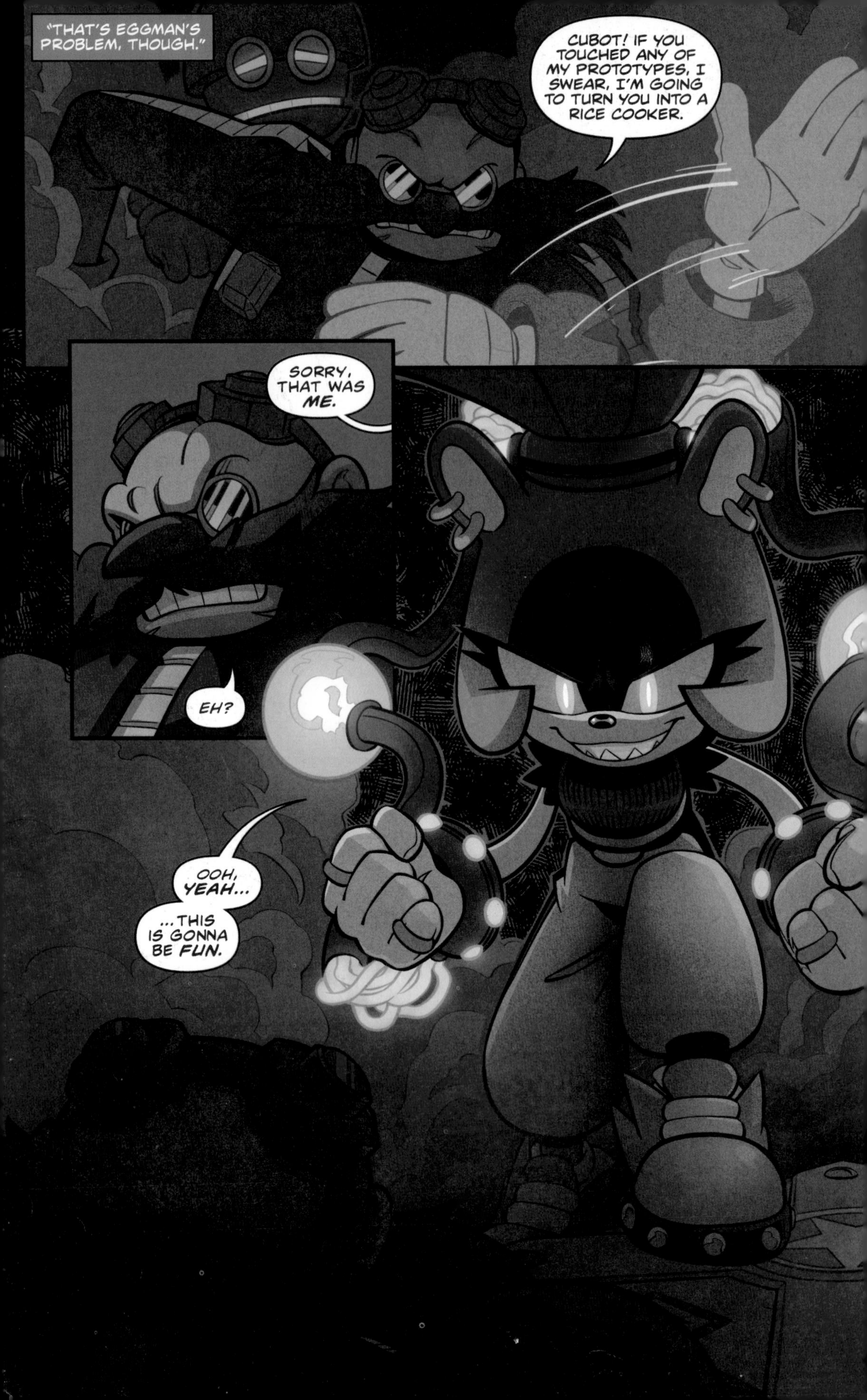
"THAT'S EGGMAN'S PROBLEM, THOUGH."
CUBOT! IF YOU TOUCHED ANY OF MY PROTOTYPES, I SWEAR, I'M GOING TO TURN YOU INTO A RICE COOKER.
SORRY, THAT WAS ME.
EH?
OOH, YEAH...
...THIS IS GONNA BE FUN.

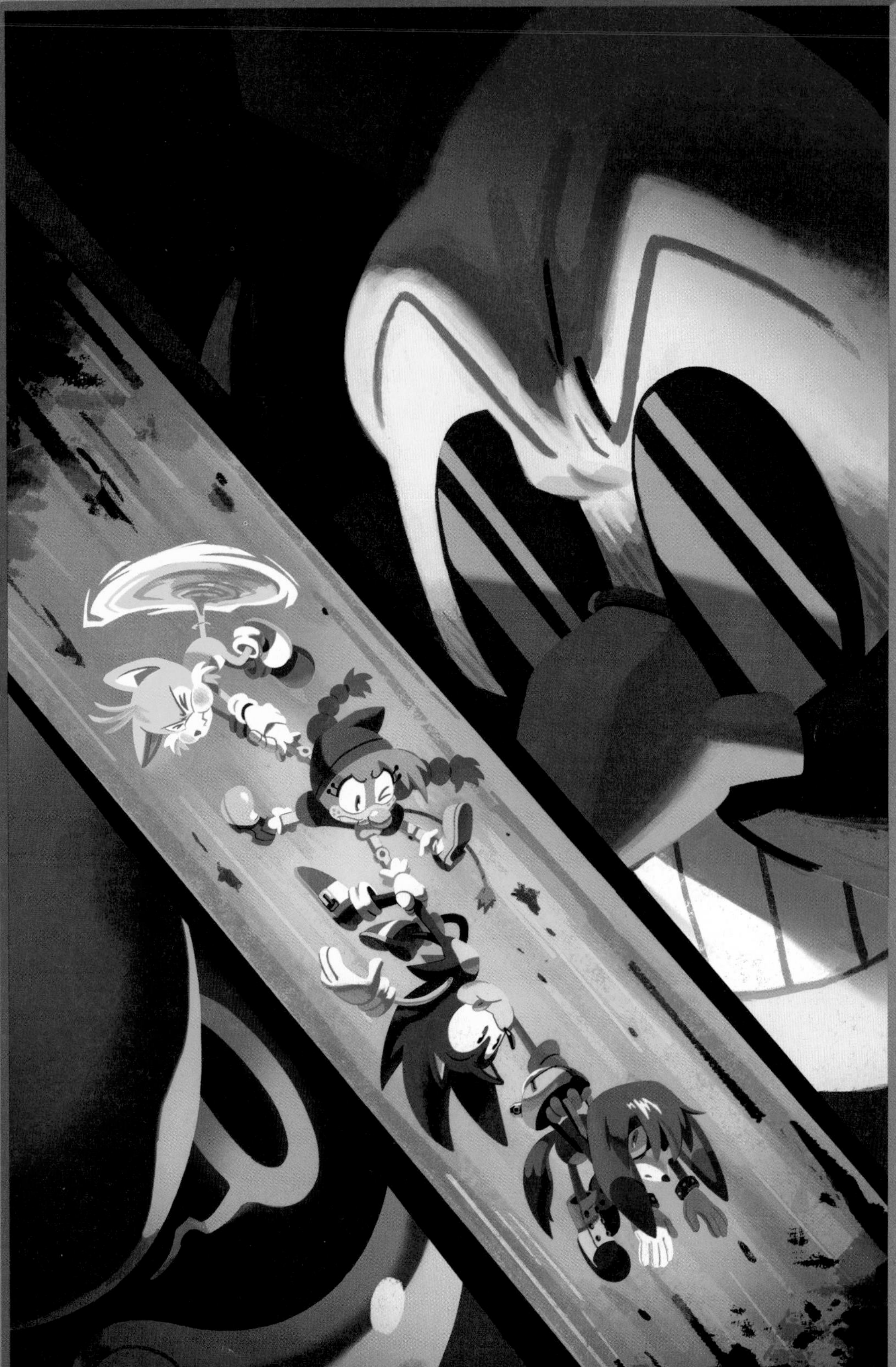

ART BY **NATHALIE FOURDRAINE**

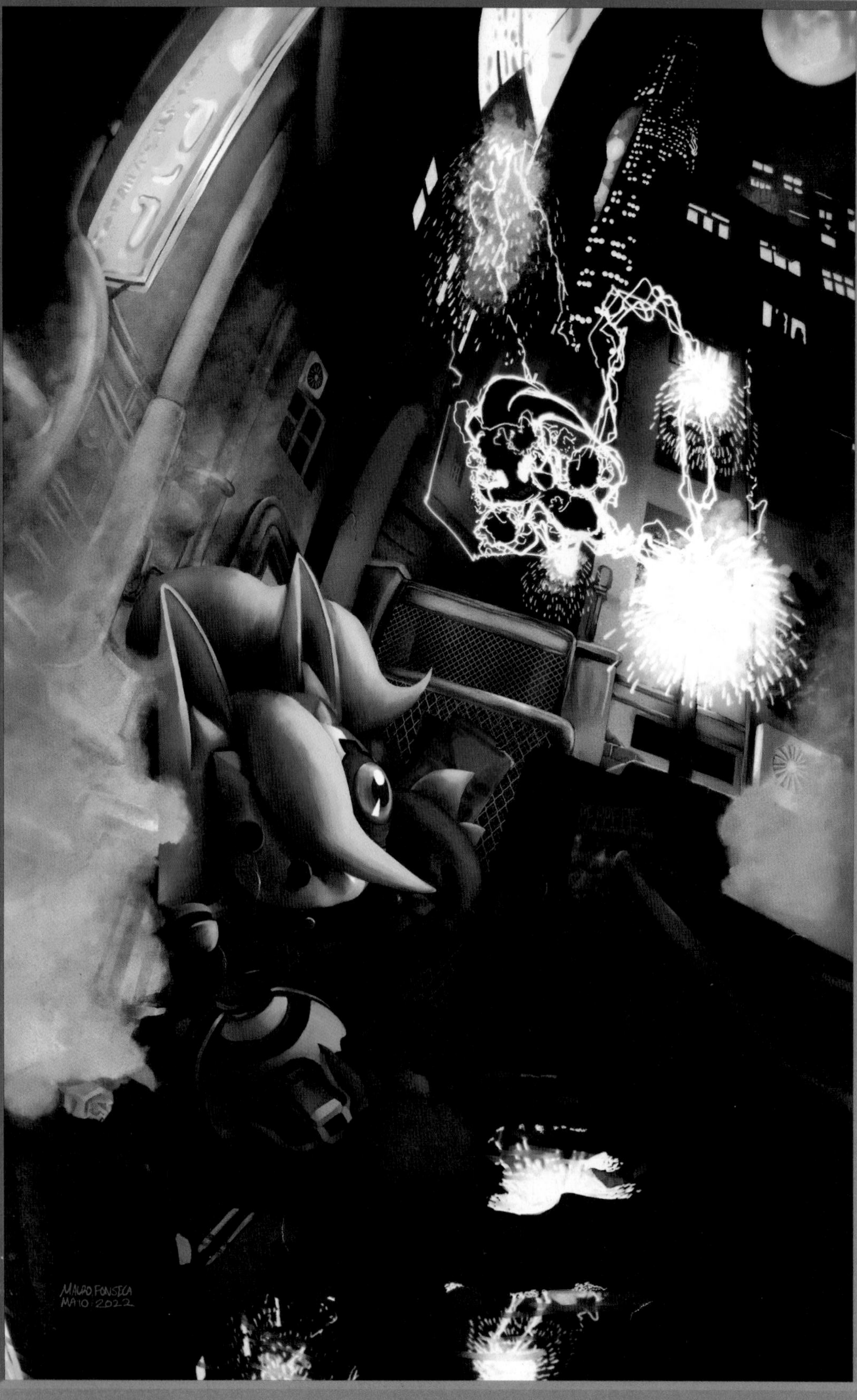
MAURO FONSECA
MAIO 2022

ART BY **MAURO FONSECA**

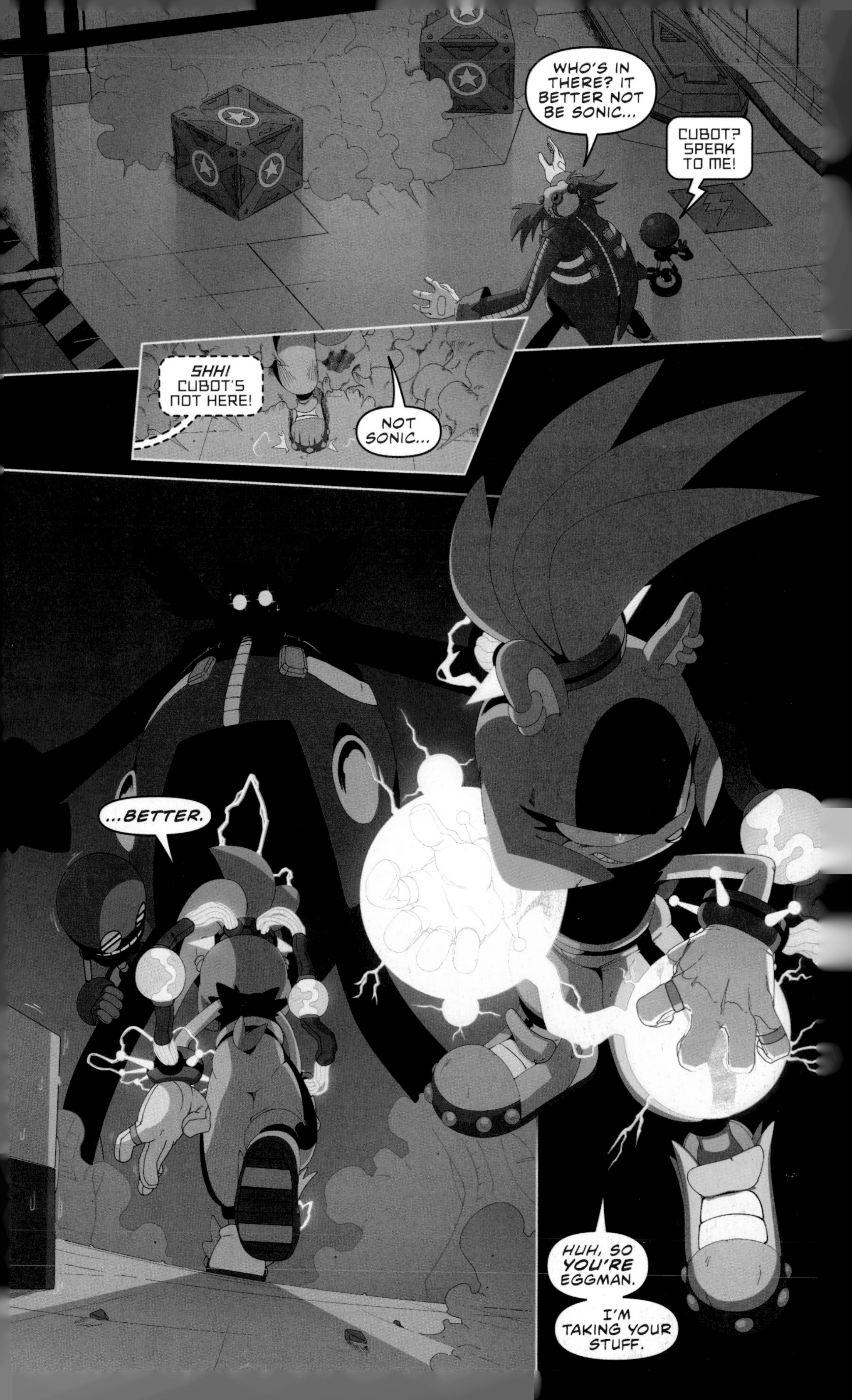
WHO'S IN THERE? IT BETTER NOT BE SONIC...
CUBOT? SPEAK TO ME!
SHH! CUBOT'S NOT HERE!
NOT SONIC...
...BETTER.
HUH, SO YOU'RE EGGMAN.
I'M TAKING YOUR STUFF.

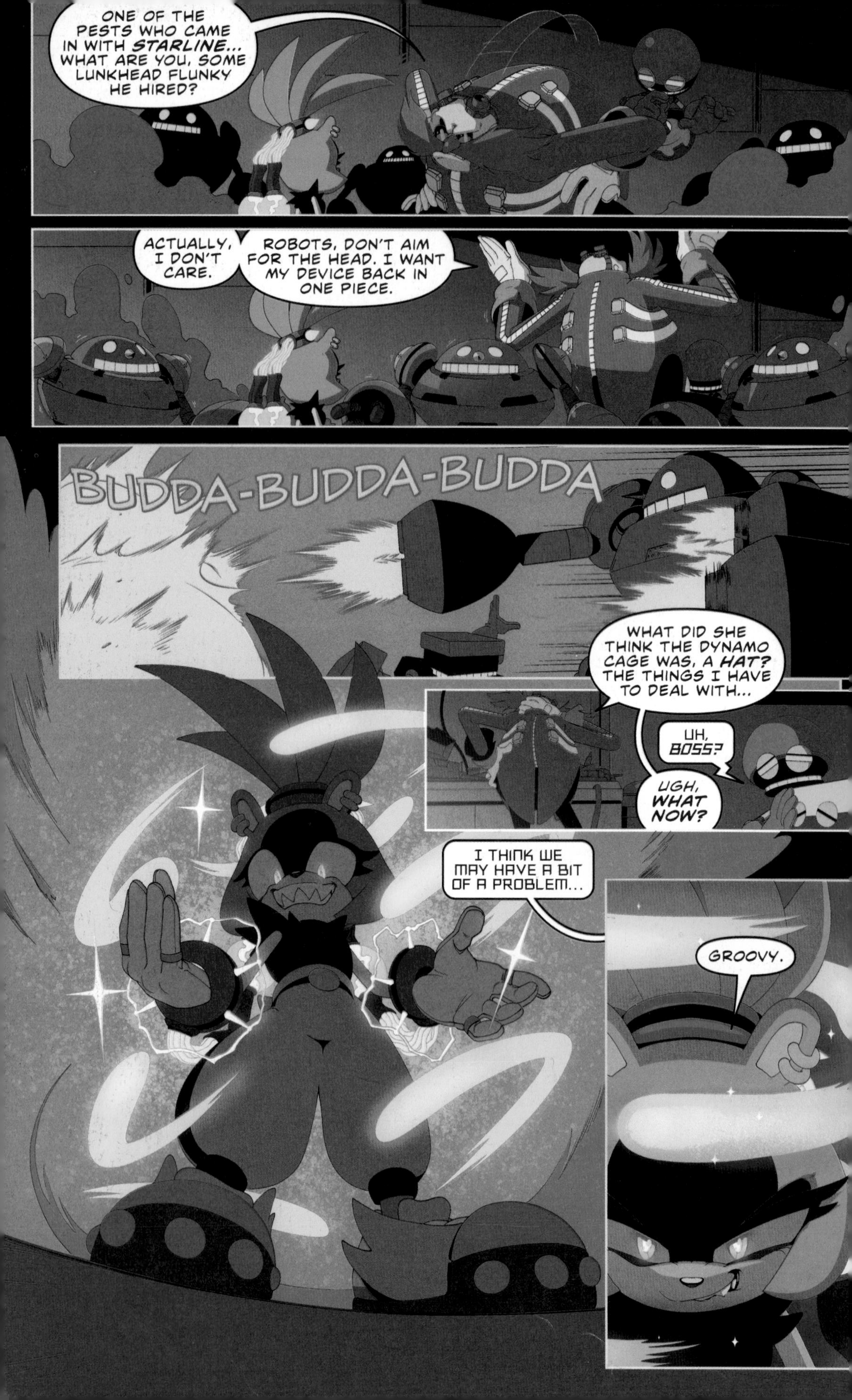
ONE OF THE PESTS WHO CAME IN WITH STARLINE... WHAT ARE YOU, SOME LUNKHEAD FLUNKY HE HIRED?
ACTUALLY, I DON'T CARE.
ROBOTS, DON'T AIM FOR THE HEAD. I WANT MY DEVICE BACK IN ONE PIECE.
BUDDA-BUDDA-BUDDA
WHAT DID SHE THINK THE DYNAMO CAGE WAS, A HAT? THE THINGS I HAVE TO DEAL WITH...
UH, BOSS?
UGH, WHAT NOW?
I THINK WE MAY HAVE A BIT OF A PROBLEM...
GROOVY.

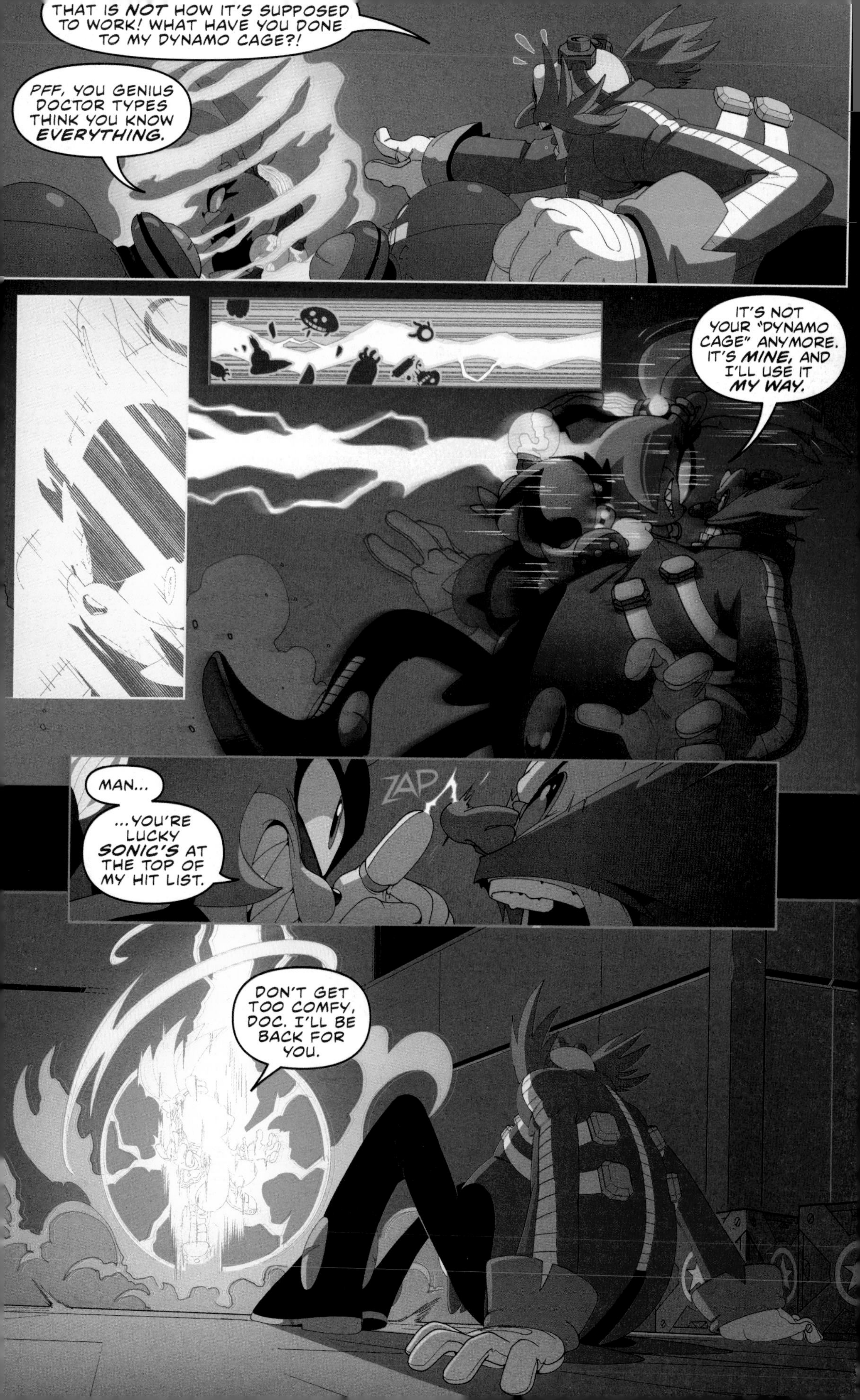
THAT IS *NOT* HOW IT'S SUPPOSED TO WORK! WHAT HAVE YOU DONE TO MY DYNAMO CAGE?!
PFF, YOU GENIUS DOCTOR TYPES THINK YOU KNOW *EVERYTHING.*
IT'S NOT YOUR "DYNAMO CAGE" ANYMORE. IT'S *MINE,* AND I'LL USE IT *MY WAY.*
MAN...
...YOU'RE LUCKY *SONIC'S* AT THE TOP OF MY HIT LIST.
ZAP
DON'T GET TOO COMFY, DOC. I'LL BE BACK FOR YOU.

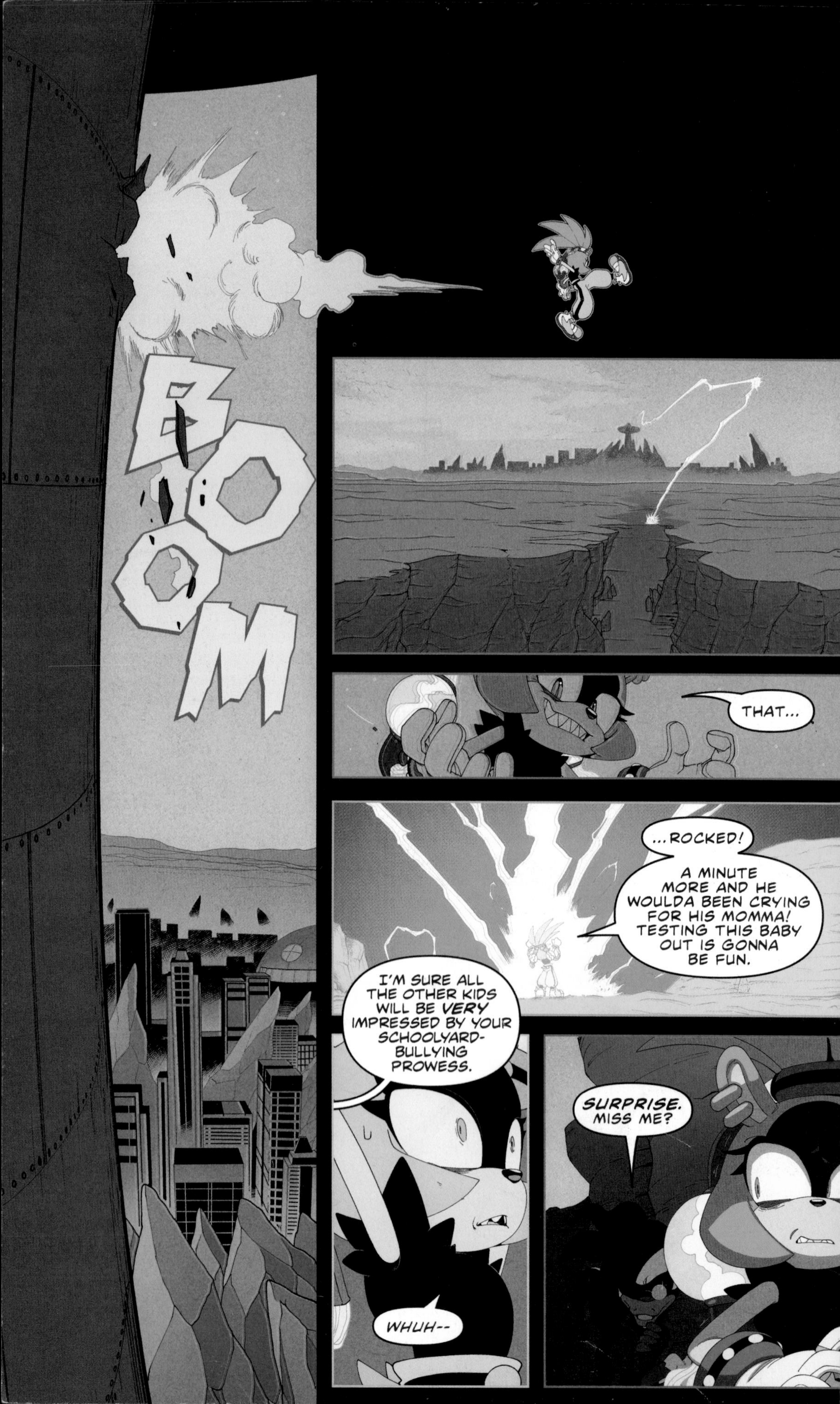
BOOM
THAT...
...ROCKED!
A MINUTE MORE AND HE WOULDA BEEN CRYING FOR HIS MOMMA! TESTING THIS BABY OUT IS GONNA BE FUN.
I'M SURE ALL THE OTHER KIDS WILL BE VERY IMPRESSED BY YOUR SCHOOLYARD-BULLYING PROWESS.
WHUH--
SURPRISE. MISS ME?

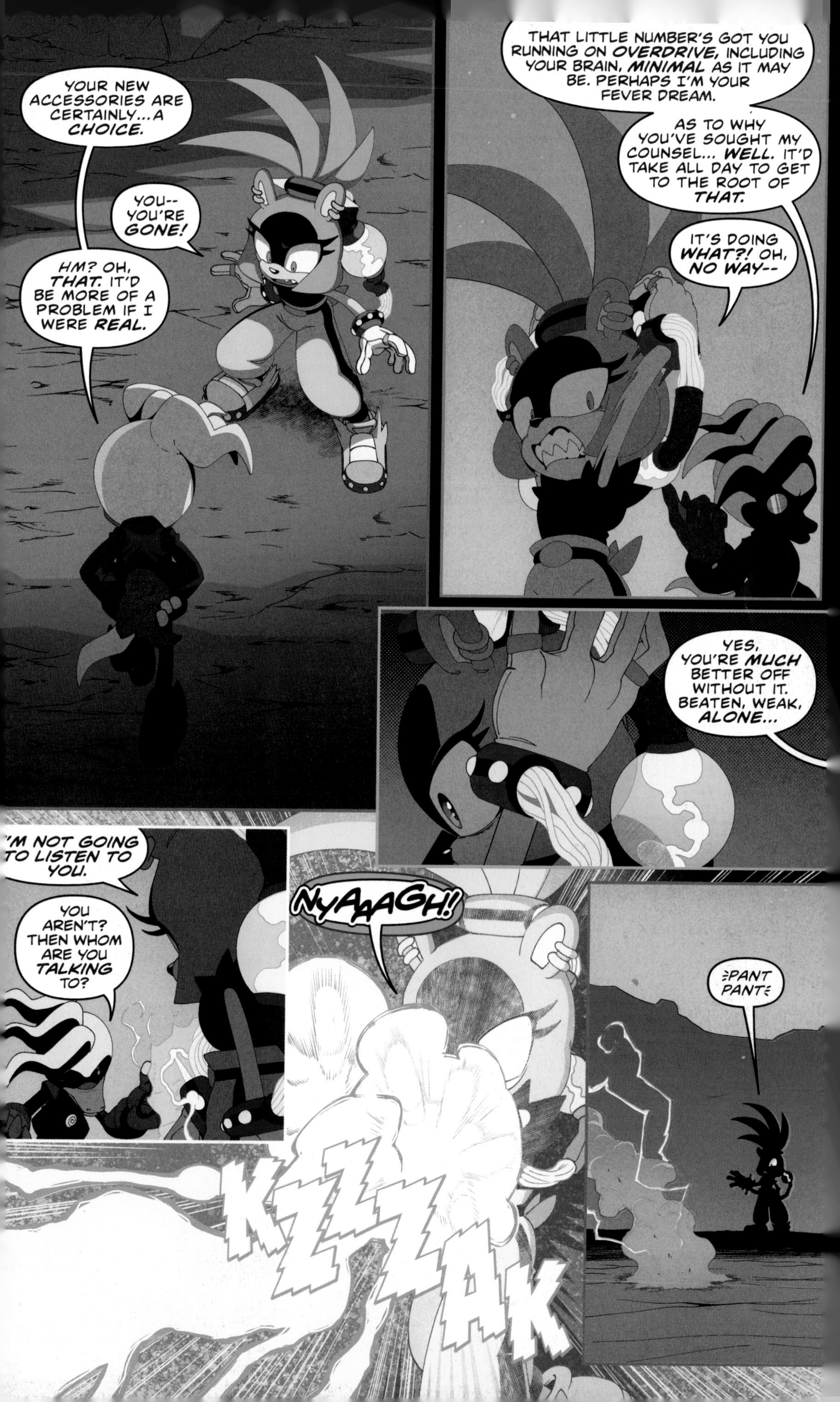
YOUR NEW ACCESSORIES ARE CERTAINLY... A CHOICE.
YOU-- YOU'RE GONE!
HM? OH, THAT. IT'D BE MORE OF A PROBLEM IF I WERE REAL.
THAT LITTLE NUMBER'S GOT YOU RUNNING ON OVERDRIVE, INCLUDING YOUR BRAIN, MINIMAL AS IT MAY BE. PERHAPS I'M YOUR FEVER DREAM.
AS TO WHY YOU'VE SOUGHT MY COUNSEL... WELL. IT'D TAKE ALL DAY TO GET TO THE ROOT OF THAT.
IT'S DOING WHAT?! OH, NO WAY--
YES, YOU'RE MUCH BETTER OFF WITHOUT IT. BEATEN, WEAK, ALONE...
I'M NOT GOING TO LISTEN TO YOU.
YOU AREN'T? THEN WHOM ARE YOU TALKING TO?
NYAAAGH!
KZZZAK
PANT PANT

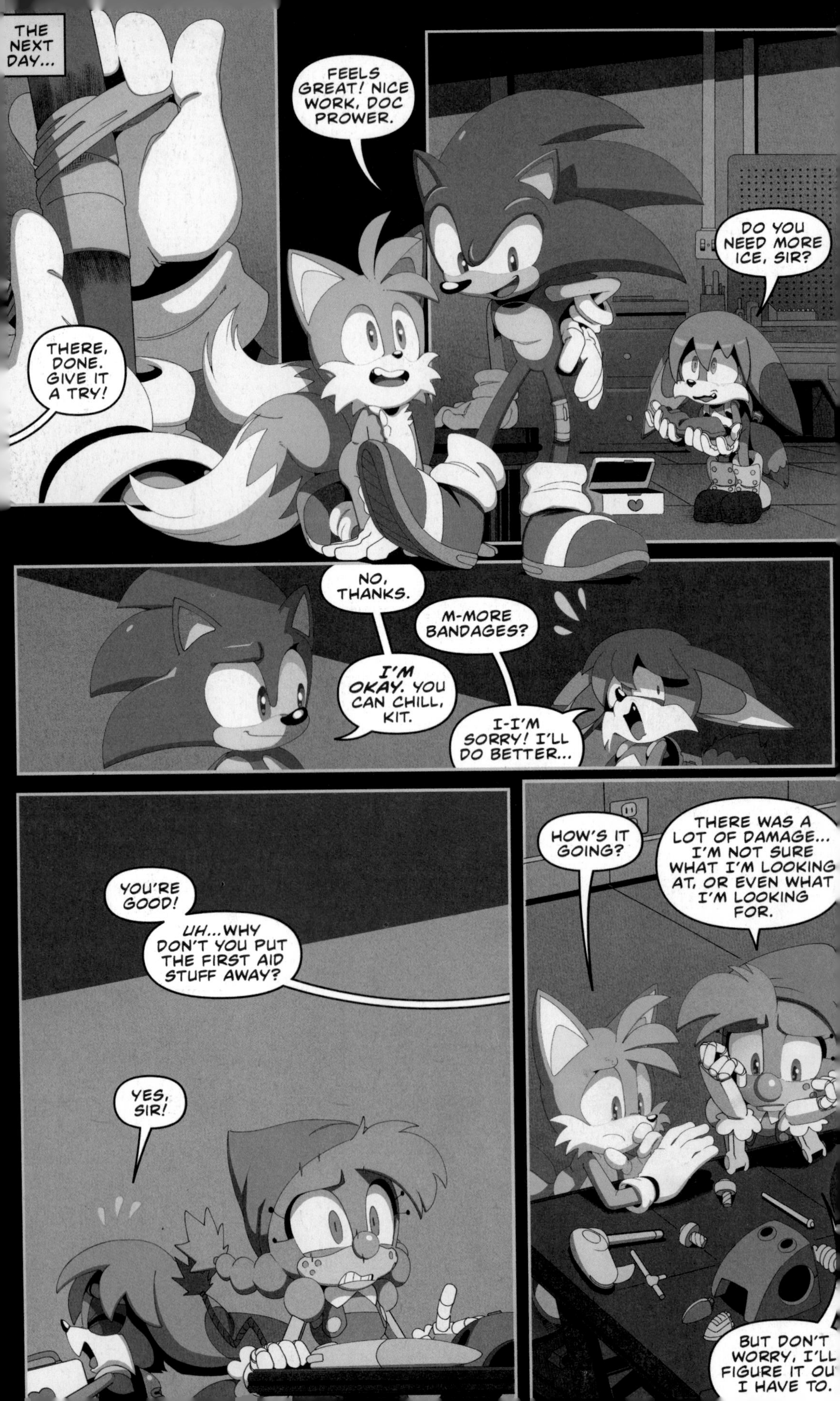
THE NEXT DAY...
THERE, DONE. GIVE IT A TRY!
FEELS GREAT! NICE WORK, DOC PROWER.
DO YOU NEED MORE ICE, SIR?
NO, THANKS.
I'M OKAY. YOU CAN CHILL, KIT.
M-MORE BANDAGES?
I-I'M SORRY! I'LL DO BETTER...
YOU'RE GOOD!
UH...WHY DON'T YOU PUT THE FIRST AID STUFF AWAY?
YES, SIR!
HOW'S IT GOING?
THERE WAS A LOT OF DAMAGE... I'M NOT SURE WHAT I'M LOOKING AT, OR EVEN WHAT I'M LOOKING FOR.
BUT DON'T WORRY, I'LL FIGURE IT OU I HAVE TO.

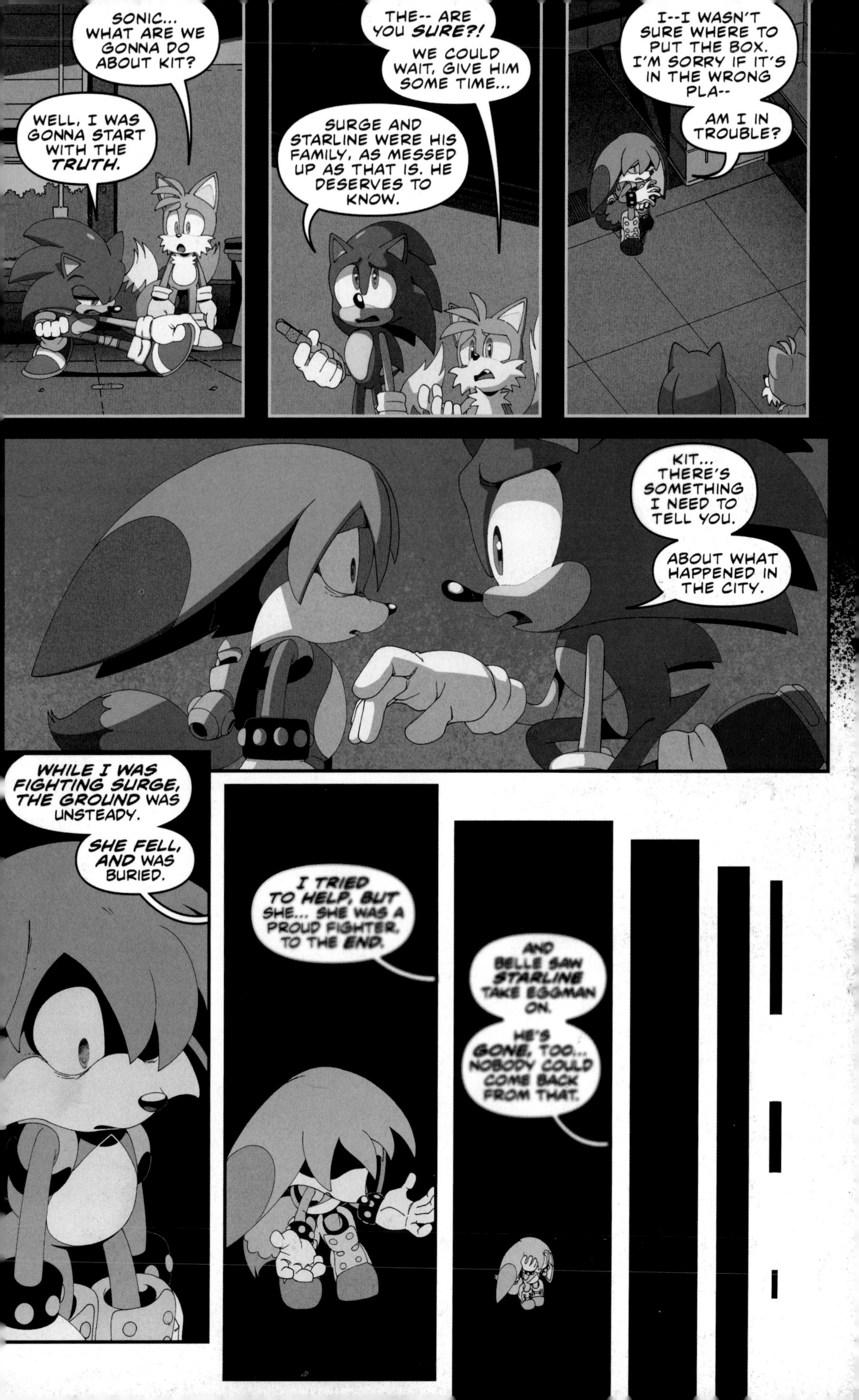
SONIC... WHAT ARE WE GONNA DO ABOUT KIT?
WELL, I WAS GONNA START WITH THE TRUTH.
THE-- ARE YOU SURE?!
WE COULD WAIT, GIVE HIM SOME TIME...
SURGE AND STARLINE WERE HIS FAMILY, AS MESSED UP AS THAT IS. HE DESERVES TO KNOW.
I--I WASN'T SURE WHERE TO PUT THE BOX. I'M SORRY IF IT'S IN THE WRONG PLA--
AM I IN TROUBLE?
KIT... THERE'S SOMETHING I NEED TO TELL YOU.
ABOUT WHAT HAPPENED IN THE CITY.
WHILE I WAS FIGHTING SURGE, THE GROUND WAS UNSTEADY.
SHE FELL, AND WAS BURIED.
I TRIED TO HELP, BUT SHE... SHE WAS A PROUD FIGHTER, TO THE END.
AND BELLE SAW STARLINE TAKE EGGMAN ON.
HE'S GONE, TOO... NOBODY COULD COME BACK FROM THAT.

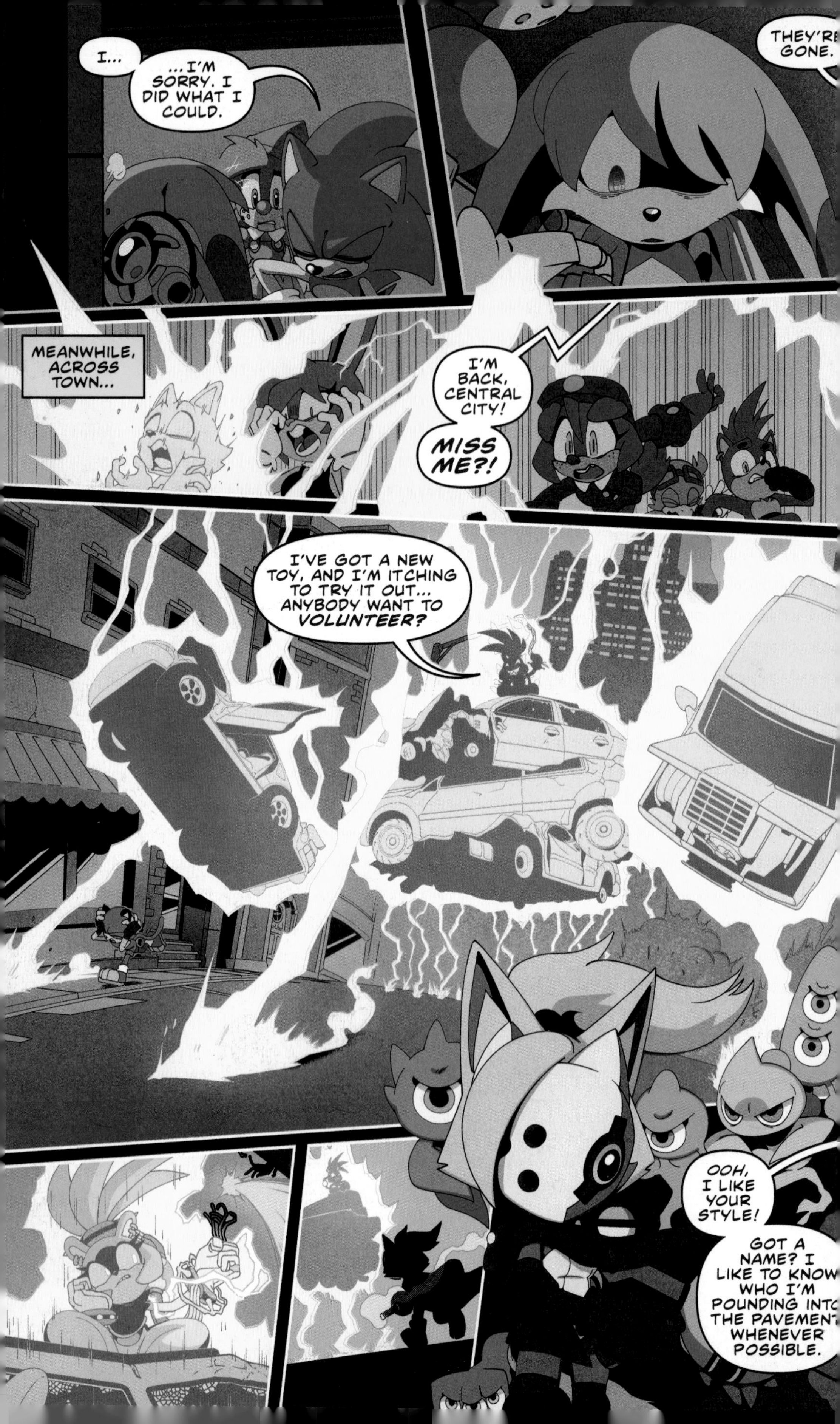
I...
...I'M SORRY. I DID WHAT I COULD.
THEY'RE GONE.
MEANWHILE, ACROSS TOWN...
I'M BACK, CENTRAL CITY!
MISS ME?!
I'VE GOT A NEW TOY, AND I'M ITCHING TO TRY IT OUT... ANYBODY WANT TO VOLUNTEER?
OOH, I LIKE YOUR STYLE!
GOT A NAME? I LIKE TO KNOW WHO I'M POUNDING INTO THE PAVEMENT WHENEVER POSSIBLE.

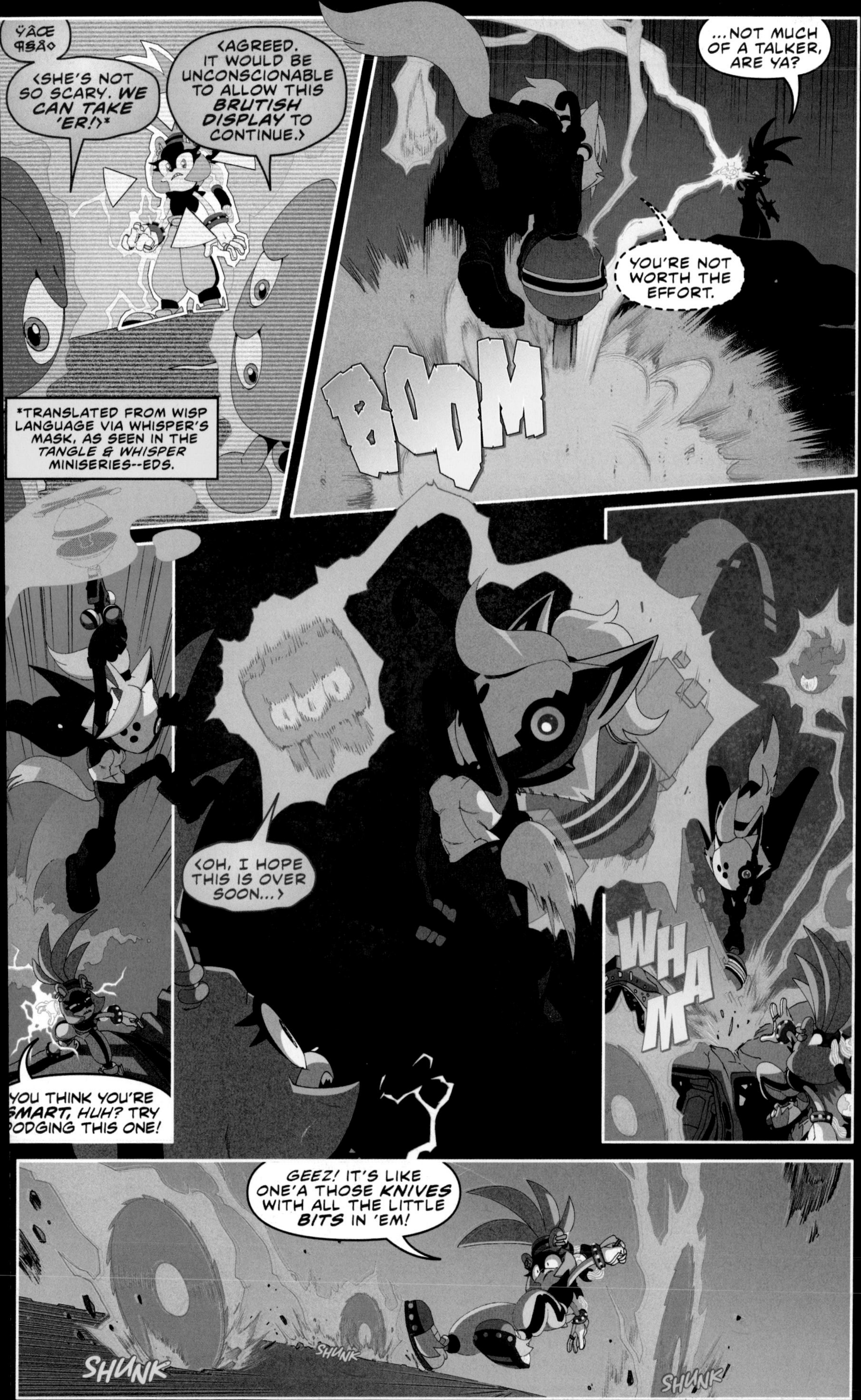

<SHE'S NOT SO SCARY. WE CAN TAKE 'ER!>*
<AGREED. IT WOULD BE UNCONSCIONABLE TO ALLOW THIS BRUTISH DISPLAY TO CONTINUE.>
*TRANSLATED FROM WISP LANGUAGE VIA WHISPER'S MASK, AS SEEN IN THE TANGLE & WHISPER MINISERIES--EDS.
...NOT MUCH OF A TALKER, ARE YA?
YOU'RE NOT WORTH THE EFFORT.
BOOM
<OH, I HOPE THIS IS OVER SOON...>
YOU THINK YOU'RE SMART, HUH? TRY DODGING THIS ONE!
WHAM
GEEZ! IT'S LIKE ONE'A THOSE KNIVES WITH ALL THE LITTLE BITS IN 'EM!
SHUNK
SHUNK
SHUNK

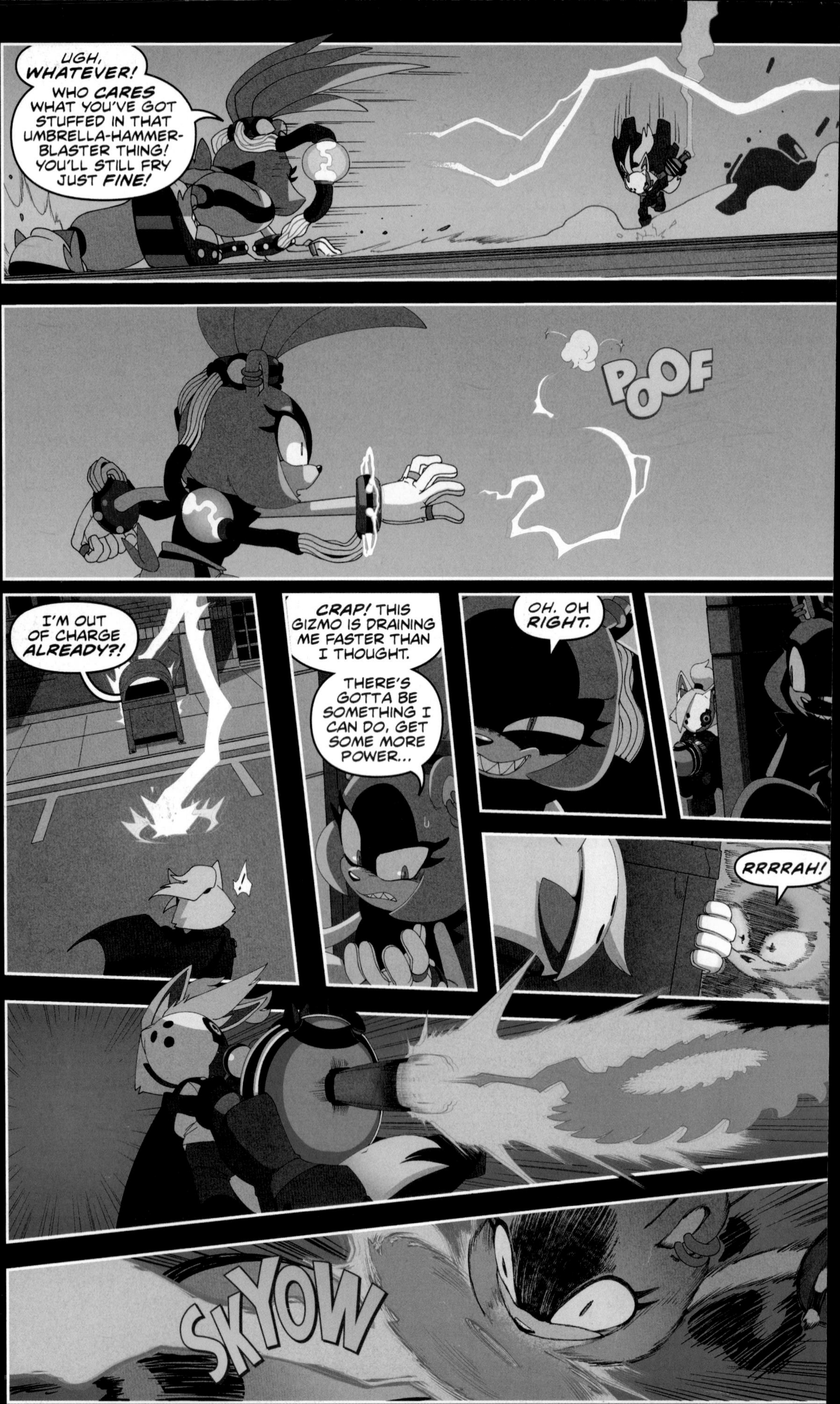
UGH, WHATEVER! WHO CARES WHAT YOU'VE GOT STUFFED IN THAT UMBRELLA-HAMMER-BLASTER THING! YOU'LL STILL FRY JUST FINE!
POOF
I'M OUT OF CHARGE ALREADY?!
CRAP! THIS GIZMO IS DRAINING ME FASTER THAN I THOUGHT.
THERE'S GOTTA BE SOMETHING I CAN DO, GET SOME MORE POWER...
OH. OH RIGHT.
RRRRAH!
SKYOW

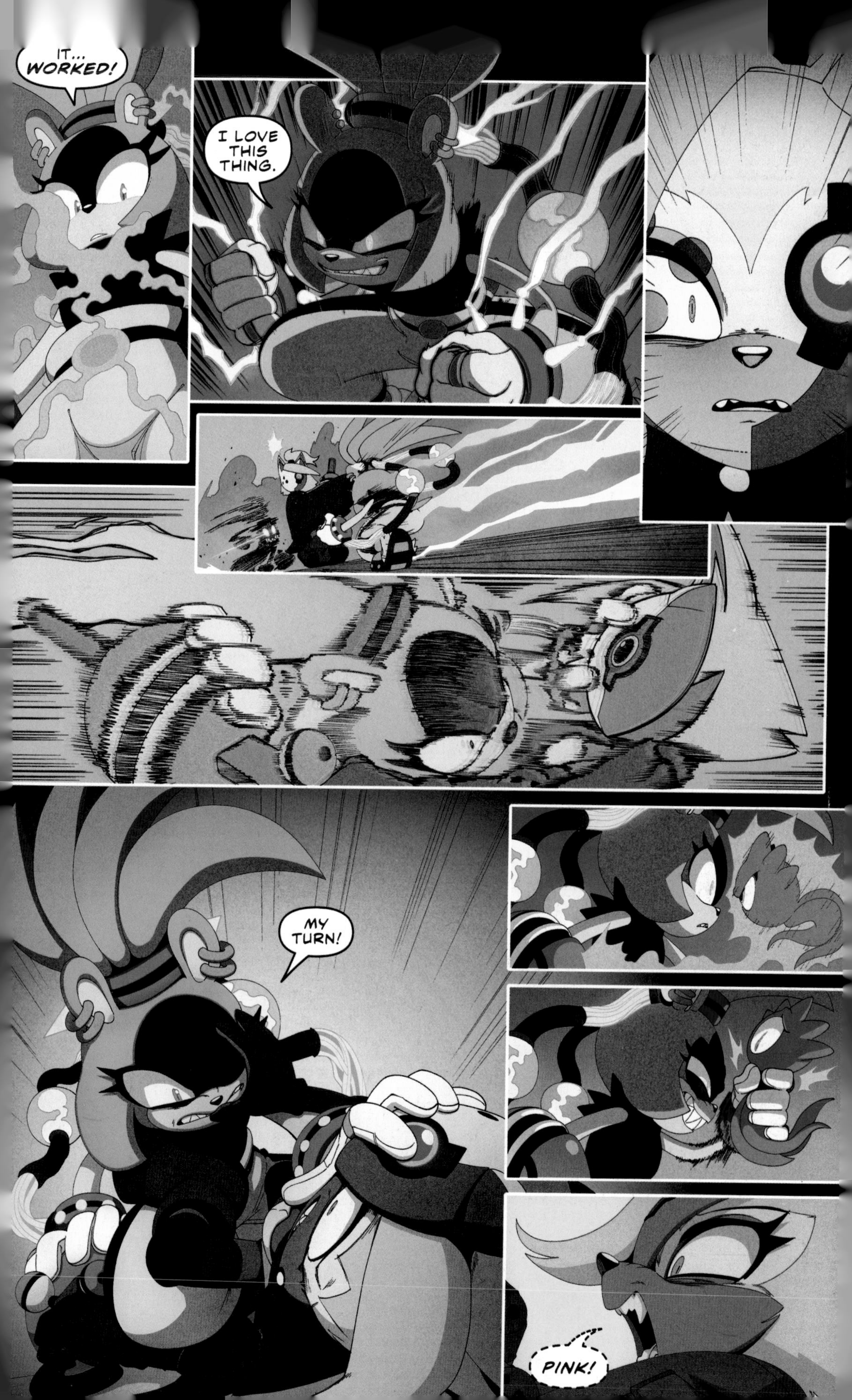
IT... WORKED!
I LOVE THIS THING.
MY TURN!
PINK!

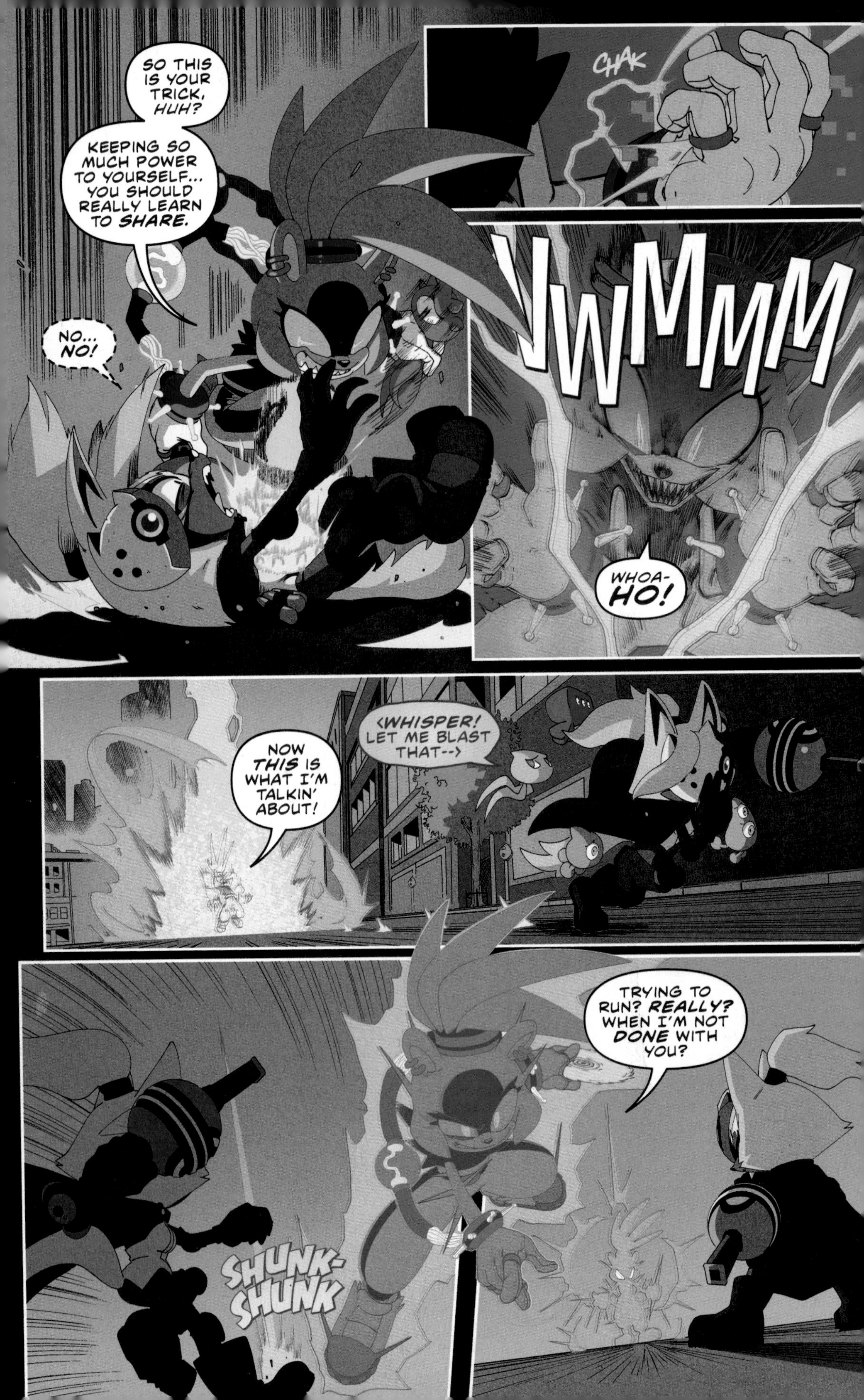

SO THIS IS YOUR TRICK, HUH?
KEEPING SO MUCH POWER TO YOURSELF... YOU SHOULD REALLY LEARN TO SHARE.
NO... NO!
CHAK
VWMMMM
WHOA-HO!
NOW THIS IS WHAT I'M TALKIN' ABOUT!
<WHISPER! LET ME BLAST THAT-->
TRYING TO RUN? REALLY? WHEN I'M NOT DONE WITH YOU?
SHUNK-SHUNK

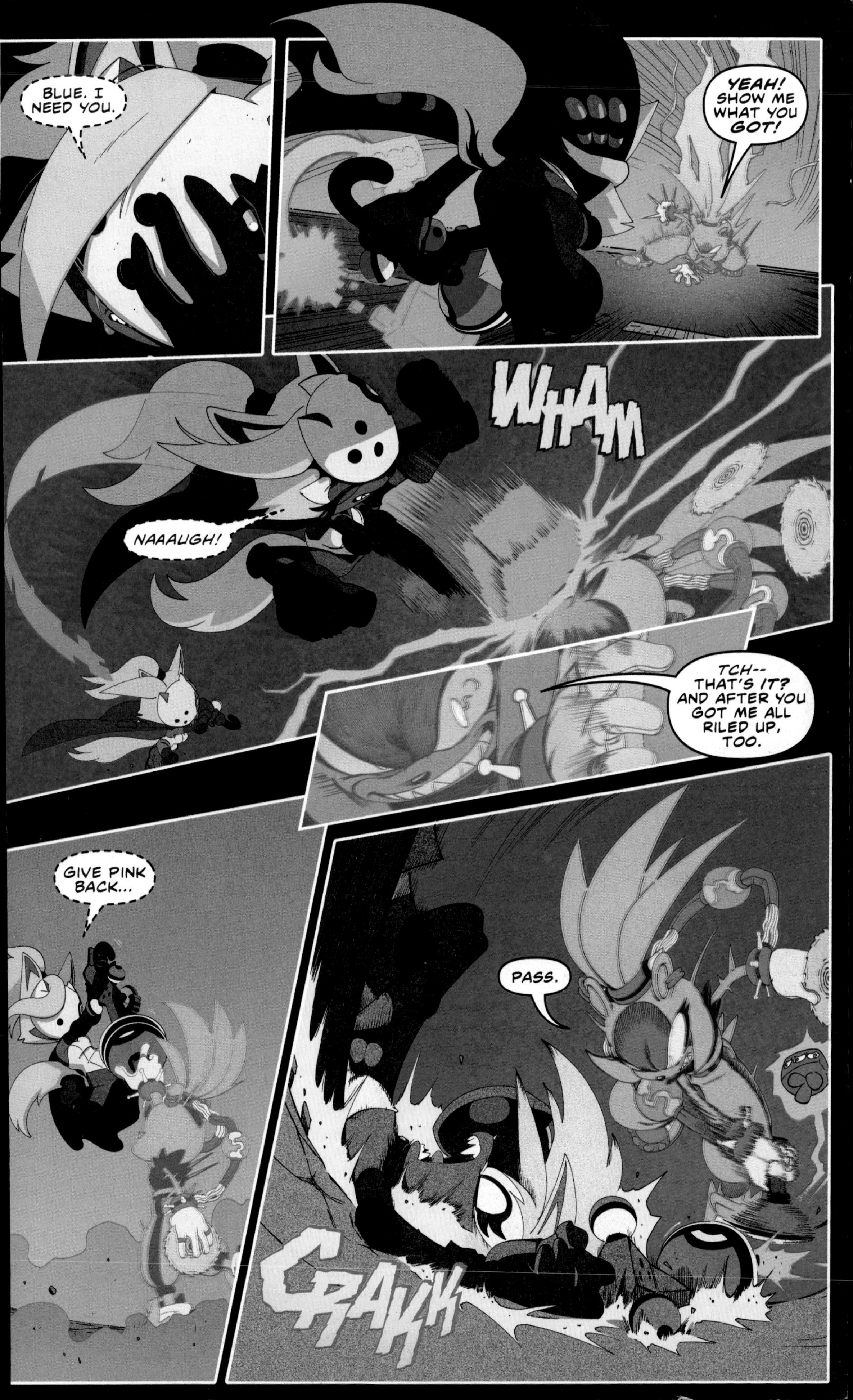
BLUE. I NEED YOU.
YEAH! SHOW ME WHAT YOU GOT!
WHAM
NAAAUGH!
TCH-- THAT'S IT? AND AFTER YOU GOT ME ALL RILED UP, TOO.
GIVE PINK BACK...
PASS.
CRAKK

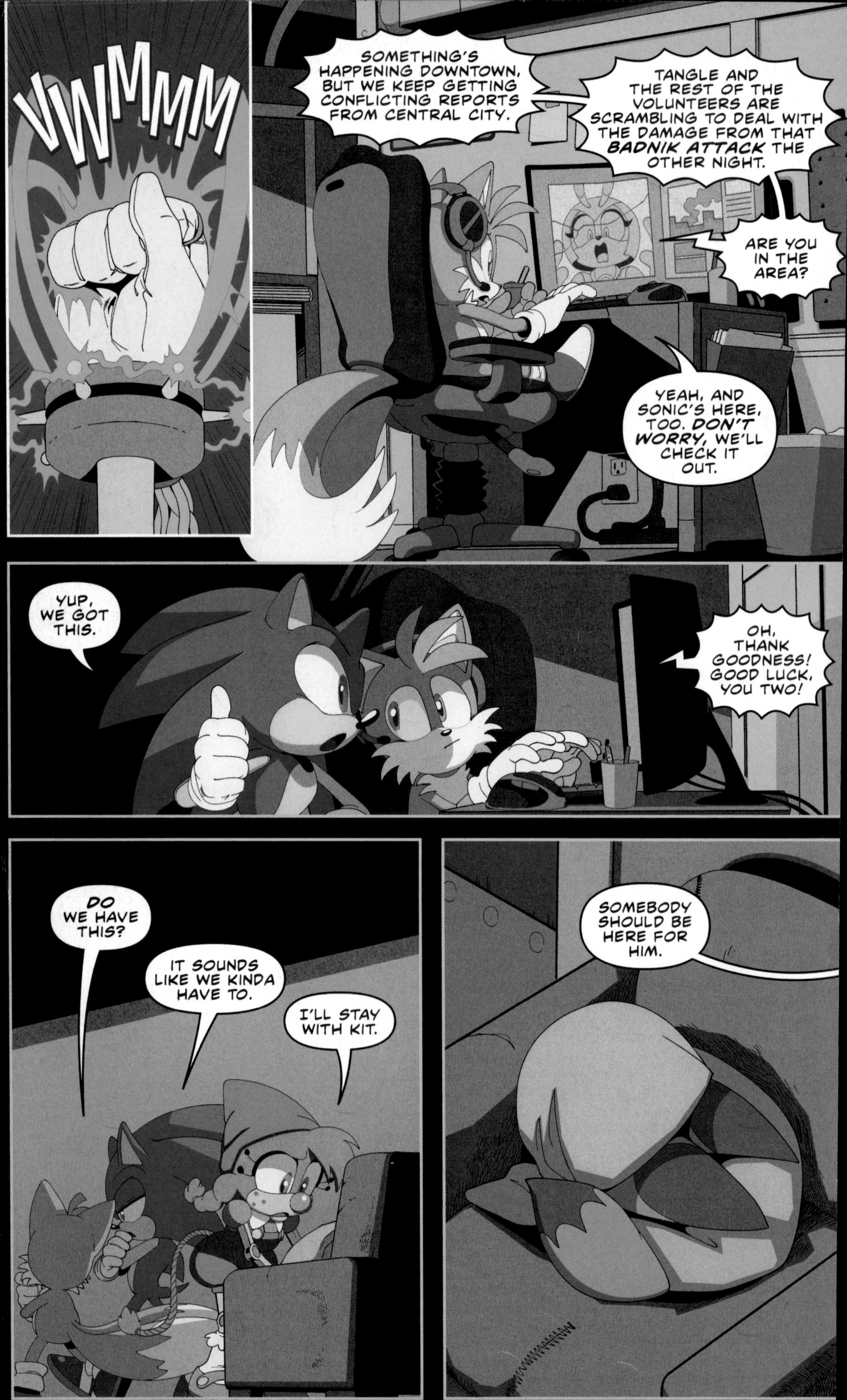
VWMMM
SOMETHING'S HAPPENING DOWNTOWN, BUT WE KEEP GETTING CONFLICTING REPORTS FROM CENTRAL CITY.
TANGLE AND THE REST OF THE VOLUNTEERS ARE SCRAMBLING TO DEAL WITH THE DAMAGE FROM THAT BADNIK ATTACK THE OTHER NIGHT.
ARE YOU IN THE AREA?
YEAH, AND SONIC'S HERE, TOO. DON'T WORRY, WE'LL CHECK IT OUT.
YUP, WE GOT THIS.
OH, THANK GOODNESS! GOOD LUCK, YOU TWO!
DO WE HAVE THIS?
IT SOUNDS LIKE WE KINDA HAVE TO.
I'LL STAY WITH KIT.
SOMEBODY SHOULD BE HERE FOR HIM.

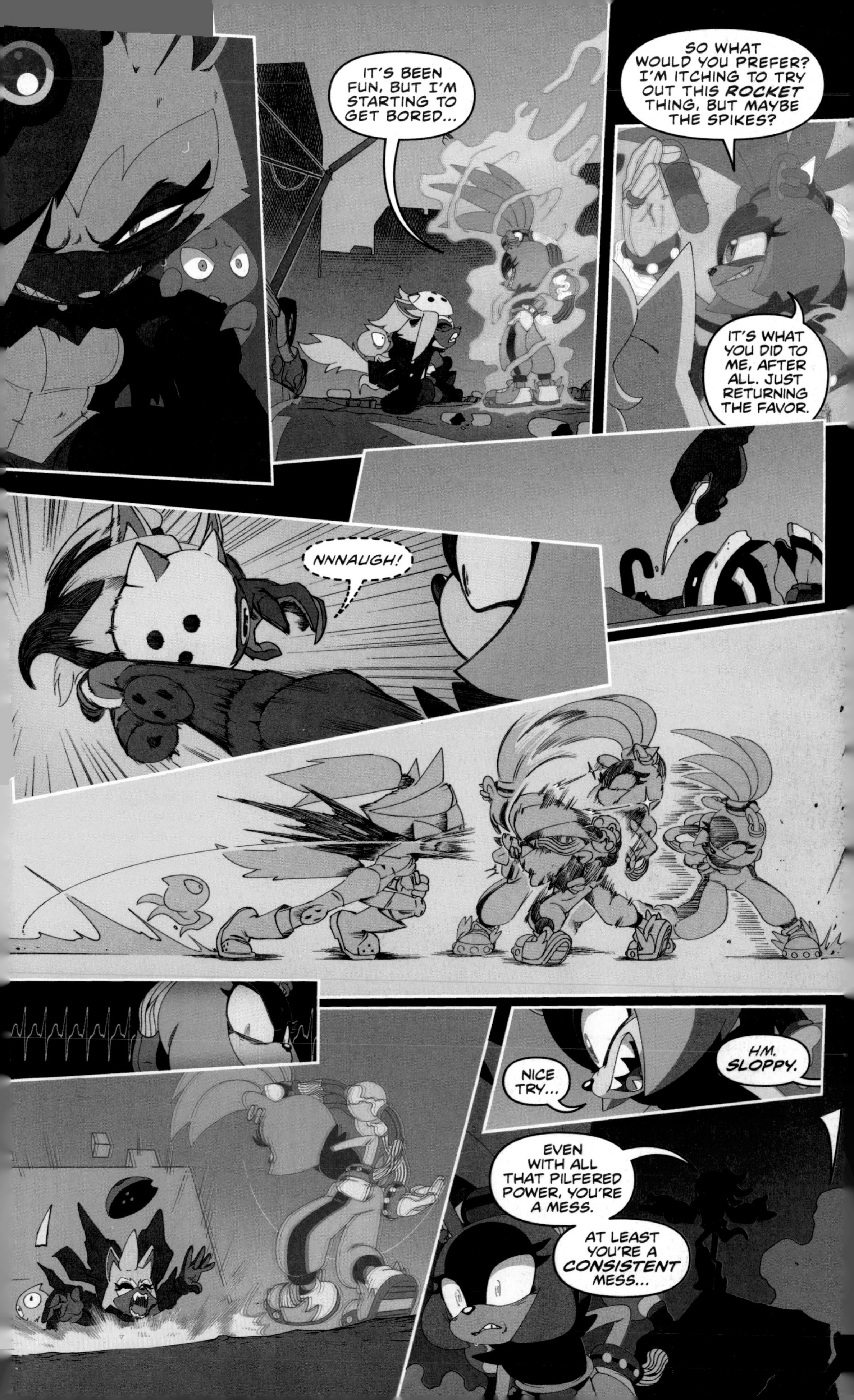
IT'S BEEN FUN, BUT I'M STARTING TO GET BORED...
SO WHAT WOULD YOU PREFER? I'M ITCHING TO TRY OUT THIS ROCKET THING, BUT MAYBE THE SPIKES?
IT'S WHAT YOU DID TO ME, AFTER ALL. JUST RETURNING THE FAVOR.
NNNAUGH!
NICE TRY...
HM. SLOPPY.
EVEN WITH ALL THAT PILFERED POWER, YOU'RE A MESS.
AT LEAST YOU'RE A CONSISTENT MESS...

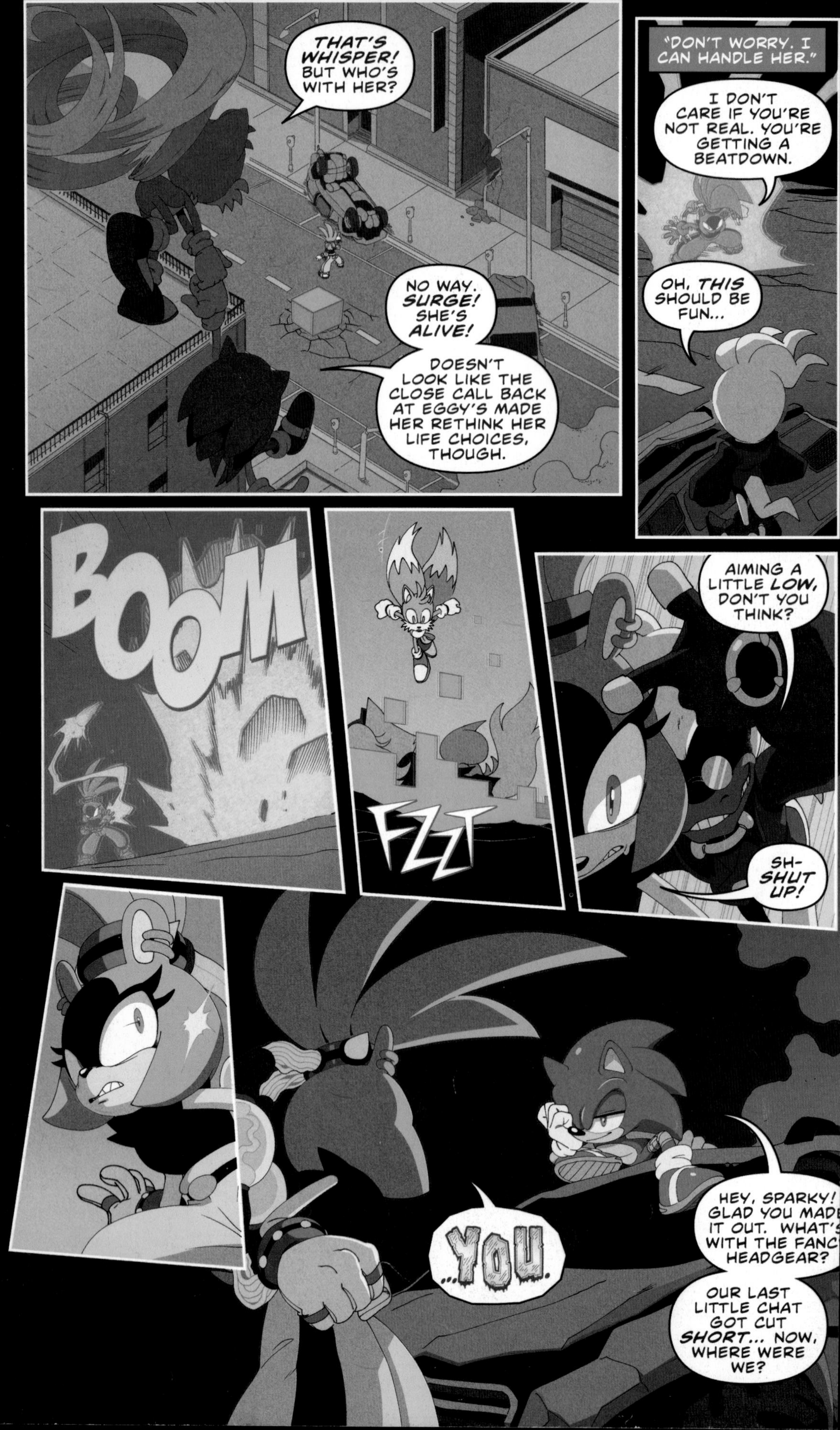
THAT'S WHISPER! BUT WHO'S WITH HER?
NO WAY. SURGE! SHE'S ALIVE!
DOESN'T LOOK LIKE THE CLOSE CALL BACK AT EGGY'S MADE HER RETHINK HER LIFE CHOICES, THOUGH.
"DON'T WORRY. I CAN HANDLE HER."
I DON'T CARE IF YOU'RE NOT REAL. YOU'RE GETTING A BEATDOWN.
OH, THIS SHOULD BE FUN...
BOOM
FZZT
AIMING A LITTLE LOW, DON'T YOU THINK?
SH-SHUT UP!
...YOU.
HEY, SPARKY! GLAD YOU MADE IT OUT. WHAT'S WITH THE FANC HEADGEAR?
OUR LAST LITTLE CHAT GOT CUT SHORT... NOW, WHERE WERE WE?

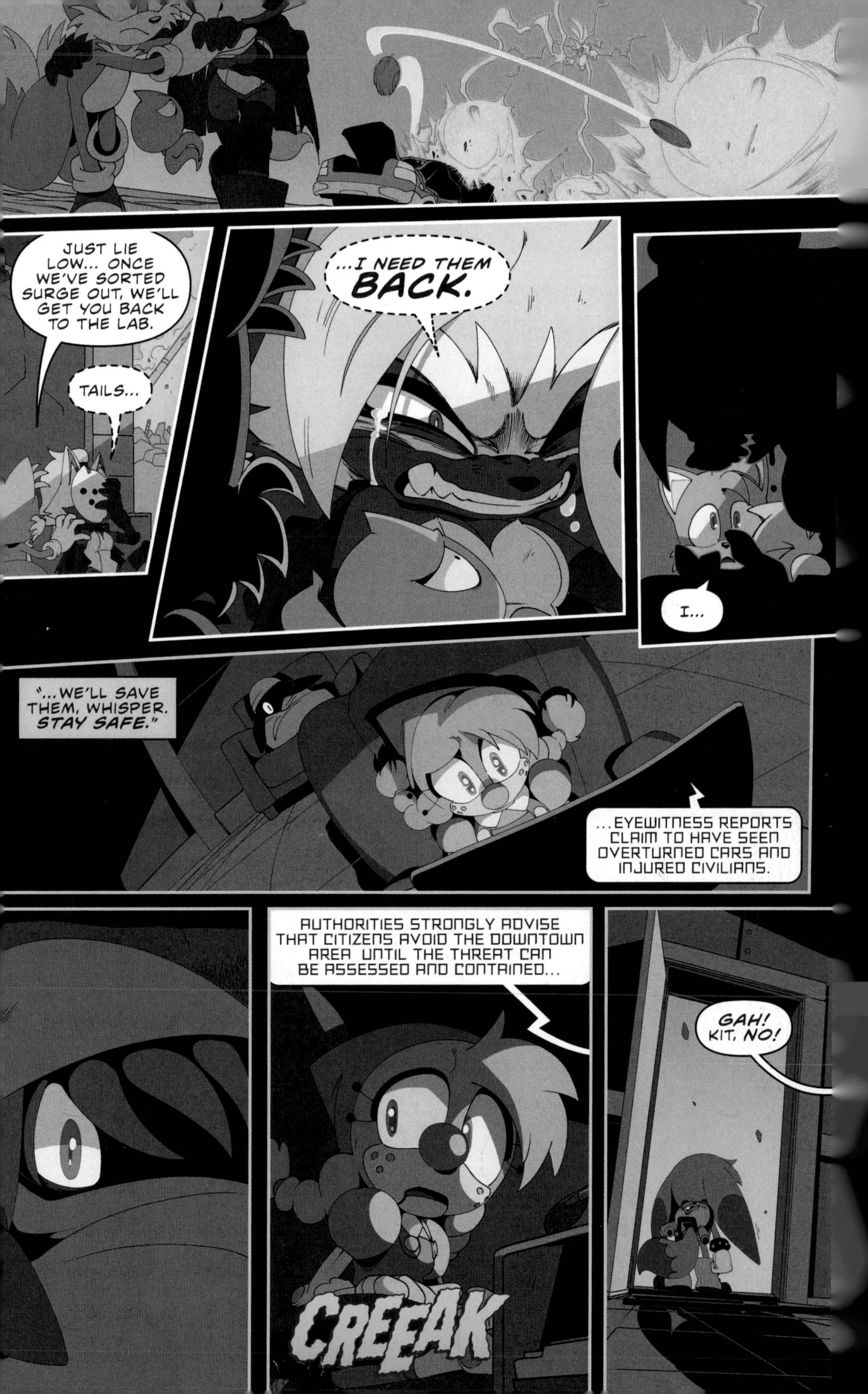
JUST LIE LOW... ONCE WE'VE SORTED SURGE OUT, WE'LL GET YOU BACK TO THE LAB.
TAILS...
...I NEED THEM BACK.
I...
"...WE'LL SAVE THEM, WHISPER. STAY SAFE."
...EYEWITNESS REPORTS CLAIM TO HAVE SEEN OVERTURNED CARS AND INJURED CIVILIANS.
AUTHORITIES STRONGLY ADVISE THAT CITIZENS AVOID THE DOWNTOWN AREA UNTIL THE THREAT CAN BE ASSESSED AND CONTAINED...
GAH! KIT, NO!
CREEAK

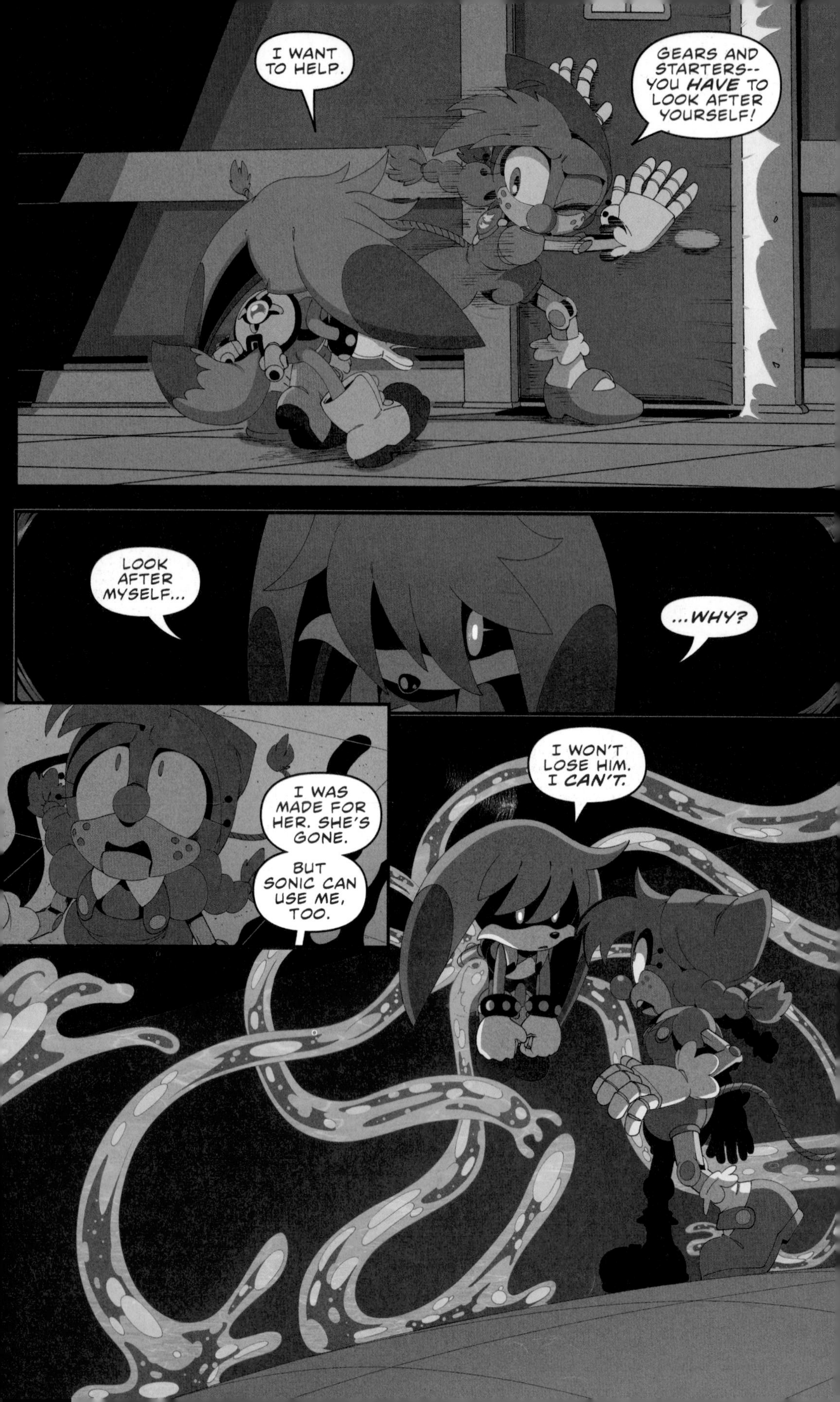
I WANT TO HELP.
GEARS AND STARTERS-- YOU *HAVE* TO LOOK AFTER YOURSELF!
LOOK AFTER MYSELF...
...*WHY?*
I WAS MADE FOR HER. SHE'S GONE.
BUT SONIC CAN USE ME, TOO.
I WON'T LOSE HIM. I *CAN'T.*

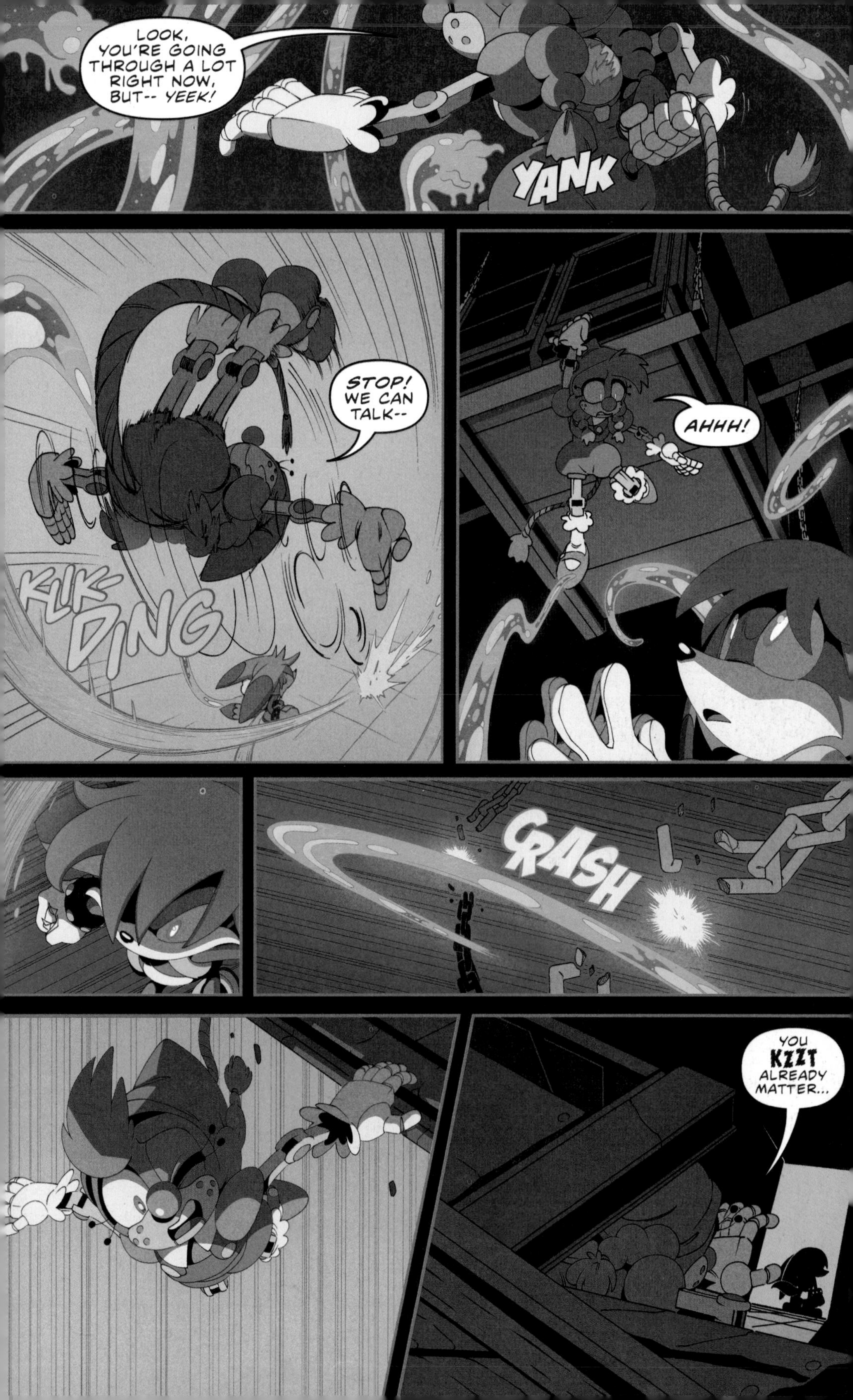
LOOK, YOU'RE GOING THROUGH A LOT RIGHT NOW, BUT-- YEEK!
YANK
STOP! WE CAN TALK--
KLIK-DING
AHHH!
CRASH
YOU KZZT ALREADY MATTER...

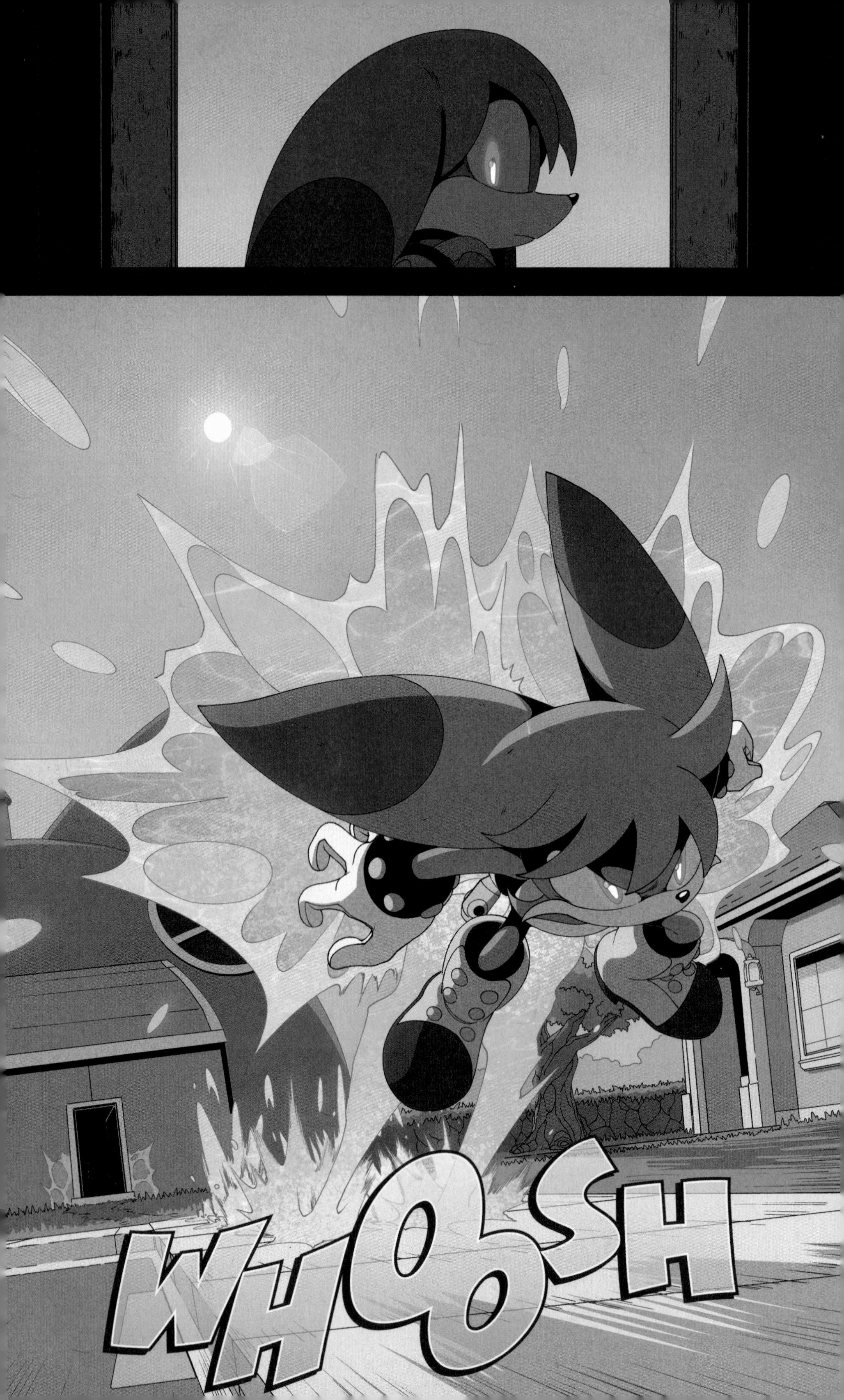
WHOOSH

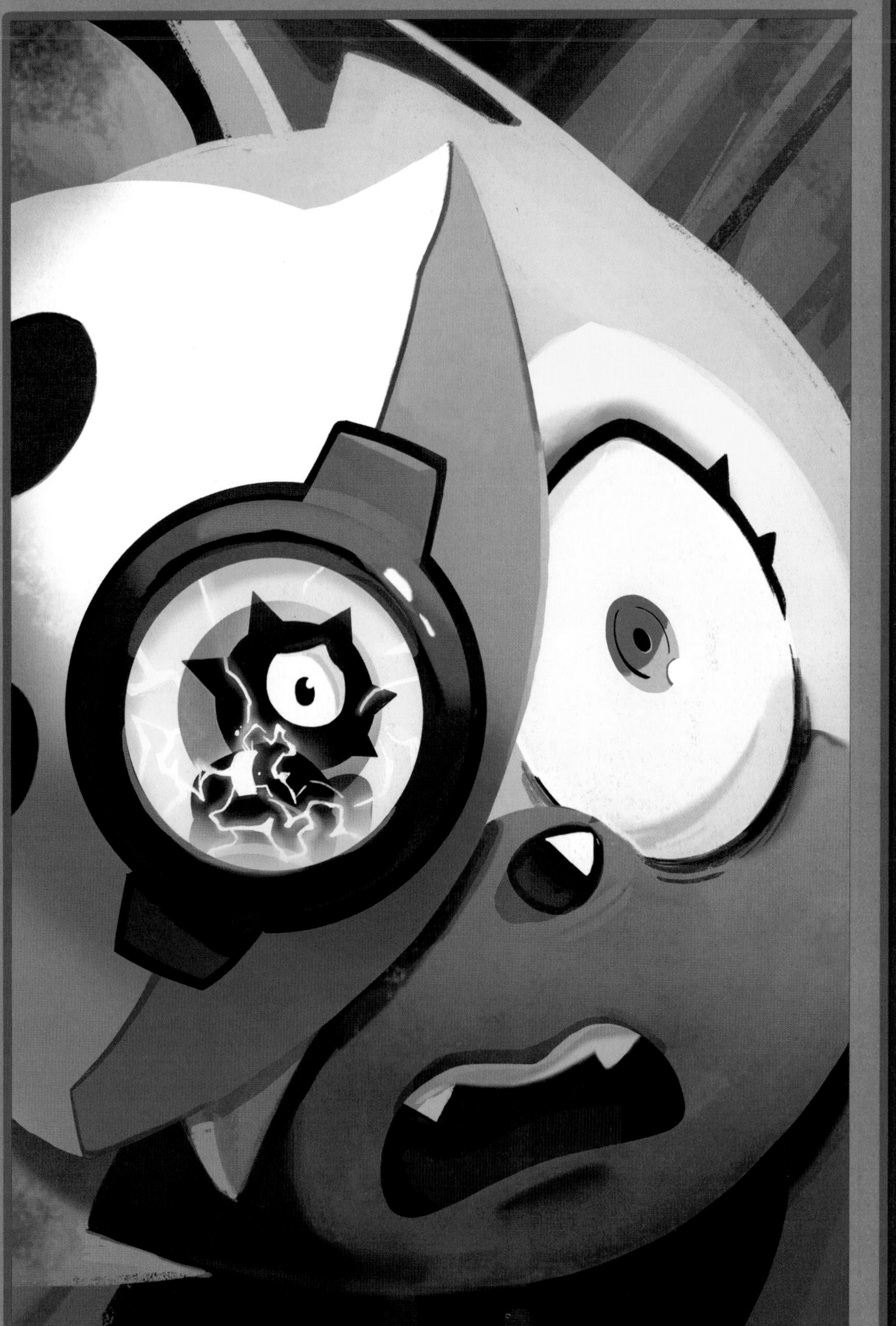

ART BY **NATHALIE FOURDRAINE**

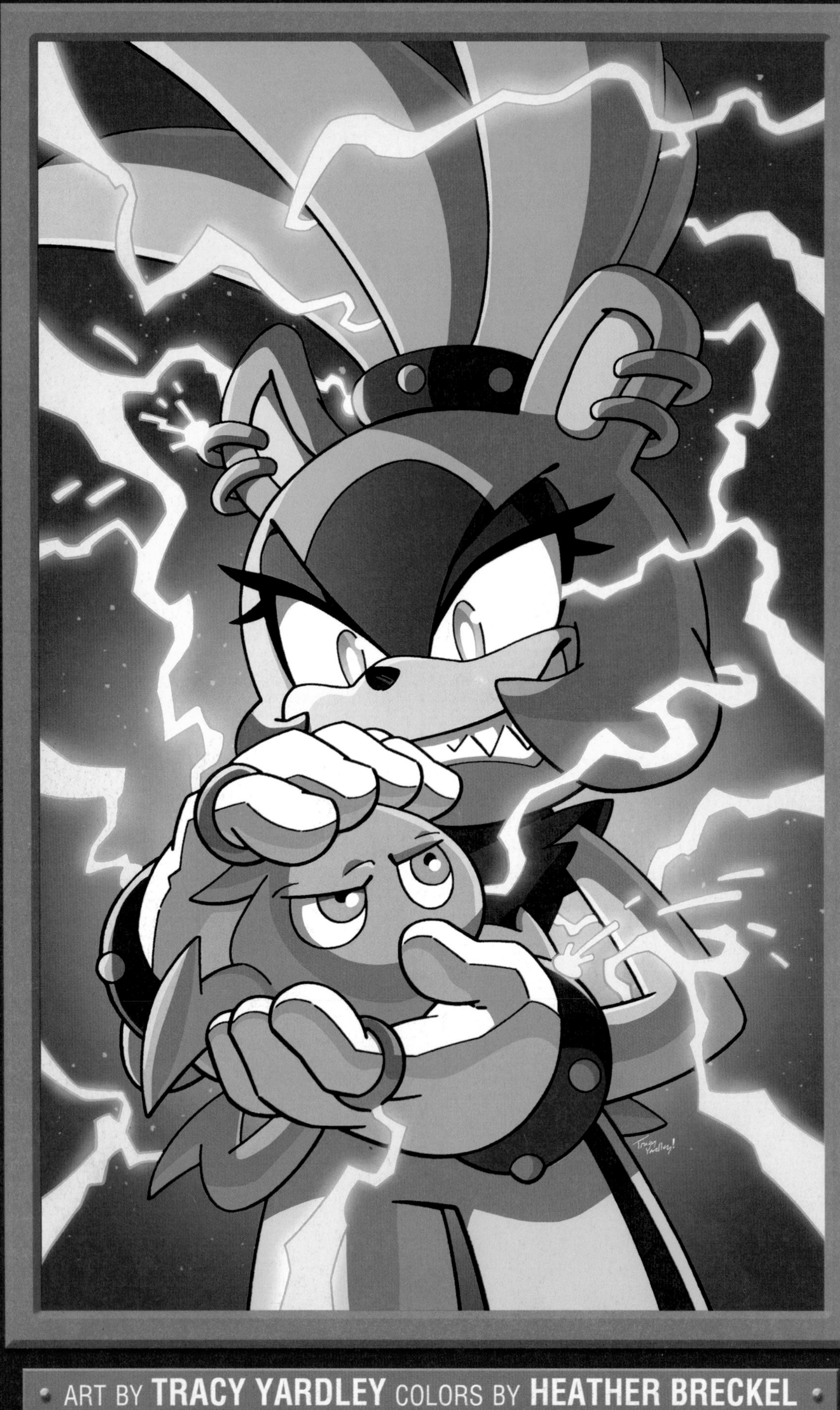

ART BY **TRACY YARDLEY** COLORS BY **HEATHER BRECKEL**

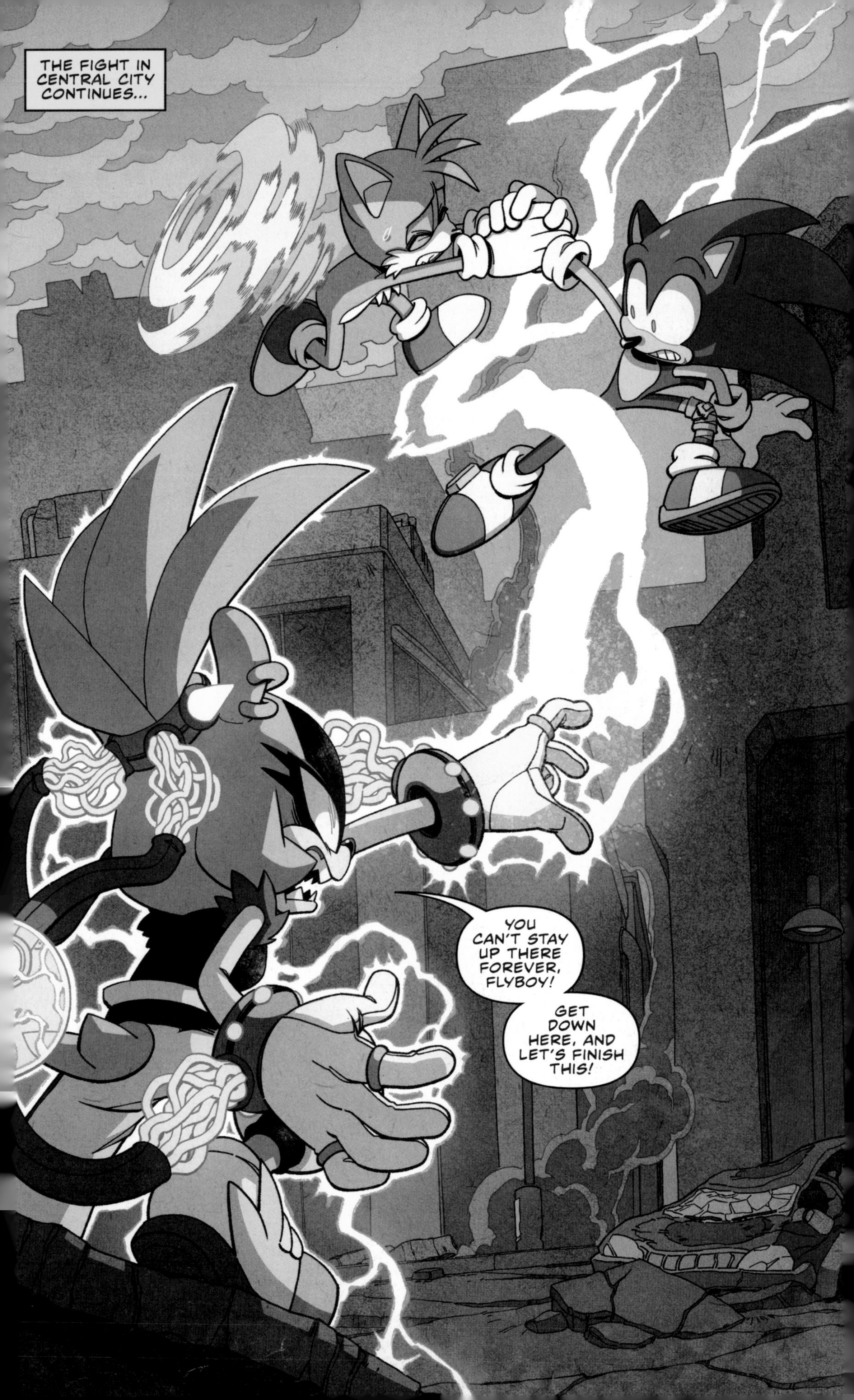
THE FIGHT IN CENTRAL CITY CONTINUES...
YOU CAN'T STAY UP THERE FOREVER, FLYBOY!
GET DOWN HERE, AND LET'S FINISH THIS!

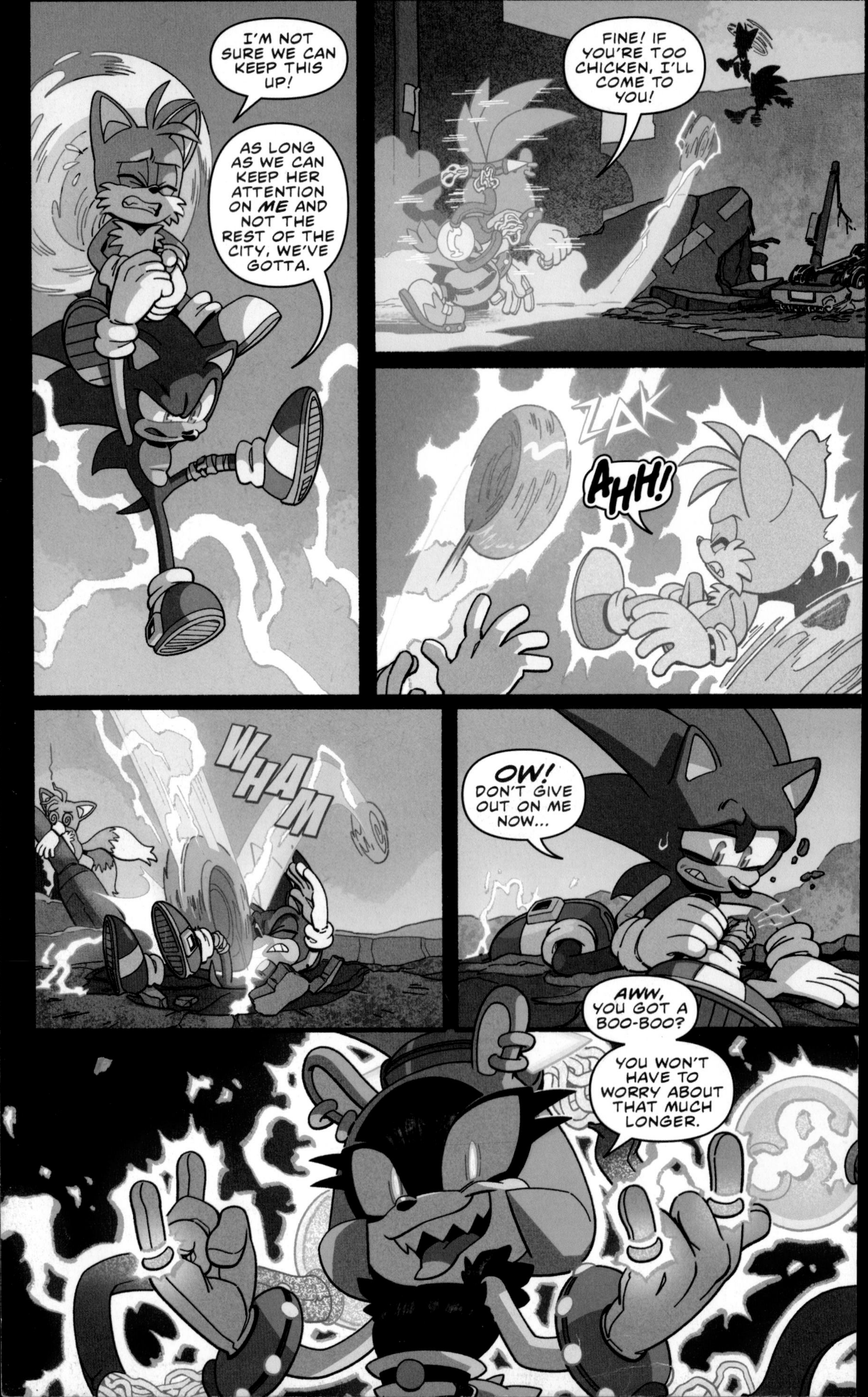
I'M NOT SURE WE CAN KEEP THIS UP!
AS LONG AS WE CAN KEEP HER ATTENTION ON *ME* AND NOT THE REST OF THE CITY, WE'VE GOTTA.
FINE! IF YOU'RE TOO CHICKEN, I'LL COME TO YOU!
ZAK
AHH!
WHAM
OW! DON'T GIVE OUT ON ME NOW...
AWW, YOU GOT A BOO-BOO?
YOU WON'T HAVE TO WORRY ABOUT THAT MUCH LONGER.

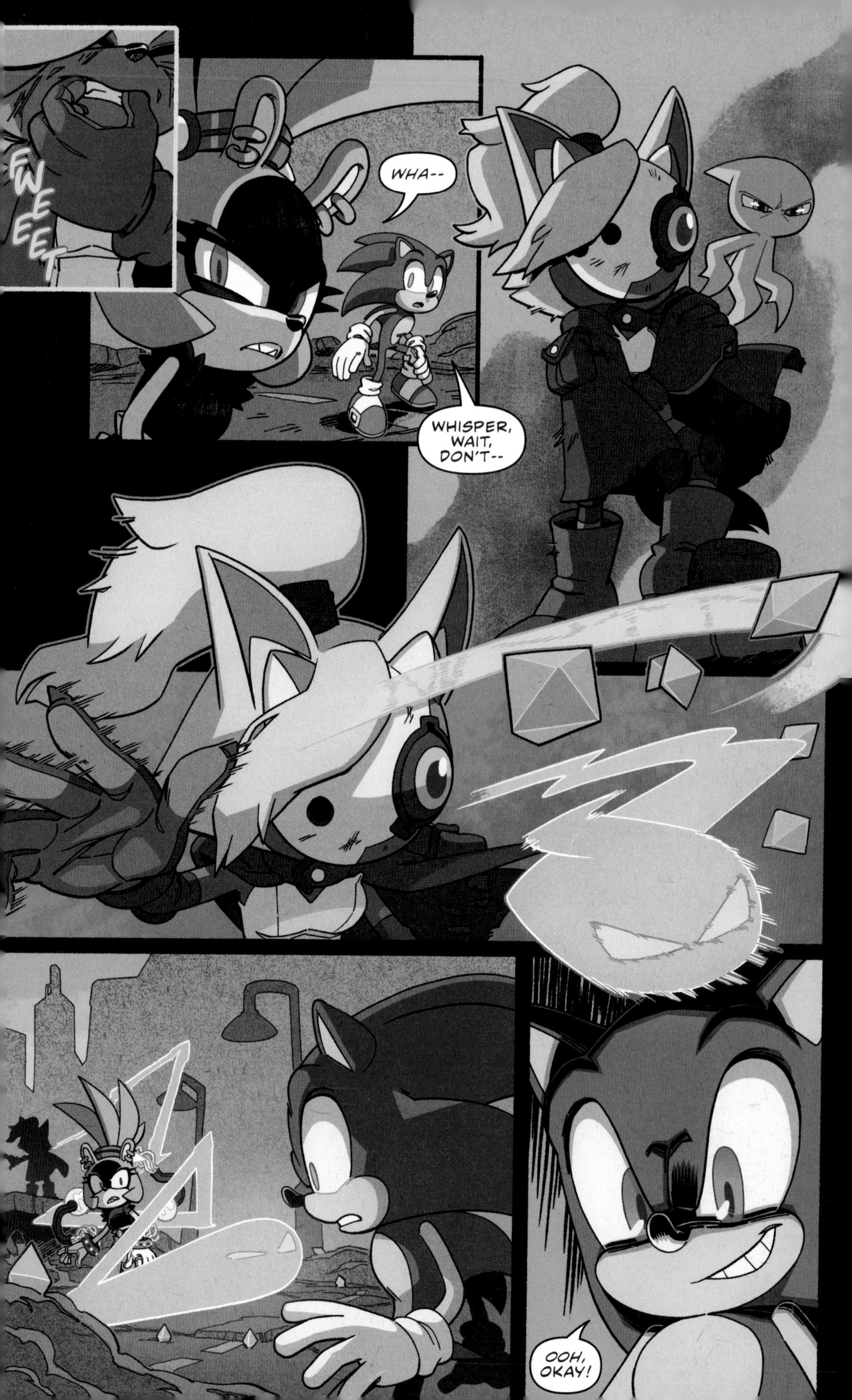
FWEEEET
WHA--
WHISPER, WAIT, DON'T--
OOH, OKAY!

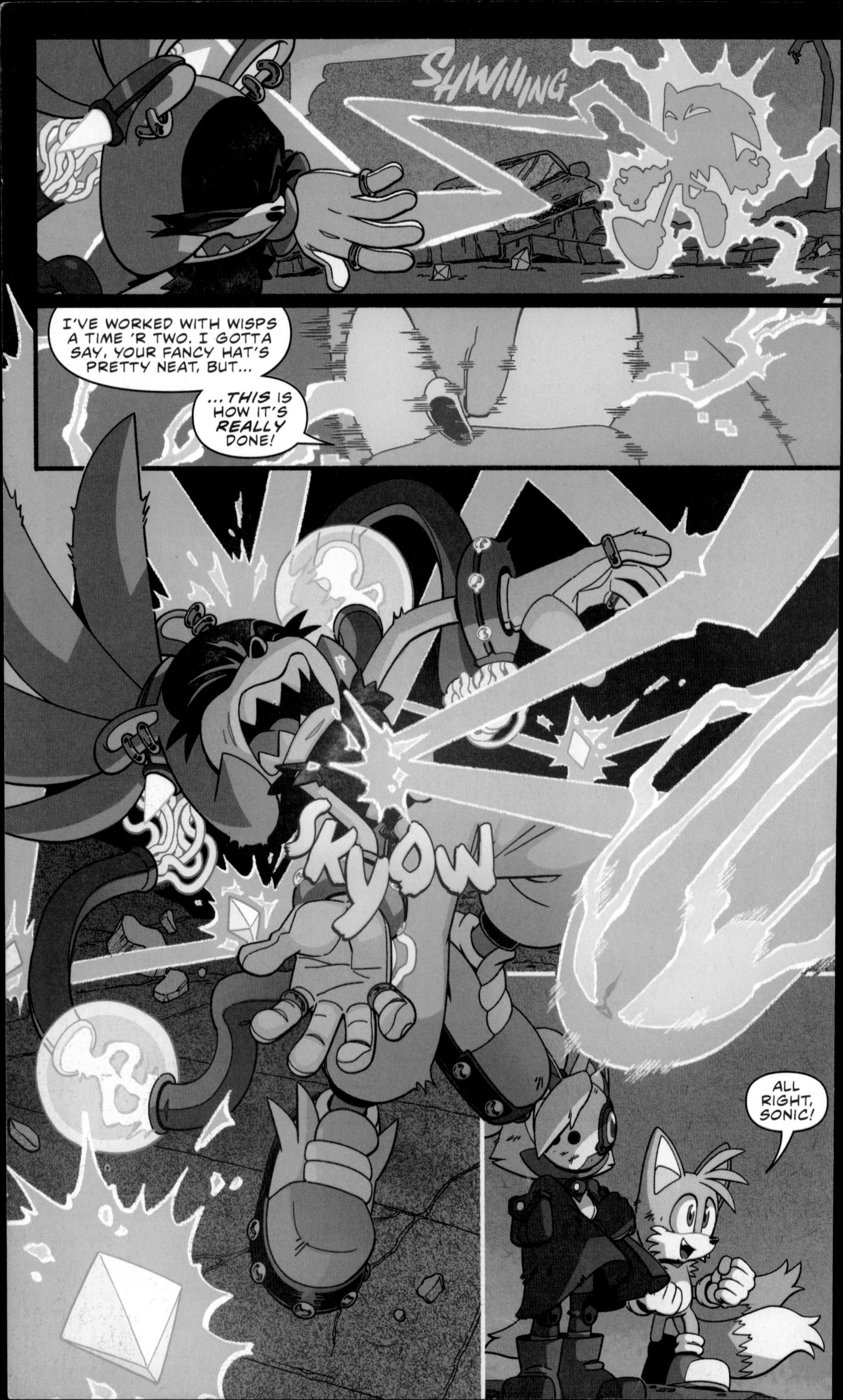
SHWING
I'VE WORKED WITH WISPS A TIME 'R TWO. I GOTTA SAY, YOUR FANCY HAT'S PRETTY NEAT, BUT...
...THIS IS HOW IT'S REALLY DONE!
SKYOW
ALL RIGHT, SONIC!

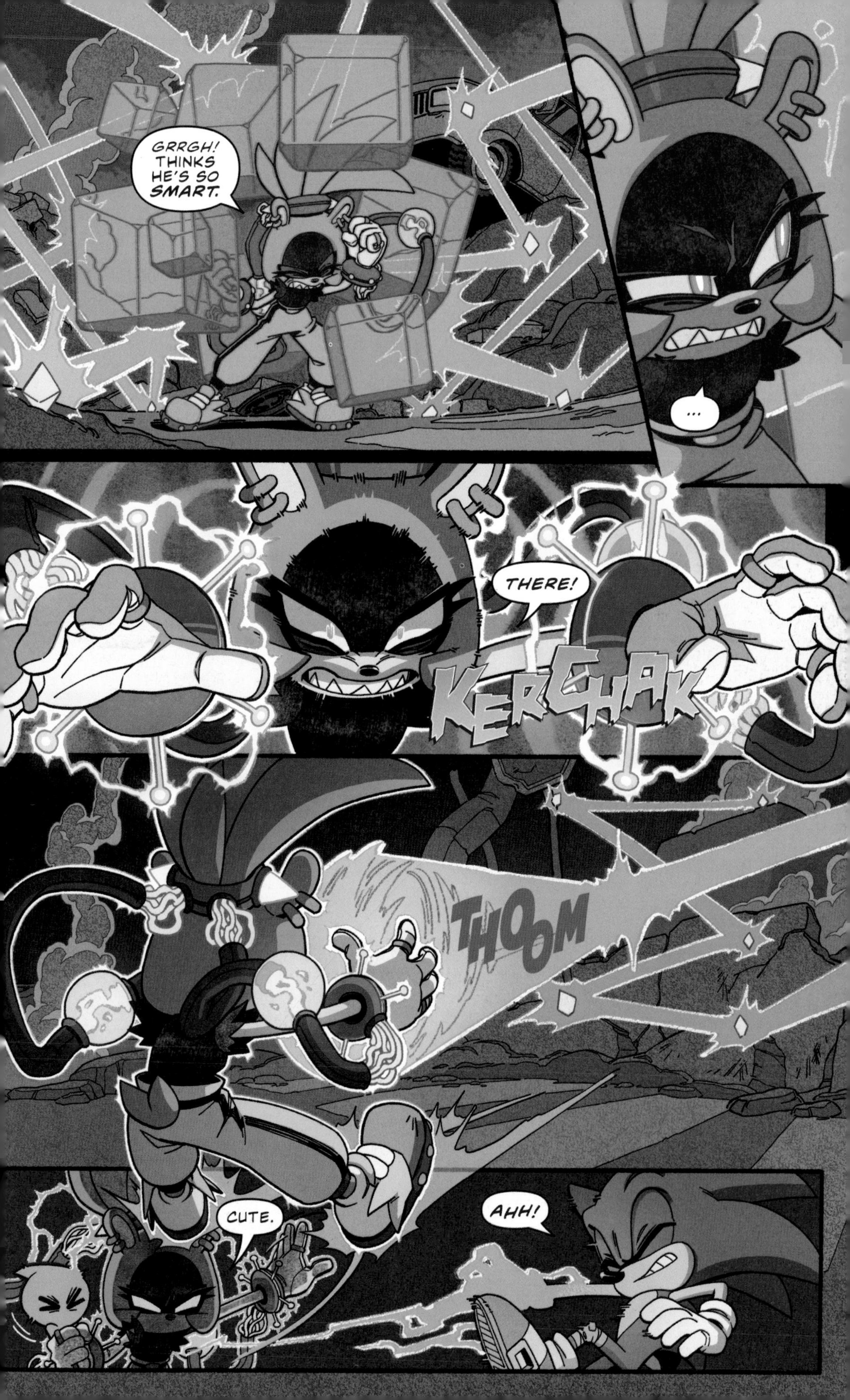
GRRGH! THINKS HE'S SO SMART.
...
THERE!
KERCHAK
THOOM
CUTE.
AHH!

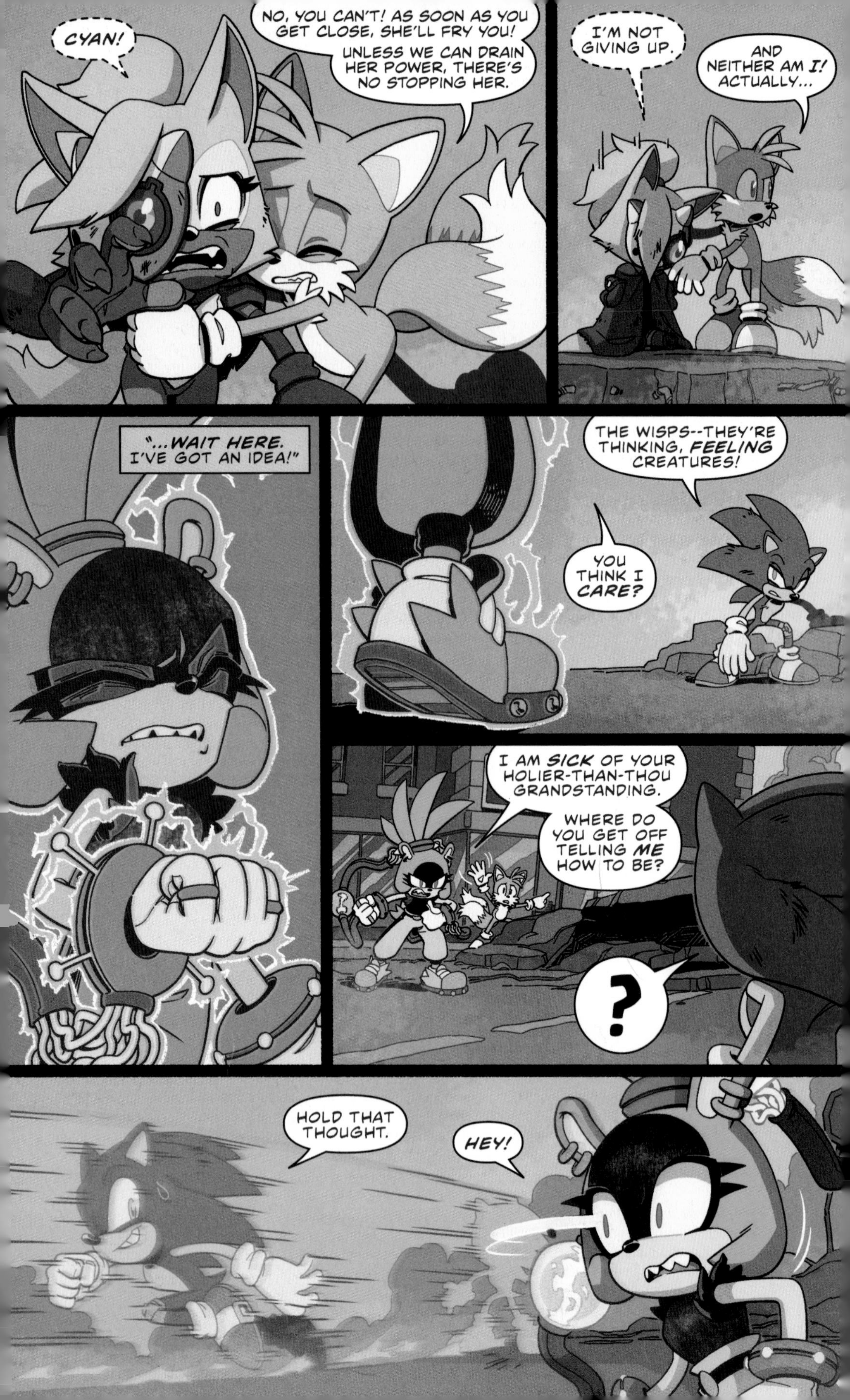

CYAN!
NO, YOU CAN'T! AS SOON AS YOU GET CLOSE, SHE'LL FRY YOU!
UNLESS WE CAN DRAIN HER POWER, THERE'S NO STOPPING HER.
I'M NOT GIVING UP.
AND NEITHER AM *I!* ACTUALLY...
"...*WAIT HERE.* I'VE GOT AN IDEA!"
THE WISPS--THEY'RE THINKING, *FEELING* CREATURES!
YOU THINK I *CARE?*
I AM *SICK* OF YOUR HOLIER-THAN-THOU GRANDSTANDING.
WHERE DO YOU GET OFF TELLING *ME* HOW TO BE?
?
HOLD THAT THOUGHT.
HEY!

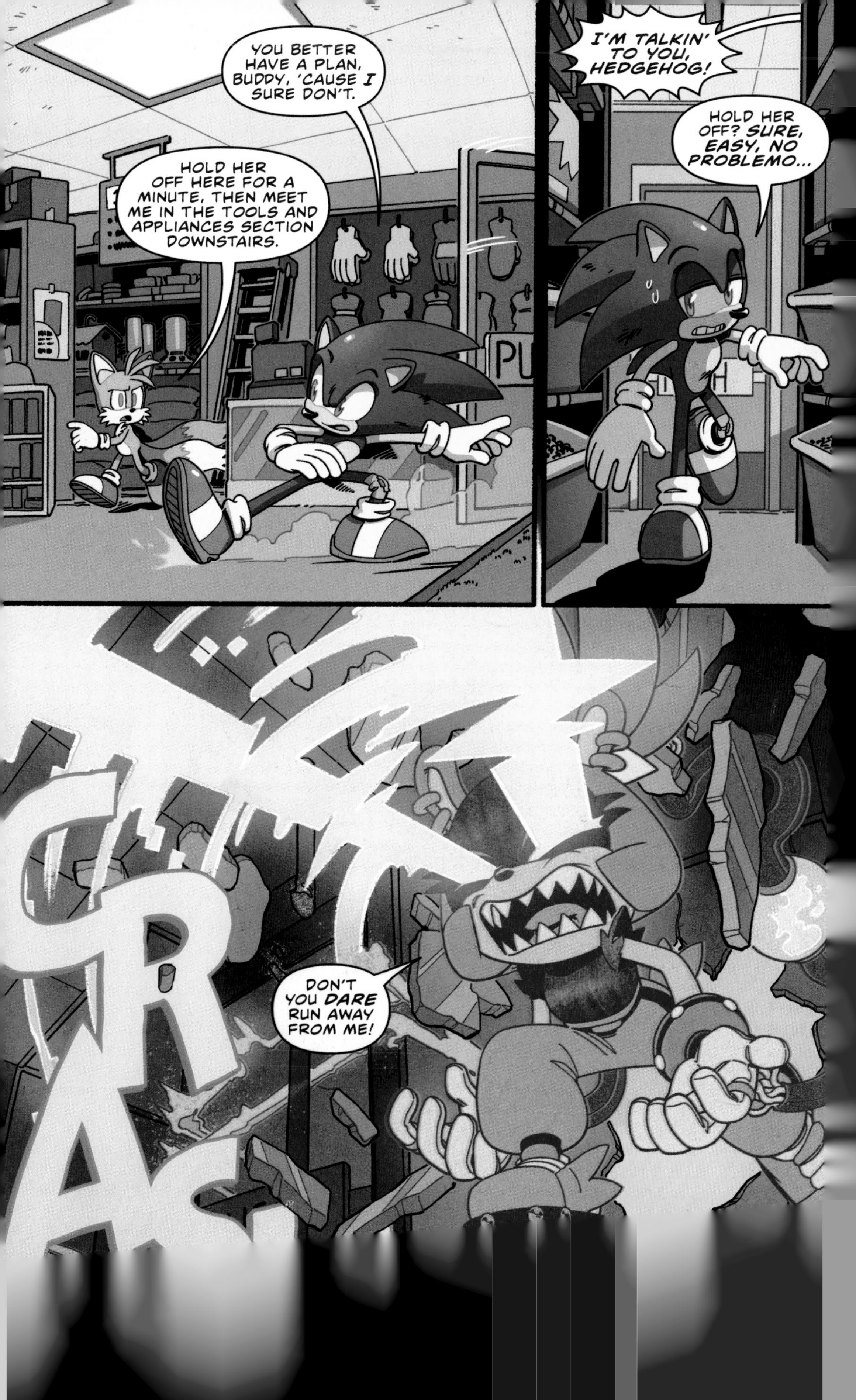
HOLD HER OFF HERE FOR A MINUTE, THEN MEET ME IN THE TOOLS AND APPLIANCES SECTION DOWNSTAIRS.
YOU BETTER HAVE A PLAN, BUDDY, 'CAUSE *I* SURE DON'T.
I'M TALKIN' TO YOU, HEDGEHOG!
HOLD HER OFF? *SURE, EASY, NO PROBLEMO...*
CRASH
DON'T YOU *DARE* RUN AWAY FROM ME!

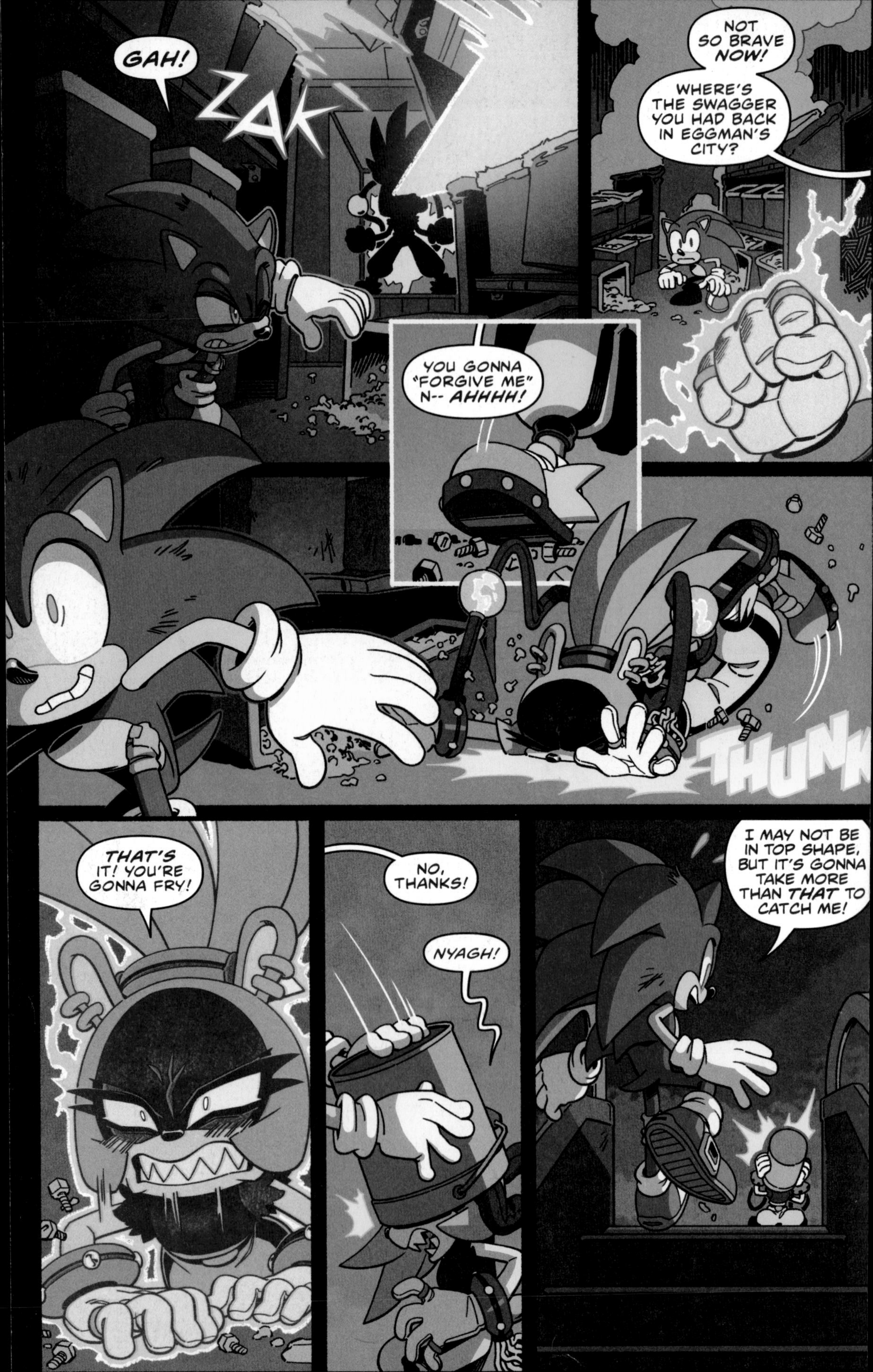
GAH!
ZAK
NOT SO BRAVE NOW!
WHERE'S THE SWAGGER YOU HAD BACK IN EGGMAN'S CITY?
YOU GONNA "FORGIVE ME" N-- AHHHH!
THUNK
THAT'S IT! YOU'RE GONNA FRY!
NO, THANKS!
NYAGH!
I MAY NOT BE IN TOP SHAPE, BUT IT'S GONNA TAKE MORE THAN THAT TO CATCH ME!

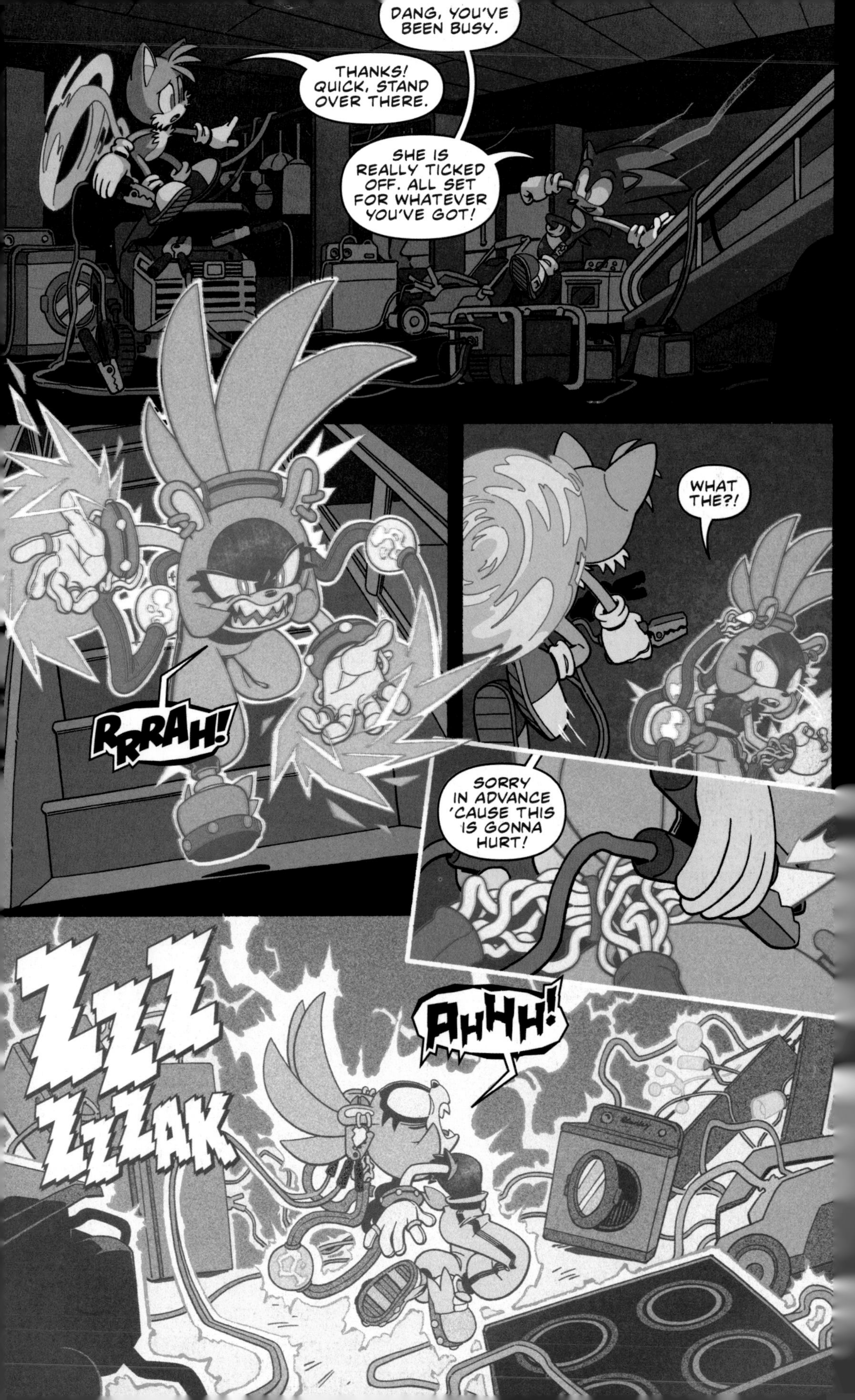
DANG, YOU'VE BEEN BUSY.
THANKS! QUICK, STAND OVER THERE.
SHE IS REALLY TICKED OFF. ALL SET FOR WHATEVER YOU'VE GOT!
RRRAH!
WHAT THE?!
SORRY IN ADVANCE 'CAUSE THIS IS GONNA HURT!
ZZZ ZZZAK
AHHH!

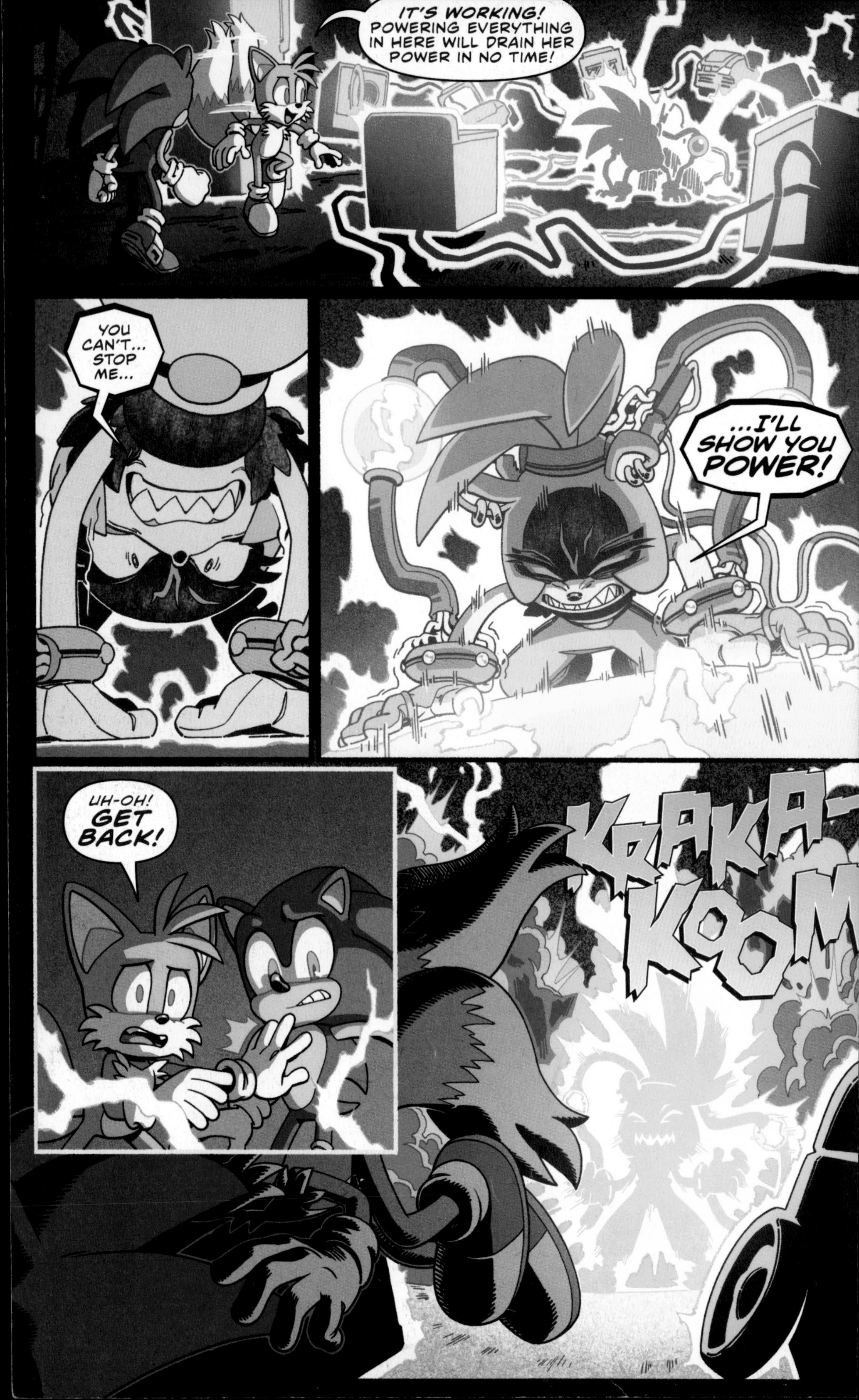
IT'S WORKING! POWERING EVERYTHING IN HERE WILL DRAIN HER POWER IN NO TIME!
YOU CAN'T... STOP ME...
...I'LL SHOW YOU POWER!
UH-OH! GET BACK!
KRAKA-KOOM

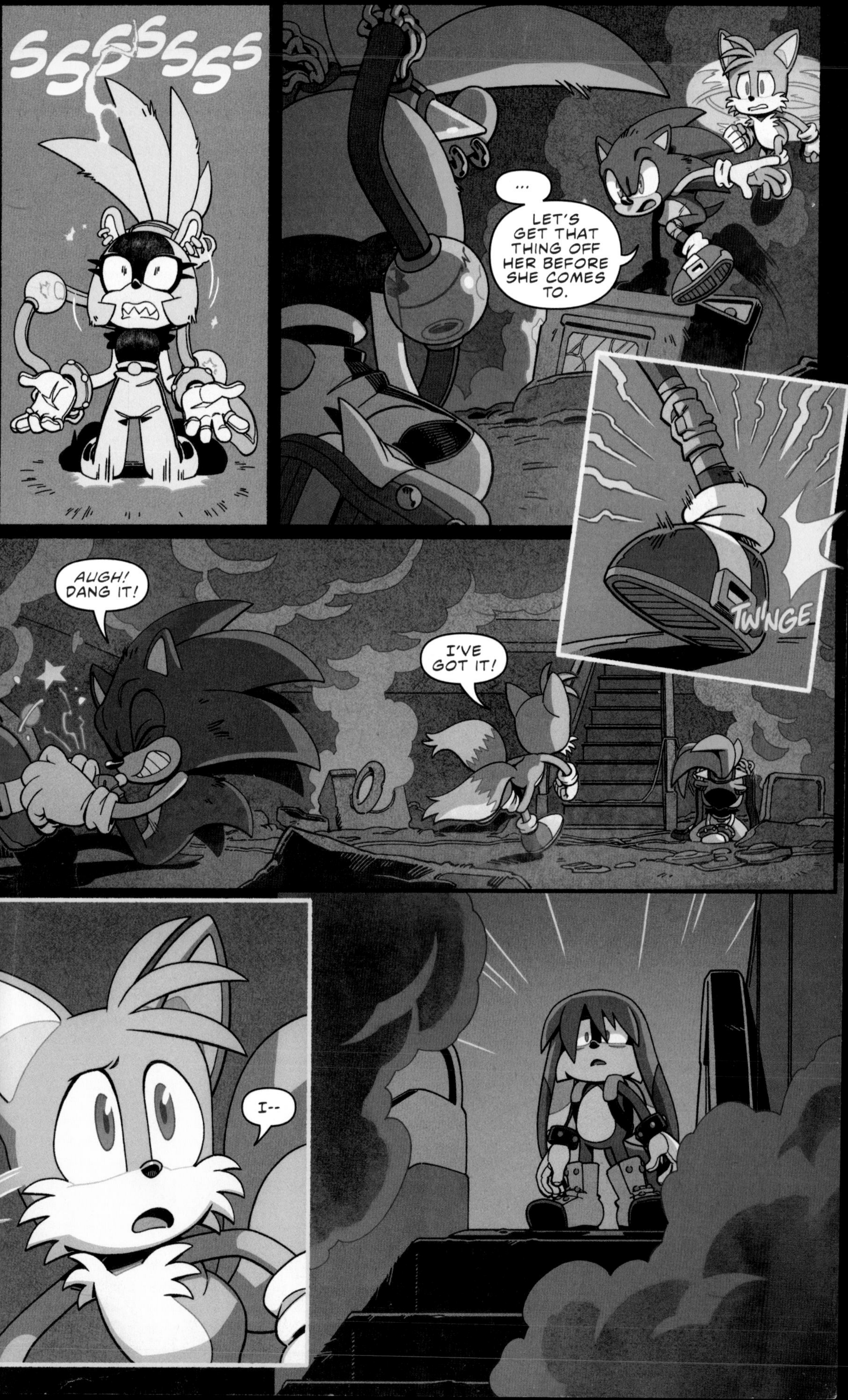
SSSSSSSSS
...
LET'S GET THAT THING OFF HER BEFORE SHE COMES TO.
TWINGE
AUGH! DANG IT!
I'VE GOT IT!
I--

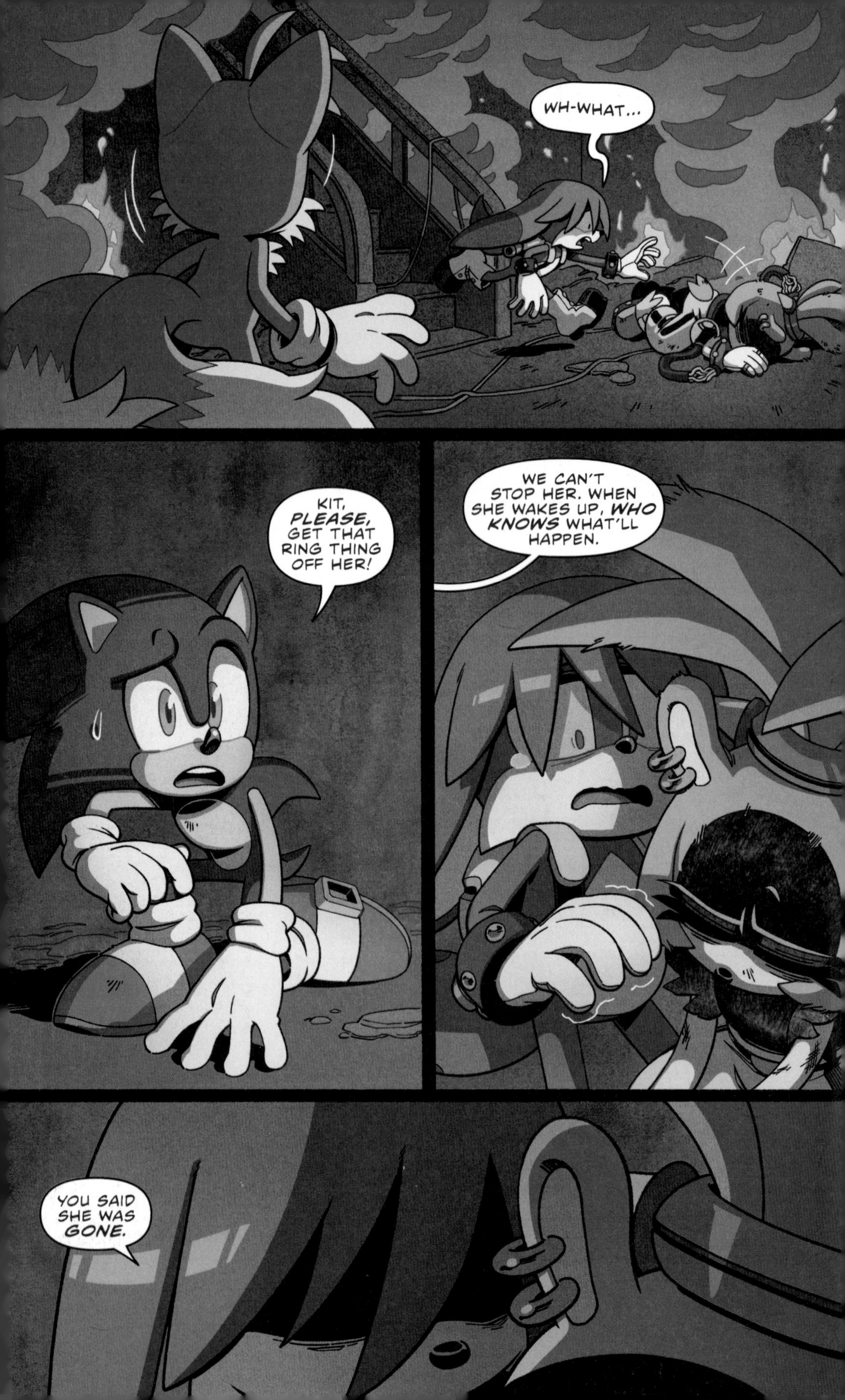
WH-WHAT...
KIT, PLEASE, GET THAT RING THING OFF HER!
WE CAN'T STOP HER. WHEN SHE WAKES UP, WHO KNOWS WHAT'LL HAPPEN.
YOU SAID SHE WAS GONE.

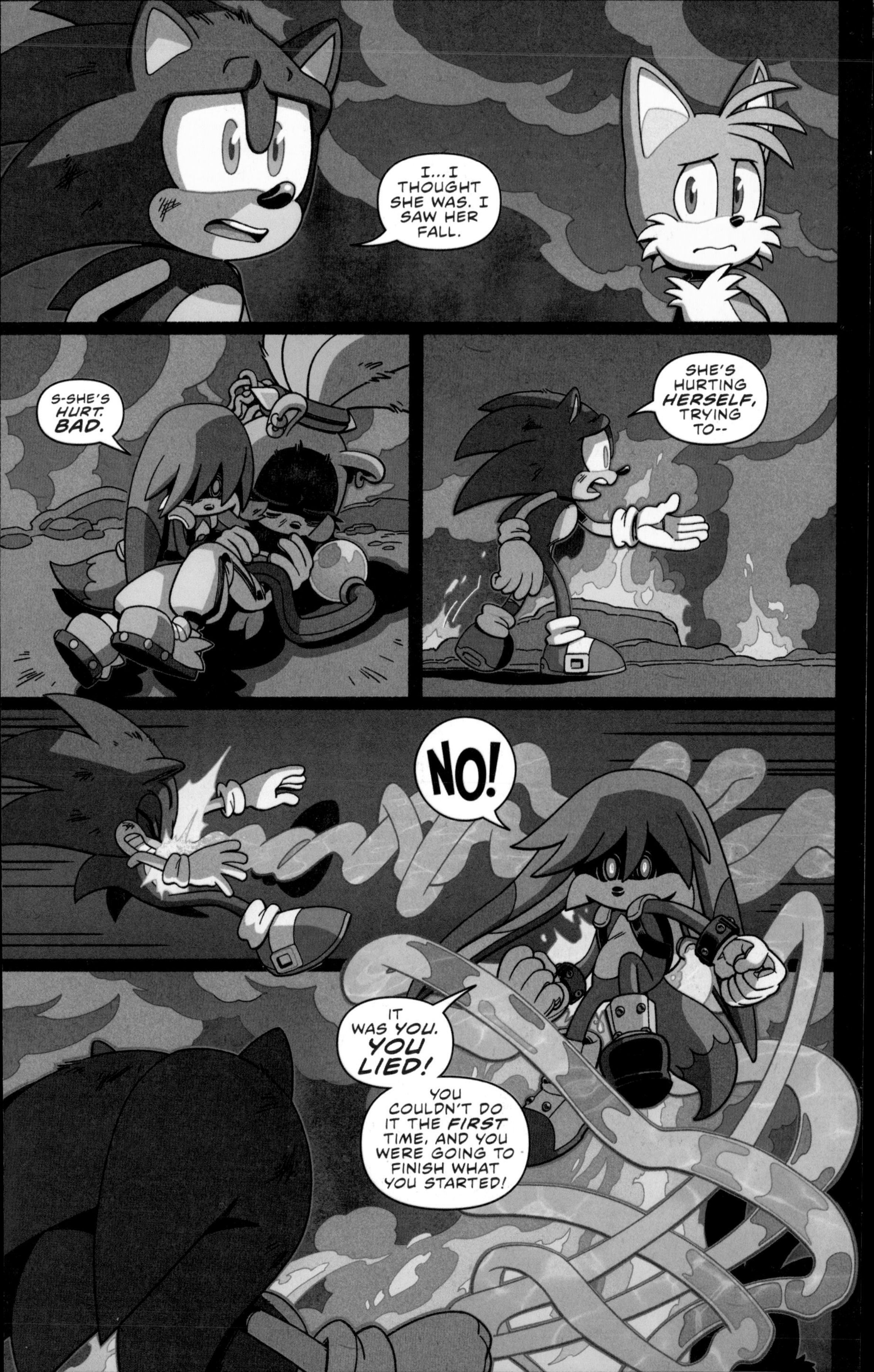
I... I THOUGHT SHE WAS. I SAW HER FALL.
S-SHE'S HURT. BAD.
SHE'S HURTING HERSELF, TRYING TO--
NO!
IT WAS YOU. YOU LIED!
YOU COULDN'T DO IT THE FIRST TIME, AND YOU WERE GOING TO FINISH WHAT YOU STARTED!

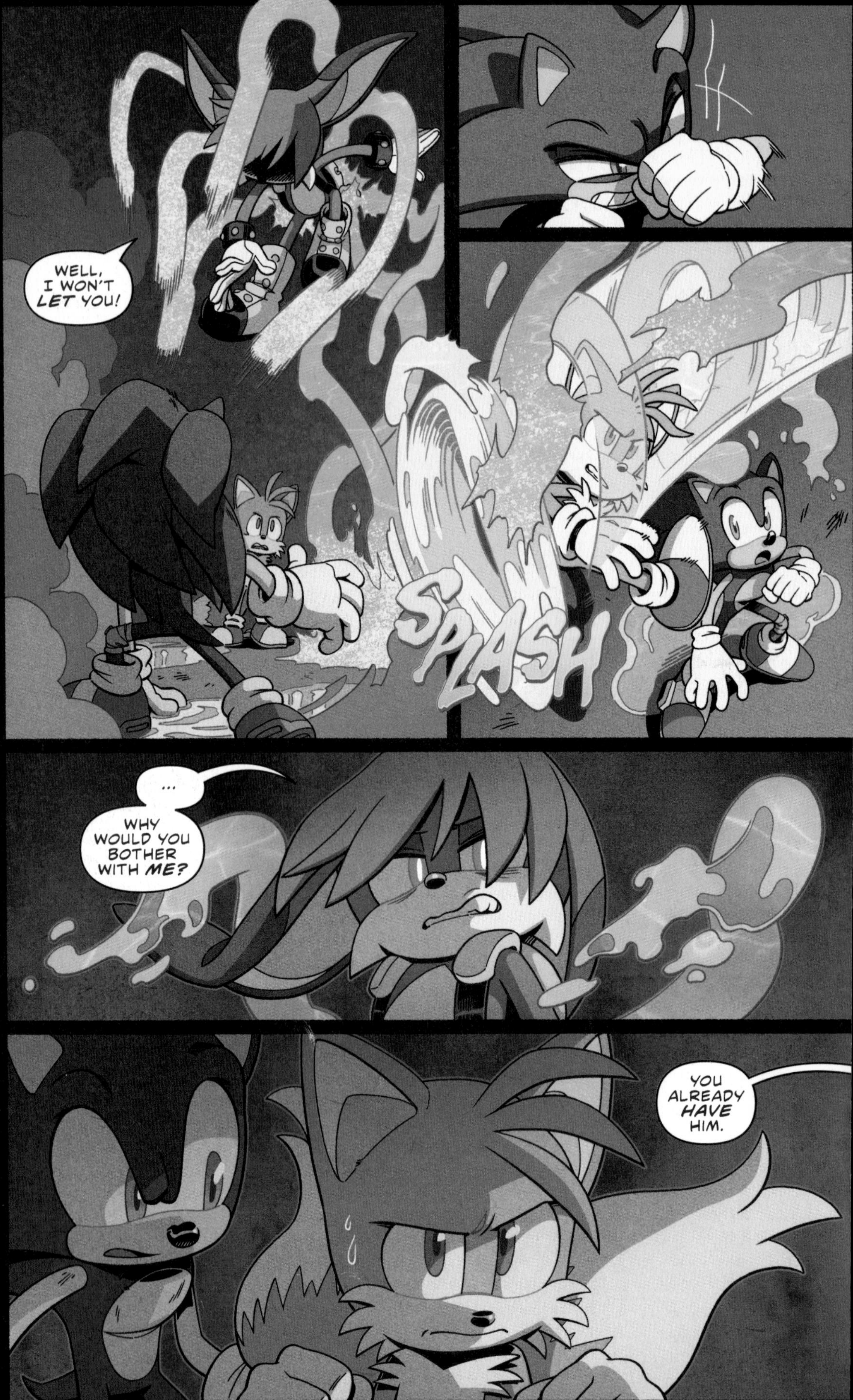
WELL, I WON'T LET YOU!
SPLASH
...
WHY WOULD YOU BOTHER WITH ME?
YOU ALREADY HAVE HIM.

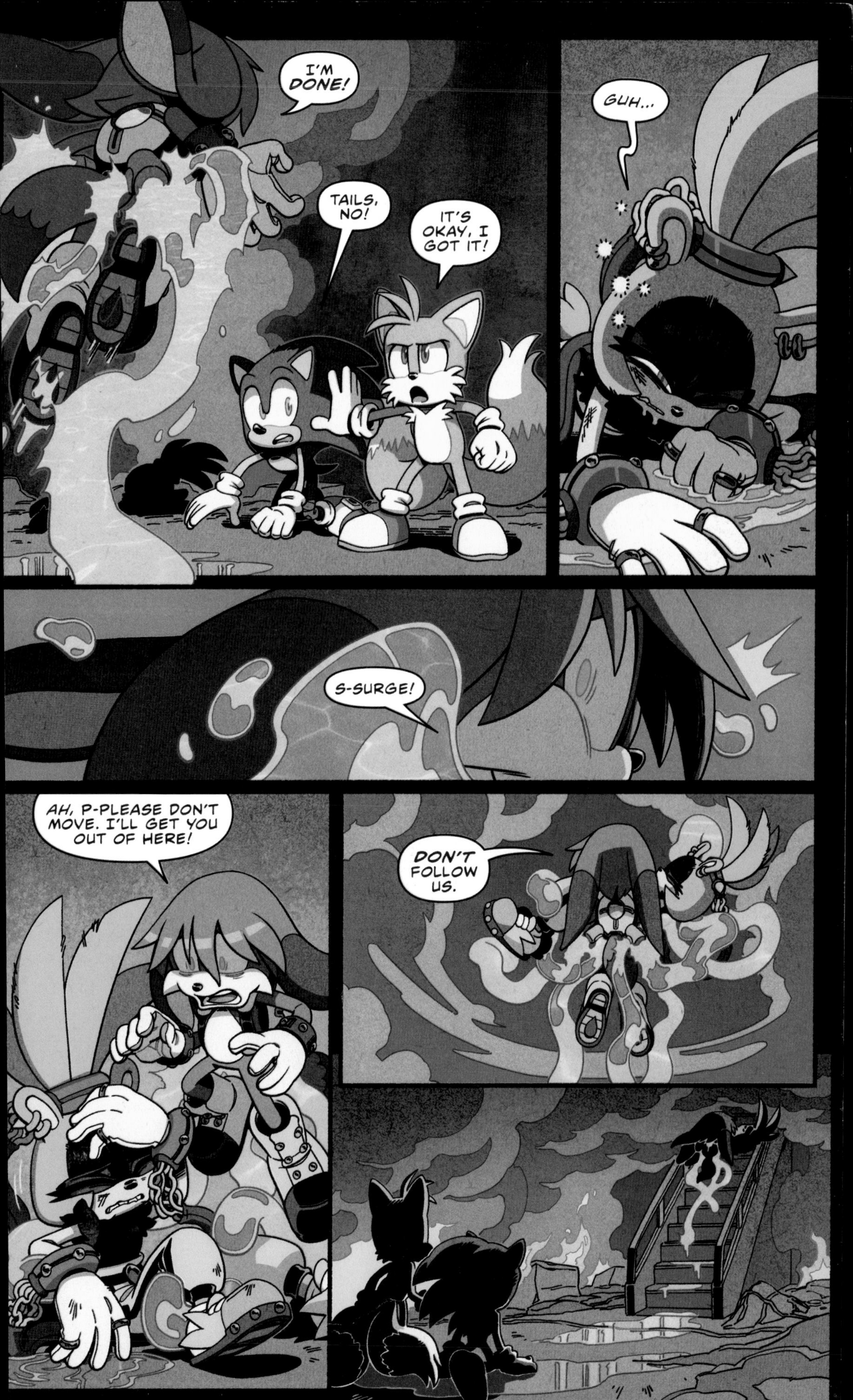
I'M DONE!
TAILS, NO!
IT'S OKAY, I GOT IT!
GUH...
S-SURGE!
AH, P-PLEASE DON'T MOVE. I'LL GET YOU OUT OF HERE!
DON'T FOLLOW US.

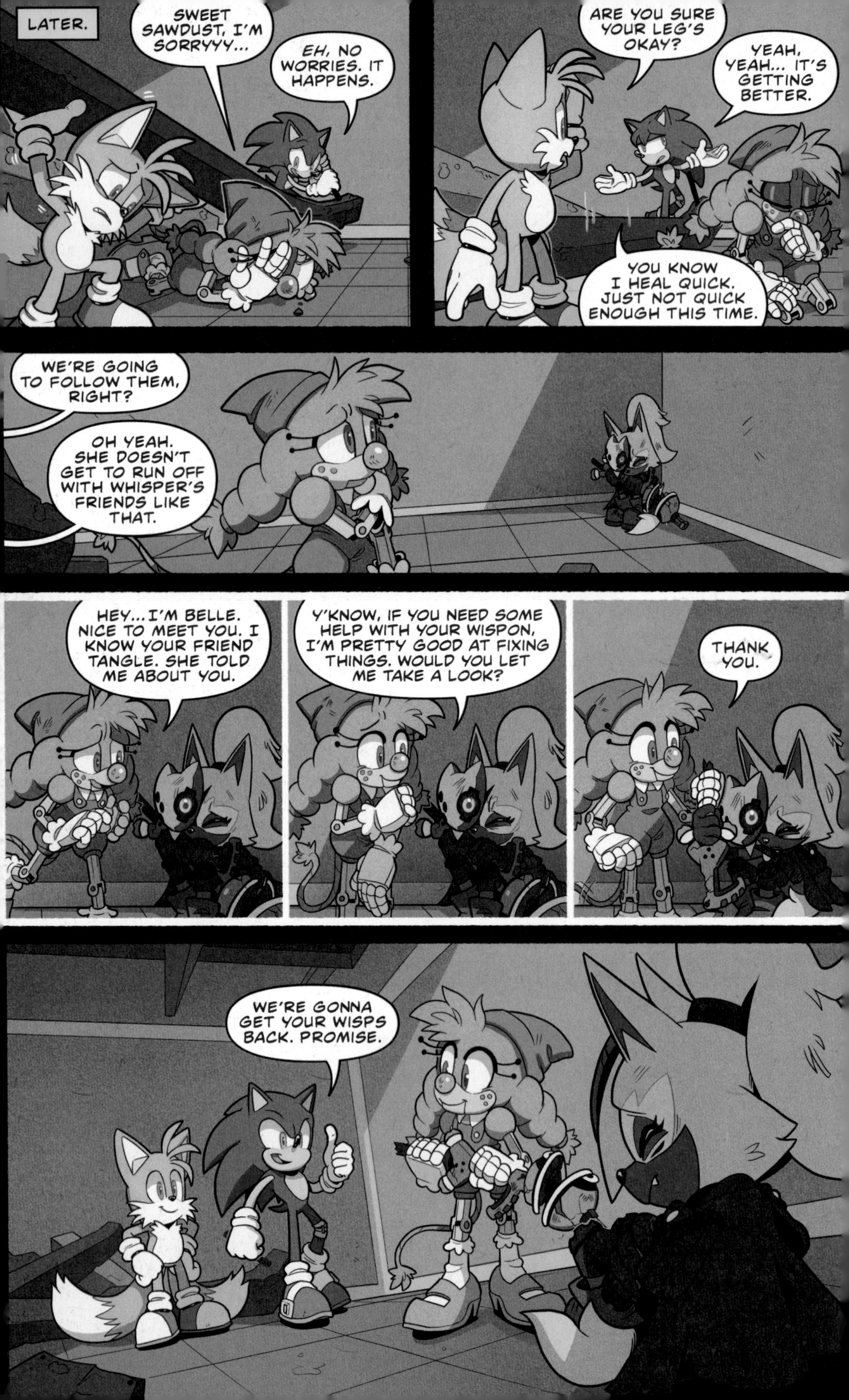
LATER.
SWEET SAWDUST, I'M SORRYYY...
EH, NO WORRIES. IT HAPPENS.
ARE YOU SURE YOUR LEG'S OKAY?
YEAH, YEAH... IT'S GETTING BETTER.
YOU KNOW I HEAL QUICK. JUST NOT QUICK ENOUGH THIS TIME.
WE'RE GOING TO FOLLOW THEM, RIGHT?
OH YEAH. SHE DOESN'T GET TO RUN OFF WITH WHISPER'S FRIENDS LIKE THAT.
HEY... I'M BELLE. NICE TO MEET YOU. I KNOW YOUR FRIEND TANGLE. SHE TOLD ME ABOUT YOU.
Y'KNOW, IF YOU NEED SOME HELP WITH YOUR WISPON, I'M PRETTY GOOD AT FIXING THINGS. WOULD YOU LET ME TAKE A LOOK?
THANK YOU.
WE'RE GONNA GET YOUR WISPS BACK. PROMISE.

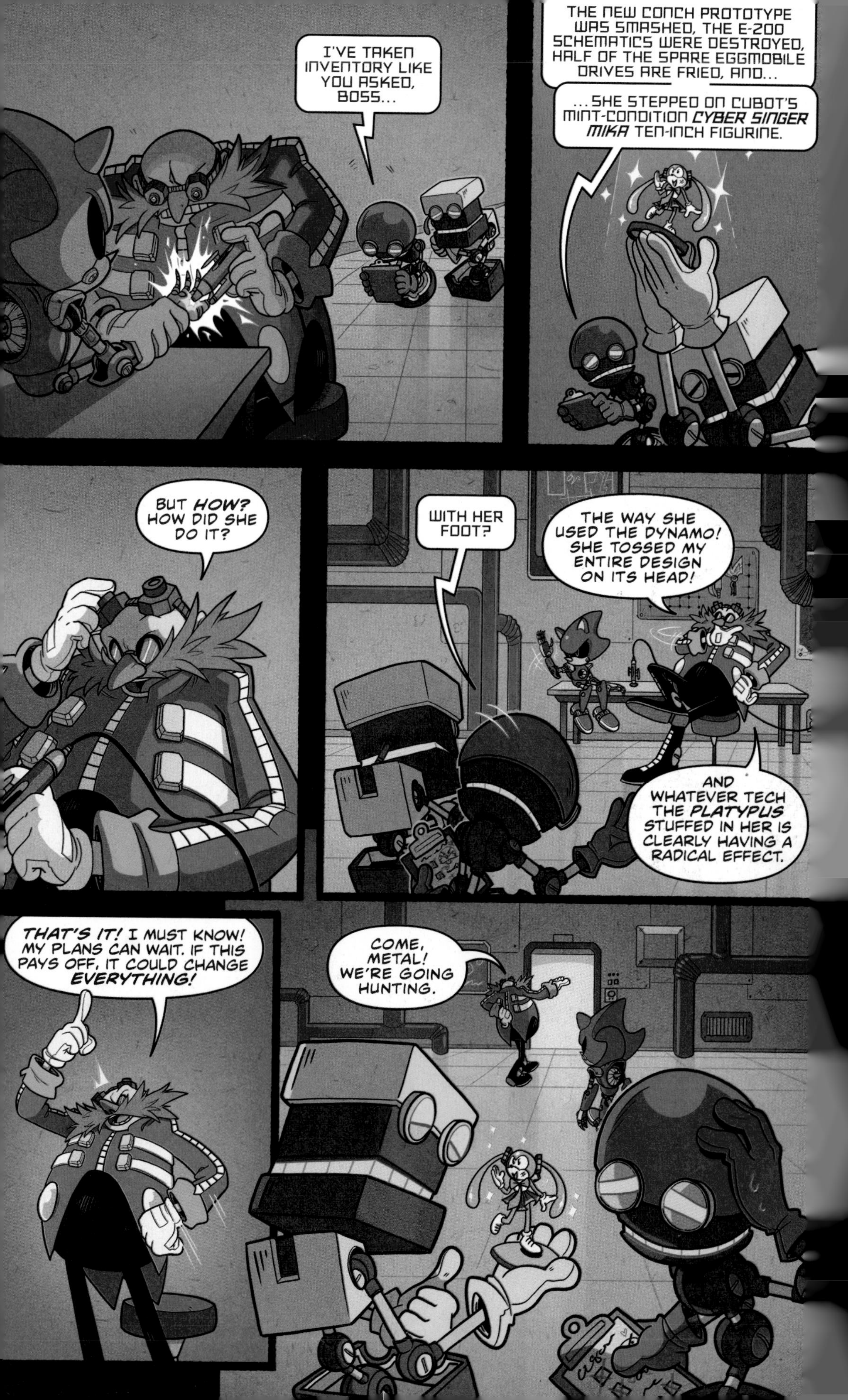
I'VE TAKEN INVENTORY LIKE YOU ASKED, BOSS...
THE NEW CONCH PROTOTYPE WAS SMASHED, THE E-200 SCHEMATICS WERE DESTROYED, HALF OF THE SPARE EGGMOBILE DRIVES ARE FRIED, AND...
...SHE STEPPED ON CUBOT'S MINT-CONDITION *CYBER SINGER MIKA* TEN-INCH FIGURINE.
BUT *HOW?* HOW DID SHE DO IT?
WITH HER FOOT?
THE WAY SHE USED THE DYNAMO! SHE TOSSED MY ENTIRE DESIGN ON ITS HEAD!
AND WHATEVER TECH THE *PLATYPUS* STUFFED IN HER IS CLEARLY HAVING A RADICAL EFFECT.
THAT'S IT! I MUST KNOW! MY PLANS CAN WAIT. IF THIS PAYS OFF, IT COULD CHANGE *EVERYTHING!*
COME, METAL! WE'RE GOING HUNTING.

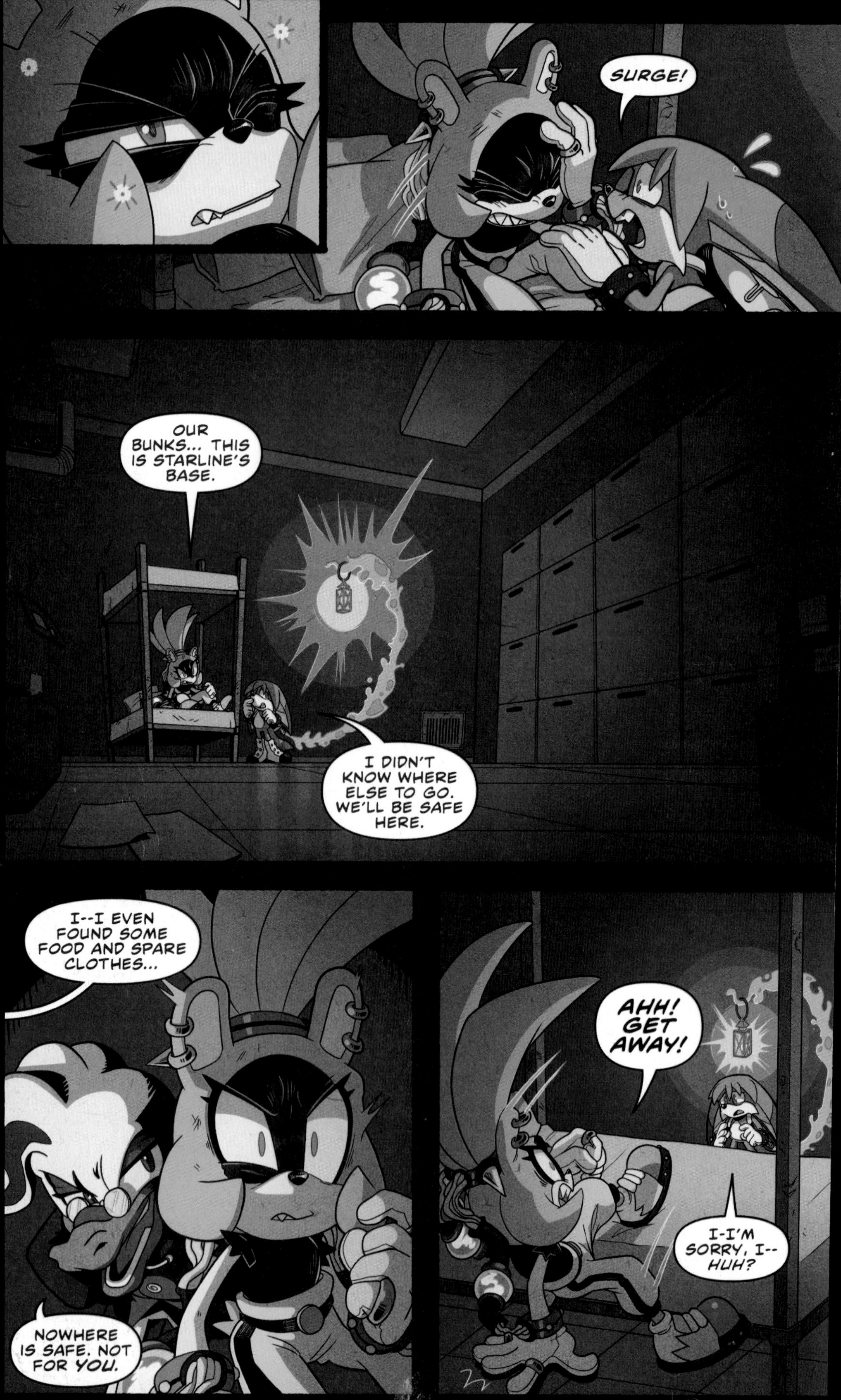
SURGE!
OUR BUNKS... THIS IS STARLINE'S BASE.
I DIDN'T KNOW WHERE ELSE TO GO. WE'LL BE SAFE HERE.
I--I EVEN FOUND SOME FOOD AND SPARE CLOTHES...
NOWHERE IS SAFE. NOT FOR YOU.
AHH! GET AWAY!
I-I'M SORRY, I-- HUH?

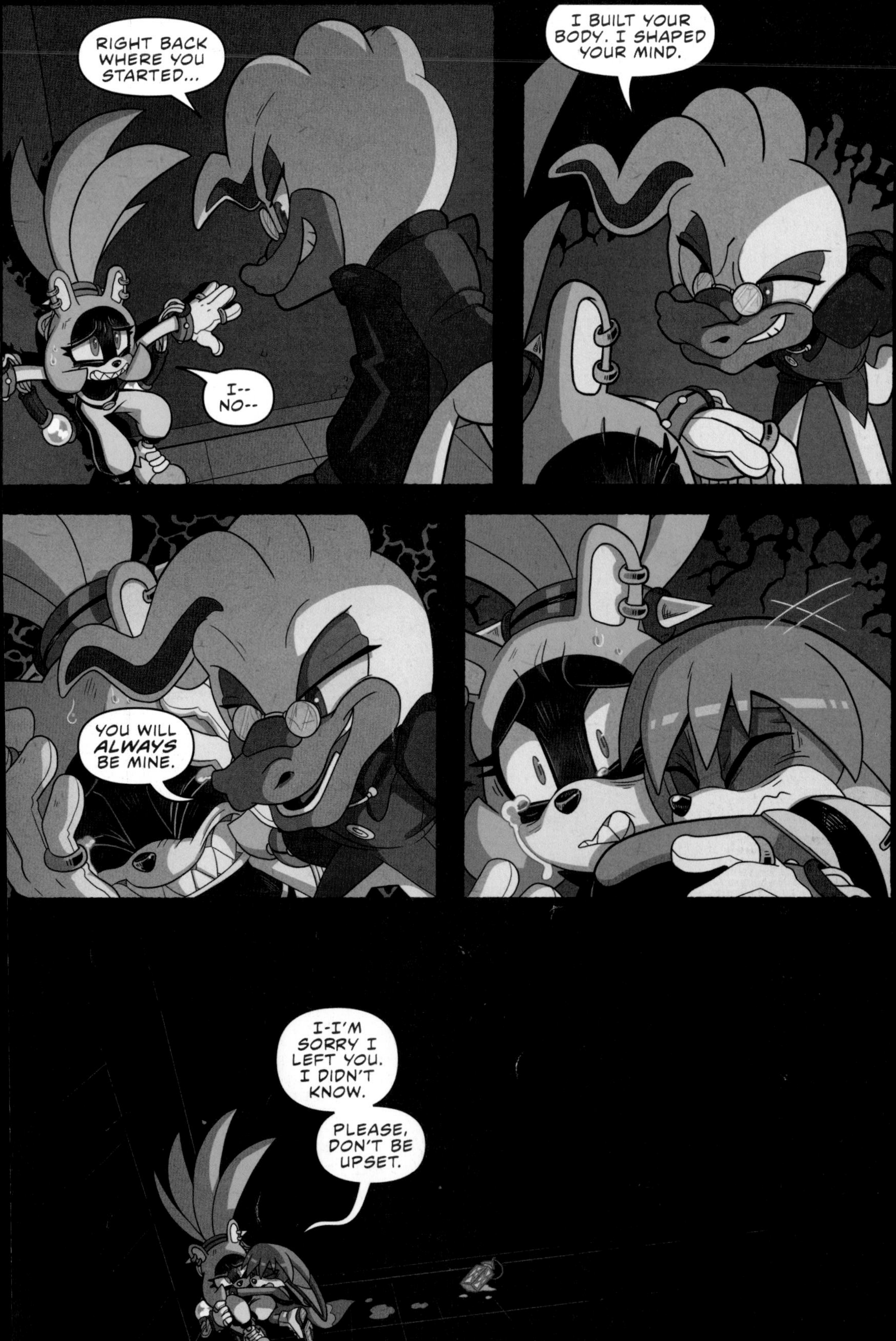
RIGHT BACK WHERE YOU STARTED...
I-- NO--
I BUILT YOUR BODY. I SHAPED YOUR MIND.
YOU WILL *ALWAYS* BE MINE.
I-I'M SORRY I LEFT YOU. I DIDN'T KNOW.
PLEASE, DON'T BE UPSET.

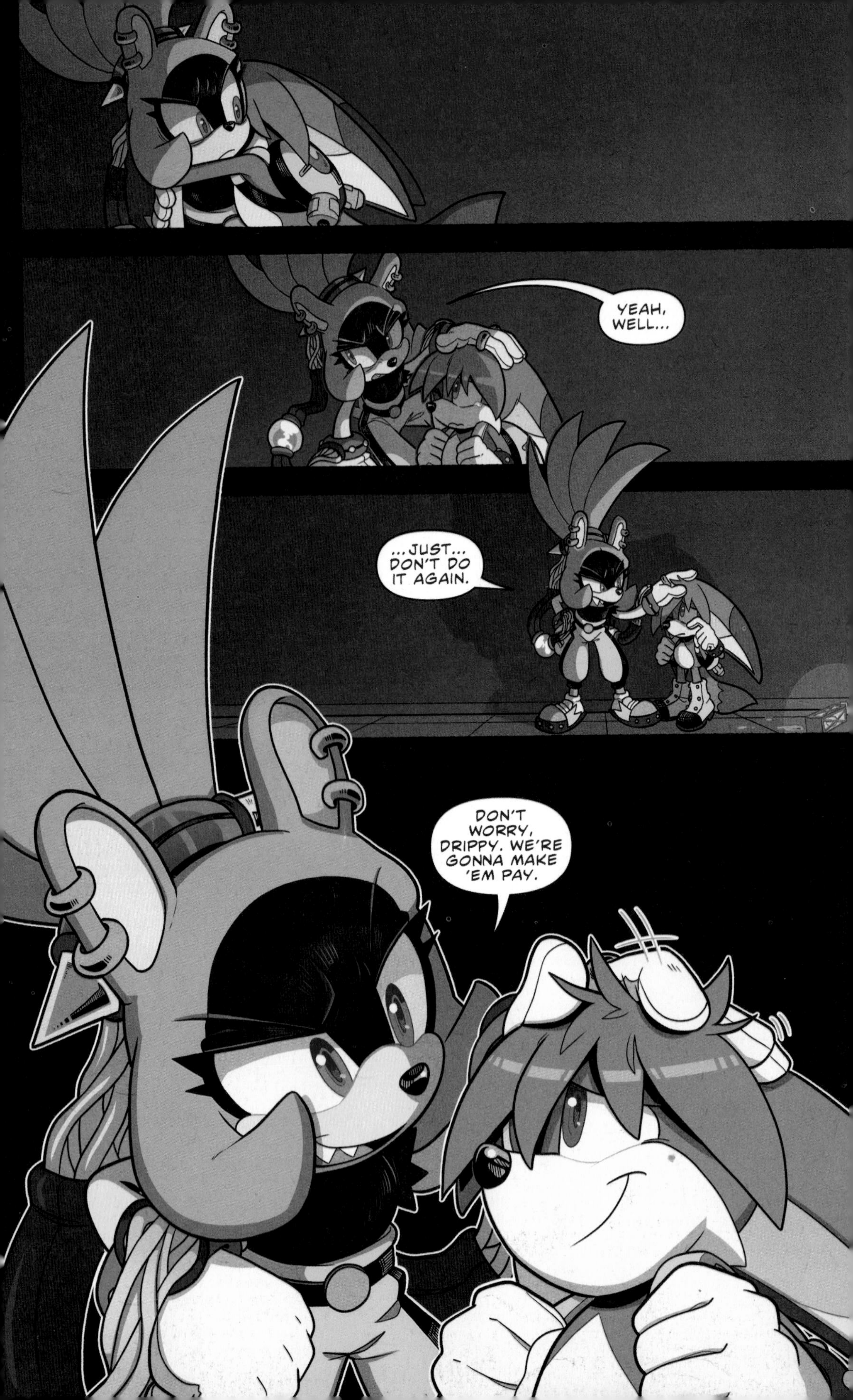
YEAH, WELL...
...JUST... DON'T DO IT AGAIN.
DON'T WORRY, DRIPPY. WE'RE GONNA MAKE 'EM PAY.

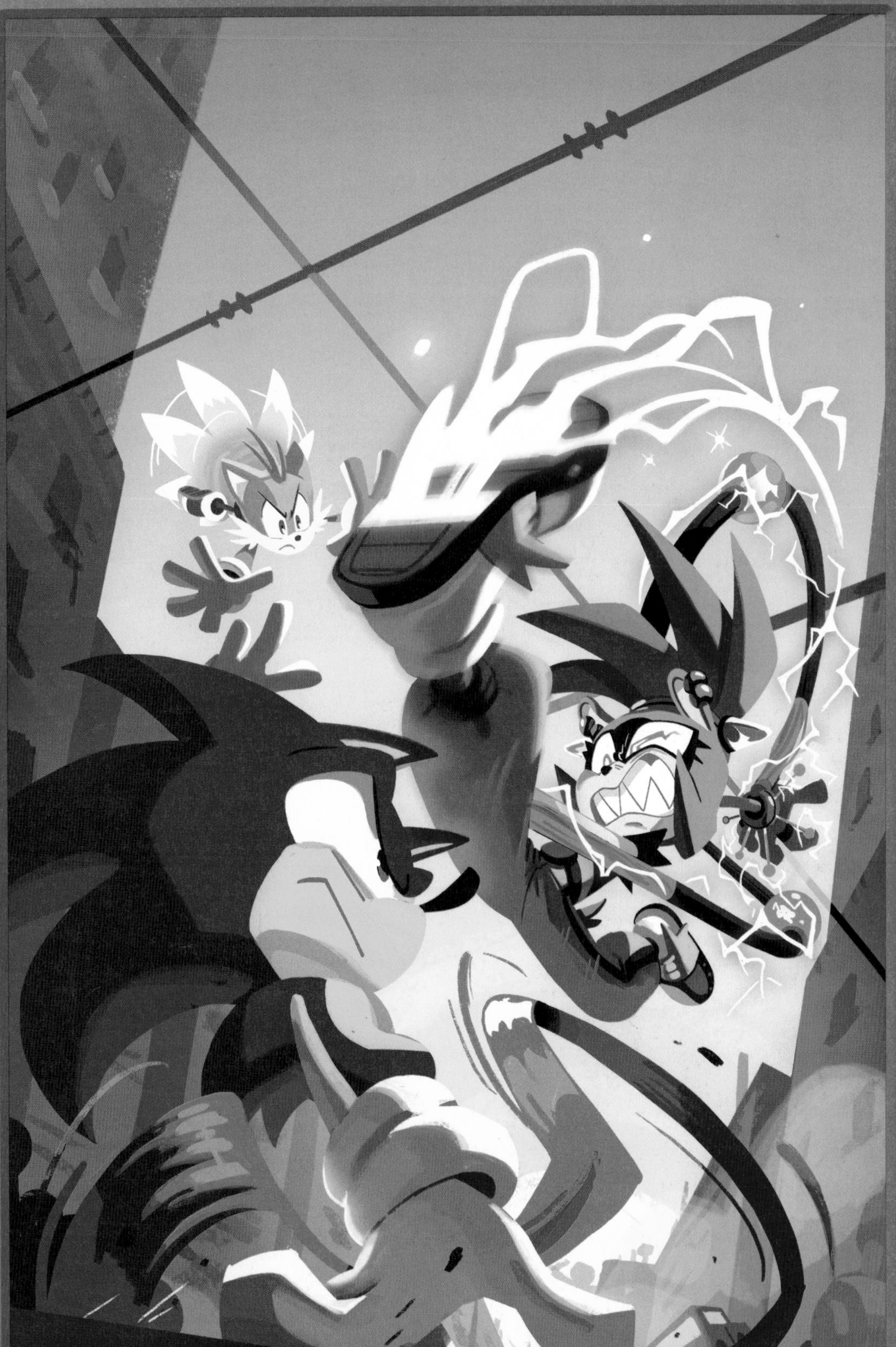

ART BY **NATHALIE FOURDRAINE**

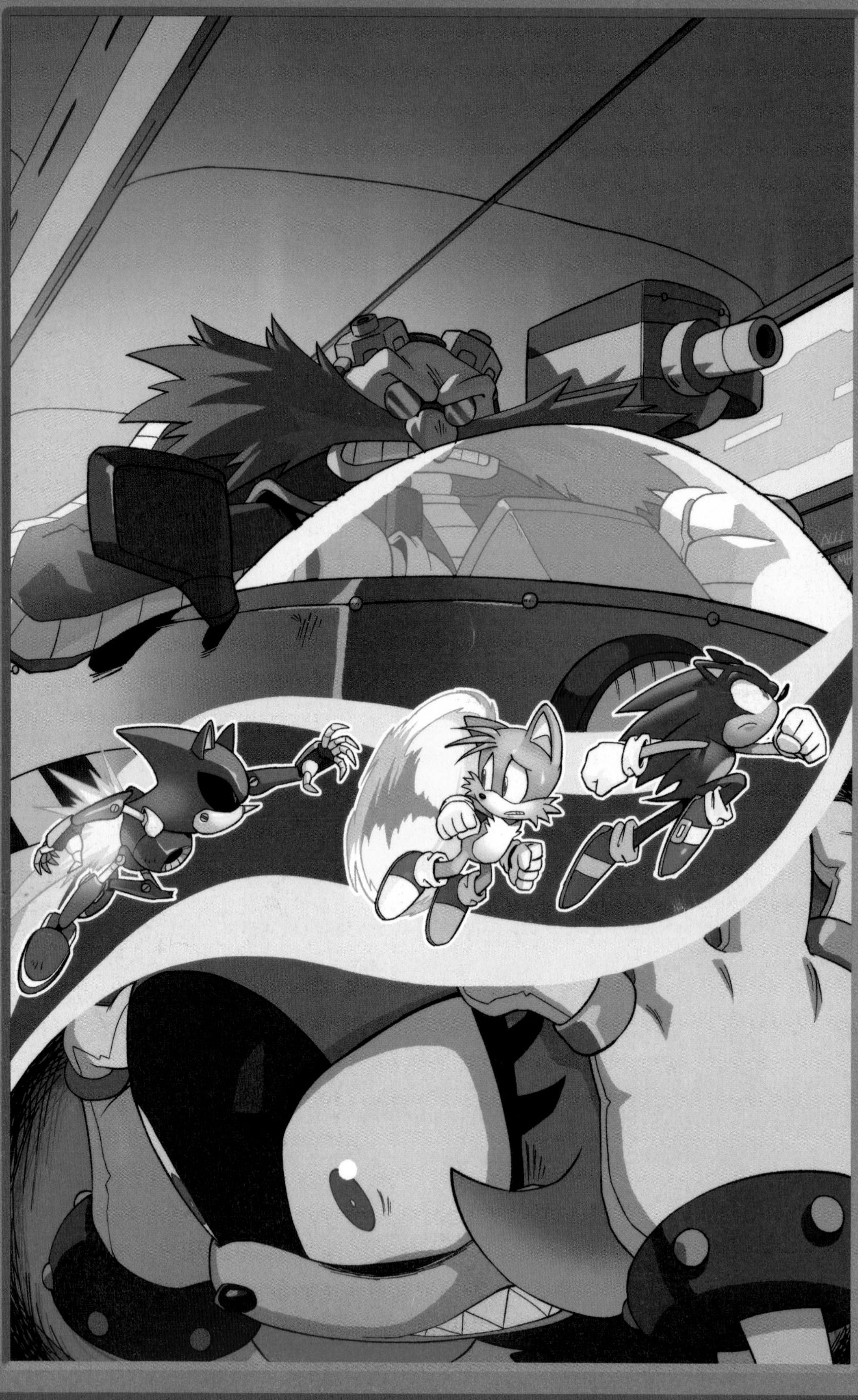

ART BY **AARON HAMMERSTROM** COLORS BY **MATT HERMS**

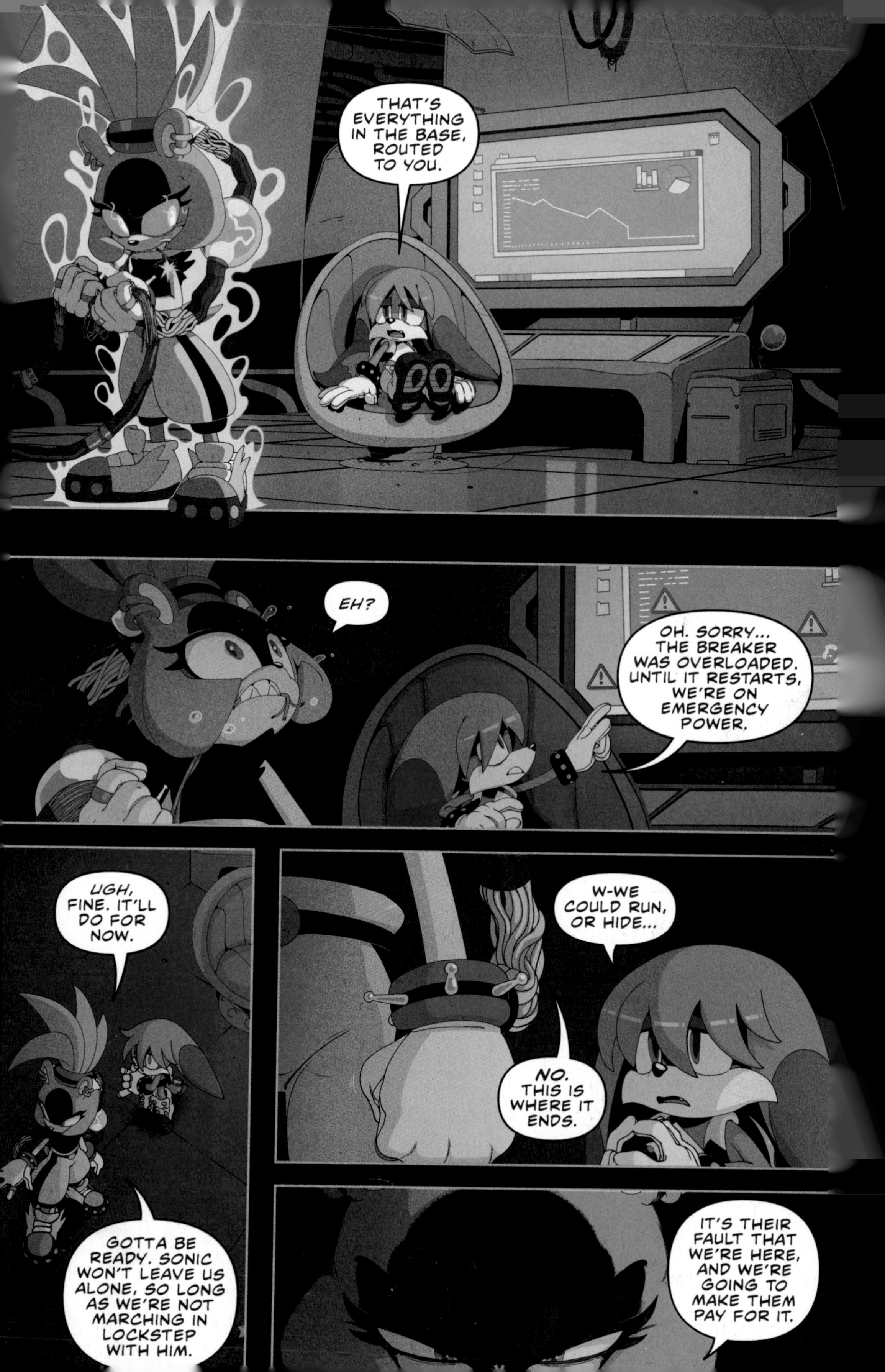
THAT'S EVERYTHING IN THE BASE, ROUTED TO YOU.
EH?
OH. SORRY... THE BREAKER WAS OVERLOADED. UNTIL IT RESTARTS, WE'RE ON EMERGENCY POWER.
UGH, FINE. IT'LL DO FOR NOW.
GOTTA BE READY. SONIC WON'T LEAVE US ALONE, SO LONG AS WE'RE NOT MARCHING IN LOCKSTEP WITH HIM.
W-WE COULD RUN, OR HIDE...
NO. THIS IS WHERE IT ENDS.
IT'S THEIR FAULT THAT WE'RE HERE, AND WE'RE GOING TO MAKE THEM PAY FOR IT.

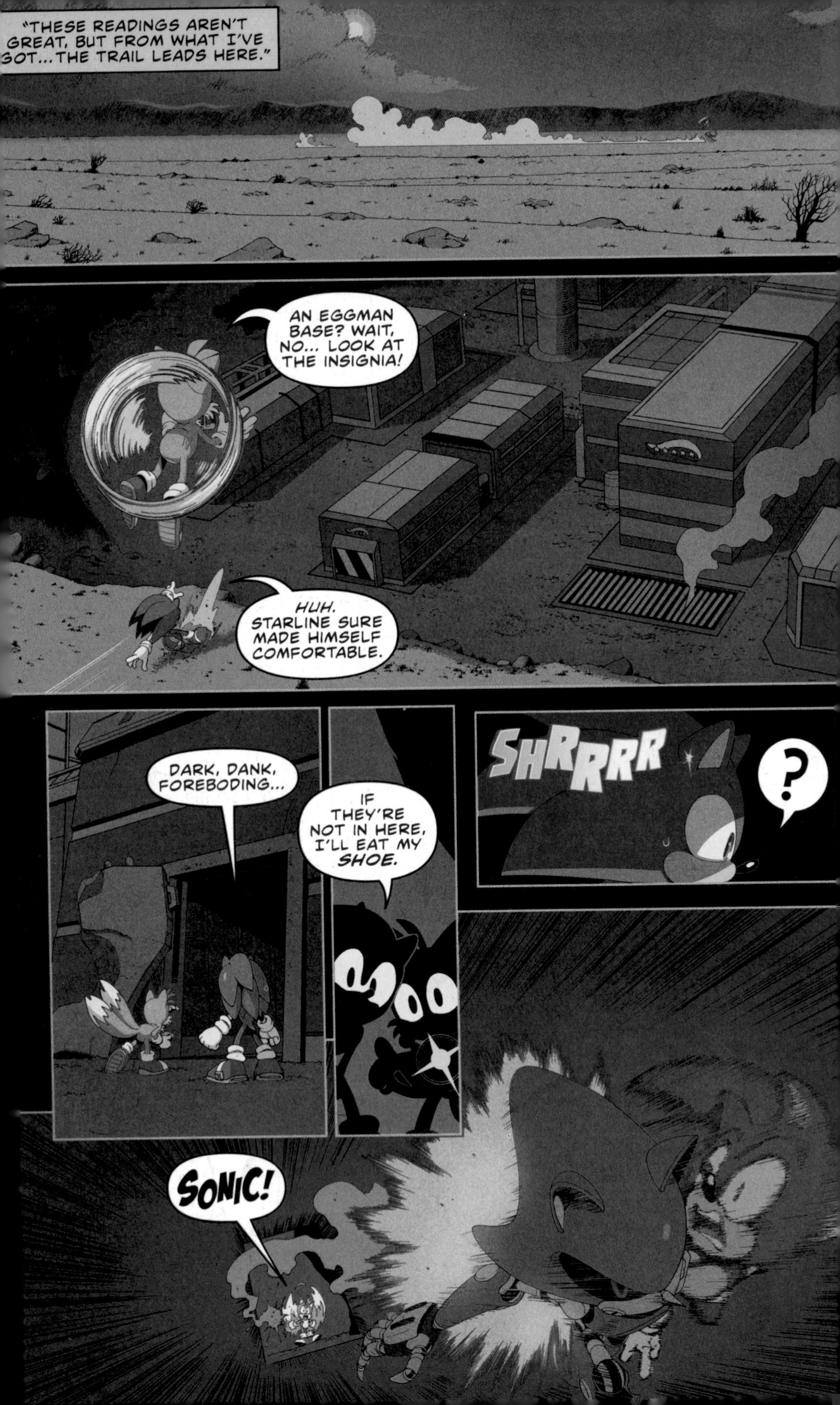
"THESE READINGS AREN'T GREAT, BUT FROM WHAT I'VE GOT... THE TRAIL LEADS HERE."
AN EGGMAN BASE? WAIT, NO... LOOK AT THE INSIGNIA!
HUH. STARLINE SURE MADE HIMSELF COMFORTABLE.
DARK, DANK, FOREBODING...
IF THEY'RE NOT IN HERE, I'LL EAT MY SHOE.
SHRRRR
?
SONIC!

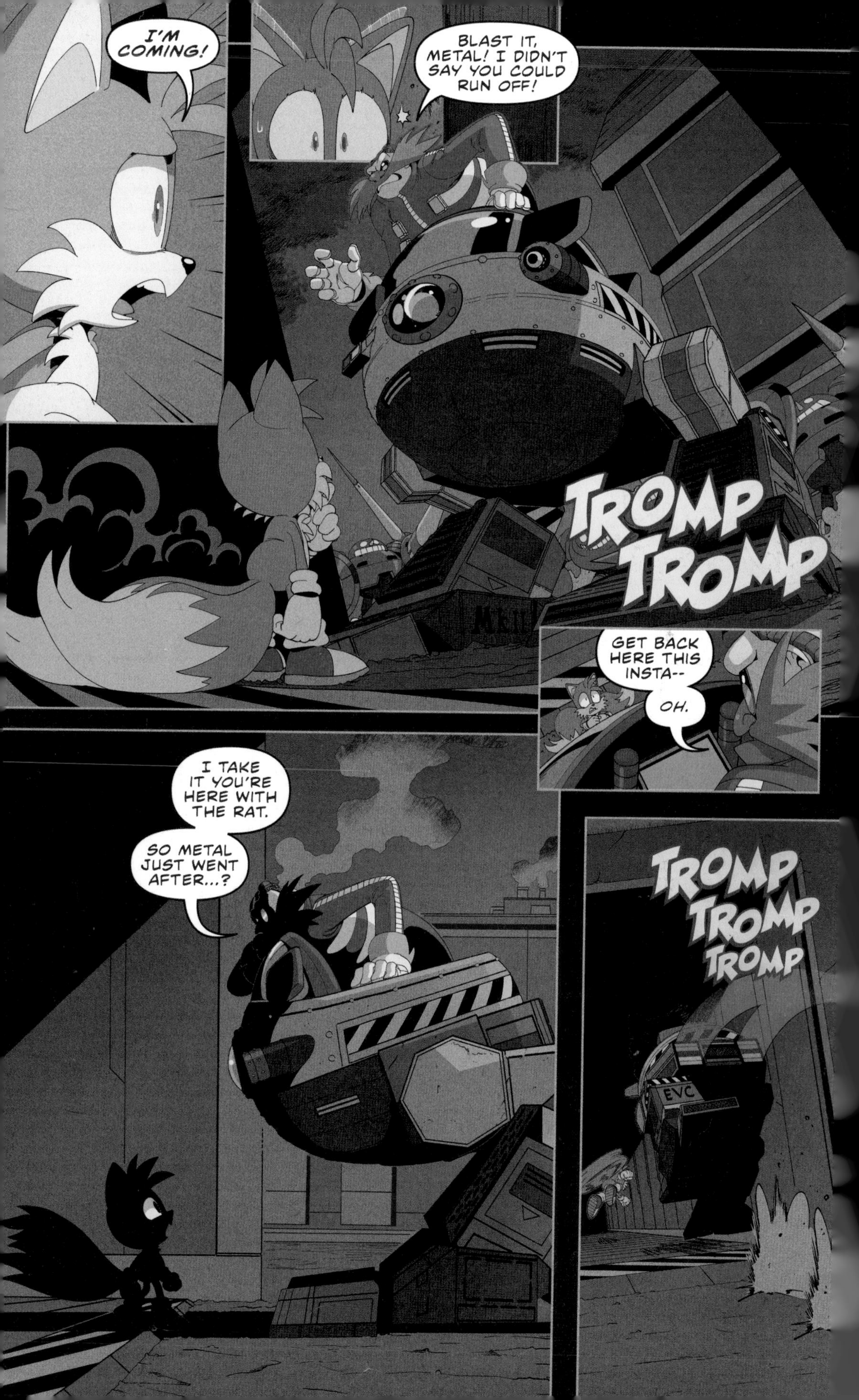
I'M COMING!
BLAST IT, METAL! I DIDN'T SAY YOU COULD RUN OFF!
TROMP TROMP
GET BACK HERE THIS INSTA--
OH.
I TAKE IT YOU'RE HERE WITH THE RAT.
SO METAL JUST WENT AFTER...?
TROMP TROMP TROMP
EVC

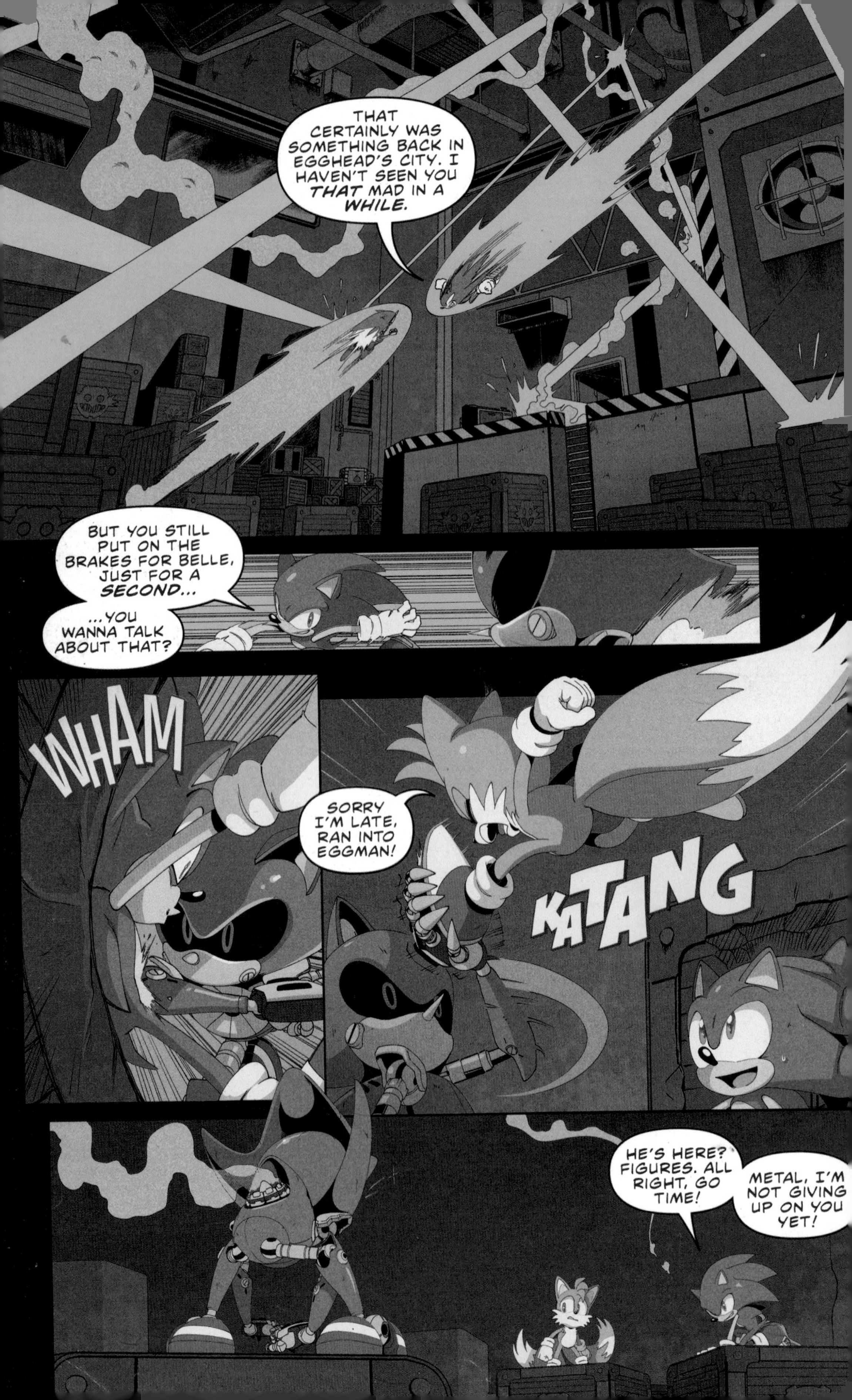
THAT CERTAINLY WAS SOMETHING BACK IN EGGHEAD'S CITY. I HAVEN'T SEEN YOU THAT MAD IN A WHILE.
BUT YOU STILL PUT ON THE BRAKES FOR BELLE, JUST FOR A SECOND...
...YOU WANNA TALK ABOUT THAT?
WHAM
SORRY I'M LATE, RAN INTO EGGMAN!
KATANG
HE'S HERE? FIGURES. ALL RIGHT, GO TIME!
METAL, I'M NOT GIVING UP ON YOU YET!

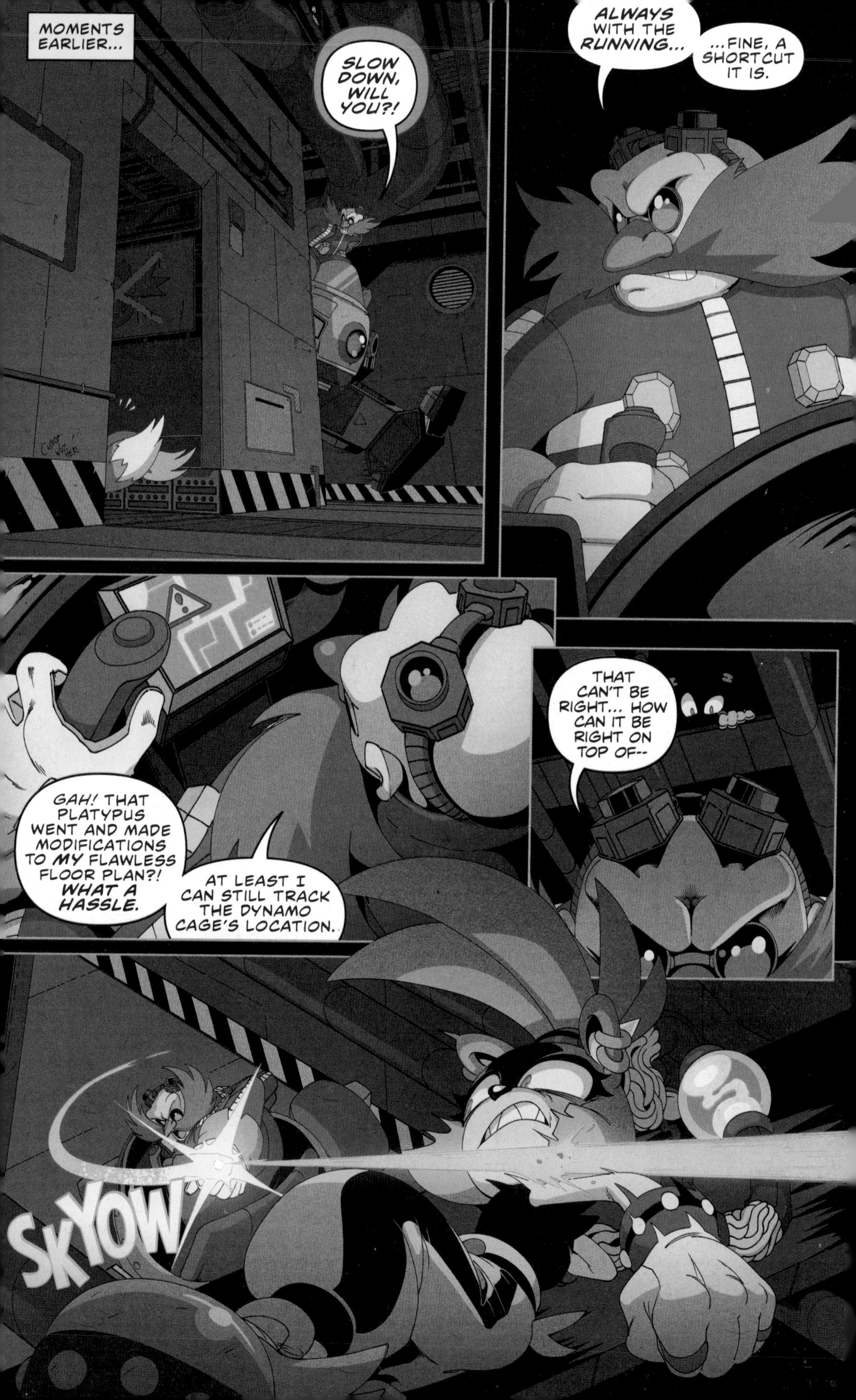
MOMENTS EARLIER...
SLOW DOWN, WILL YOU?!
ALWAYS WITH THE RUNNING...
...FINE, A SHORTCUT IT IS.
GAH! THAT PLATYPUS WENT AND MADE MODIFICATIONS TO MY FLAWLESS FLOOR PLAN?! WHAT A HASSLE.
AT LEAST I CAN STILL TRACK THE DYNAMO CAGE'S LOCATION.
THAT CAN'T BE RIGHT... HOW CAN IT BE RIGHT ON TOP OF--
SKYOW

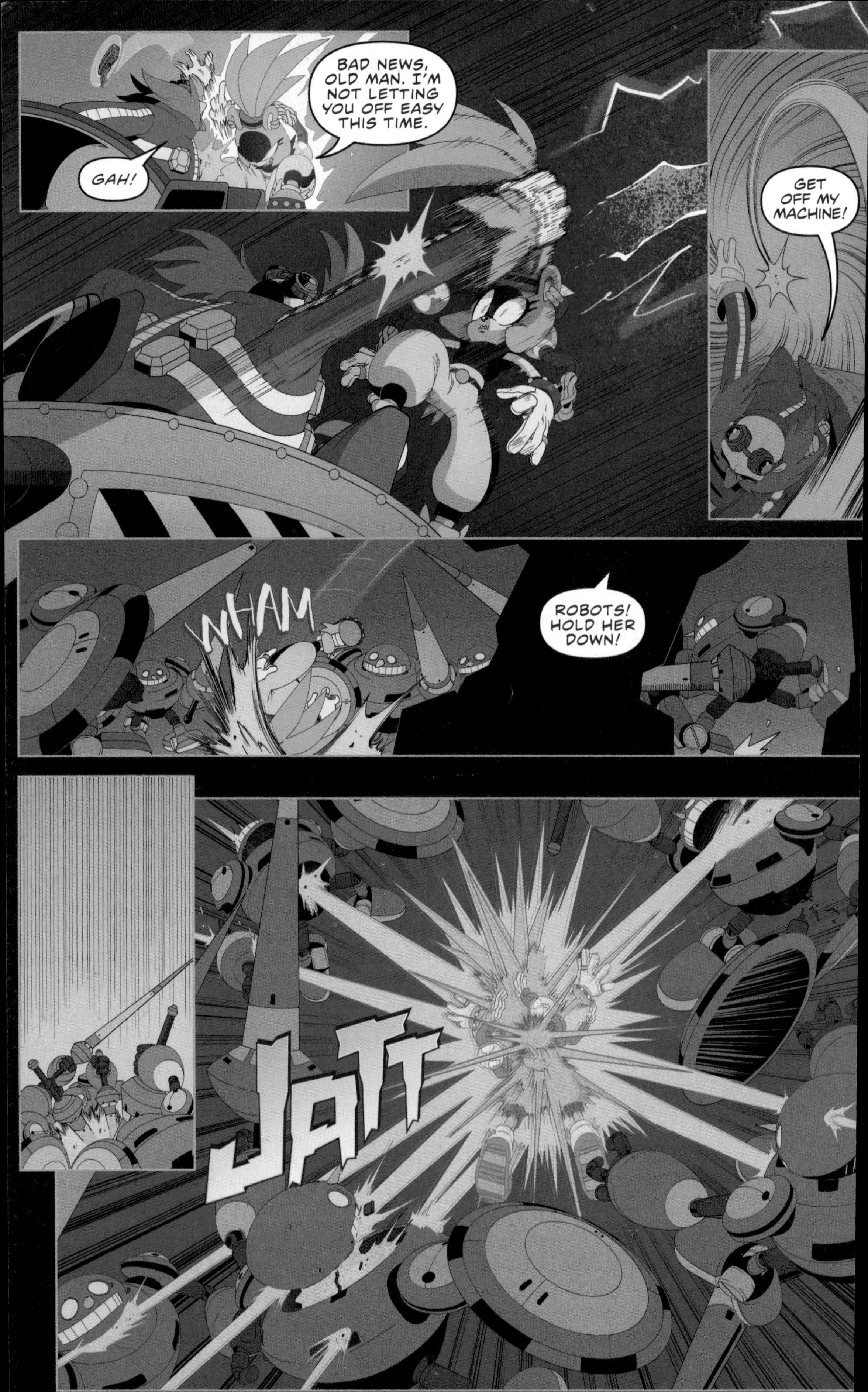
BAD NEWS, OLD MAN. I'M NOT LETTING YOU OFF EASY THIS TIME.
GAH!
GET OFF MY MACHINE!
WHAM
ROBOTS! HOLD HER DOWN!
JATT

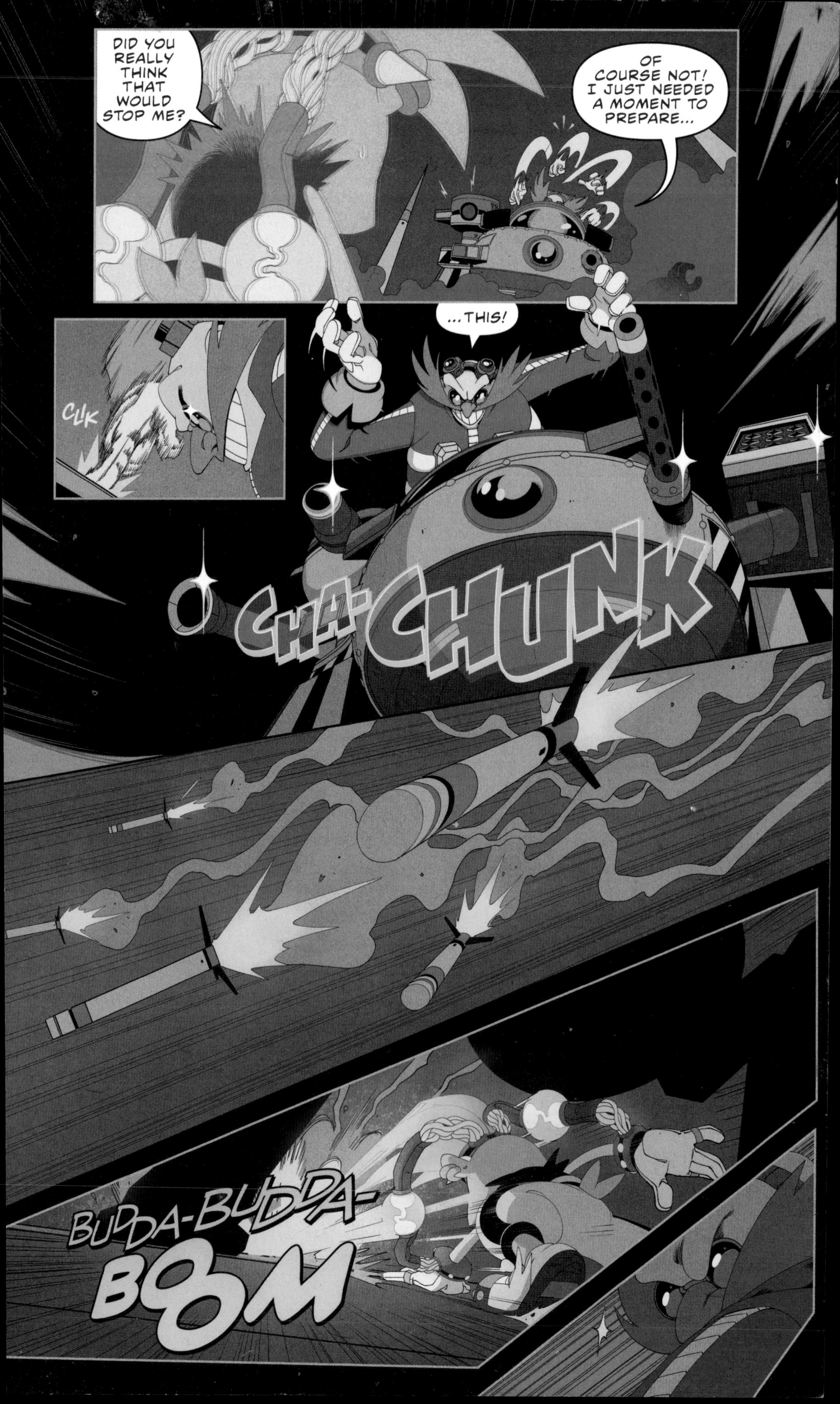
DID YOU REALLY THINK THAT WOULD STOP ME?
OF COURSE NOT! I JUST NEEDED A MOMENT TO PREPARE...
...THIS!
CLIK
CHA-CHUNK
BUDDA-BUDDA-BOOM

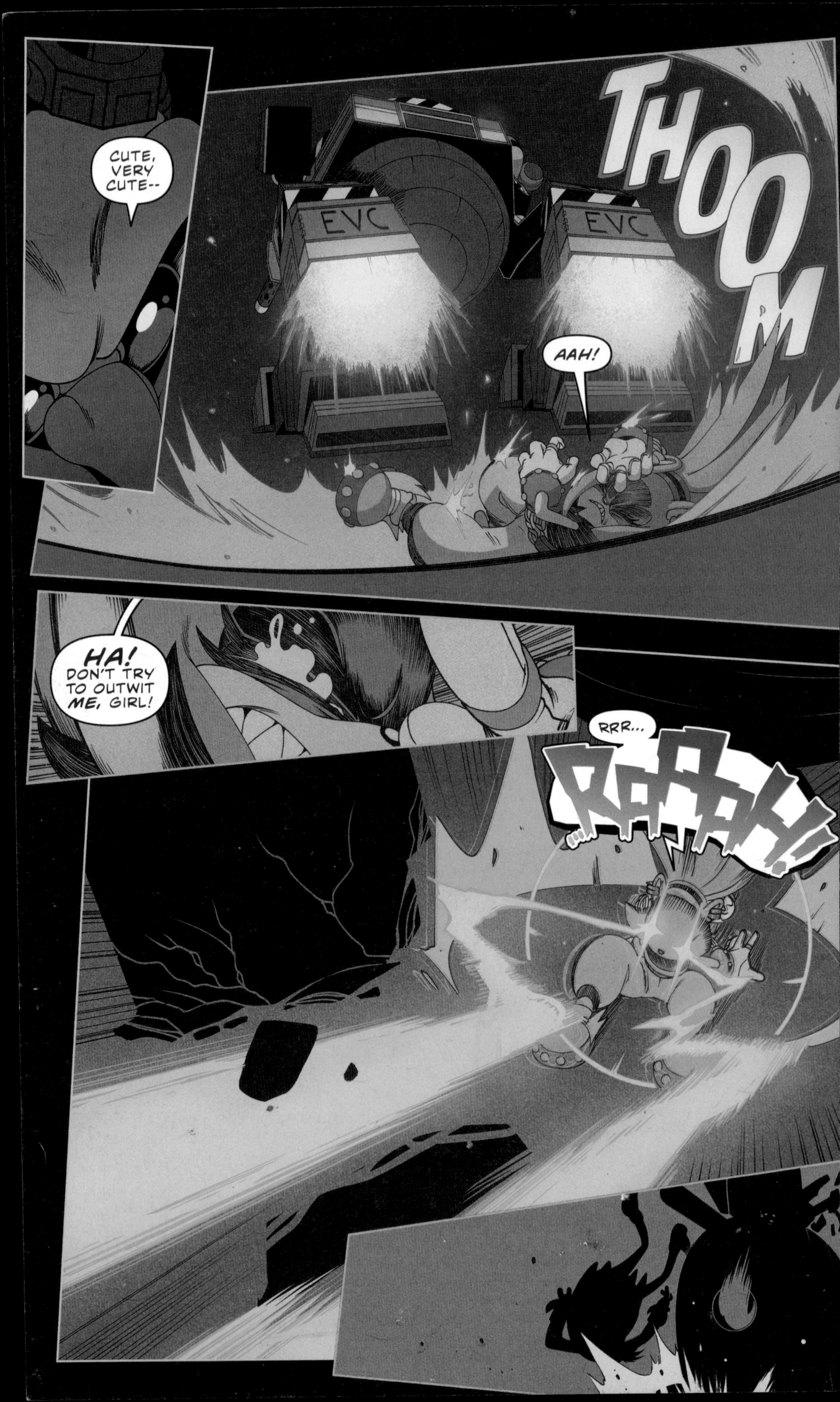
CUTE, VERY CUTE--
THOOM
AAH!
HA! DON'T TRY TO OUTWIT ME, GIRL!
RRR...
RAAAH!

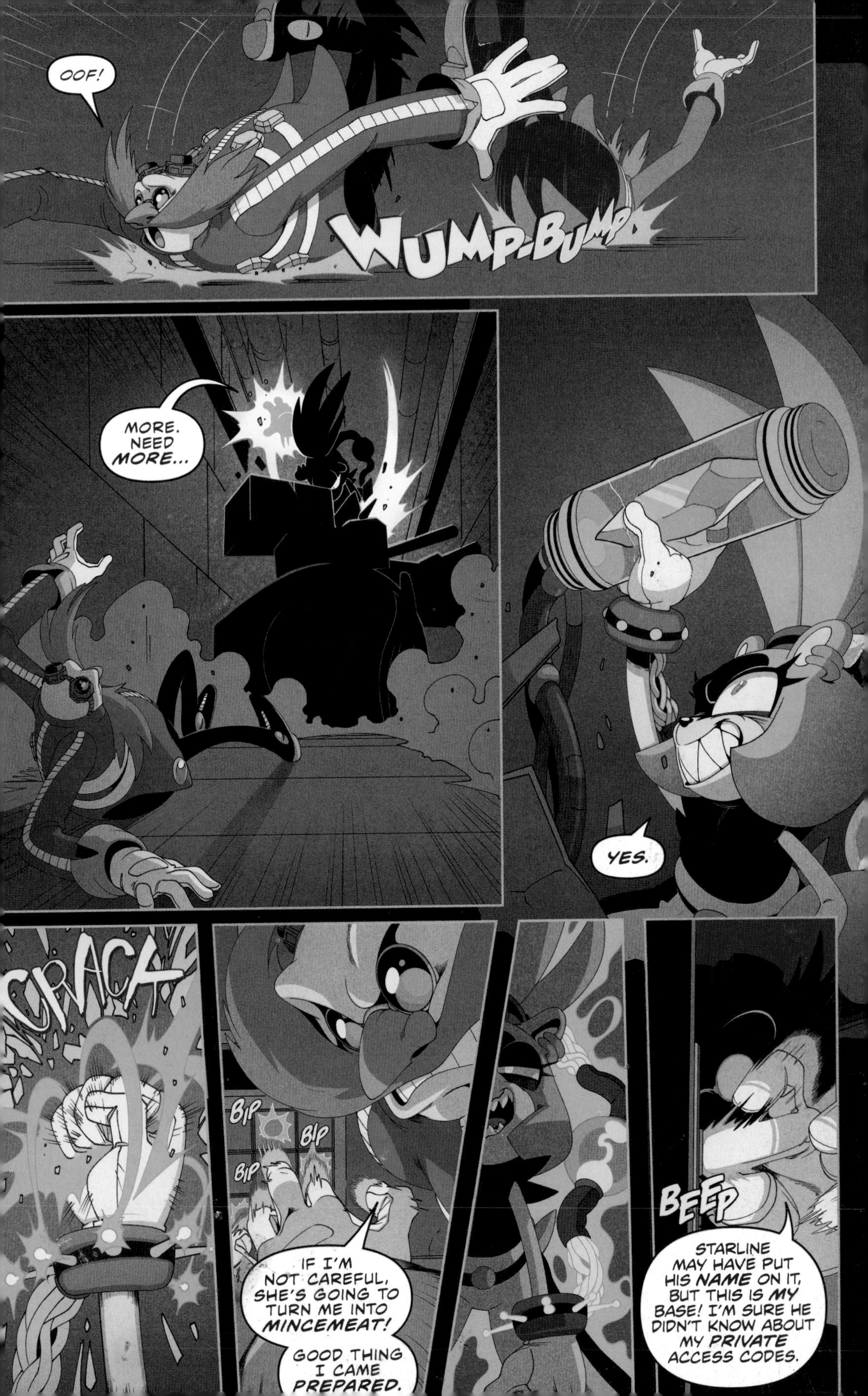
OOF!
WUMP-BUMP
MORE. NEED MORE...
YES.
CRACK
BIP
BIP
BIP
IF I'M NOT CAREFUL, SHE'S GOING TO TURN ME INTO MINCEMEAT!
GOOD THING I CAME PREPARED.
BEEP
STARLINE MAY HAVE PUT HIS NAME ON IT, BUT THIS IS MY BASE! I'M SURE HE DIDN'T KNOW ABOUT MY PRIVATE ACCESS CODES.

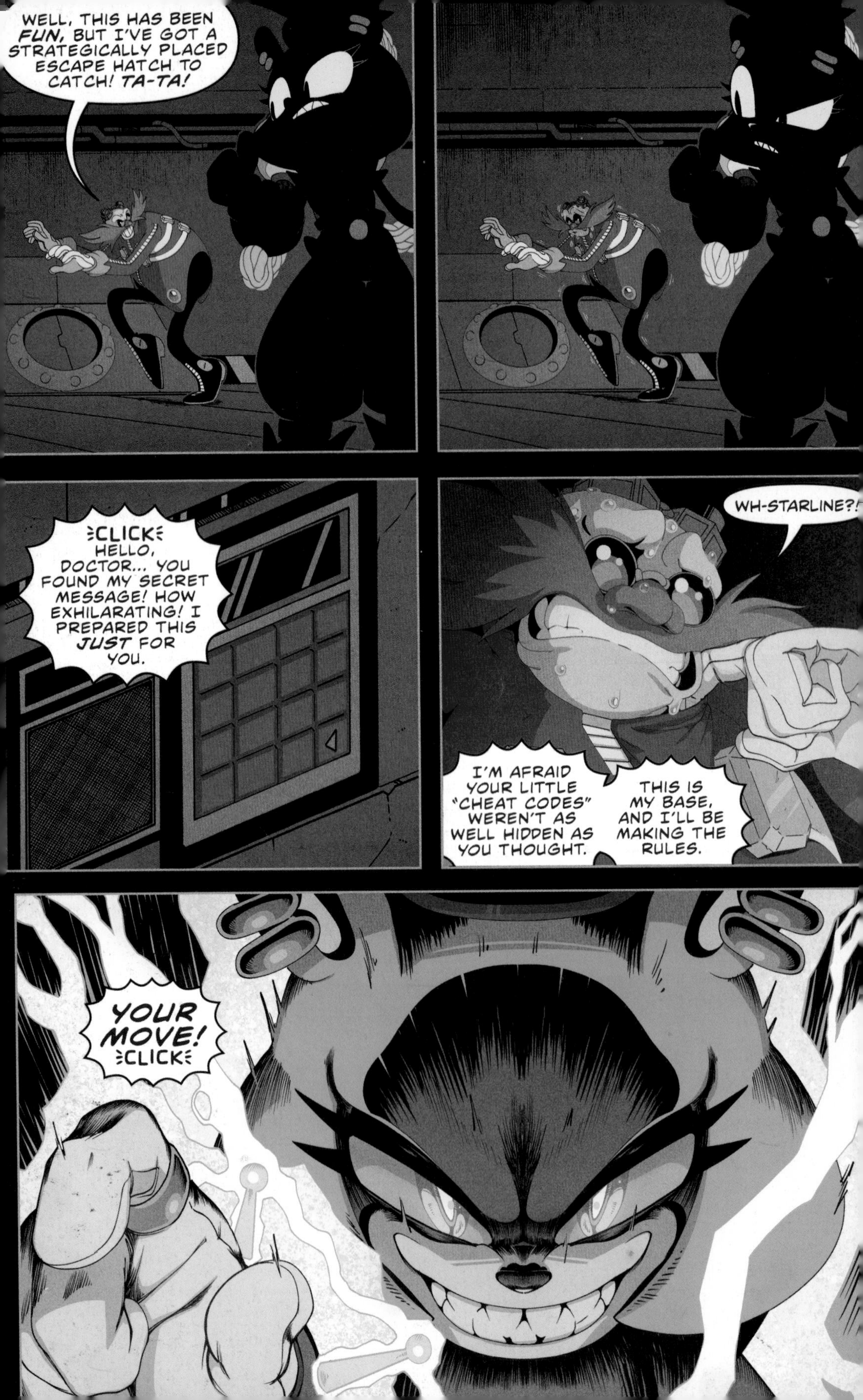

WELL, THIS HAS BEEN FUN, BUT I'VE GOT A STRATEGICALLY PLACED ESCAPE HATCH TO CATCH! TA-TA!
CLICK HELLO, DOCTOR... YOU FOUND MY SECRET MESSAGE! HOW EXHILARATING! I PREPARED THIS JUST FOR YOU.
WH-STARLINE?!
I'M AFRAID YOUR LITTLE "CHEAT CODES" WEREN'T AS WELL HIDDEN AS YOU THOUGHT.
THIS IS MY BASE, AND I'LL BE MAKING THE RULES.
YOUR MOVE! CLICK

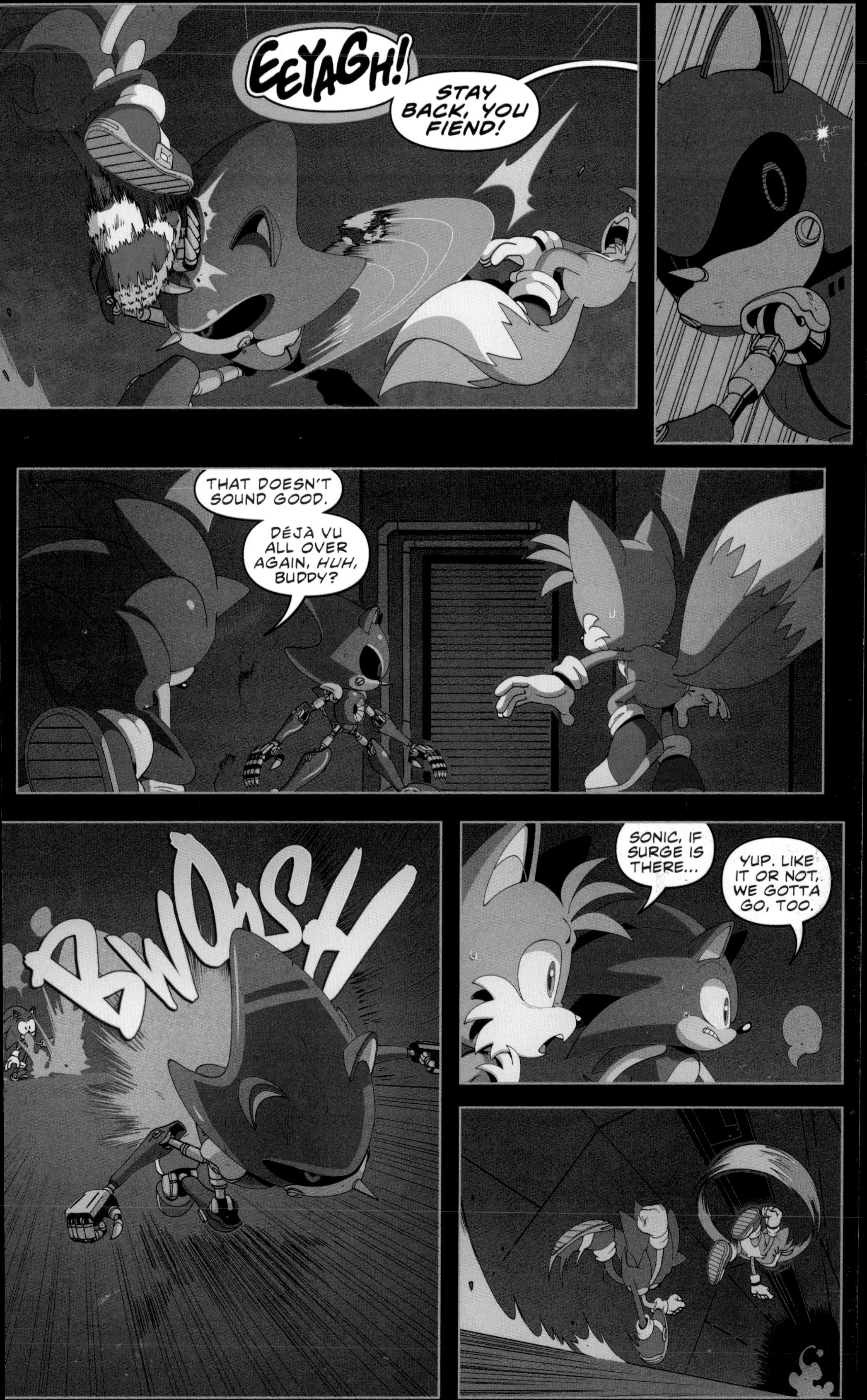
EEYAGH!
STAY BACK, YOU FIEND!
THAT DOESN'T SOUND GOOD.
DÉJÀ VU ALL OVER AGAIN, *HUH,* BUDDY?
BWOOSH
SONIC, IF SURGE IS THERE...
YUP. LIKE IT OR NOT, WE GOTTA GO, TOO.

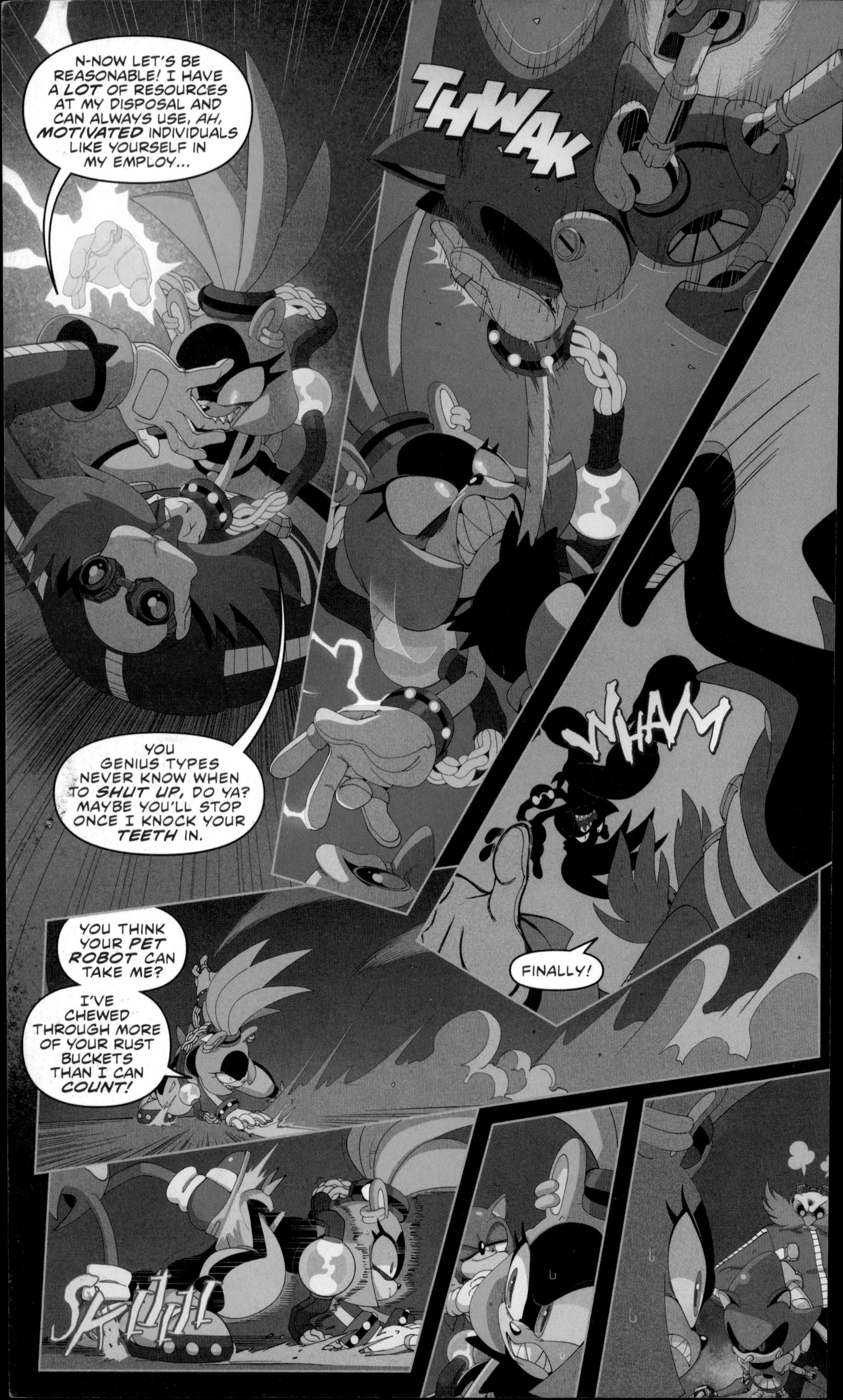
N-NOW LET'S BE REASONABLE! I HAVE A LOT OF RESOURCES AT MY DISPOSAL AND CAN ALWAYS USE, AH, MOTIVATED INDIVIDUALS LIKE YOURSELF IN MY EMPLOY...
THWAK
YOU GENIUS TYPES NEVER KNOW WHEN TO SHUT UP, DO YA? MAYBE YOU'LL STOP ONCE I KNOCK YOUR TEETH IN.
WHAM
FINALLY!
YOU THINK YOUR PET ROBOT CAN TAKE ME?
I'VE CHEWED THROUGH MORE OF YOUR RUST BUCKETS THAN I CAN COUNT!
SKRITTT

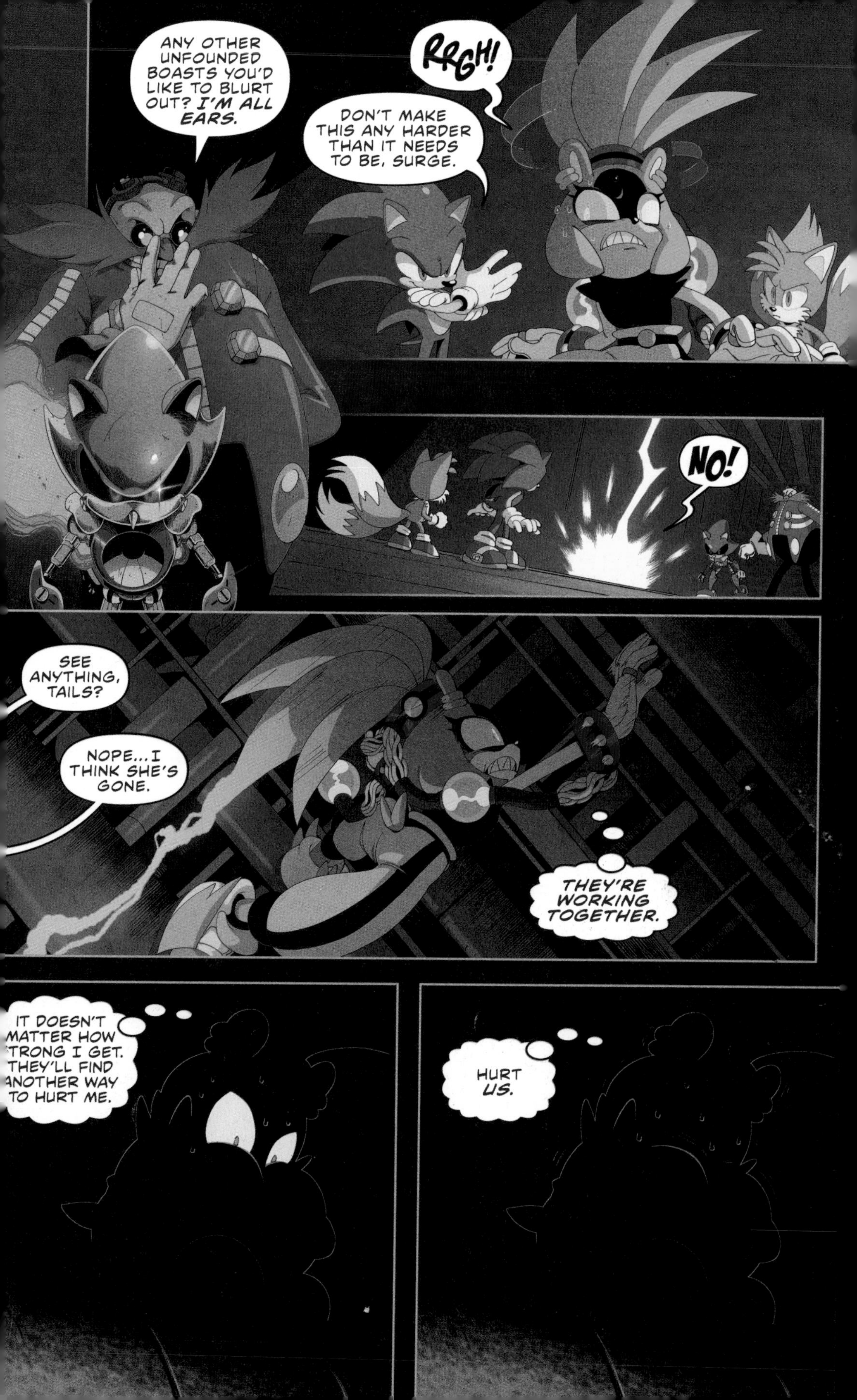
ANY OTHER UNFOUNDED BOASTS YOU'D LIKE TO BLURT OUT? I'M ALL EARS.
RRGH!
DON'T MAKE THIS ANY HARDER THAN IT NEEDS TO BE, SURGE.
NO!
SEE ANYTHING, TAILS?
NOPE... I THINK SHE'S GONE.
THEY'RE WORKING TOGETHER.
IT DOESN'T MATTER HOW STRONG I GET. THEY'LL FIND ANOTHER WAY TO HURT ME.
HURT US.

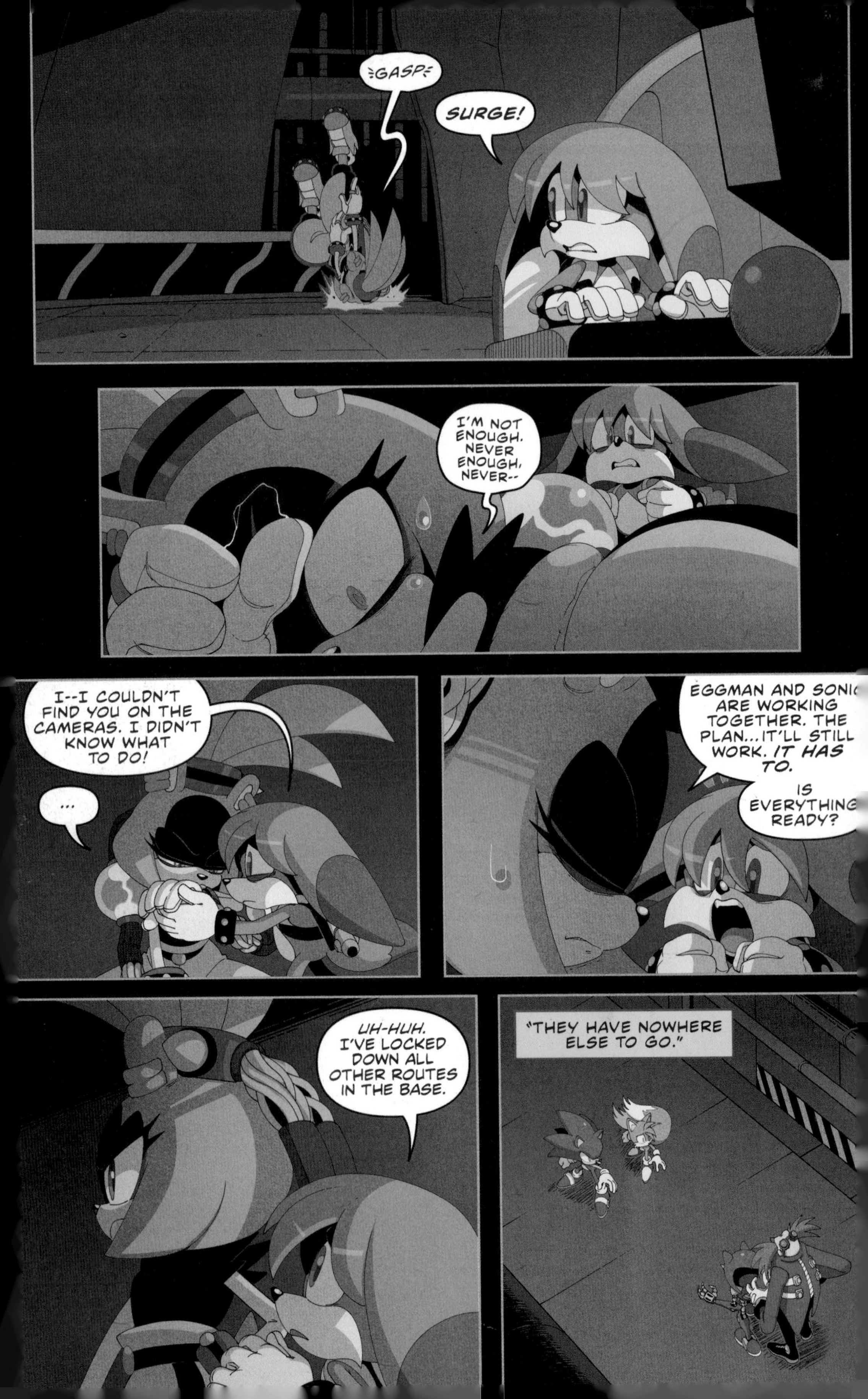
GASP
SURGE!
I'M NOT ENOUGH. NEVER ENOUGH, NEVER--
I--I COULDN'T FIND YOU ON THE CAMERAS. I DIDN'T KNOW WHAT TO DO!
...
EGGMAN AND SONIC ARE WORKING TOGETHER. THE PLAN... IT'LL STILL WORK. IT HAS TO.
IS EVERYTHING READY?
UH-HUH. I'VE LOCKED DOWN ALL OTHER ROUTES IN THE BASE.
"THEY HAVE NOWHERE ELSE TO GO."

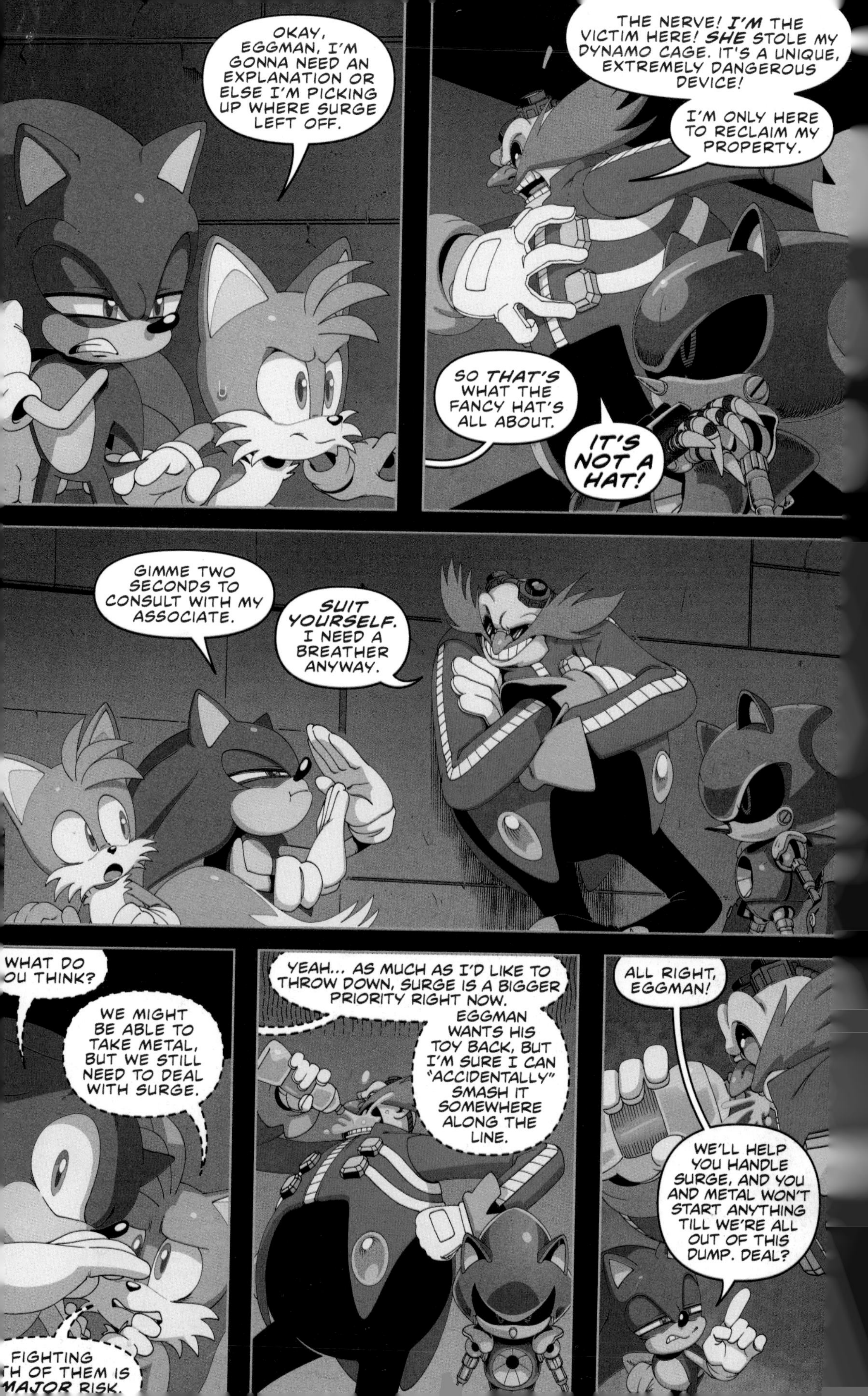

OKAY, EGGMAN, I'M GONNA NEED AN EXPLANATION OR ELSE I'M PICKING UP WHERE SURGE LEFT OFF.
THE NERVE! I'M THE VICTIM HERE! SHE STOLE MY DYNAMO CAGE. IT'S A UNIQUE, EXTREMELY DANGEROUS DEVICE!
I'M ONLY HERE TO RECLAIM MY PROPERTY.
SO THAT'S WHAT THE FANCY HAT'S ALL ABOUT.
IT'S NOT A HAT!
GIMME TWO SECONDS TO CONSULT WITH MY ASSOCIATE.
SUIT YOURSELF. I NEED A BREATHER ANYWAY.
WHAT DO OU THINK?
WE MIGHT BE ABLE TO TAKE METAL, BUT WE STILL NEED TO DEAL WITH SURGE.
FIGHTING TH OF THEM IS MAJOR RISK.
YEAH... AS MUCH AS I'D LIKE TO THROW DOWN, SURGE IS A BIGGER PRIORITY RIGHT NOW.
EGGMAN WANTS HIS TOY BACK, BUT I'M SURE I CAN "ACCIDENTALLY" SMASH IT SOMEWHERE ALONG THE LINE.
ALL RIGHT, EGGMAN!
WE'LL HELP YOU HANDLE SURGE, AND YOU AND METAL WON'T START ANYTHING TILL WE'RE ALL OUT OF THIS DUMP. DEAL?

A TRUCE, EH?

ABSOLUTELY! OF COURSE, METAL SONIC *COULD* HANDLE THE SITUATION, BUT YOUR SUPPORT WILL BE *QUITE* USEFUL.

I'LL BE WATCHING YOU.

AND I'LL ABSOLUTELY CRUSH YOU... *EVENTUALLY.*

JUDGING BY MY MAP, THERE'S ONLY ONE WAY THAT'S OPEN FOR US TO GO.

OOH, A *TRAP!* SOUNDS LIKE FUN.

DOES IT?

IF I'D KNOWN YOU WERE *ENJOYING* THEM, I WOULDN'T HAVE MADE SO MANY.

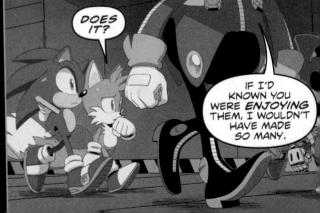

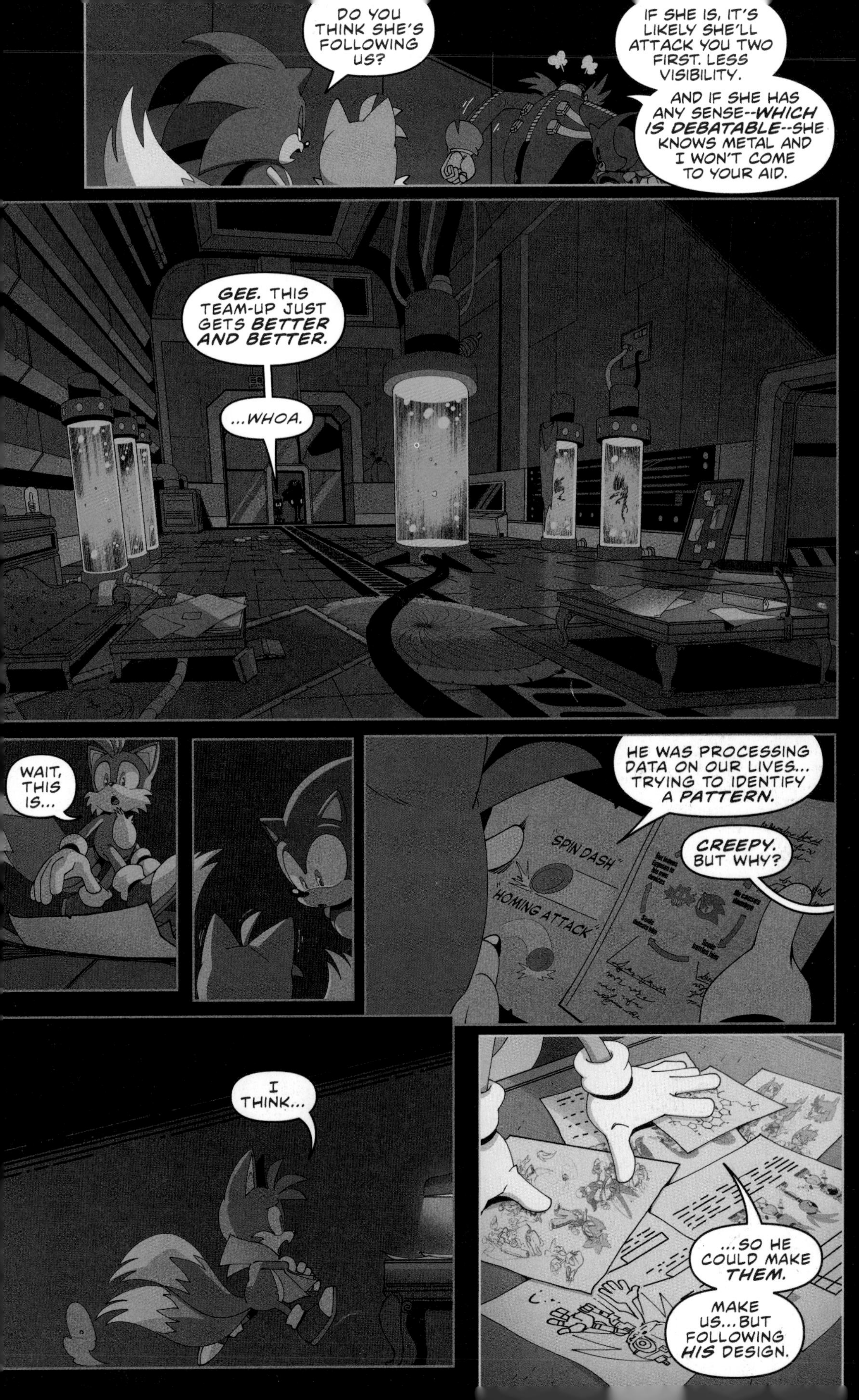
DO YOU THINK SHE'S FOLLOWING US?
IF SHE IS, IT'S LIKELY SHE'LL ATTACK YOU TWO FIRST. LESS VISIBILITY.
AND IF SHE HAS ANY SENSE--*WHICH IS DEBATABLE*--SHE KNOWS METAL AND I WON'T COME TO YOUR AID.
GEE. THIS TEAM-UP JUST GETS *BETTER AND BETTER.*
...WHOA.
WAIT, THIS IS...
HE WAS PROCESSING DATA ON OUR LIVES... TRYING TO IDENTIFY A *PATTERN.*
"SPIN DASH"
"HOMING ATTACK"
CREEPY. BUT WHY?
I THINK...
...SO HE COULD MAKE *THEM.*
MAKE US...BUT FOLLOWING *HIS* DESIGN.

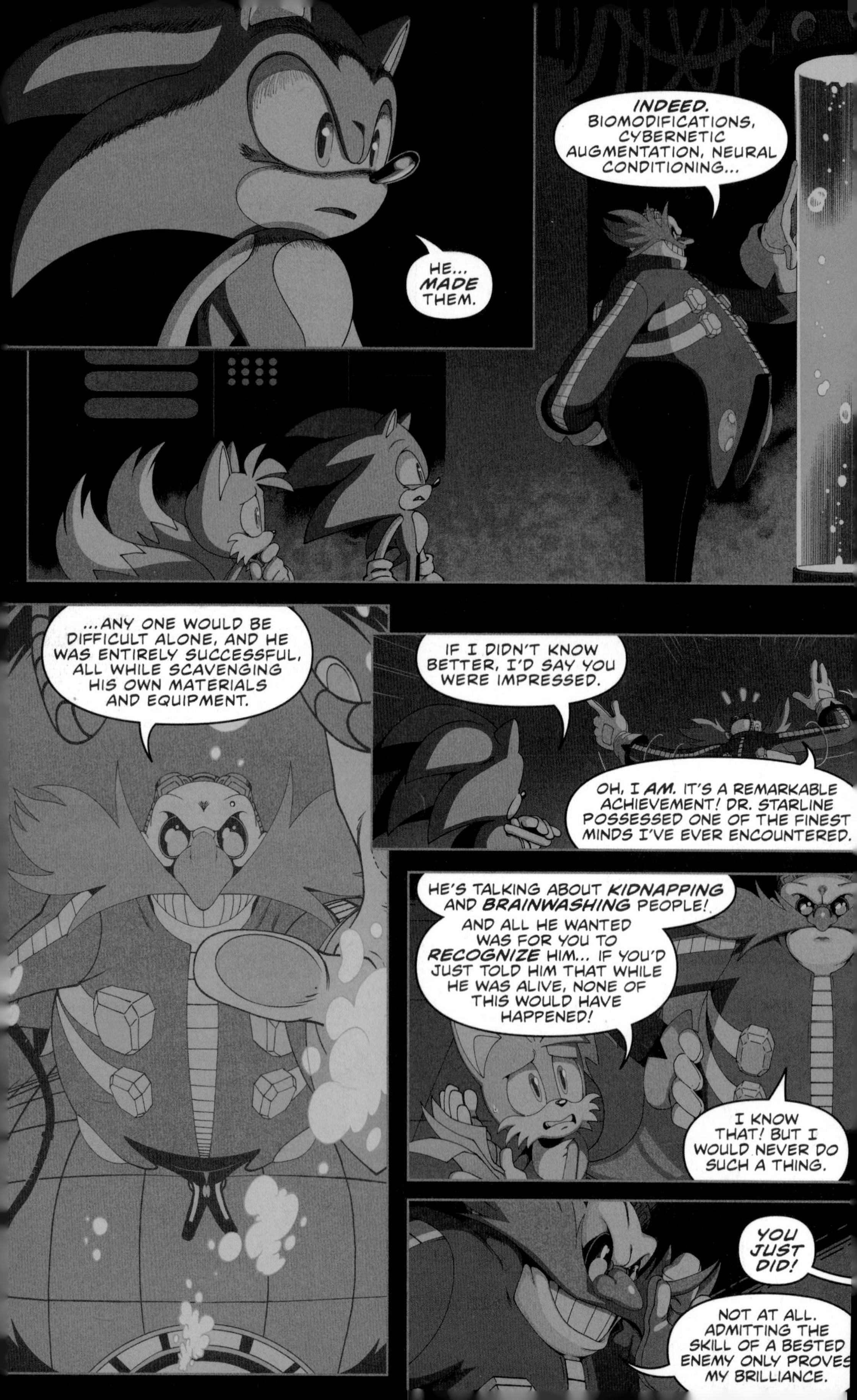
HE... MADE THEM.
INDEED. BIOMODIFICATIONS, CYBERNETIC AUGMENTATION, NEURAL CONDITIONING...
...ANY ONE WOULD BE DIFFICULT ALONE, AND HE WAS ENTIRELY SUCCESSFUL, ALL WHILE SCAVENGING HIS OWN MATERIALS AND EQUIPMENT.
IF I DIDN'T KNOW BETTER, I'D SAY YOU WERE IMPRESSED.
OH, I AM. IT'S A REMARKABLE ACHIEVEMENT! DR. STARLINE POSSESSED ONE OF THE FINEST MINDS I'VE EVER ENCOUNTERED.
HE'S TALKING ABOUT KIDNAPPING AND BRAINWASHING PEOPLE!
AND ALL HE WANTED WAS FOR YOU TO RECOGNIZE HIM... IF YOU'D JUST TOLD HIM THAT WHILE HE WAS ALIVE, NONE OF THIS WOULD HAVE HAPPENED!
I KNOW THAT! BUT I WOULD NEVER DO SUCH A THING.
YOU JUST DID!
NOT AT ALL. ADMITTING THE SKILL OF A BESTED ENEMY ONLY PROVES MY BRILLIANCE.

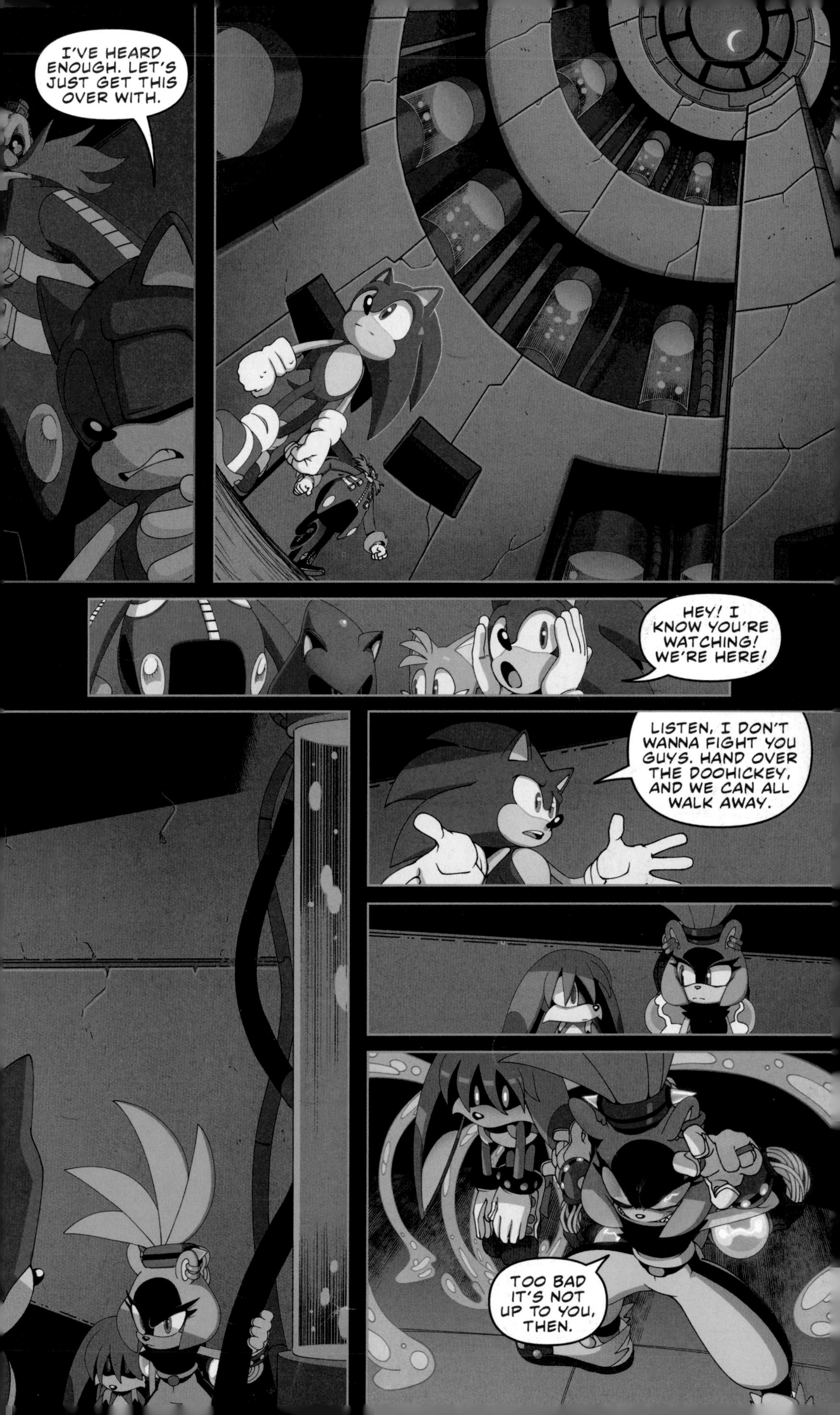
I'VE HEARD ENOUGH. LET'S JUST GET THIS OVER WITH.
HEY! I KNOW YOU'RE WATCHING! WE'RE HERE!
LISTEN, I DON'T WANNA FIGHT YOU GUYS. HAND OVER THE DOOHICKEY, AND WE CAN ALL WALK AWAY.
TOO BAD IT'S NOT UP TO YOU, THEN.

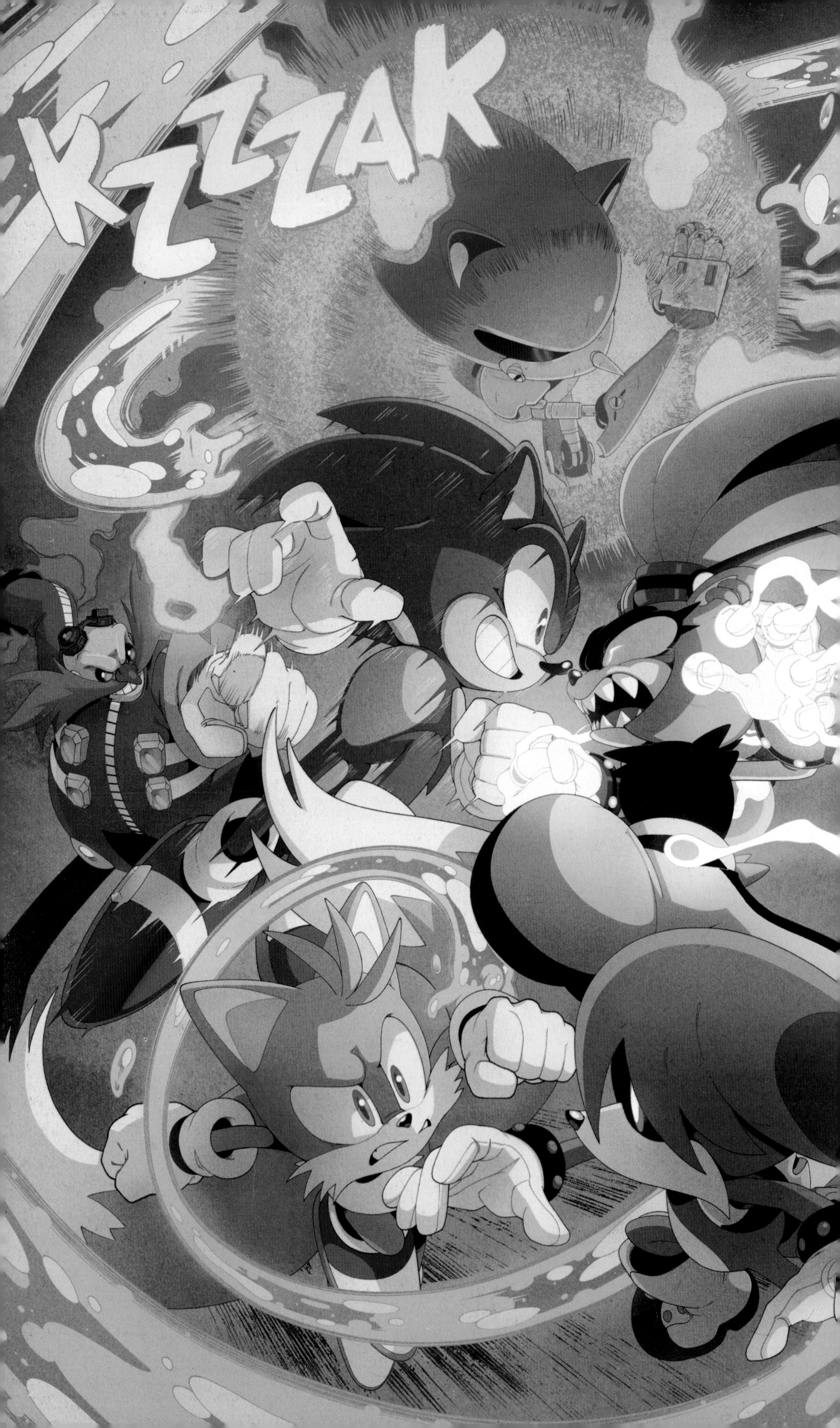
KZZZAK

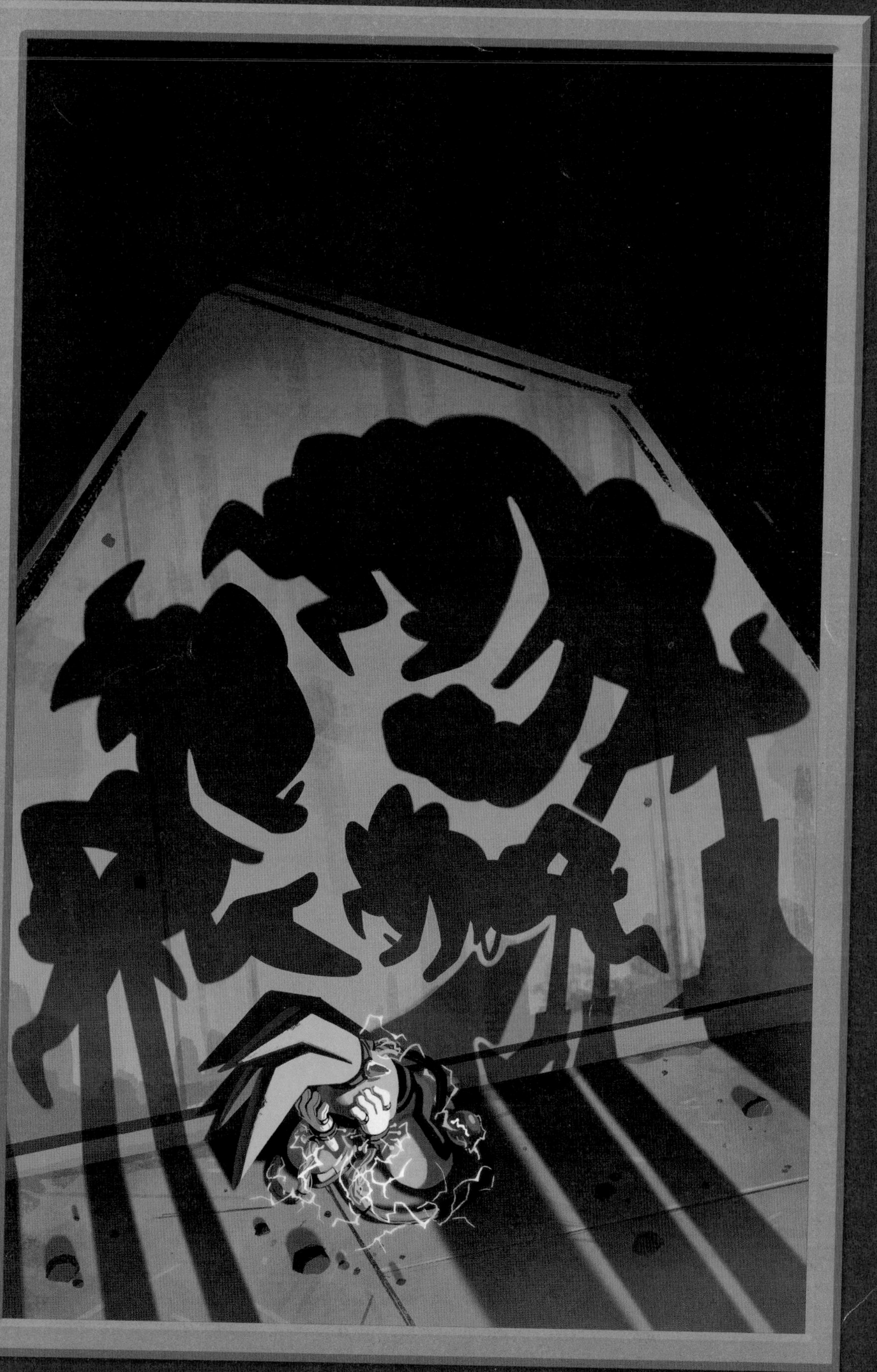

ART BY **NATHALIE FOURDRAINE**

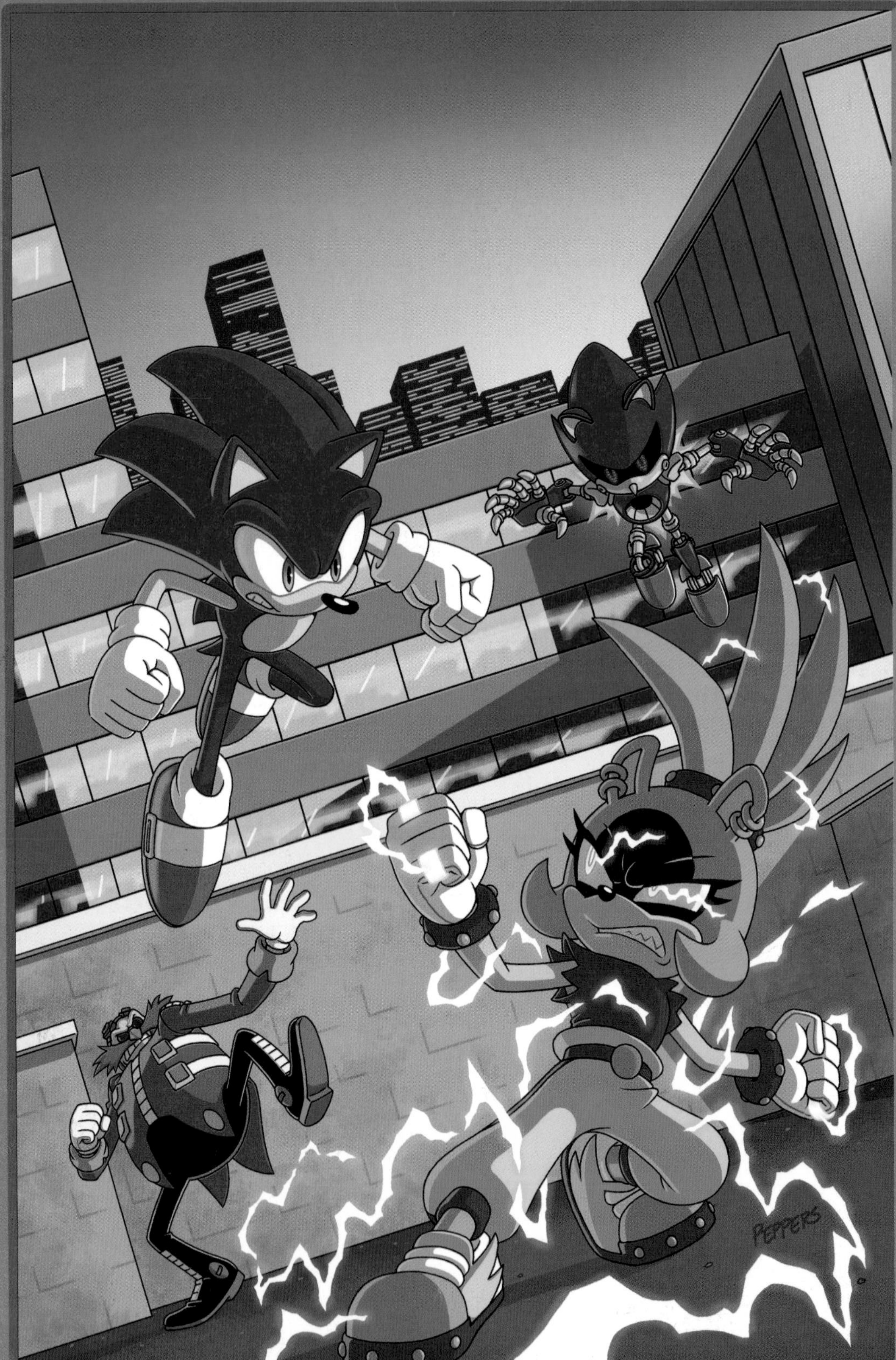
PEPPERS

ART BY **JAMAL PEPPERS**

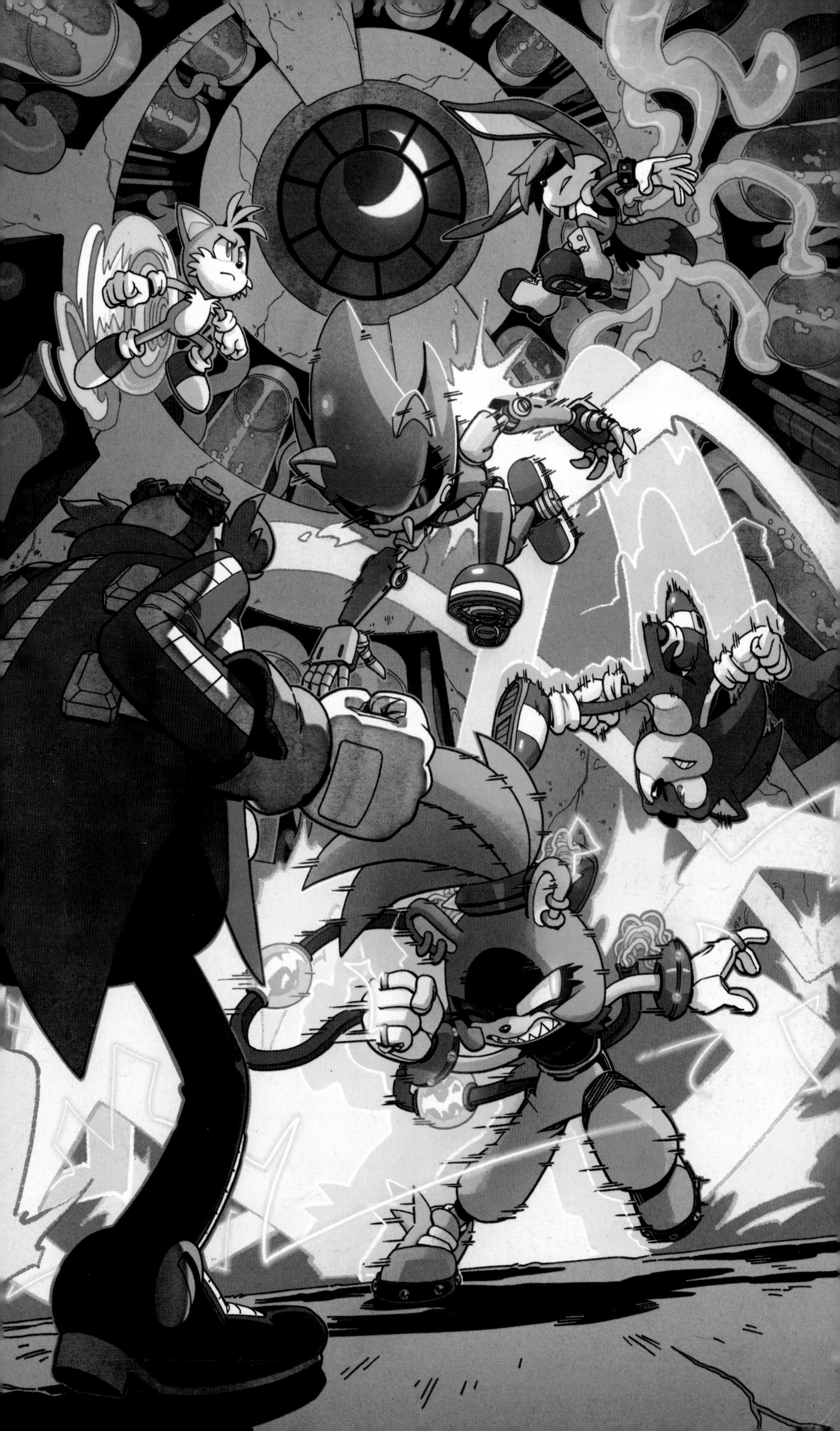

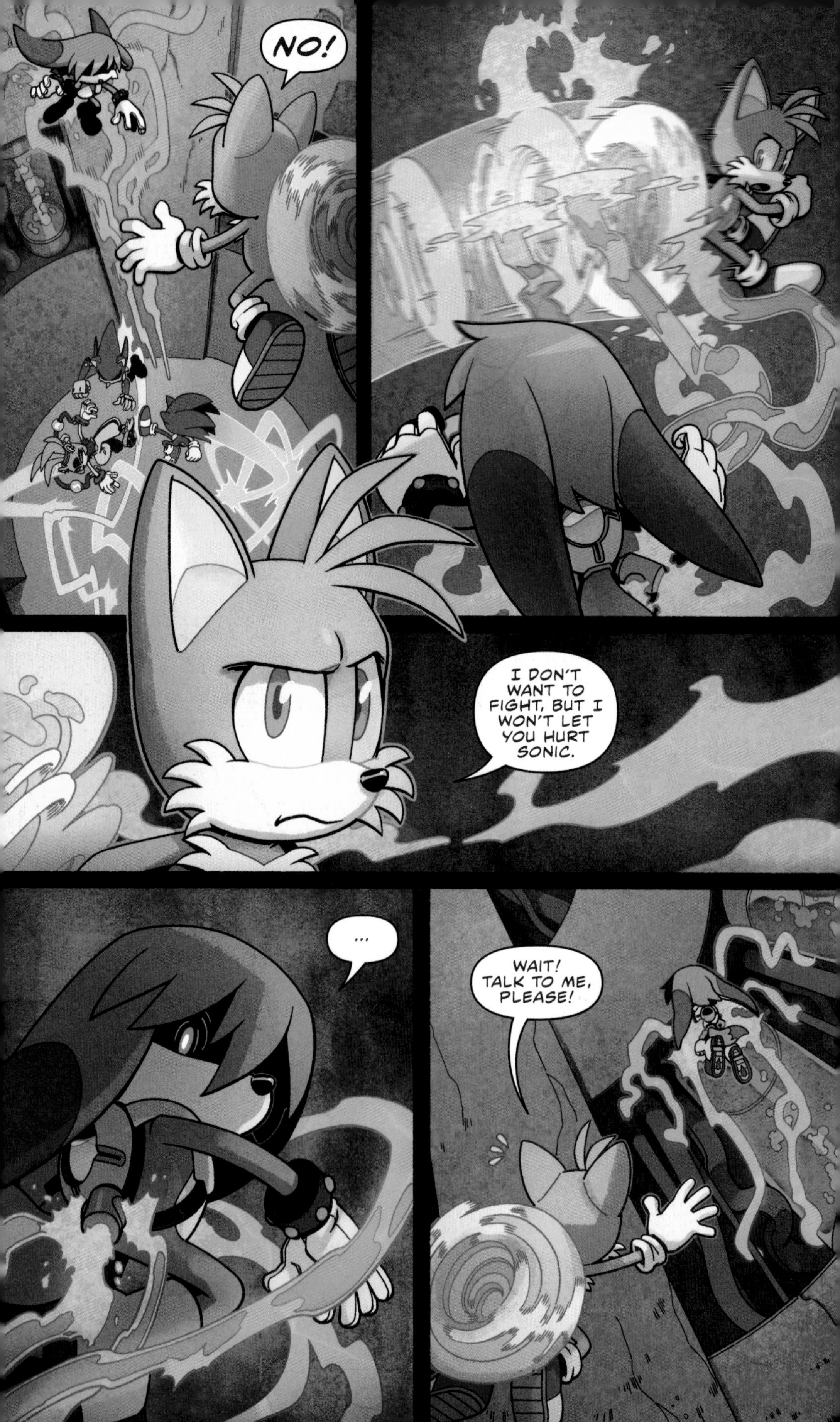
NO!
I DON'T WANT TO FIGHT, BUT I WON'T LET YOU HURT SONIC.
...
WAIT! TALK TO ME, PLEASE!

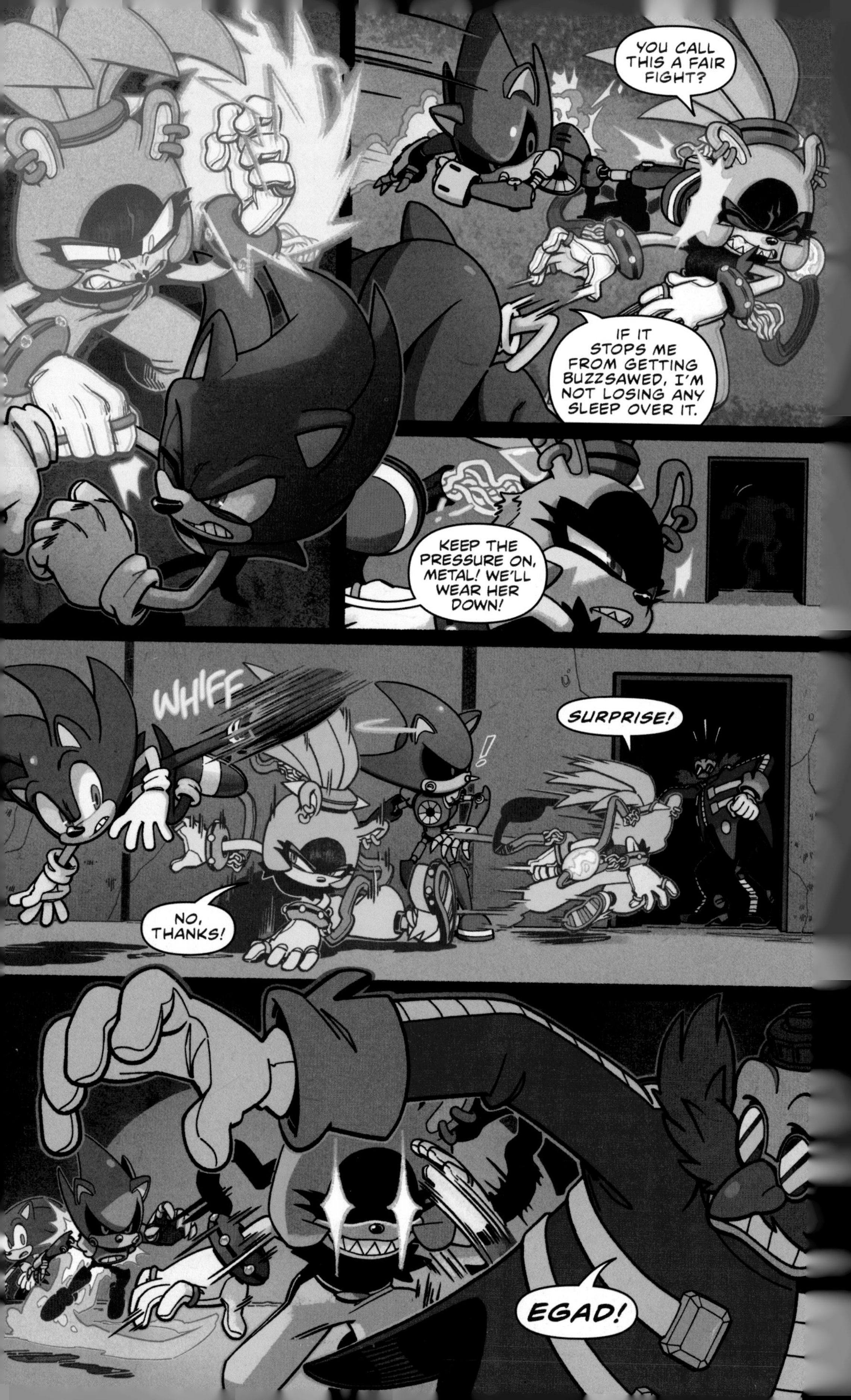
YOU CALL THIS A FAIR FIGHT?
IF IT STOPS ME FROM GETTING BUZZSAWED, I'M NOT LOSING ANY SLEEP OVER IT.
KEEP THE PRESSURE ON, METAL! WE'LL WEAR HER DOWN!
WHIFF
SURPRISE!
NO, THANKS!
EGAD!

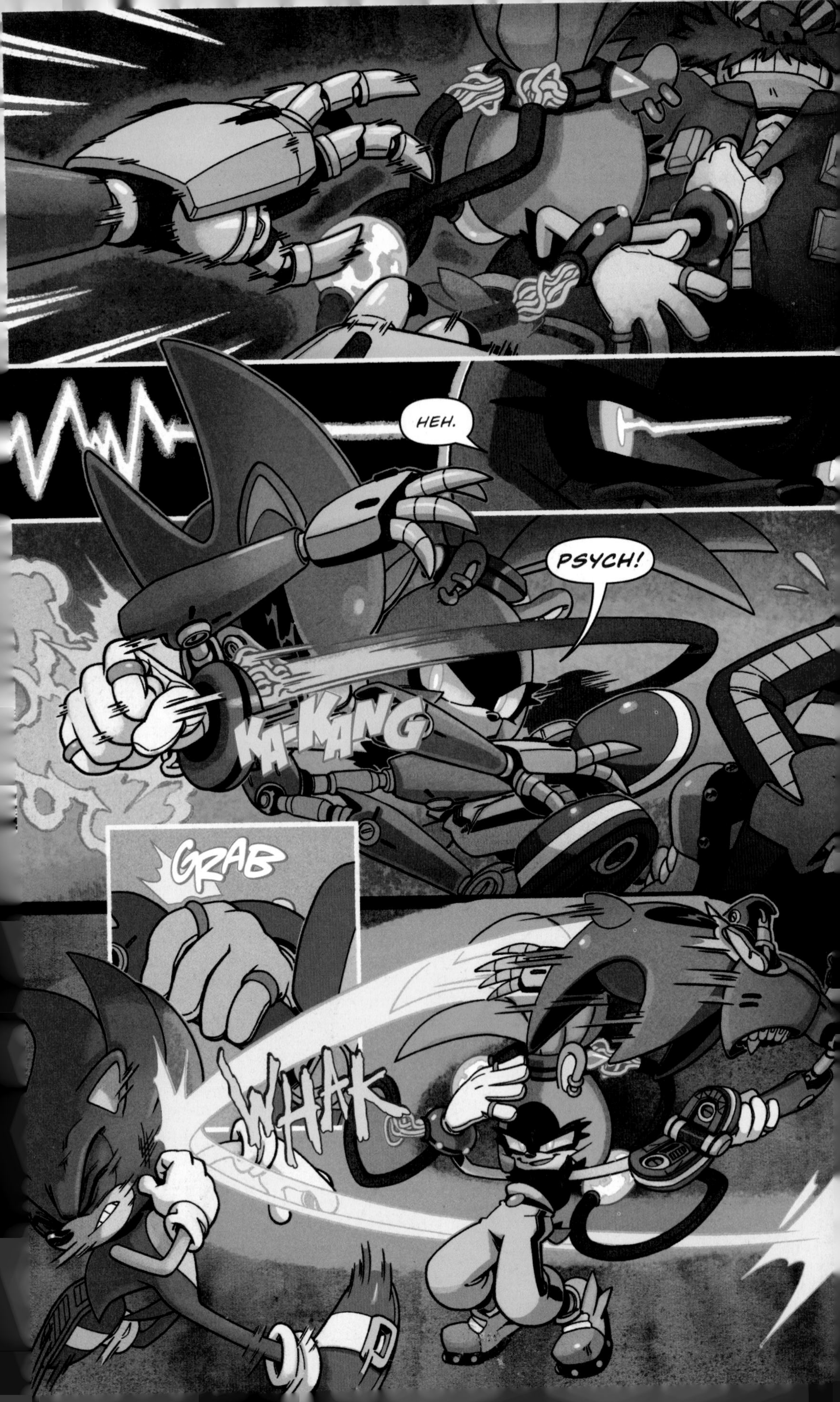
HEH.
PSYCH!
KA-KANG
GRAB
WHAK

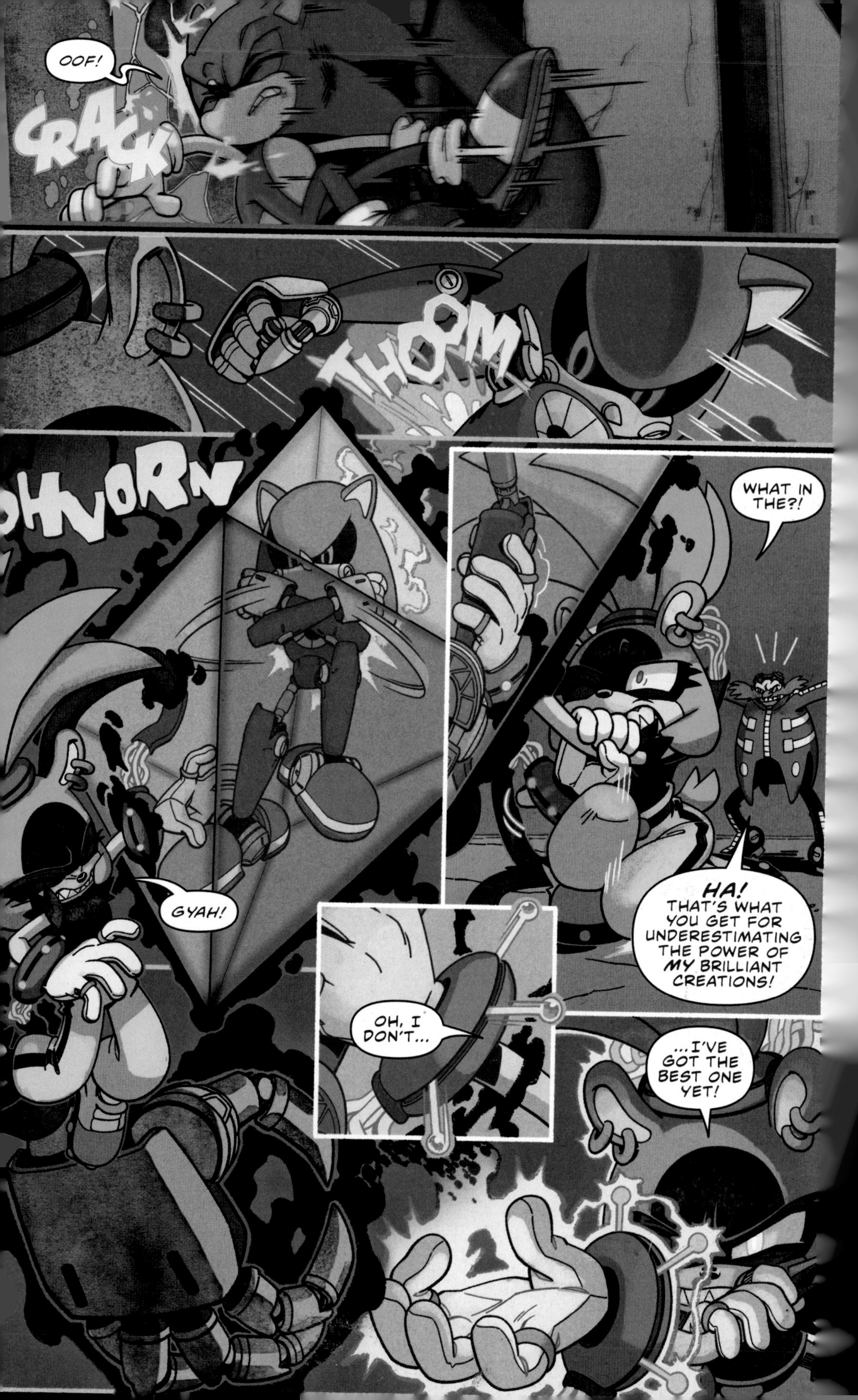
OOF!
CRACK
THOOM
OHVORN
WHAT IN THE?!
GYAH!
HA! THAT'S WHAT YOU GET FOR UNDERESTIMATING THE POWER OF MY BRILLIANT CREATIONS!
OH, I DON'T...
...I'VE GOT THE BEST ONE YET!

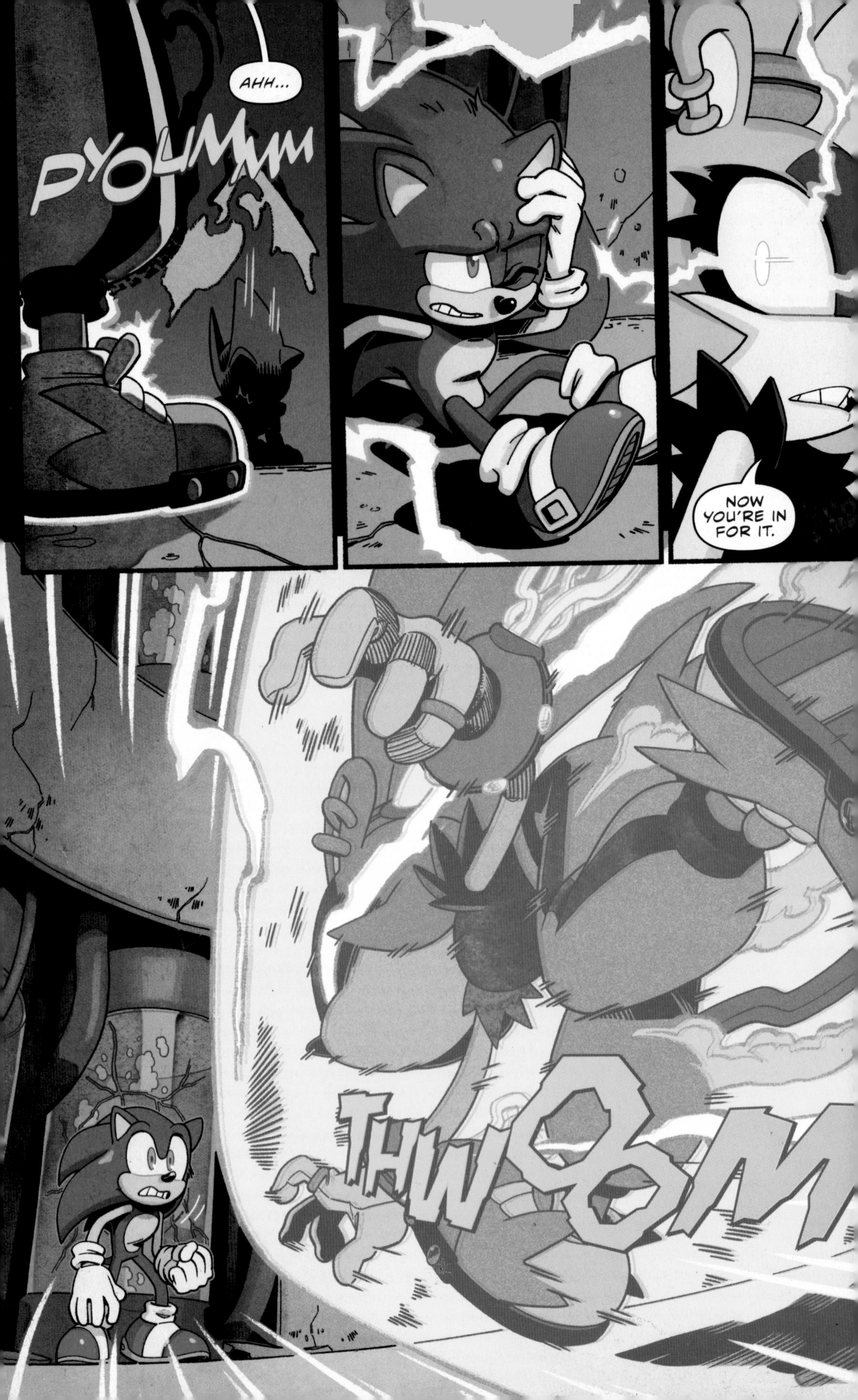
AHH...
PYOUMMM
NOW YOU'RE IN FOR IT.
THWOOMM

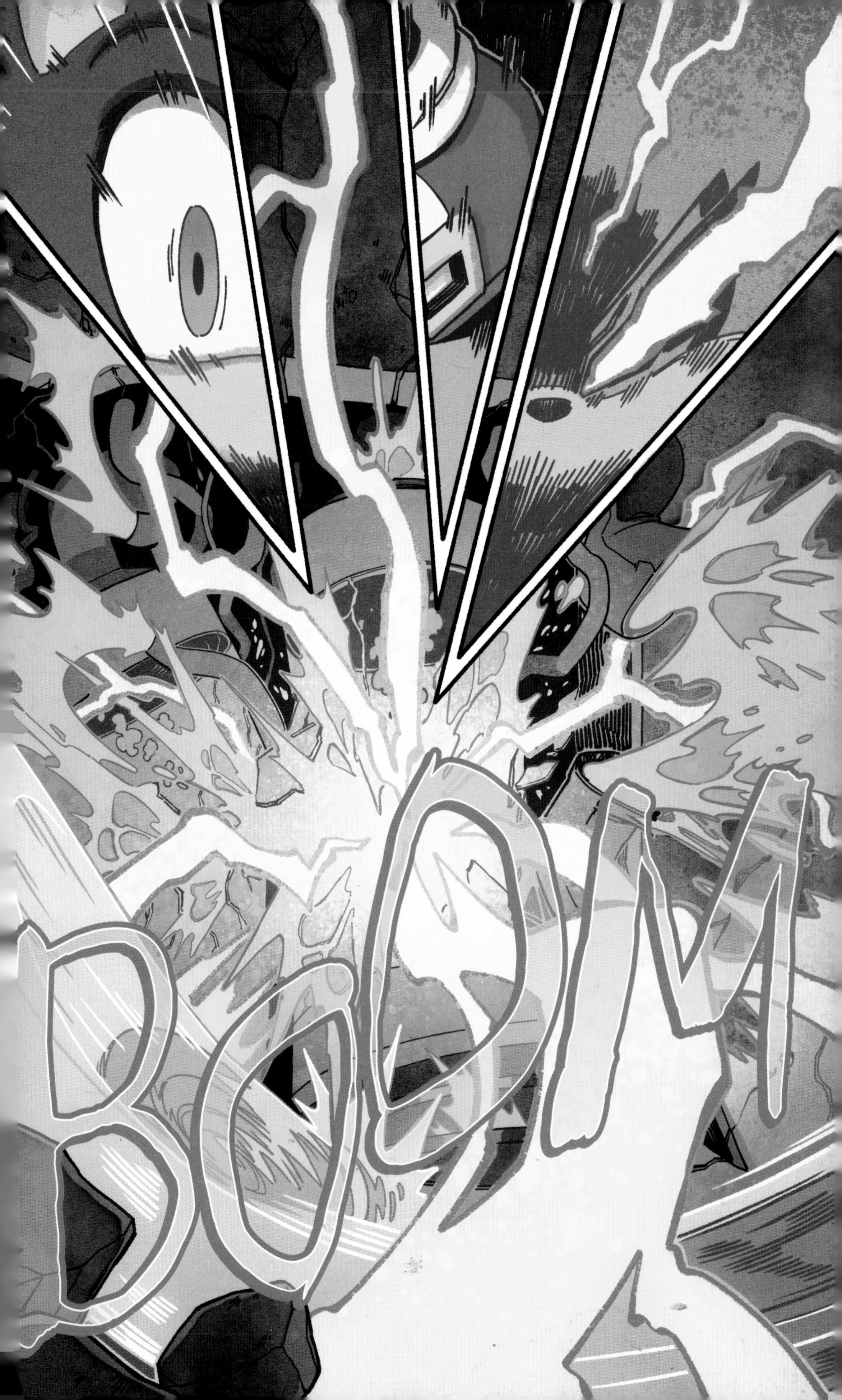
BOOM

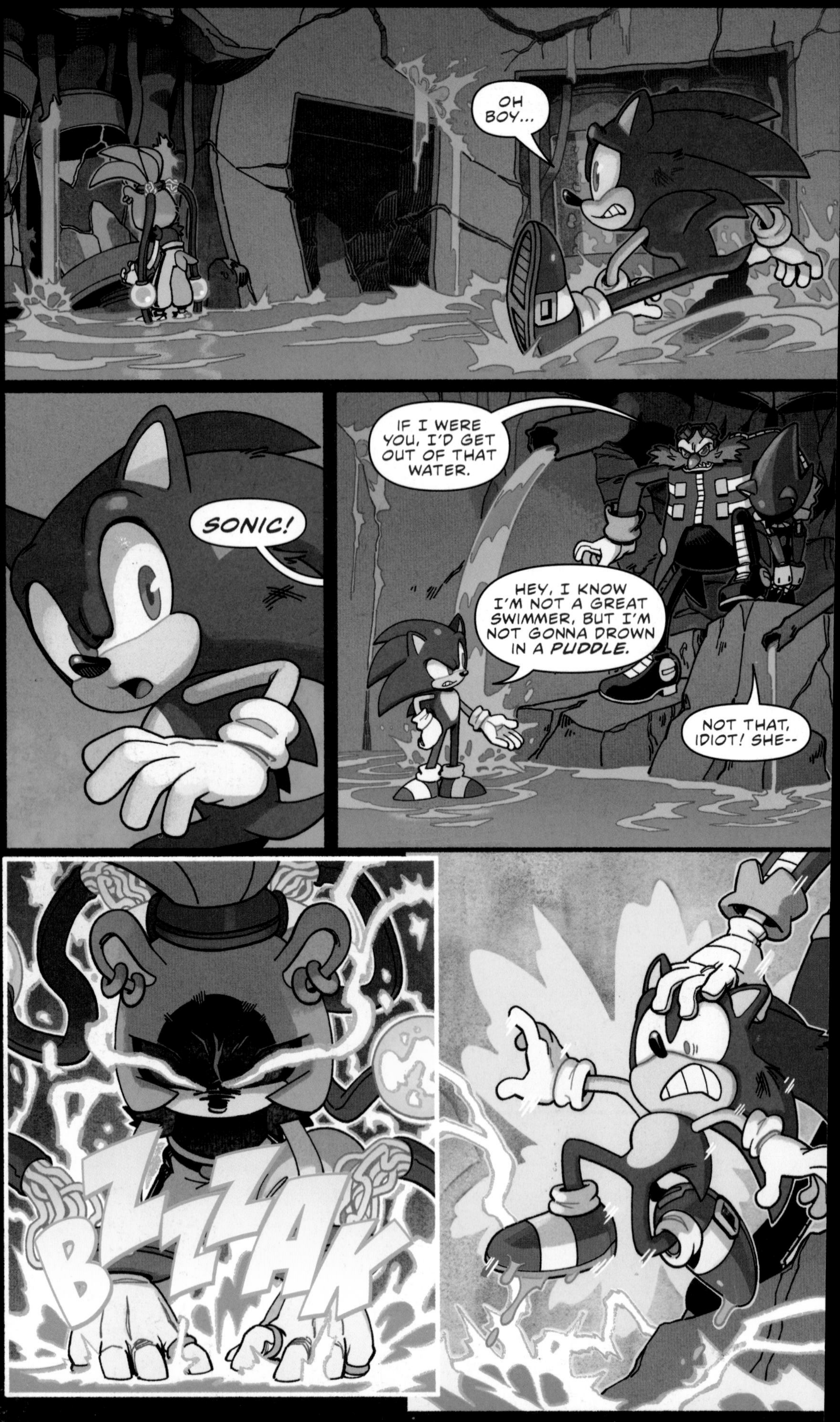
OH BOY...
SONIC!
IF I WERE YOU, I'D GET OUT OF THAT WATER.
HEY, I KNOW I'M NOT A GREAT SWIMMER, BUT I'M NOT GONNA DROWN IN A *PUDDLE*.
NOT THAT, IDIOT! SHE--
BZZZAK

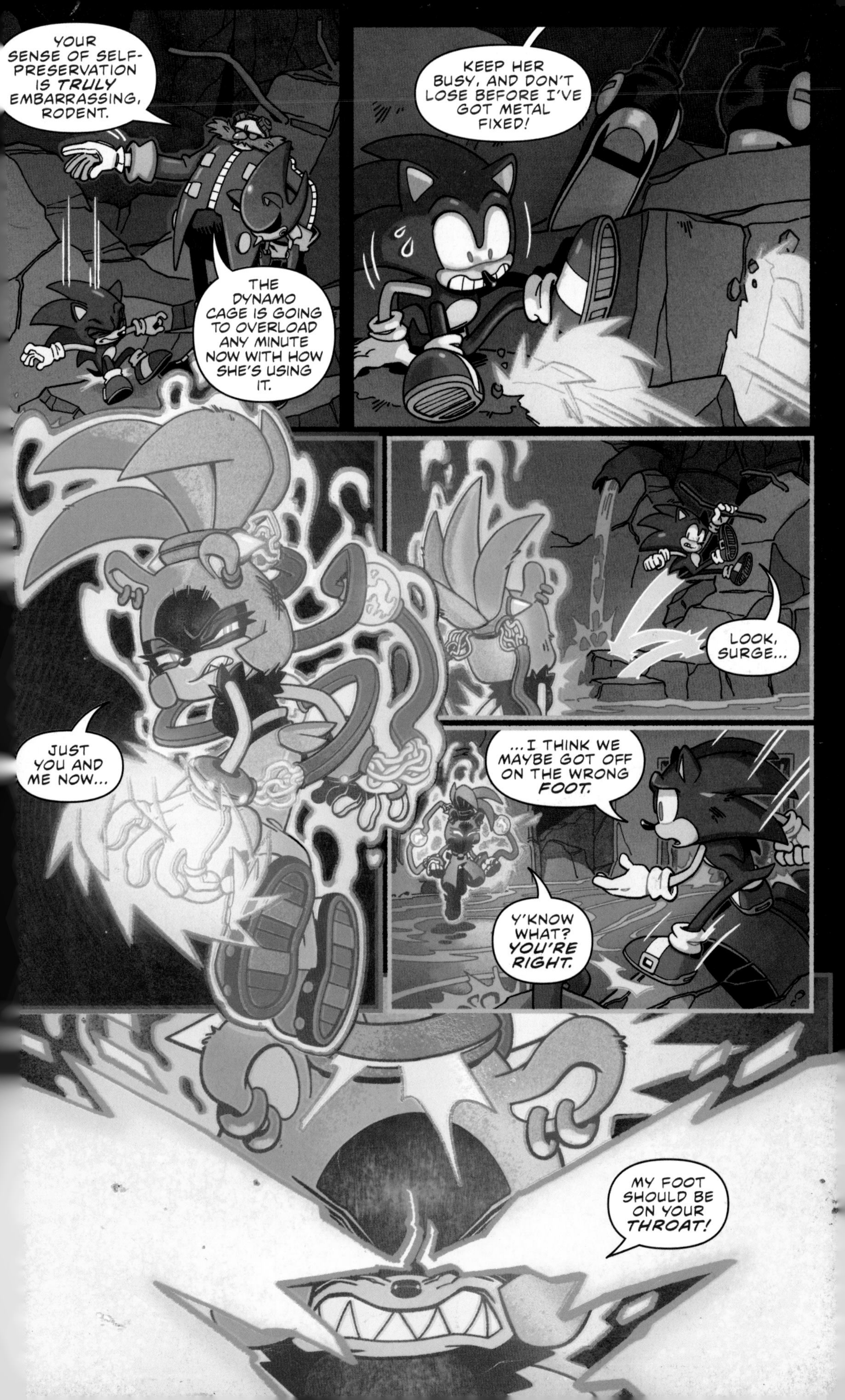
YOUR SENSE OF SELF-PRESERVATION IS TRULY EMBARRASSING, RODENT.
THE DYNAMO CAGE IS GOING TO OVERLOAD ANY MINUTE NOW WITH HOW SHE'S USING IT.
KEEP HER BUSY, AND DON'T LOSE BEFORE I'VE GOT METAL FIXED!
JUST YOU AND ME NOW...
LOOK, SURGE...
...I THINK WE MAYBE GOT OFF ON THE WRONG FOOT.
Y'KNOW WHAT? YOU'RE RIGHT.
MY FOOT SHOULD BE ON YOUR THROAT!

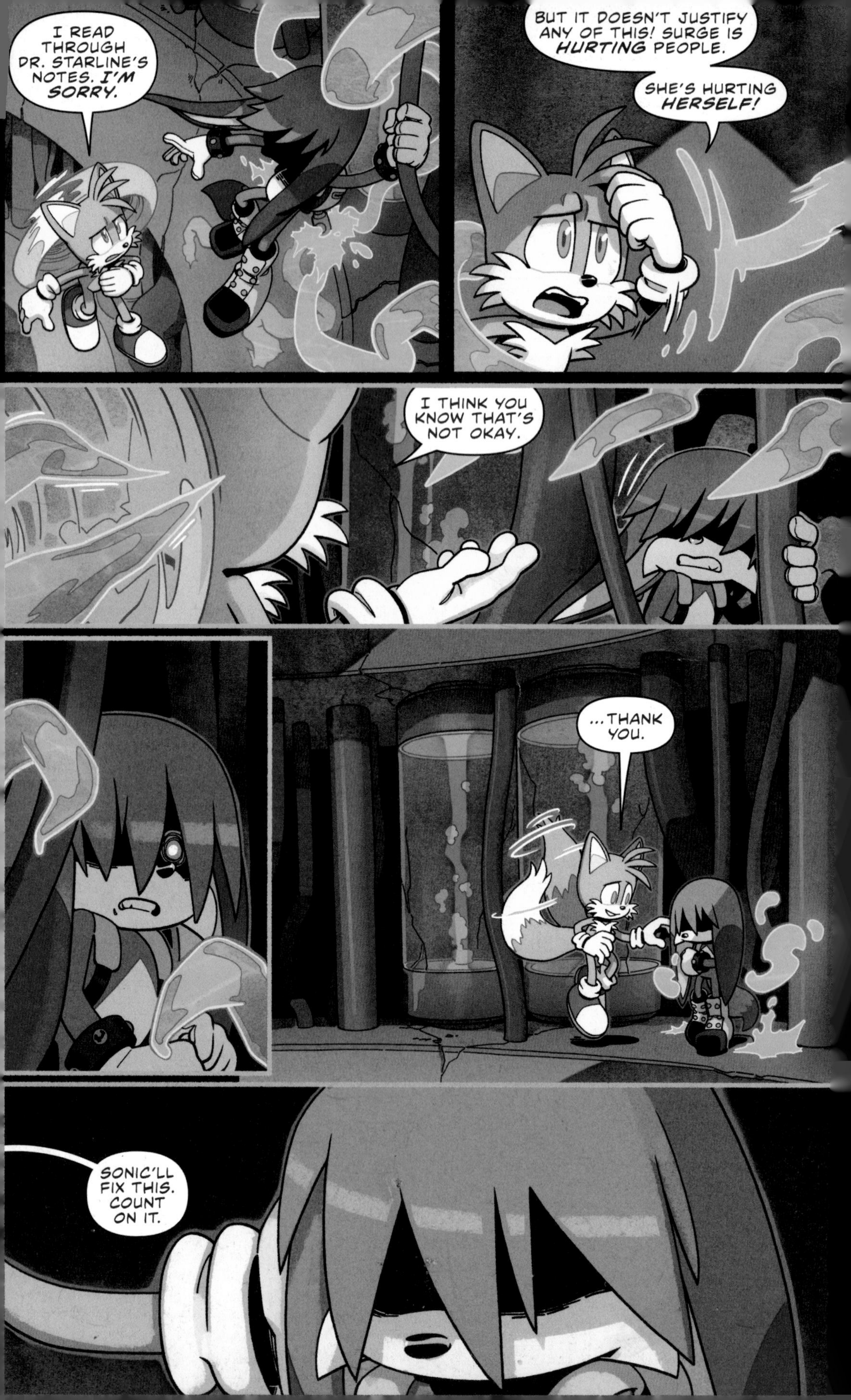
I READ THROUGH DR. STARLINE'S NOTES. *I'M SORRY.*
BUT IT DOESN'T JUSTIFY ANY OF THIS! SURGE IS *HURTING* PEOPLE.
SHE'S HURTING *HERSELF!*
I THINK YOU KNOW THAT'S NOT OKAY.
...THANK YOU.
SONIC'LL FIX THIS. COUNT ON IT.

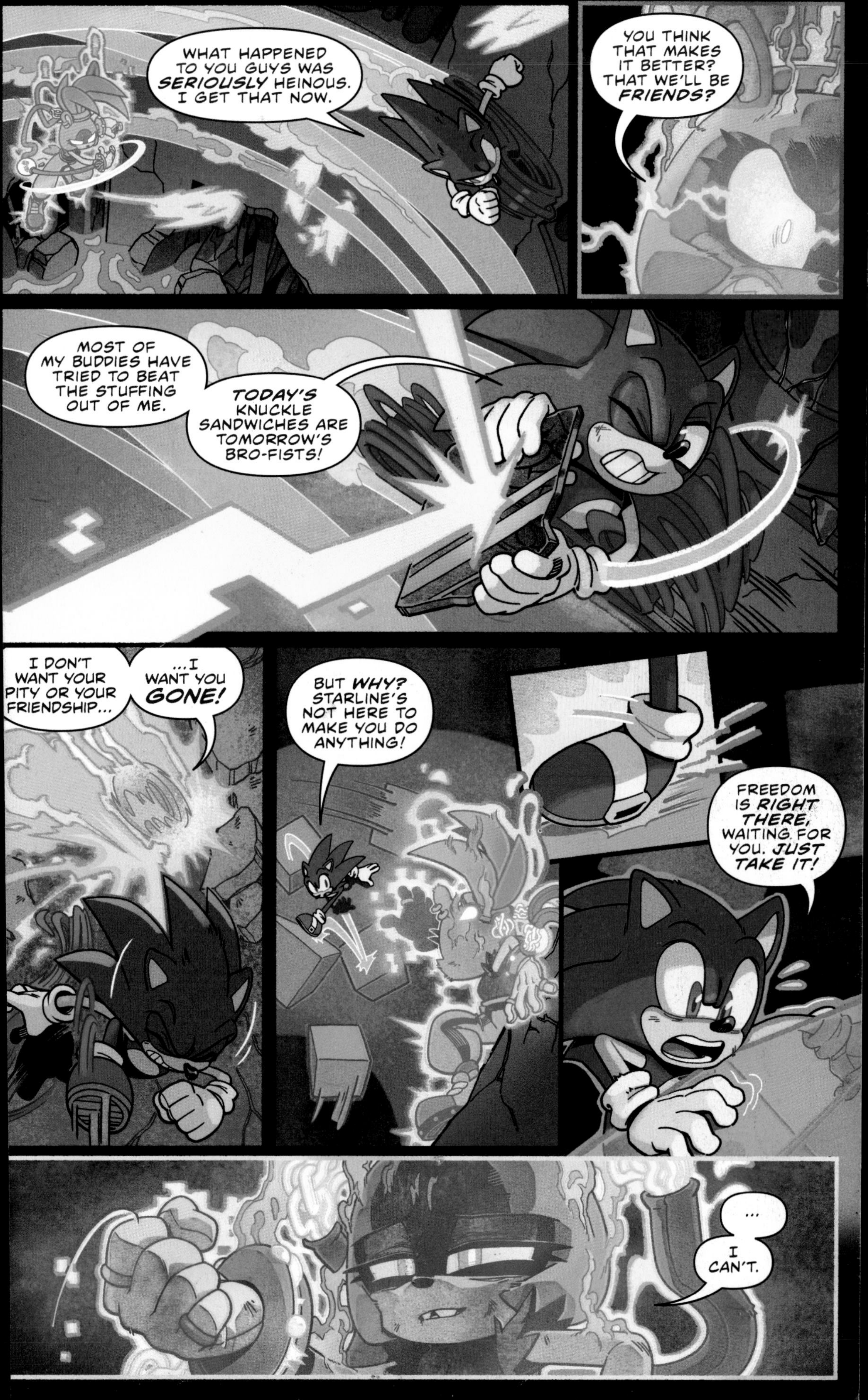
WHAT HAPPENED TO YOU GUYS WAS *SERIOUSLY* HEINOUS. I GET THAT NOW.
YOU THINK THAT MAKES IT BETTER? THAT WE'LL BE *FRIENDS?*
MOST OF MY BUDDIES HAVE TRIED TO BEAT THE STUFFING OUT OF ME.
TODAY'S KNUCKLE SANDWICHES ARE TOMORROW'S BRO-FISTS!
I DON'T WANT YOUR PITY OR YOUR FRIENDSHIP...
...I WANT YOU *GONE!*
BUT *WHY?* STARLINE'S NOT HERE TO MAKE YOU DO ANYTHING!
FREEDOM IS *RIGHT THERE,* WAITING FOR YOU. *JUST TAKE IT!*
...
I CAN'T.

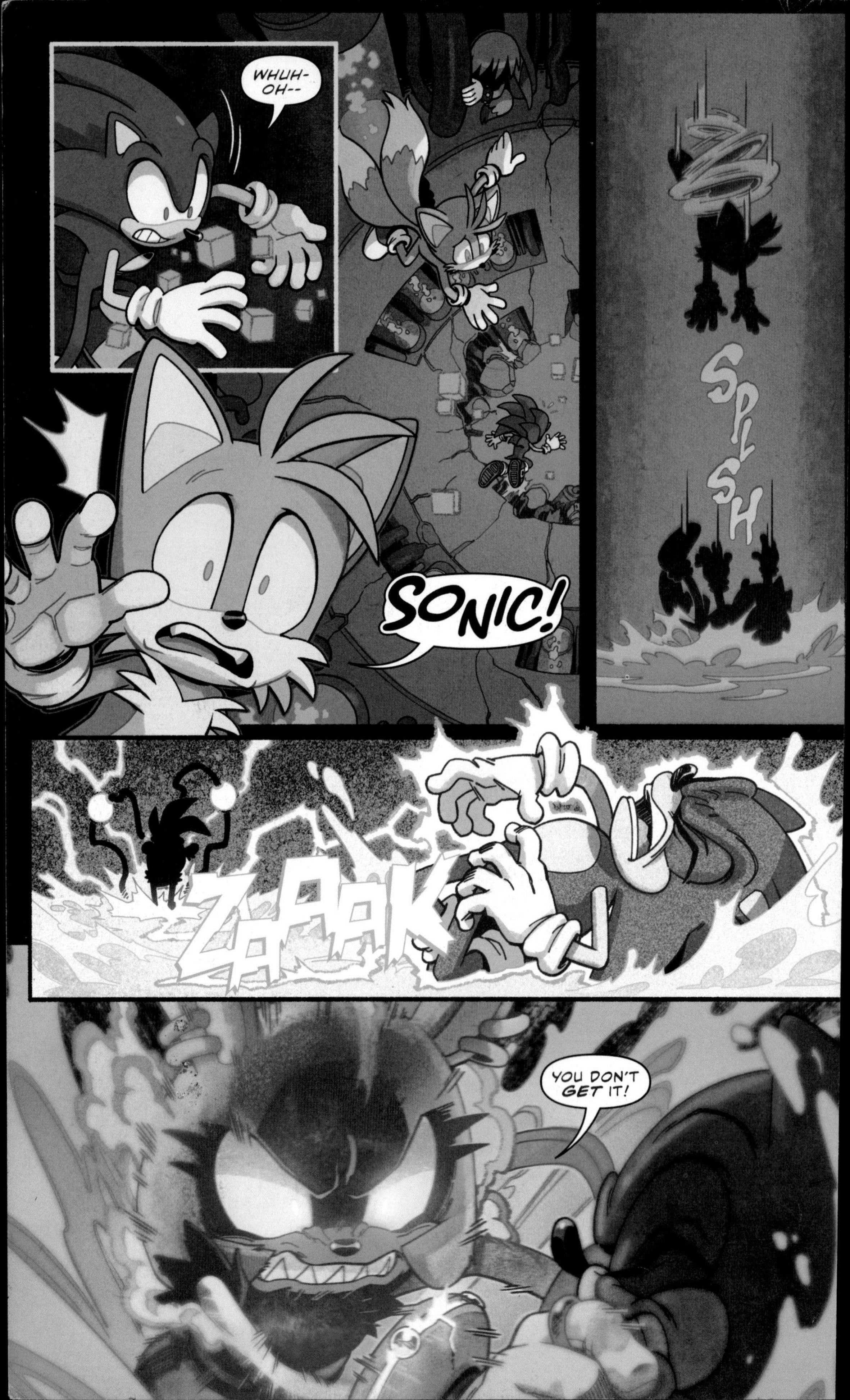
WHUH-OH--
SONIC!
SPLSH
ZAAAK
YOU DON'T GET IT!

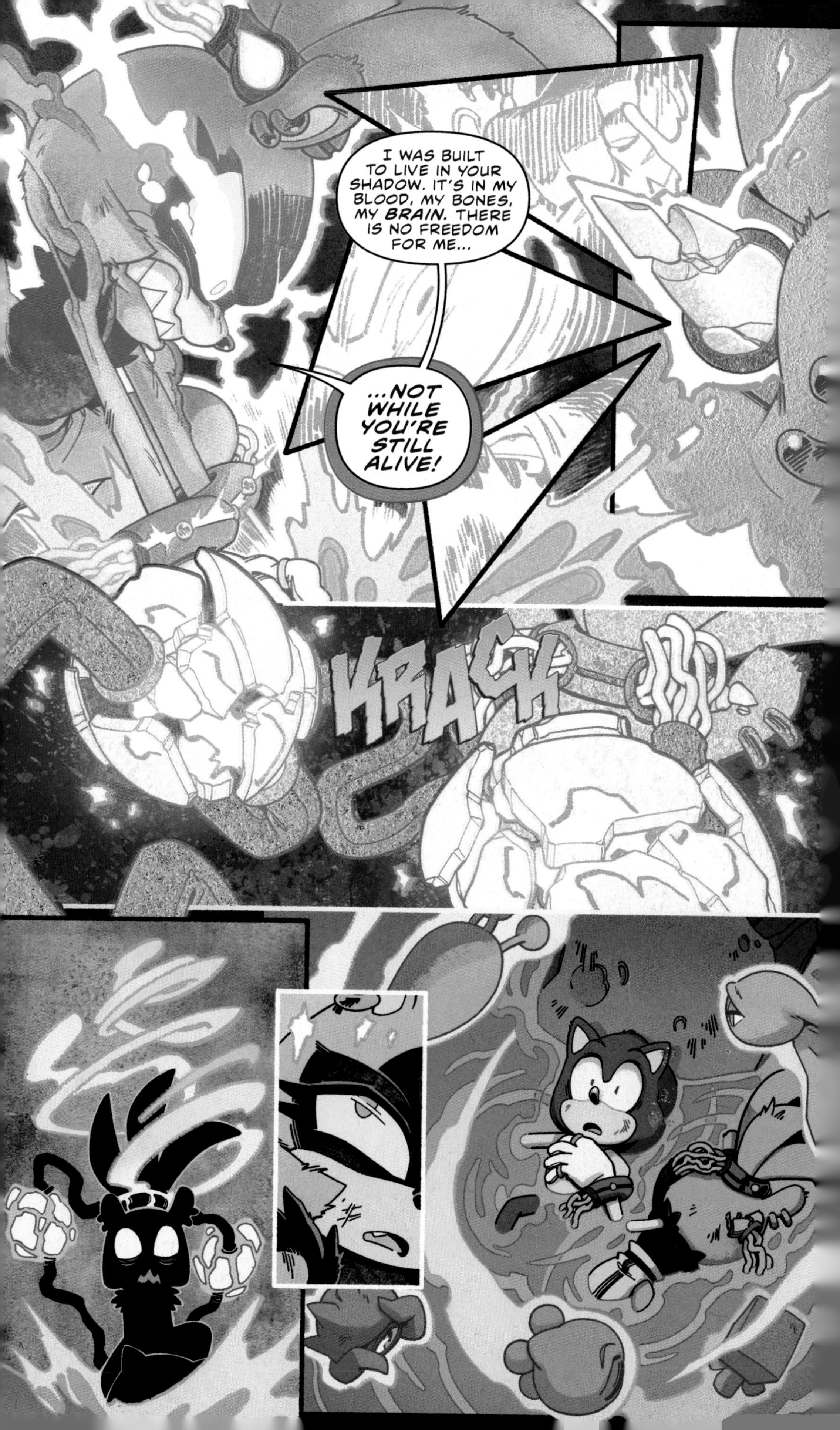
I WAS BUILT TO LIVE IN YOUR SHADOW. IT'S IN MY BLOOD, MY BONES, MY *BRAIN*. THERE IS NO FREEDOM FOR ME...
...*NOT WHILE YOU'RE STILL ALIVE!*
KRACK

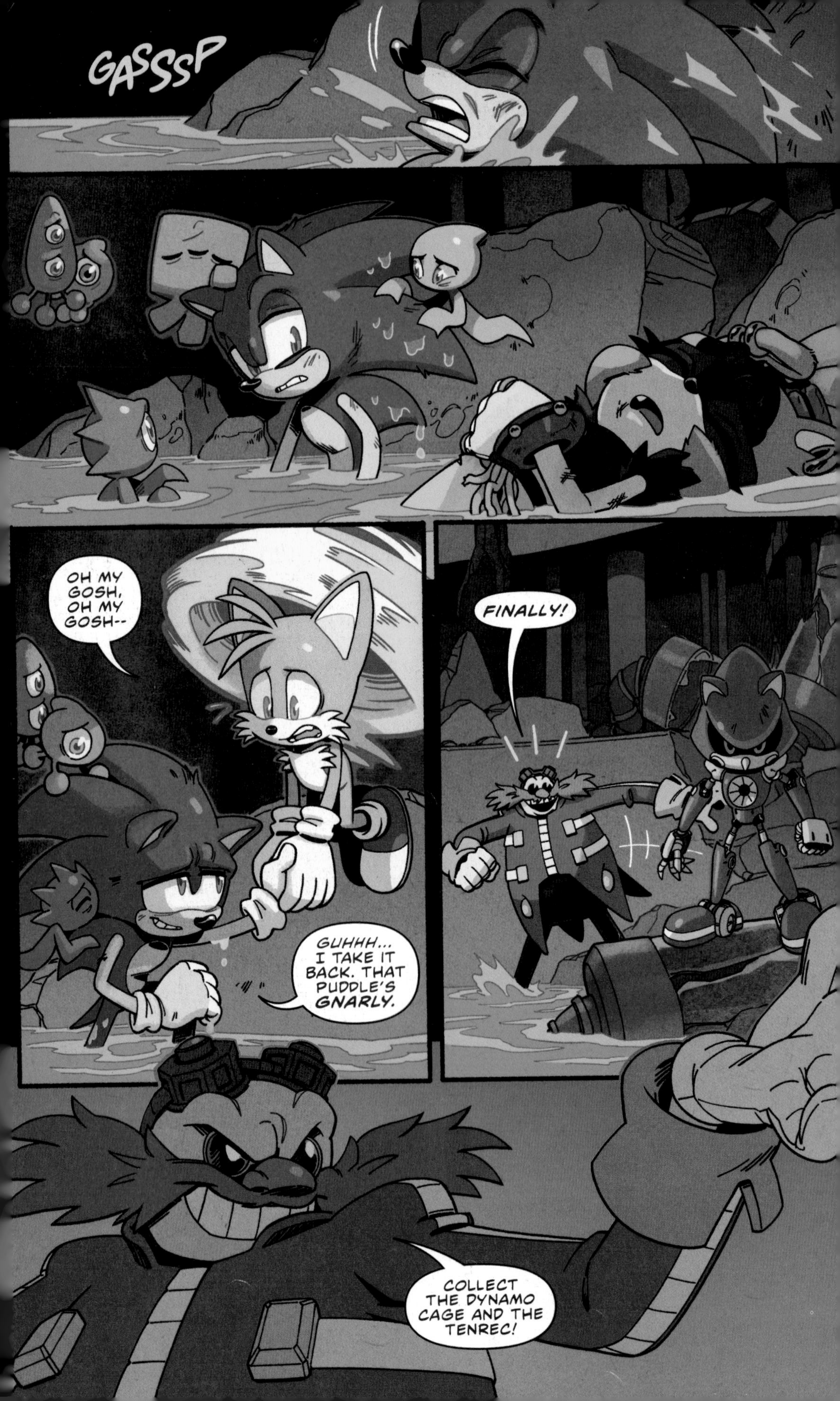
GASSSP
OH MY GOSH, OH MY GOSH--
GUHHH... I TAKE IT BACK. THAT PUDDLE'S GNARLY.
FINALLY!
COLLECT THE DYNAMO CAGE AND THE TENREC!

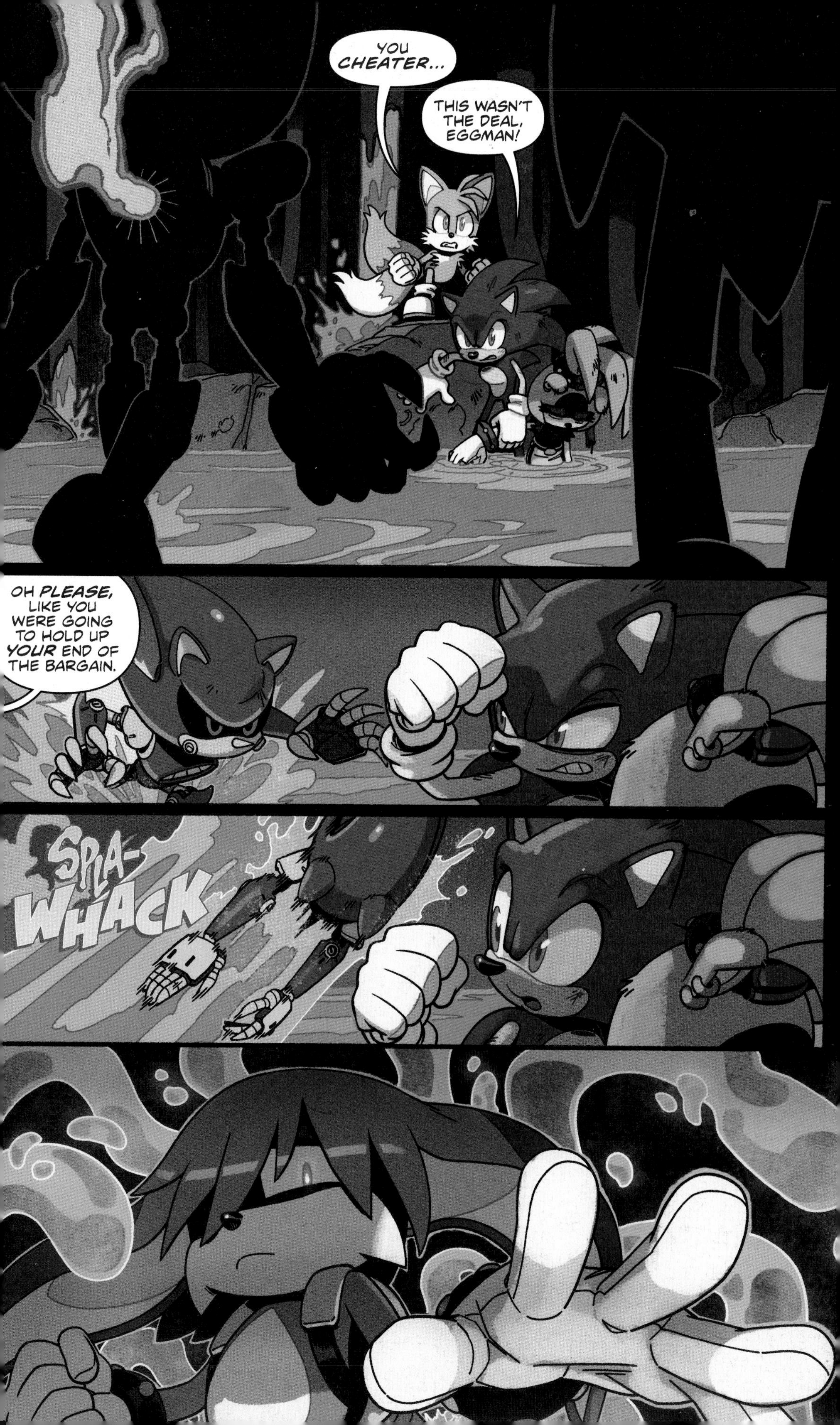
YOU CHEATER...
THIS WASN'T THE DEAL, EGGMAN!
OH PLEASE, LIKE YOU WERE GOING TO HOLD UP YOUR END OF THE BARGAIN.
SPLA-WHACK

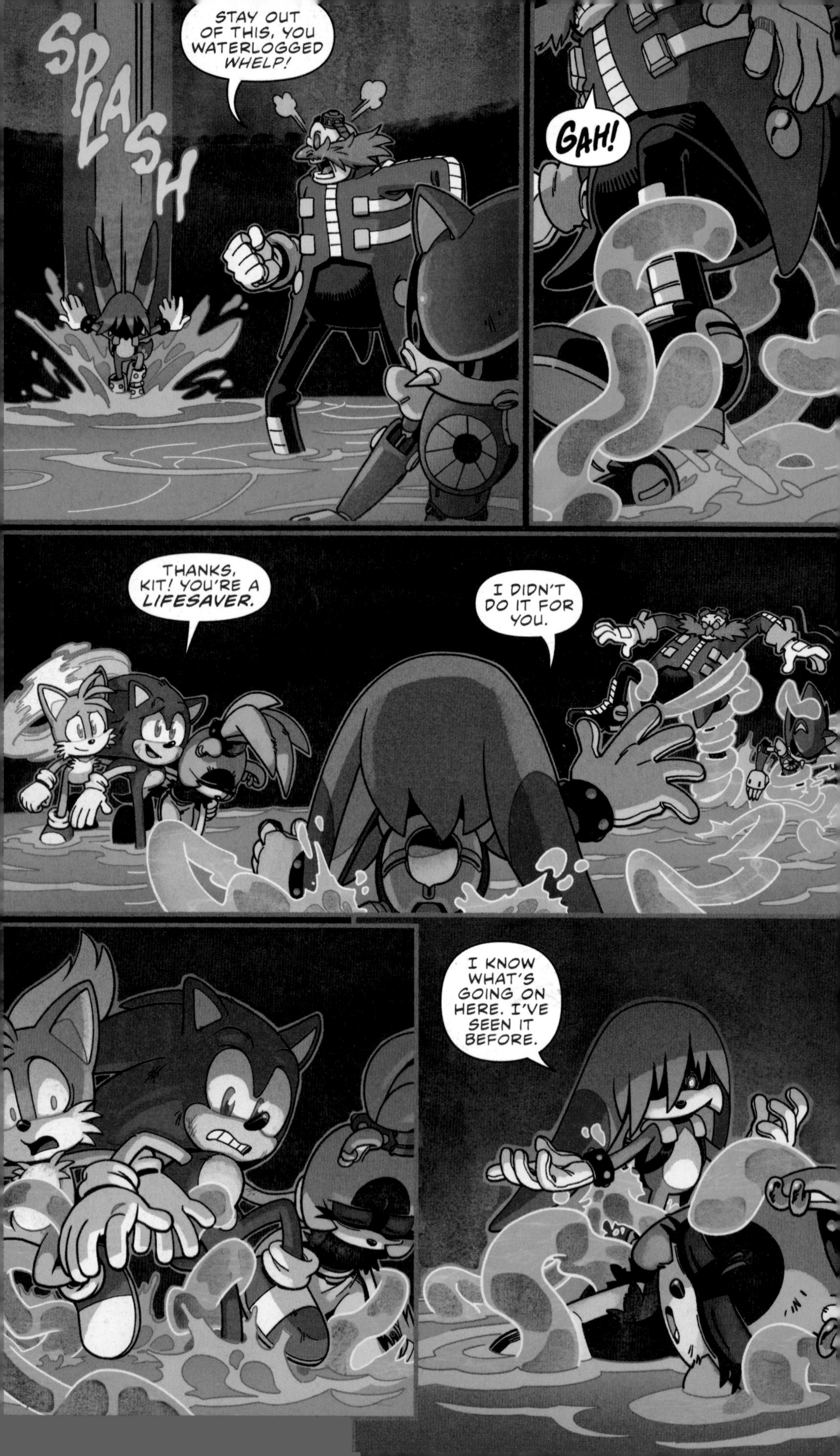
SPLASH
STAY OUT OF THIS, YOU WATERLOGGED WHELP!
GAH!
THANKS, KIT! YOU'RE A *LIFESAVER*.
I DIDN'T DO IT FOR YOU.
I KNOW WHAT'S GOING ON HERE. I'VE SEEN IT BEFORE.

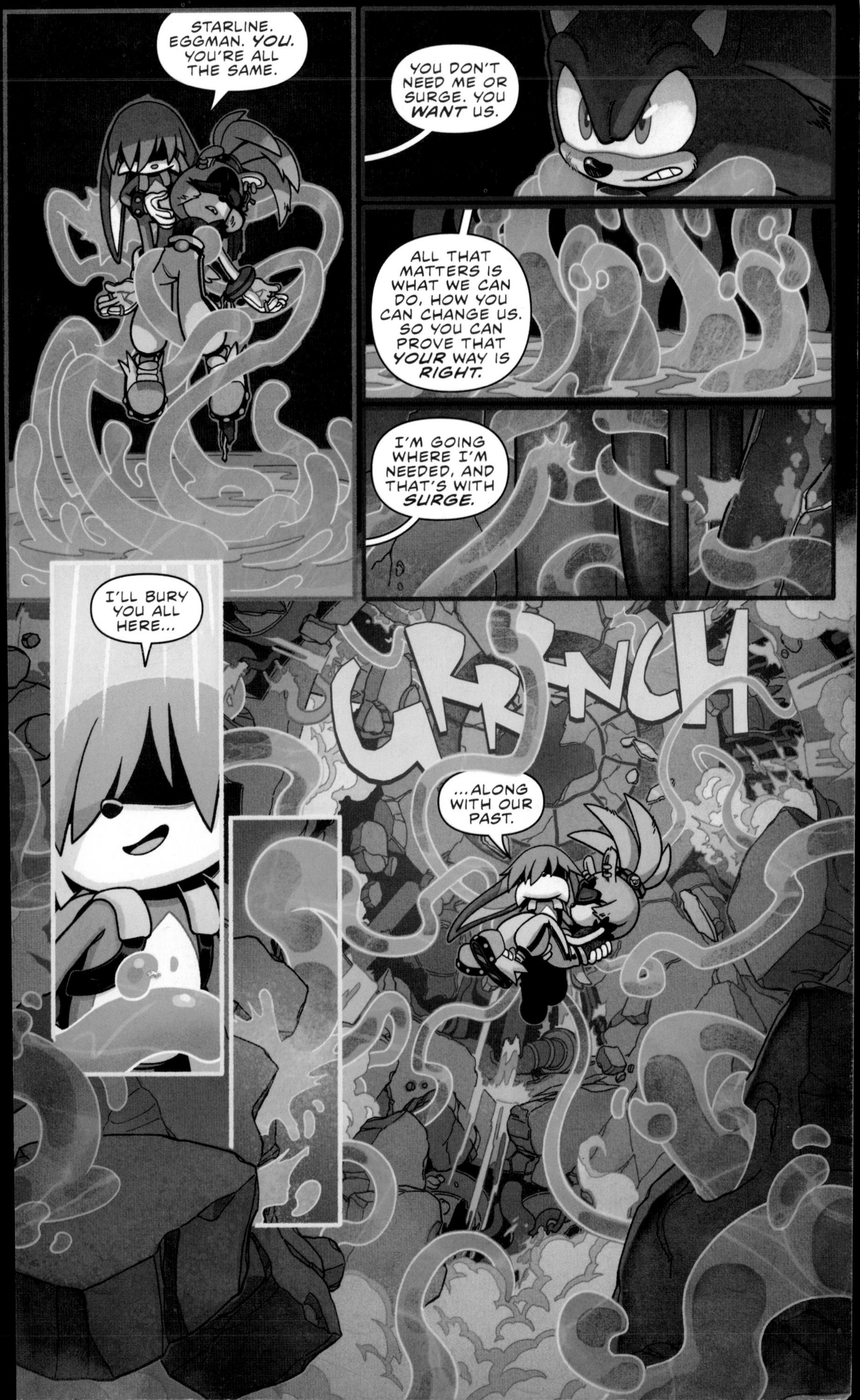
STARLINE. EGGMAN. *YOU.* YOU'RE ALL THE SAME.
YOU DON'T NEED ME OR SURGE. YOU *WANT* US.
ALL THAT MATTERS IS WHAT WE CAN DO, HOW YOU CAN CHANGE US. SO YOU CAN PROVE THAT *YOUR* WAY IS *RIGHT.*
I'M GOING WHERE I'M NEEDED, AND THAT'S WITH *SURGE.*
I'LL BURY YOU ALL HERE...
CRUNCH
...ALONG WITH OUR PAST.

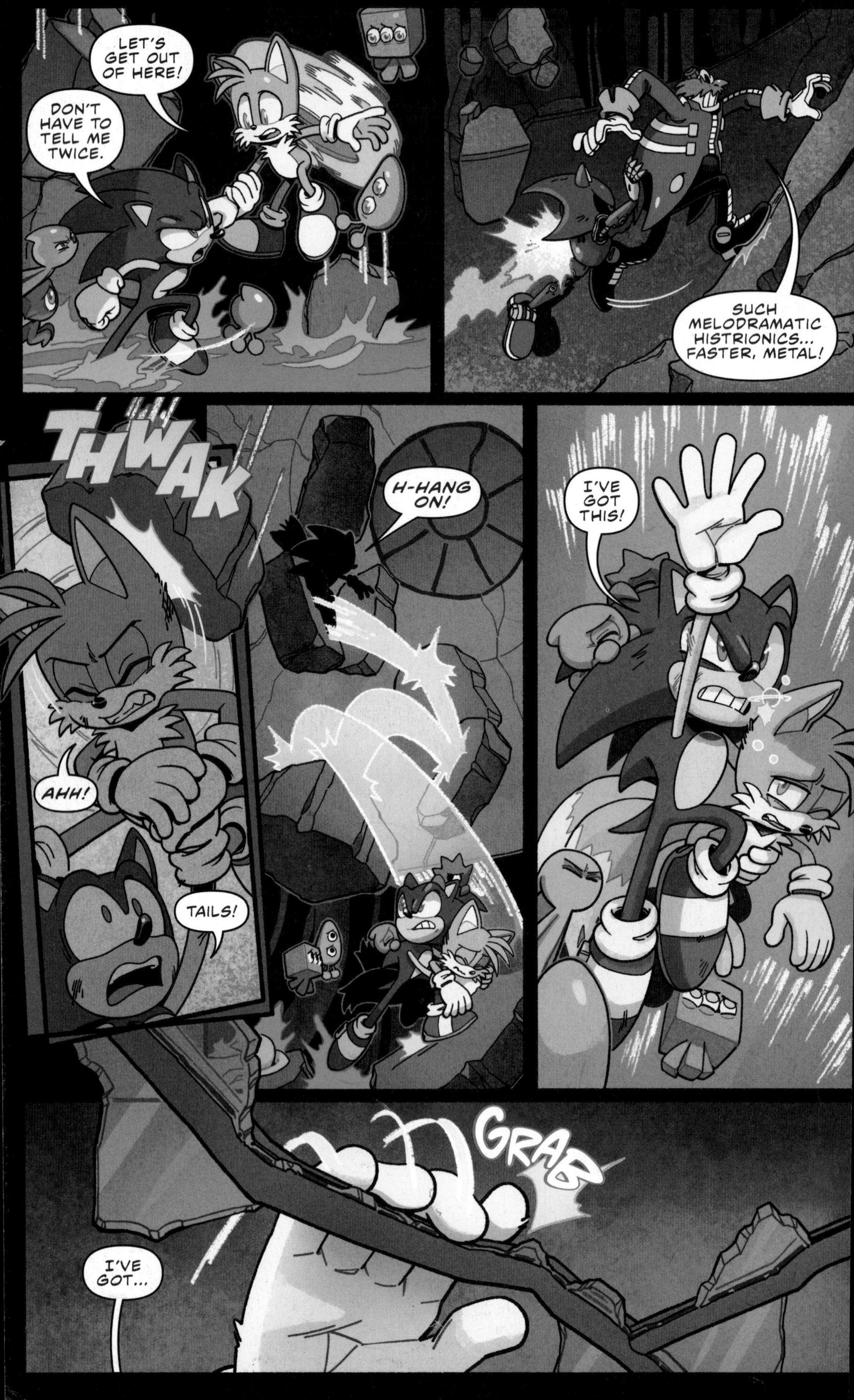
LET'S GET OUT OF HERE!
DON'T HAVE TO TELL ME TWICE.
SUCH MELODRAMATIC HISTRIONICS... FASTER, METAL!
THWAK
AHH!
TAILS!
H-HANG ON!
I'VE GOT THIS!
GRAB
I'VE GOT...

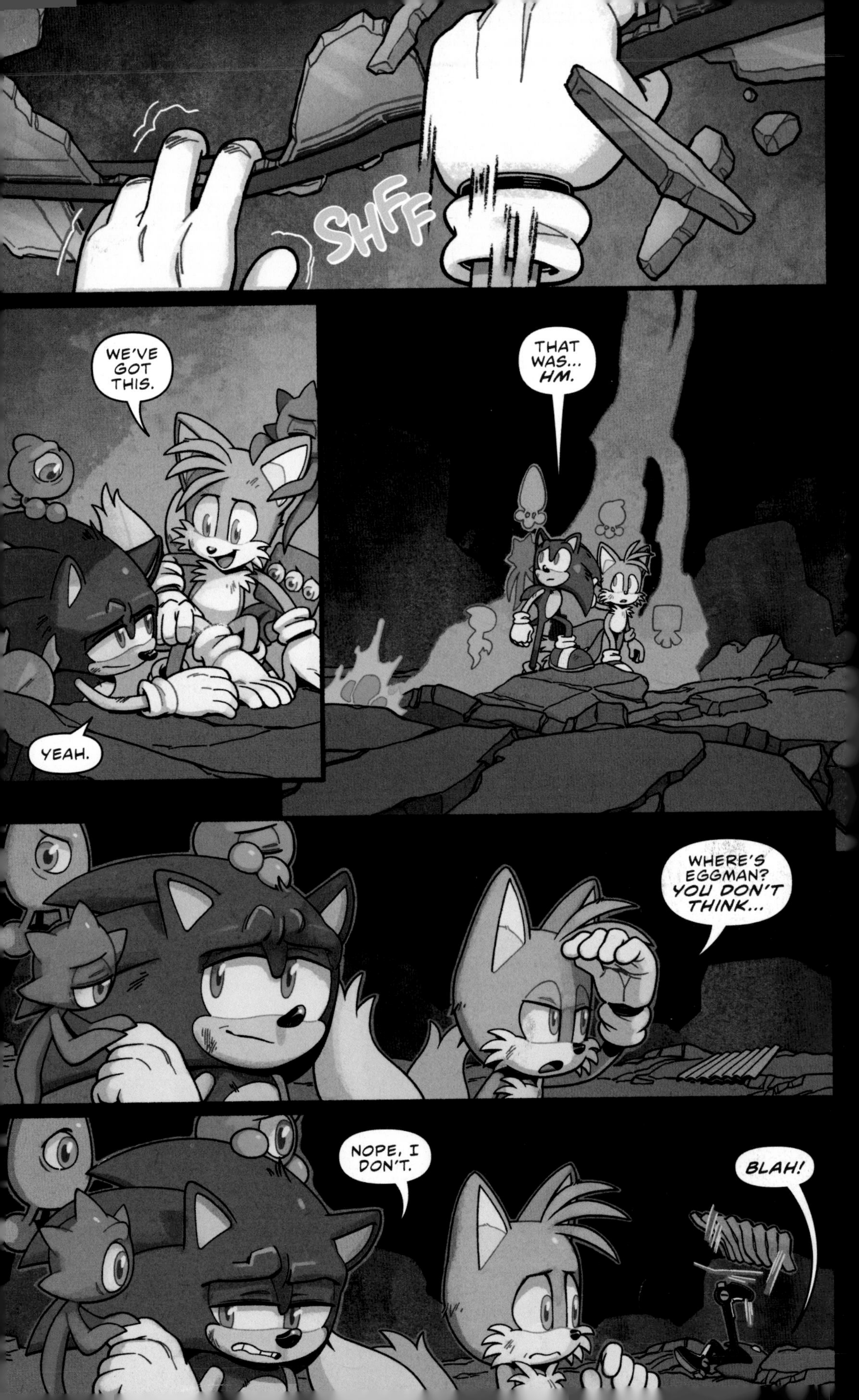
SHFF
WE'VE GOT THIS.
YEAH.
THAT WAS... HM.
WHERE'S EGGMAN? YOU DON'T THINK...
NOPE, I DON'T.
BLAH!

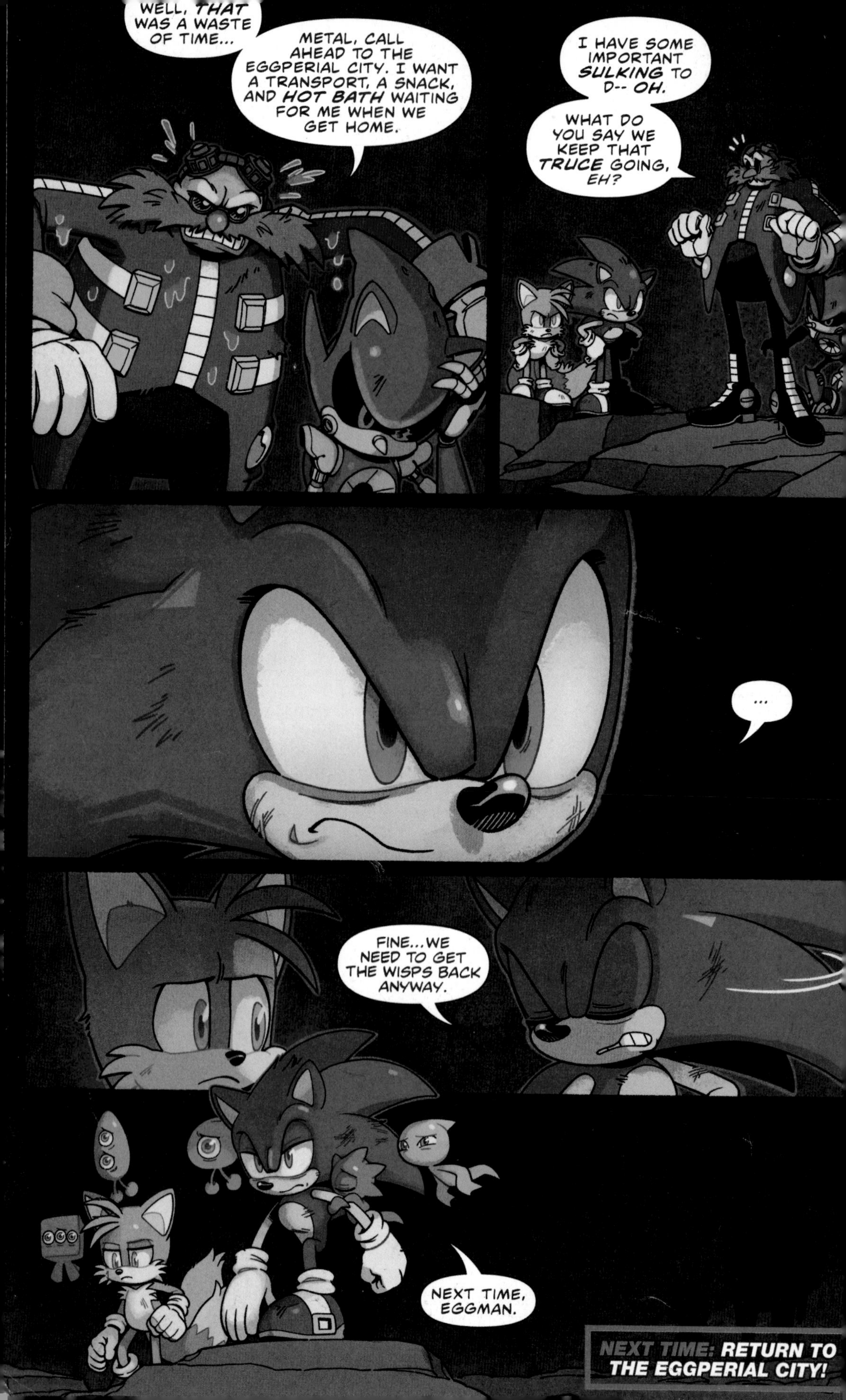
WELL, THAT WAS A WASTE OF TIME...
METAL, CALL AHEAD TO THE EGGPERIAL CITY. I WANT A TRANSPORT, A SNACK, AND HOT BATH WAITING FOR ME WHEN WE GET HOME.
I HAVE SOME IMPORTANT SULKING TO D-- OH.
WHAT DO YOU SAY WE KEEP THAT TRUCE GOING, EH?
...
FINE...WE NEED TO GET THE WISPS BACK ANYWAY.
NEXT TIME, EGGMAN.
NEXT TIME: RETURN TO THE EGGPERIAL CITY!

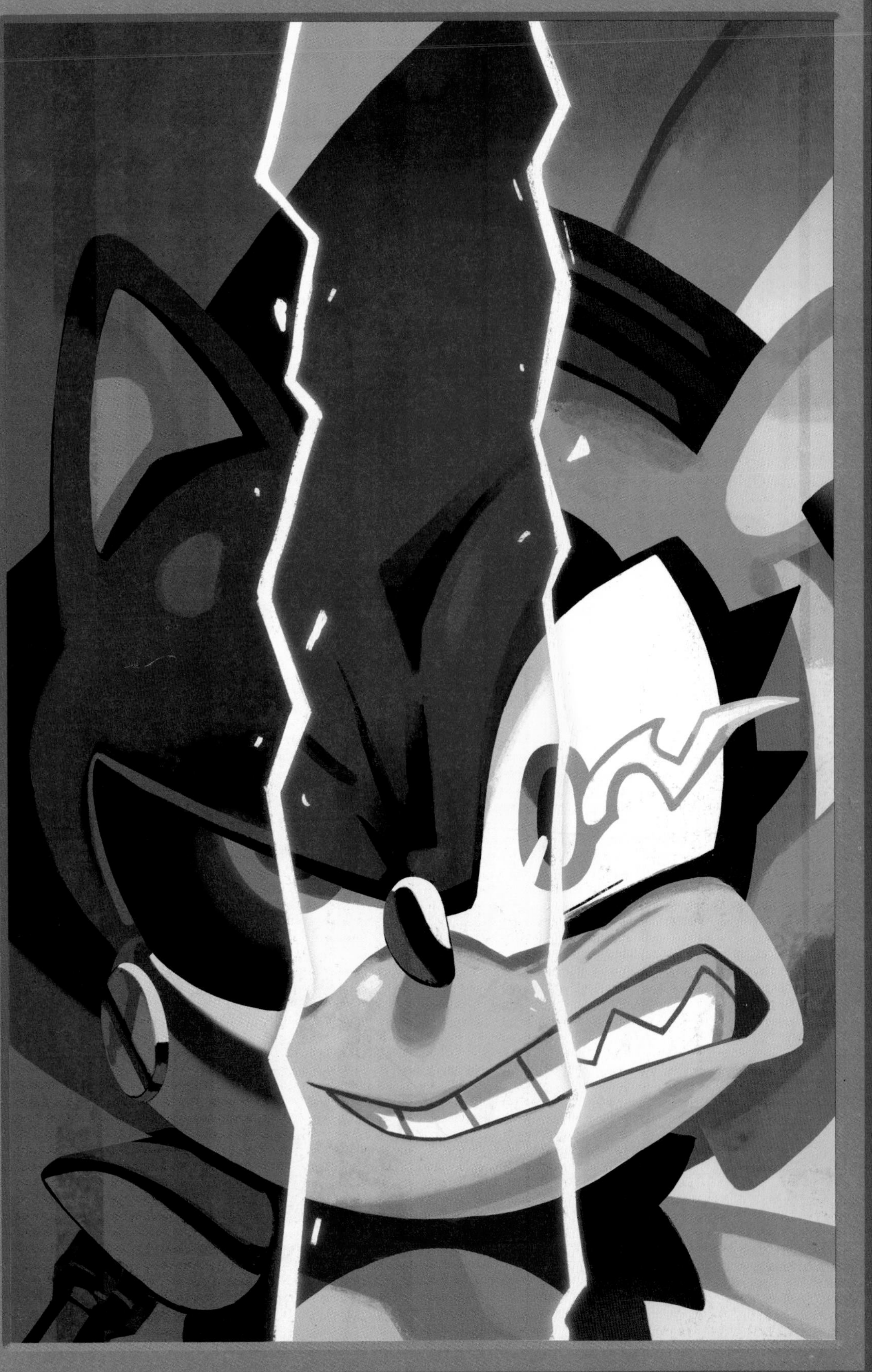

ART BY **NATHALIE FOURDRAINE**

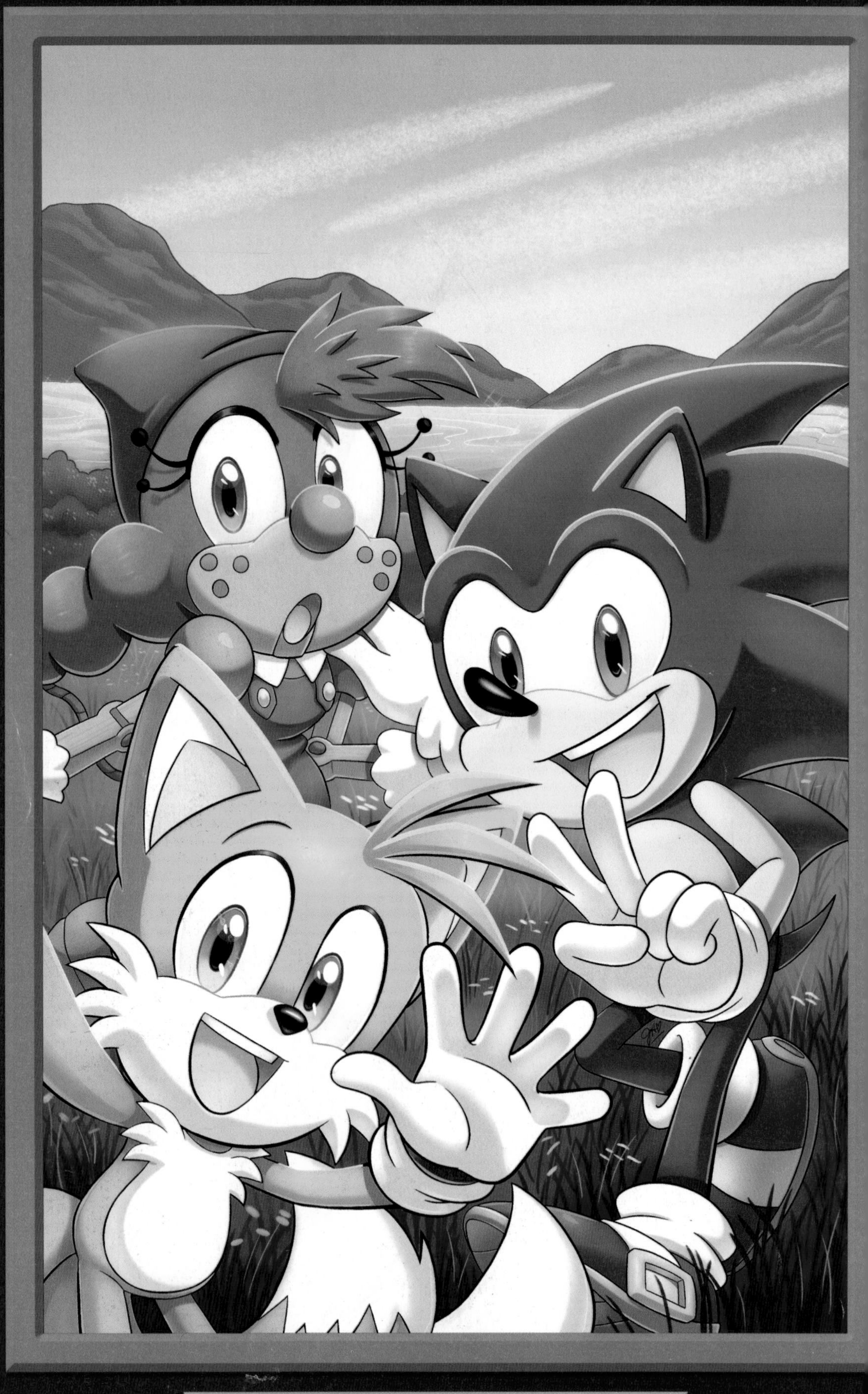

ART BY JENNIFER HERNANDEZ

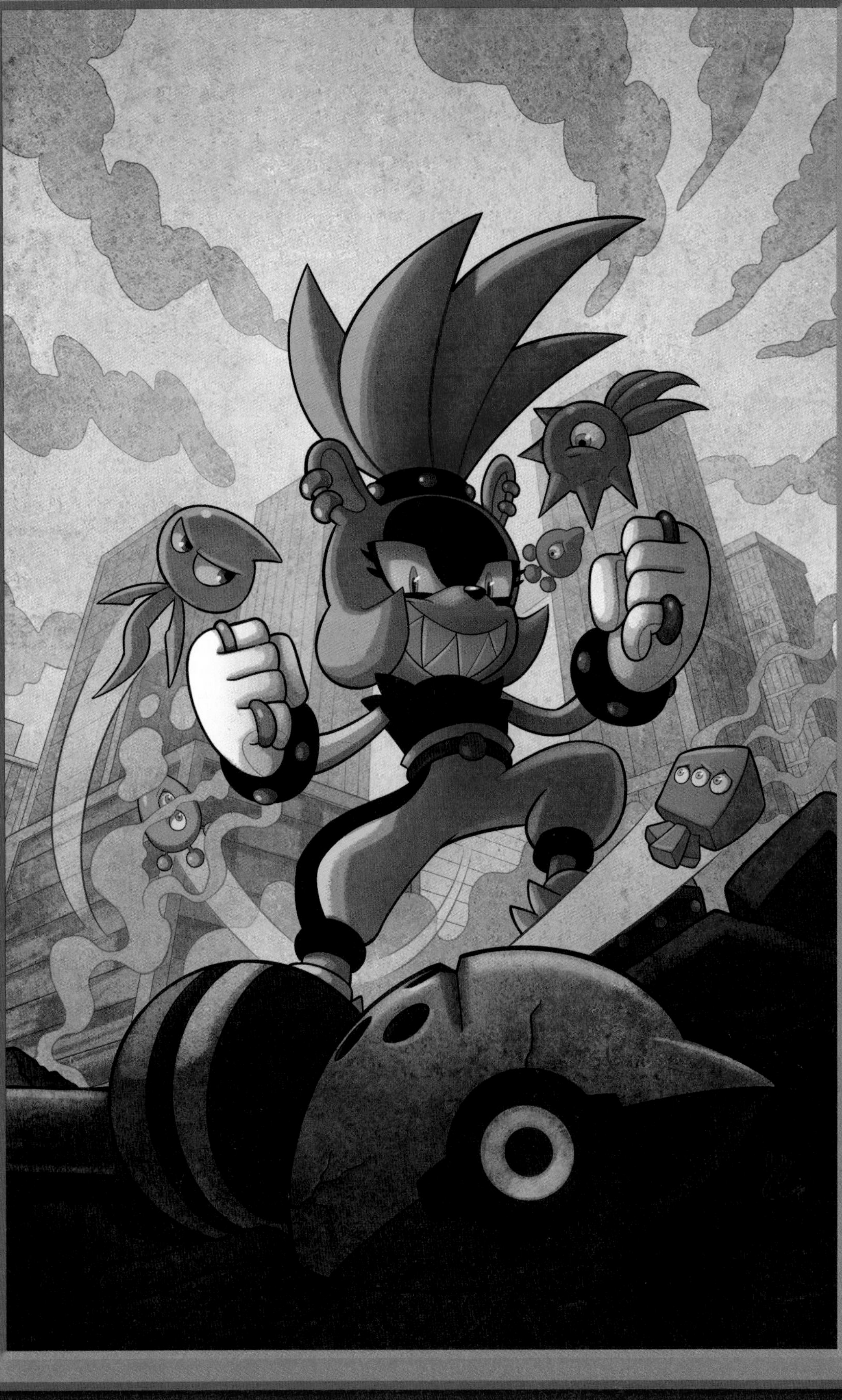

ART BY **ABBY BULMER** COLORS BY **REGGIE GRAHAM**

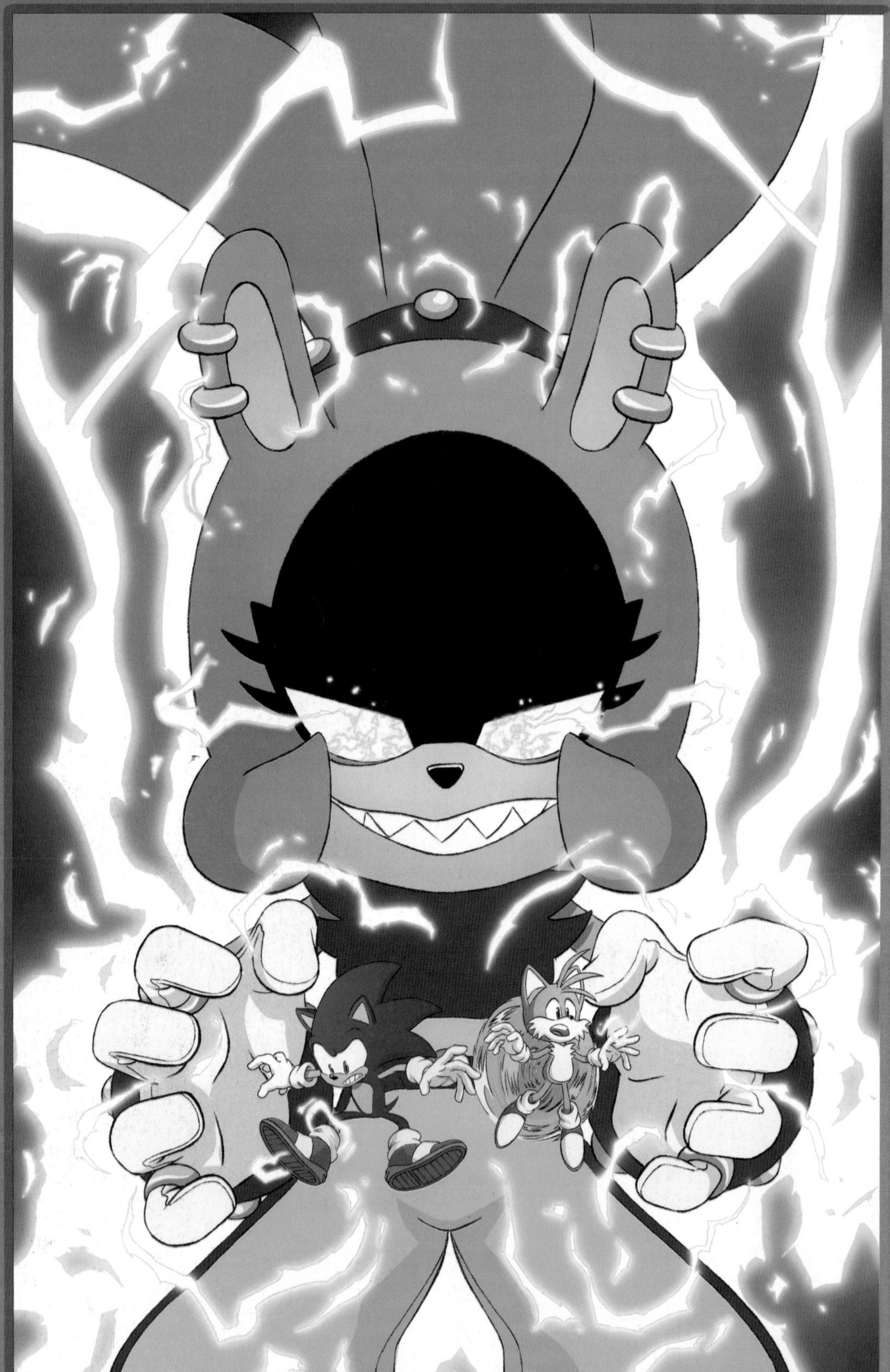

ART BY **DAN SCHOENING** COLORS BY **LUIS ANTONIO DELGADO**

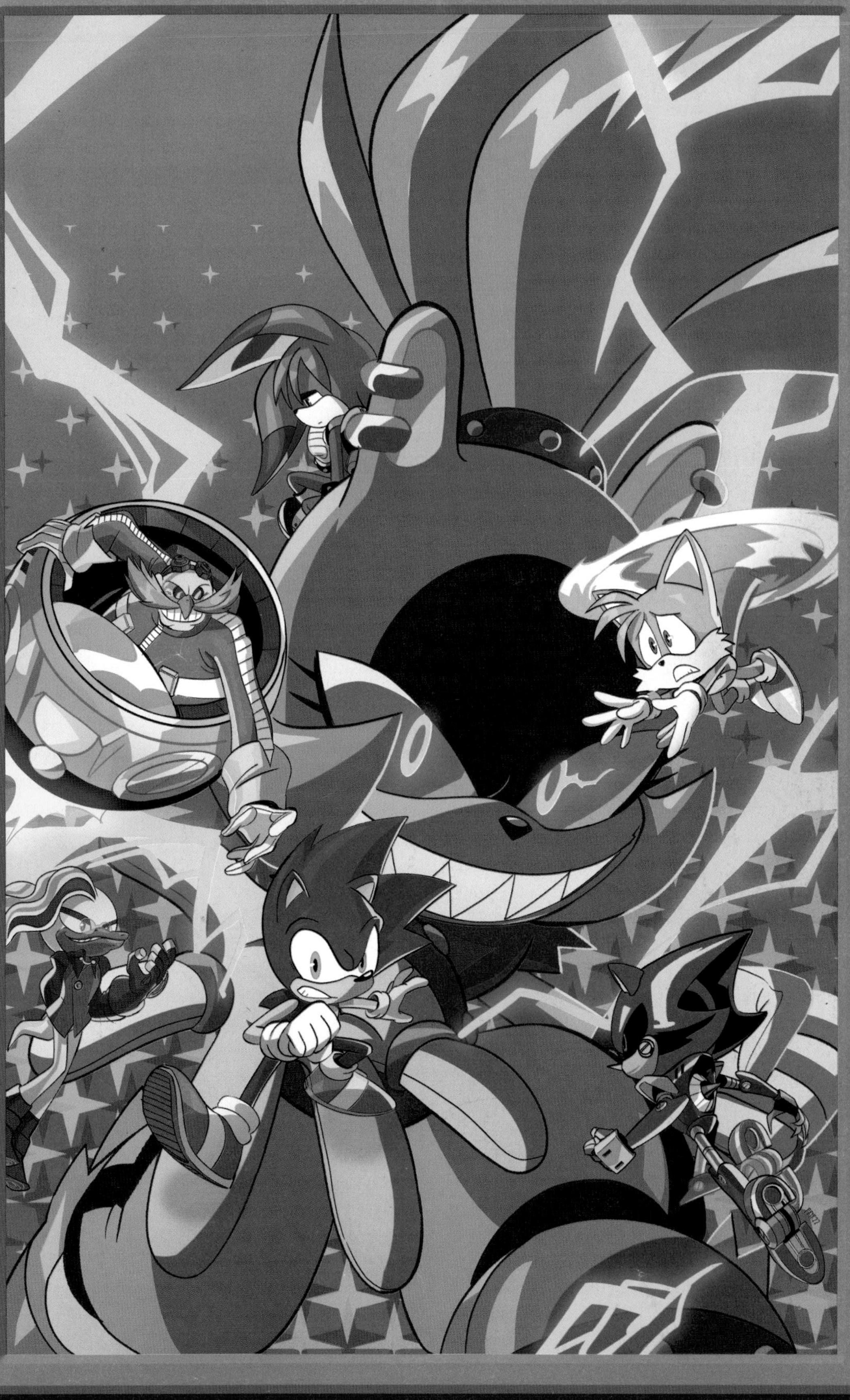

ART BY **PRISCILLA TRAMONTANO**

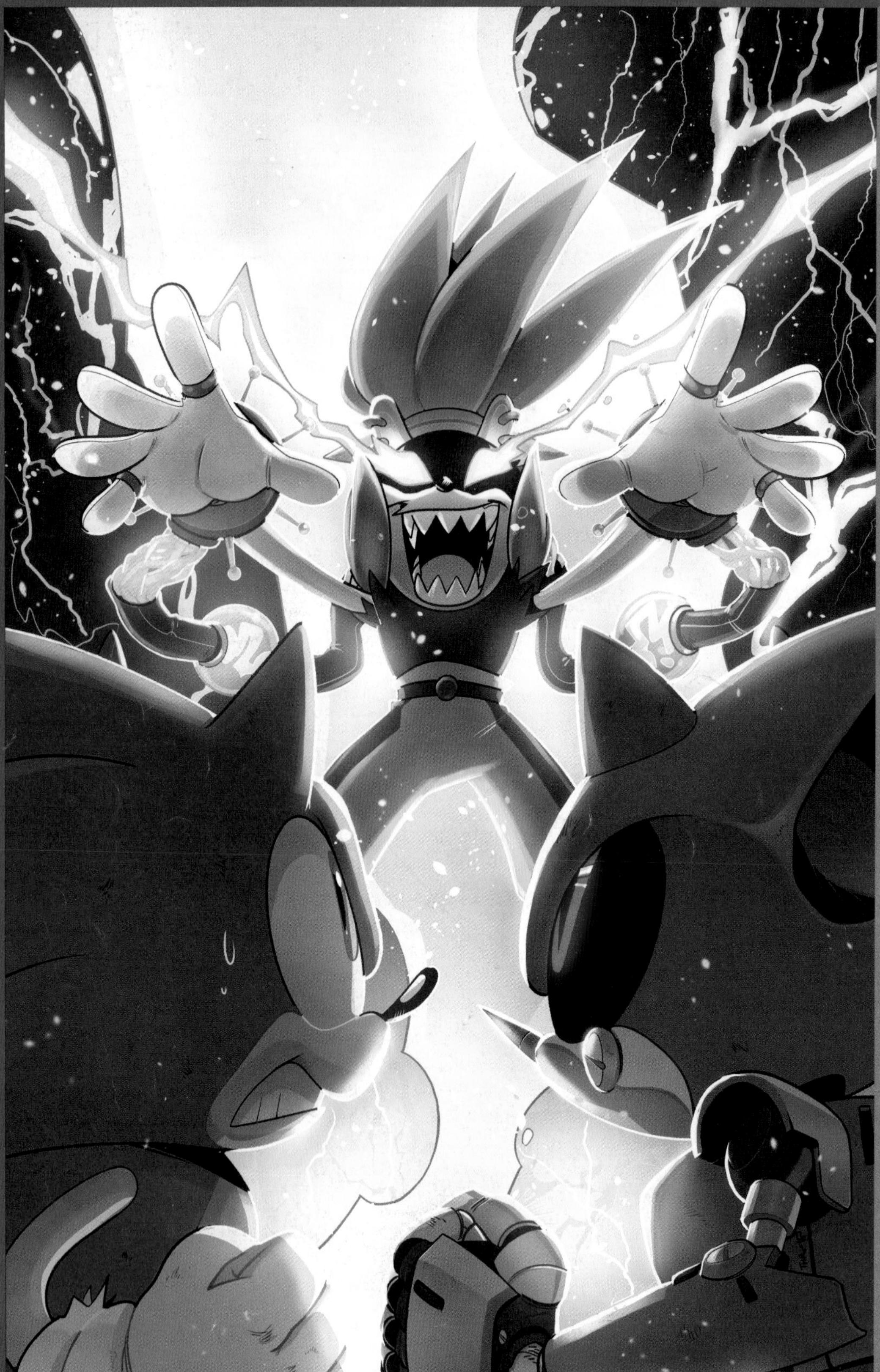

ART BY **THOMAS ROTHLISBERGER** COLORS BY **VALENTINA PINTO**

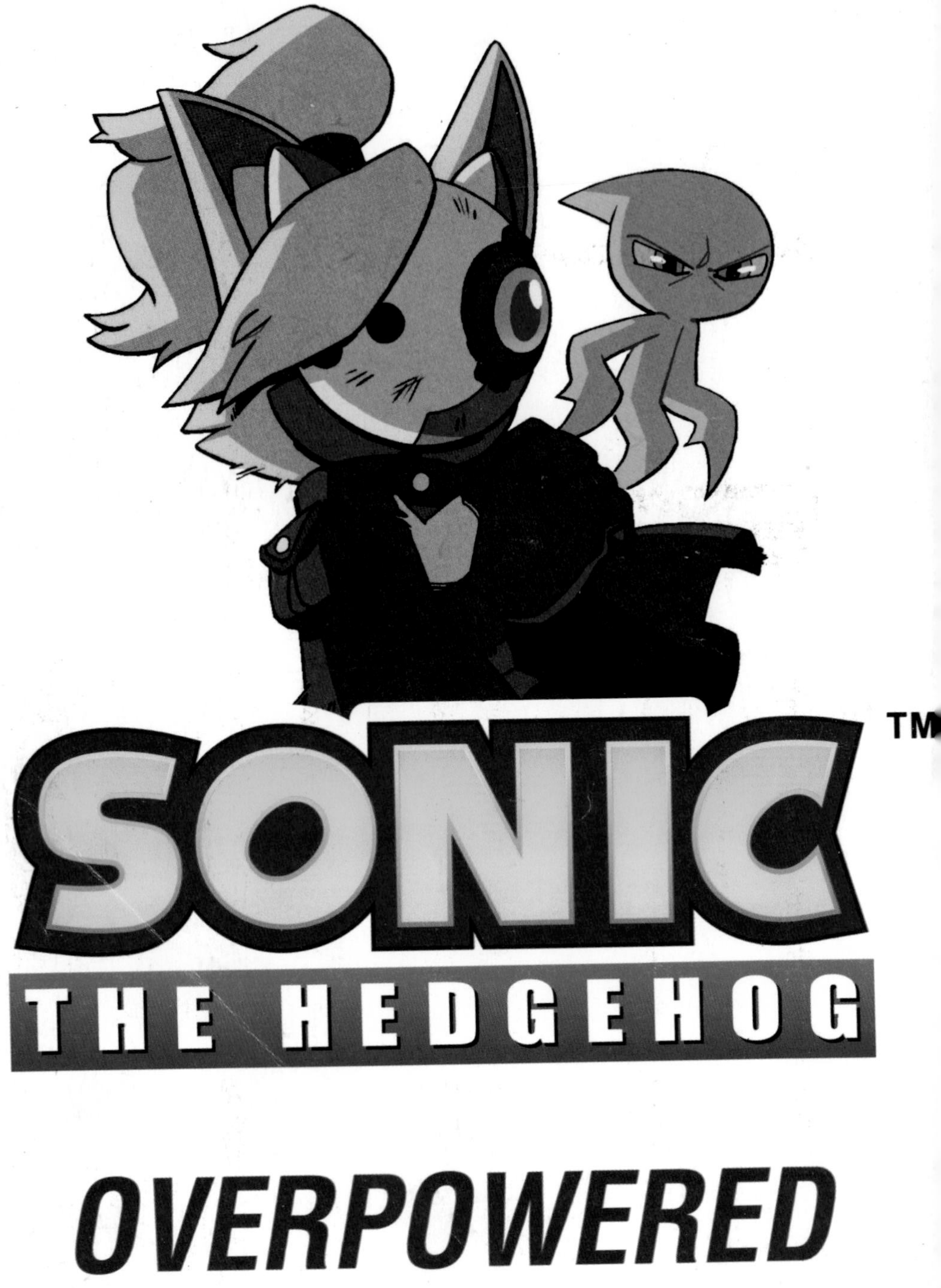

SONIC™ THE HEDGEHOG

OVERPOWERED

SEGA®